INTO TH.

This is my first try at a novel. Writing it was an inexpensive and effective form of therapy. Everything in this book is fictional but true.

Jonas Send
Munich, 2022

Cover design by Aleksandra Bilic

ISBN: 978-1-09-949991-3

INTO THE VOID

JONAS SEND

To the night you saved my life.

And so long as you haven't experienced
this: to die and so to grow,
you are only a troubled guest
on the dark earth.

Johann Wolfgang von Goethe
The Holy Longing

1

I was woken up by the rattling noise of a jackhammer
booming through the half-open window next to my
bed. I was hot and dizzy, and the moist bedlinen stuck
to my skin. I opened my eyes. The plain hospital room
was covered in stripes of light that the unforgiving
Spanish sun sent through the shutter. The other bed
in the room was empty but not permanently, judging
by its ruffled sheets. It took me a while to pick up my
aching body before I could drag my bare feet over the
linoleum floor towards the bathroom. I froze when I
saw myself in the mirror above the sink. The left
half of my face was swollen, and my cheek badly
grazed. My left eye was half shut from the swelling
and surrounded by a big, purple bruise. With my
tongue, I felt bone splinters piercing the mucosa between my left cheek and my upper row of teeth. My
left nostril was clogged with clotted blood. The swollen knuckles of my right hand hurt, and the thin skin
between the knuckles of my left hand was burst. From
what the doctor had told me this morning, I knew my

cheekbone was broken in three places: just in front of my ear, behind my eye, and from the eye socket down to my teeth. My lingering hangover didn't help either. I made faces in the mirror until the nagging pain that hummed through my skull grew too heavy. I must have gotten into a fight. Again. My brain felt as though it was wrapped in cotton wool. There was a black hole where the memory of the events that had led to my hospitalisation should have been.

I knew today was my fourth day in Barcelona. I also knew that yesterday I had ended up on somewhat of a bender with Alberto, a graduate student from California whom I had met in Sofia about a month ago. Over a couple of beers, we had exchanged our favourite conspiracy theories on the balcony of our hostel. Later that night, we went on to a bar that served a hundred different shots, some of which involved setting the whole table on fire. I didn't remember the bar's name but retained vague memories of a long, dark, and narrow room and a blue neon sign outside. In a state of mindless exuberance, Alberto and I downed shot after shot, shouting and laughing hysterically. At one point, Alberto climbed onto the table and started singing *The Internationale*. After another shot, he told a story from his time in Oxford, when he had been forced to jump stark naked out of a bathroom window and run home through the nocturnal streets. With a wild burst of facial expressions and gesticulations using all of his compact body, he cursed the drunk lover who had forgotten to tell him the minor detail that she had a boyfriend who enjoyed staging surprise late-night visits. Alberto somehow transitioned effortlessly into a slurred rant about the Queen's role in the preservation of the English class structure. He was a whirlwind of a man. After we had drunk our way through the shot menu, we wound up at a 'Fucking Monday' party in a large-scale disco called Gràcia Getaway at the Plaça de Catalunya with beer pong, free sangria, and confetti. I was already drunk enough to dance to soulless chart house music and hit on wasted Erasmus girls, both to rather mild success. The last image I had of last night was of Alberto and me at the bar ordering a bottle of vodka with an ice bucket full of energy drinks. The rest was blackness.

This morning, the contagiously friendly girl from the hostel reception had woken me up. Someone I shared the room with had informed her that a man covered in blood was lying in the bunk below. Although I was above all hungry and dying of thirst, the concerned staff of the hostel urged me to go straight to the hospital. One of the housekeepers kindly drove me to one nearby in his run-down SEAT, which was plastered with punk band stickers. On my arrival at the hospital, I was told to wait. I used the time to finally get some food—cereal bars and a sandwich from a vending machine. I also washed some of the blood off my face and hands. After a woozy wait that felt like it lasted for seconds and days at the same time, I was X-rayed and had to deal with some insurance issues. In the end, I was confined to bed to be monitored for potential brain damage.

My disfigured self still looked back at me from the mirror. My dark blond hair had grown quite a bit since I left London three months before. I was also sporting a full beard, which I had always found too patchy to wear around the office. All I had on were boxer shorts. When I flexed my muscles, I was pleased to see I was still in decent shape despite the revelry of

3

the past few months. My right knee and elbow were scuffed and a little swollen. Two ribs on my right side were bruised but not broken. I started shadow-boxing the pathetic creature in the mirror. A wave of debilitating dizziness forced me to stop immediately. With cramping hands, I held onto the sink and took a deep breath that hurt my scorched lungs. I cursed my drunk, nicotine-dependent self. It only took a mo-ment for the dizziness to become tolerable again. Whom had I fought? Was Alberto doing all right? He hadn't answered his phone this morning. I was afraid I might never hear from him again. As I stared at myself in the mirror, I felt as though I had been here before—in a past life, or maybe in another version of this one. Was time a circle? Would I end up in this stuffy hospital toilet, gazing at my bruised face, again and again and again, forever? I felt depressed. The drug-fuelled night out and the resulting mayhem had drained me. I forced myself to smile, to trick my brain into being happy—something I had taught myself as a depressed teenager. It worked to some degree. I had to stop looking at my wrecked face.

On the way back to my bed, a middle-aged, tough-looking nurse entered the room. I tried to put on a polite smile and said, 'Sorry, do you happen to have a phone charger?'

With a stern look, the nurse replied, '*Yo no hablo inglés.*'

I was lost—and a little angry at myself for acting like a damned tourist. I picked up my phone and pointed at its charger socket, sheepishly smiling at the nurse. She gave me a look I could not interpret and talked to me some more in what sounded like Catalan. She pointed at me and then to the bed. I followed her gesticulated orders. Despite my dizziness, a vague

feeling of guilt, the jackhammer outside still clattering, and feeling hungry again, I fell asleep before the
nurse finished her check-up.

When I woke up, a young nurse was bringing in my
dinner. Hospital food smells the same wherever you
go—sickeningly sweet, with the odour of hot plastic.
The noise echoing from the construction site had
stopped. The stuffy air was still scorching hot, and my
pillow was wet.

The nurse put the food on the table next to my bed,
moved it over to me, and said with a Spanish accent,
'Are you the one who needs the phone charger?'

So, the old woman had understood. The young
nurse's smile was a little wry but cute. She brushed a
strand of curly dark hair that had escaped its braid
behind her ear. I was glad when she held up the
charger type I needed.

'Yeah, perfect, thank you,' I said and turned to
devour overcooked pasta with undersalted tomato
sauce.

When she came back to pick up the dishes, I tried
to start a conversation with her. But she was busy, so
I left her alone. The other bed in the room was still
empty and now looked as if it might stay that way
tonight.

When I got to switch on my phone again, I saw
multiple missed calls from Ben, one of my best friends
from home. I called him back.

'Hey, man, how are you?'

'Hey, Ben. I'm good.' I hesitated. 'Well, I'm in
hospital. But I'm all right.'

'What happened?'

'I think I kind of got into a drunken fight. It's all a
bit of a blur.'

'No way! How many guys did you fight with? Are you badly hurt?'

'My cheekbone is broken, and I have a couple of bruises. I'm all right though, just a bit dizzy and hung-over . . . I think they'll only keep me in for tonight.'

'And you don't remember how it happened?'

'Not a clue. I suppose I was rather royally wasted.'

'No shit! Oh man, this reminds me of the time you broke your arm back home.'

His voice sounded half worried and half-amused, and I had to smile. I said, 'Yeah, I know . . . '

'But you're going to be all right?'

'I guess so. They said I probably won't need surgery since it's all pretty much stayed in place.'

'Good to hear! Listen, do you have a minute? If it's okay with your concussion and all . . . '

'Go ahead.'

'When do you plan on wrapping up your travelling?'

'I haven't given it a thought yet, but I have no plans after Barcelona. Why?'

'Remember I told you about this new job opportunity? For two weeks now, I've been working in the equity valuation unit at the bank. It's amazing. We're testing a new valuation model that uses vast data-sets—super challenging! I know these guys from before, and I've told them about you—best in class and all that.'

'Second best.'

'Yeah, whatever.' He chuckled. 'Anyway, they were impressed by what I told them and want to talk to you. They're keen on adding someone with knowledge in machine learning to their team. Do you think you could come to Frankfurt or at least take a Skype call with them next week?'

'I don't know. I'll have to think about it. I mean, it's basically what I did in London . . . Can I get back to you?'

'Look, I know you were pissed off by your job at Phorcys in the City. But Frankfurt is a different scene. You could crash at our place at the beginning and, who knows, maybe you'll like it. It might be less money, but also fewer hours. At least talk to them! It's not like your trip seems to be going awfully well, either. Maybe this episode is a sign that you should be getting back to work. Maybe you should start figuring out what you want to do.'

'Yeah. I don't know . . . I can't think clearly about these things right now . . . Maybe I'll end up as a dis-illusioned bartender in Cuba after all.'

We both chuckled at our old inside joke.

'Okay, but please think about it and let me know, will you?'

'Yes. And thanks, Ben, I appreciate it.'

'No worries. By the way, how was Italy with Alice?'

'I don't want to talk about it now, to be honest.'

'I see . . . Will you finally go back home now to get some rest? I'm sure it would make your family really happy. Your mum even asked me about you when I was home two weeks ago. Are you still not talking?'

'No.' I felt dizzy. 'I'm not sure yet. Maybe I'll stay here for a bit and relax at the beach. Wanna come? They still have the volleyball courts right on the beach.'

'Oh, I'd love to! But I don't see myself taking time off anytime soon. Listen, I have to go. I have a date with a friend at the gym. Think about the offer and let me know what you decide. Call me! And take care!'

'I will, thanks. And can you please not tell every-body about my latest mishap?'

'Sure thing! Bye!'

Ben hung up. Sometimes I wished I had the optimistic pragmatism with which he approached life. But working for another bank? I enjoyed pushing numbers around and writing code. I liked solving complex problems. And I loved the triumphant sensation I got every time the computer spat out an accurate result. But making rich people richer, kowtowing to arrogant superiors, cashing in before the next big, inevitable crash, certain that everyone would be rescued by tax money, again? No thanks. I wasn't in the mood to waste any thought on the old rat race. I felt dizzy, and now my cheek started hurting as well. I had declined painkillers.

I turned to my phone and grazed my social media accounts. Giving likes, numbly noticing received likes, scrolling through endless feeds of irrelevance. Then, I received a Facebook message—from Alice. Nervously, I tapped on it.

'Hej! How are you? How was Marseille with your friend? I'm still in Rome, but we're coming to Barcelona the day after tomorrow. Are you already there? Do you want to meet? You could stay in the Airbnb apartment we booked. It has a rooftop garden! P.S. I still love the sunglasses you bought me.'

I felt my heart pounding in my chest. So far, today had been the first day in weeks I hadn't spent thinking of Alice all the time. And now she had me, once more. Seeing her again, so soon? That had come out of nowhere—and not a single word about our fight. When I had driven away from her in Rome, I hadn't been sure whether I would ever see her again. Whether I ever *wanted* to see her again after what she had said to me. Why the hell was she coming to Barcelona? And who the hell were *we*? In my skull

8

painfully vibrated the image of Alice, bathing in the dark water of the Elbe in the moonlight of our first night together—gleaming deep-brown eyes, the black rose blossoming between her breasts. I needed distraction. Again, I tried to call Alberto. Again, to no avail. My disfigured face looked back at me from the black mirror in my hands. Ben was probably right; I should figure out what I wanted to do with my life. But where to wander in this uncertain world? What purpose to believe in in this pointless existence? How to breathe in this smothering summer night? Why not wait for Alice, and let her set the horizons of my heart ablaze? I closed my eyes. As my bed spun in the hollow darkness of the stuffy hospital room, I slowly fell asleep.

The dream I had that night was feverish. I was on the deck of a cruise ship, drifting through an ocean glowing with a red hue. Meteors came crashing down from the warped sky, gleaming orange, and thundered into the sea, causing the massive ship to rock. Alice was standing next to me, holding my hand. I ran my fingers through her thick brown hair and across her soft, full lips.

She looked at me with piercing eyes and whispered, 'Let's go inside. I'm bored.'

I followed her into a hallway, aflame with blue light, stretching into infinity. On both sides were countless doors with mystic runes on them. We were roller-skating down the corridor, and Alice opened every door we passed. Behind each door was a small cabin with a bed and steamy bodies glimmering with sweat—men and women entwined in all imaginable combinations. Alice laughed and dragged me into one of the cabins. She joined two men on the bed—

a golden-locked Adonis and a dark Persian warrior. I froze in jealous paralysis. As Alice moaned in ecstasy, locked in between the bodies of the two beautiful statuesque men, black ants started crawling across my body and face. The image of Alice making love to other men and the itching of the ants' spiky legs on my face filled me with boiling madness. My body melted and dripped into nothingness and through infinite darkness, and dropped, in the shape of a man, onto a red leather bench. Across a white metal table, Alice was studying a menu. We were in a roadside diner somewhere in the wasteland. Through the window, I could see the desert, torrid and hostile to life. We had the diner to ourselves, except for a few weary truckers who sat hunched over the counter and stared at their empty plates in empty silence. I was mad at Alice but couldn't remember why.

She looked up and said with a smile, 'Close your eyes and make a wish.'

I closed my eyes and wished for forgiveness. A warm wave ran through my body, and I felt over-whelmingly secure. When I opened my eyes again, I was still in the diner, but now Emma, my first love, was sitting in front of me. She smiled at me merci-fully—those adorable dimples in both her cheeks. I knew her innocent face was hiding a complex gloom that frightened me.

With her gentle voice, Emma said, 'I'm going to order some ice cream for both of us.'

I looked outside. A vast meteor was hurtling straight towards us, already darkening the desert as it began to eclipse the sun. I was happy. I knew we still had some time left.

The young nurse who had lent me her charger woke me up twice that night and asked my name to check that my brain was still functioning. In the dim blue light coming from the hall, she looked like a tropical angel.

The next morning, my old friend, the jackhammer, woke me up, rupturing the asphalt that had become porous over many years in the Mediterranean sun. My dream still confused me. Fortunately, the rattling of dishes and the smell of hospital coffee cut short any contemplations. The door flew open, and, to my pleasant surprise, it was the young nurse. They must have awfully long shifts here. After she had prepared my breakfast and I had gratefully returned her charger, I tried to spark another conversation.

'Do you think they'll let me out today?'

'Sorry, but you must talk to the doctor. But it's important you get more rest. I guess you don't live here; will you go home after the hospital?' She looked exhausted; by now, her braid had lost control over most of her curly hair. It must have been close to the end of her shift. I found it all the kinder of her to take some time to talk to me.

'Yeah, I'm staying in a hostel, but I have no idea where I will go from here. Would you like to take care of me for a couple of days?' I gave her what I hoped was a winning grin. It hurt my cheek.

'Well, I'm sure my boyfriend would be happy to share our bed with one of the patients.'

She looked at me with a defiant smile.

'Fair enough. Thanks for everything.'

'You're welcome. And remember: get some rest.'

When she left the room, the door stayed open. A moment later, a nurse I hadn't seen before helped an obese man with a broken leg and arm into the bed next to me. After the nurse left, I said, 'Hi,' but the big-boned one gave me a frown. I settled for listening to his alarmingly heavy breathing.

A doctor visited me an hour later and assured me I didn't need corrective surgery. He told me I was good to go. I felt as if he wanted to get rid of me. I put on my clothes, collected some insurance paperwork, and went to the reception desk and let them call me a taxi. I stepped outside onto the small square in front of the hospital and found a pleasant spot on a bench in the shade of a tree with thick, oily leaves. It was still morning, but the sun was already relentless. I watched topless construction workers frying in the heat, asphalt dust settling on their dark, leathery skin. A Mossos car slowly drove past, serving as a reminder of the fractionality of the Kingdom of Spain that is sometimes easy to forget as a foreigner. Recently, the rupture between the separatist Catalans and the centralist Spaniards had reopened, with both sides showing little readiness for compromise. Maybe the summer sun was melting their brains. It was abnormally hot for mid-September. A record-breaking heatwave had its grip on most of Western Europe. I had seen the smoke columns of wildfires during my bus ride from Marseille to Barcelona. My head started spinning again. The prospect of returning to the hot, airless hostel room I had already paid for five more days wasn't particularly appealing. Thinking of Ben's offer, I saw myself in a suit, smooth-shaven and with short hair, making cynical jokes about how screwed-up the whole financial system was. I tried to picture myself at last reuniting with my family, but I couldn't do it. I visualised Alice's arrival and saw a bizarre tantra retreat in a farmstead somewhere in rural Aragon she would probably drag me to. I caught a glimpse of the emotional distress her reappearance in my life would likely cause. I saw the young nurse waiting for me in our bed after a long day, her curls falling on the soft pillow like dark velvet. My thoughts were engulfed by the familiar, diffuse humming of the concussion. I needed some sleep before I could decide which direction to get lost in.

* * *

There are certain queer times and occasions in this strange mixed affair we call life when a man takes this whole universe for a vast practical joke, though the wit thereof he but dimly discerns, and more than suspects that the joke is at nobody's expense but his own.

Herman Melville
Moby-Dick

2

It was a Friday afternoon at the beginning of June in Brighton. I was sitting at a small table in The Post & Telegraph Wetherspoon, one of those cheap pubs that don't play music. The air in the spacious split-level room was filled with the slurring of drunk men of all ages who had been here since before noon. The faint smell of sweat and urine tickled my nose. With a smirk, I observed the casual cross-generational day-time drinking—the kind that can only be found on the English-speaking islands. My friend Chris came back from the bar, balancing four pints. As he placed them carefully on our table, I gave him a quizzical look.

'I don't want to walk to the bar all the time!' he explained with a laugh and raised his glass. 'All right, here's to your newfound freedom.'

'Cheers.'

We both took deep sips of the cold beer. It was a little flat. Chris gave me a penetrating gaze and said,

'Okay, tell me what happened.'

'Well, I woke up one day and didn't feel like going to work anymore—into that hellhole of late-stage capitalism. So, I quit—end of story.'

'And that was last week?'

'Yeah, I quit last Friday. My managing director said that if I wanted to leave, I had to leave immediately. I also got a nice little payoff. It took me about ten seconds to find a new tenant for my flat who also agreed to buy all my furniture; it's still London, after all. Then, I slept for three days straight, handed over the keys, and took the train here this morning.'

Chris laughed his ringing laugh. 'I never would've thought you would quit your job like that! You've always been so reasonable and disciplined. This makes an old ne'er-do-well like me feel good!'

'I'm glad I can be of service. Although I remember us doing some unreasonable things together back in Stockholm.'

Chris smirked at me knowingly. 'You've had your moments of insanity, I'll give you that.' He chuckled, and we touched glasses. 'Do you already have plans for what you'll do after Brighton? Don't get me wrong, you can crash on my sofa as long as you can tolerate it.'

'Thanks, I appreciate that. I have plans to go to Bristol to see Theresa on Monday, and I've booked a flight to Hamburg in a week.'

'Ah, you're still dating that business bird? Nice!'

'I haven't seen Theresa in a while, but I need some tenderness.'

'*Tenderness*—man, you kill me sometimes.' He chuckled. 'If you're looking for *tenderness*, I will hook you up with someone tonight. I tell you, these girls are crazy!'

'We'll see about that.'

'You don't have to talk to them too much, don't worry. You can still get your insightful thoughts from your books tomorrow. Tonight, we drink!'

We touched glasses again and soon moved on to the second round.

'What are you going to do in Hamburg?'

'I have no clue yet. I might meet some people I know from my master's. I found a good flight, and it's cheap to get to Sweden from there, where I was also thinking of going.'

'Ah, the old playground . . . So, no work for you anytime soon?'

'I haven't given it any thought yet. I don't even know what I want to be doing.'

'Travelling sounds like a good plan to me, then. I'm jealous. I'd join you, but I'm super busy and short on money—saving up for the dream!'

'You texted me you still work in that bar. Are you still a bike courier as well?'

'No, I've upgraded to driving a car, mate! I'm working as an Uber driver and a freelance postman.'

I laughed. 'You've got to love the gig economy.'

Chris looked at me with playful indignation. 'These gigs pay for the sofa on which you will make love to a beautiful girl tonight! And once my road-bike business starts taking off, I won't need any of them anymore.'

'I'm sorry. At least you have three and a half more jobs than me.'

We both chuckled and looked around the bar, marvelling at the old men with dozens of empty pint glasses on their tables.

Soon our glasses were empty as well, and I went to the bar to get the next round. While waiting for our drinks, I looked at Chris across the room, which was characterised by a patterned, greenish-carpeted floor and ugly chandeliers hanging from its high ceiling. Naturally, Chris was already chatting up the two women in their late forties to early fifties who had just taken a seat at the table next to us. They seemed flattered by his extroverted charm and impressed by his rugged, virile looks. Chris wore jeans, a white V-neck T-shirt that displayed his dark chest hair, and a black leather jacket, although it was 25 degrees outside. Had I ever encountered him in any other clothes, even in the cold Swedish winters? I hadn't seen Chris since one of his legendary birthday parties more than a year ago, which was probably the last time I had spent the whole day drinking. We had met in Stockholm, where we had both been studying Business Administration and Political Science for our bachelor's. At our first university party, Chris had run around shirtless with a bloody mouth, asking every-one whether they had seen his missing incisor. To this day, he couldn't remember how he had lost the tooth. That night, I brought the drunkard home and let him crash on my Ikea sofa. It turned out he had no place to stay and had been sleeping at the homes of random acquaintances. Consequently, he lived at my place for a while, and soon we became best friends. For two years, we never missed a chance to get wasted, and I always wondered how I still had been able to get good grades. Then Chris dropped out of university and returned to Brighton, where he had grown up. Soon afterwards, I met Emma, and my life became a little calmer. For all I knew, Chris had been working odd jobs and picking up shady girls at the bar he worked at ever since. I returned to the table with our beers and jumped into the conversation with the two women. They smelled of heavy perfume and old smoke. Chris was telling them about his plans to open up a second-hand bike shop where he would restore old road bikes to rip off the hipster children of rich parents.

When we finished our drinks, one of the women brushed a lock of fake blonde hair behind her bejewelled ear and said in a husky voice, 'Let me buy you darlings another round.'

Chris chuckled, 'Sorry, sweetheart, but my melancholic friend here needs to get his stuff to my place. And I have a rule not to drink more than five beers on first dates.'

The woman gave a short, breathy laugh and said, 'That's a real shame.'

'Surely two charming ladies like yourselves will have no problem finding new company.'

Chris took a bow. The women looked at him with flattered smiles. I grabbed the big, washed-out yellow backpack I had inherited from my dad, and we left.

We walked through the vibrant, narrow streets in North Laine and went for a piece of cake in Kensington Gardens. After we wallowed in some Stockholm memories, we decided to take the bus to Chris' flat in Hove.

On his kitchen table, I discovered a spacious, low-ceilinged terrarium, bathed in red light and filled with wood chips, dry tree branches, and moss. The tail of a snake stuck out of a small cave formed by overlapping branches. The animal was black and covered with golden blotches. I turned to Chris and asked, 'What is that?'

'That's Herbert.'

'What's Herbert doing in your kitchen?'

'Herbert lives here.'

I nodded, looked at the snake, then back at Chris and inquired, 'Why did you get a snake?'

'He's a royal python! One of the regulars from the bar emigrated to Argentina and was looking for a new host for Herbert. And I couldn't say no—Herbert's such a lovely chap.'

'Are you even sure it's a dude?'

'Spencer—the guy who gave him to me—said so. Oh, and Herbert's great with the ladies. They always want to do photoshoots when they hear I have a royal python. He gets me laid all the time.'

I shook my head and chuckled. I sat down at the kitchen table next to Herbert and watched Chris get a bottle of white wine out of the fridge and some opaque bags out of the freezer. When I got up to offer my help to prepare dinner, Chris ordered me to sit back down and start drinking. I obeyed. Chris began his chaotic cooking efforts. About an hour later, they resulted in surprisingly tasty tagliatelle with prawns and spinach in a white wine cream sauce, accompanied by two bottles of Chenin Blanc and two Rusty Nails.

It ended up being rather late after we finished eating and drinking. We went straight to a beachside club near the pier to meet the girls Chris had advertised. It was a dark and sweaty place under the promenade. Minimal techno was clanking from the overcharged speakers. A stroboscope made the experience more hypnotic. Condensed water was dripping from Victorian arches. Chris introduced me to four young girls as the 'boxing banker I told you about'. I had a tough time telling them apart since they all wore black outfits with ugly white trainers, ponytails, and nose rings. They looked like a caricature of an electro-punk girl band. After doing a couple of shots, we went outside to have a smoke. I was the classic party smoker; I would never dream of having a cigarette in the morning, but after one glass of alcohol, the addiction centre in my brain was activated, and I craved that soothing smoke in my lungs. I tried to initiate a conversation with one of the foursome, Phoebe—at least I thought that was her name. But I soon gave up, seeing how I was boring her with my uninspired 'what do you do' and 'where are you from' questions. After going back inside, the girl group disappeared around a corner, and Chris dragged me to the sleazy men's room and into a cubicle covered in graffiti. He pulled out a small plastic sachet with little green pills with rabbits printed on them. He looked at me with a conspiratorial grin and said, 'Let's get this party started!'

I hesitated. 'No, thanks, I'm good.'

'Don't worry, mate, I've tried these before, they're fine.'

'I don't know, man. I've never done MDMA before, and I don't think I want to try it when I'm already wasted.'

'No pressure. But I'm sure you would enjoy the girls more, too.'

'I don't know. Maybe next time.'

'You can start with a half if you want?'

'No, thanks, really.'

'Okay, no worries, mate.'

Chris swallowed one of the pills. We went to the booming dancefloor, where we met up with the girls. For about an hour, we danced together. The beat was relentless. If you listen to techno music long enough and move to the rhythm, it puts you in a trance from which you can hardly escape. Phoebe moved close to me, put her hands on my arms, and kissed me. I closed my eyes and let her tongue play skilfully with mine. Her hands were all over me, from time to time running through my hair. Her ecstatic exploration of my body, carefully investigating the texture of my jeans and T-shirt, made me realise she was on ecstasy too. I broke away from her yearning kiss. The rest of the group was exchanging kisses and touches, too. Chris gave me a happy, knowing look. Phoebe pulled me back into our kiss. I enjoyed it but soon felt she wanted more from me than I could give. I stepped away from the dancefloor. I needed to encourage my-self with a gin and tonic. When I returned from the bar with a drink in my hand, Phoebe was making out with another guy, who seemed more grateful than I had been. I started dancing next to the others. Chris was highly engaged with one of the girls, and the other two were entangled with each other. They didn't notice me. I had one of those odd moments in which I soberly realised how drunk I was. I put aside my drink and walked out of the club, leaving the high lovebirds to themselves.

During the walk to Chris' flat, I wondered whether drugged-up infatuation was the only remnant of love in our nihilistic times—depressed thoughts, as tottering as my steps. Chris kept a spare key beneath his doormat, and I went straight into his tiny living room, closed the door, and dropped onto his battered sofa. I was asleep before my head hit the pillow.

The next morning, Chris woke me up with a glass of water in his hand and a wide grin on his three-day-stubbled face. I never knew where the guy got all his energy from.

'Why did you suddenly leave yesterday? You missed one hell of a party!'

'I was tired. You seemed to have fun, though.'

'You could say that.' He smirked. 'You seem to be out of practice, buddy. The rat race has made you weak! I'm making breakfast, if you can eat.'

I got up. My head was heavy, and I was hungry and a little nauseated at the same time. On our way to the kitchen, we passed the two girls who had been making out with each other last night and said goodbye as they headed out. Chris had had sex with more girls that night than I had in seven months.

After breakfast, we planned to meet up for dinner, and Chris left for his job as a postman. I resisted the temptation to go back to sleep and took a bus into town to visit some of the places I hadn't seen in quite some time. I walked through the narrow, colourful Lanes of Brighton, crammed with shops and bars. Everybody and their dog were out, enjoying the beautiful English summer day. My stroll took me down to the pier, where I wandered around the attractions. I threw some coins into a slot machine I didn't understand in the arcade and had a crab sandwich for lunch. On the beach, my attention was captured by the old West Pier, which had been deteriorating for decades and had burnt down in 2003. I was always fascinated by the black steel skeleton protruding from the sea. What a sight it must have been in the late 19th century, when millions of tourists would pilgrimage to the pier for good sea air and entertainment. It was a comical spectacle to watch some nearby surfers fruitlessly trying to catch one of the tiny waves. I spent the afternoon in a beach chair, reading *Scar Tissue*, the autobiography of Red Hot Chili Peppers frontman Anthony Kiedis. His remorseless tales of passion and addiction gave me an undirected thirst for action. Where was my 'young Kentucky girl in a push-up bra' hiding?

At eight, I had a date with Chris at the bar where he worked, The Orange Zest. We ate chicken wings and had some beers before he started his shift. The cocktail bar was a contorted, multi-storey place with a little rooftop terrace and was hidden at the end of a narrow alley. Sometime after ten, an aghast quietness fell over the bar as news filtered through of terrorists running over pedestrians and stabbing people to death in London—pictures of blood-soaked civilians circulated on smartphone screens. But soon, order was restored with rounds of soothing alcohol.

That night, the bar was hopelessly overcrowded, and the air was soon filled with an aggressive tension. In the laboratory, when you confine too many rats to too little space, they become stressed and turn on each other, even cannibalising each other. Young, drunk men, newly frustrated when it dawns on them that they will most likely go home alone that night, are not all that different. After a guy involved in a fight next to me slapped the glass out of my hand and spilt my drink over my trousers, I left. Through the mild summer night, I walked to a little pub called Fisherman's Wharf in a dark side alley between the Lanes and Hove. Two of Chris's skateboarding friends I already knew from previous visits were there. I found Kenny and Mr Hofstadter sitting at a thick wooden table in a corner of the murky, dusty pub. They invited me to take a seat and join their game of Jenga. They were down-to-earth, funny people and infected me with their playful competitiveness. From time to time, the morose barman limped over from the bar, where the only other patron was sitting, and refilled our beer pitcher. He didn't say a single word. Songs from Led Zeppelin and the Who were swirling through the bar, oddly muffled, without a determinable origin.

At half past one, Kenny and Mr Hofstadter headed home; they flew to Guangzhou and Shenzen for a skating trip the next morning. I finished my beer and brought the packed-up game to the bar. I looked at the man sitting there, a bottle of Bushmills three-quarters empty in front of him. He was a heavily built biker in his fifties with long, untamed grey hair. He looked back at me and said, in a deep, throaty voice, 'Wanna have one?' and pointed at the bottle.

For a moment, I hesitated. But then I joined him at the bar. The biker introduced himself as Menno and poured me a generous glass with his bearish paw. The tired eyes that looked out above his thick full beard radiated an angry sadness. After five minutes of drinking in silence next to each other, I asked, 'What are you trying to forget?'

He looked at me hauntingly with a brief hint of surprise and said, calmly, 'That I might have killed a man today.'

I glanced at the barman, numbly gazing nowhere, and turned back to Menno. 'What happened?'

'He's my mother's upstairs neighbour and has been terrorising her for months—throwing parties, piling rubbish in the stairwell, insulting her; showing no respect, you know? Today, I had enough of it. He won't listen, so I bash him up. When I'm done, he doesn't move—might have pushed his nose up his brain.'

I didn't know what to say. I nodded and took another sip of whiskey. For the first time, I noticed the heavily bruised knuckles of the ursine hands clinging to his glass. I asked, 'What are you going to do now?'

'Now, I drink. Tomorrow, I find out if the pigs want me. If they do, I ride until they catch me.'

'Doesn't sound like your first time,' I said, naively.

'I've had a demon on my shoulder since I was a kid.'

I finished my whiskey and said goodbye, and the two lost souls answered with slow nods. Outside, I lit a cigarette. I had accepted my weakness earlier that day and had bought a pack. I started on my way to Chris' flat. After I had walked through the lonely alleys on the quiet side of the city for a while, I felt watched. I turned around and, at the end of the street, I could see the biker from the bar slowly walking towards me. When he realised I was looking at him, he stopped, about 50 metres away. For several breaths, we stood there and looked at each other, both illuminated by the yellow light of a street lamp. With another slow nod, Menno turned and disappeared into the night. My heart was pounding as I walked home, looking over my shoulder at every corner. I lay awake for a while on Chris' sofa that night and thought about Menno. Forbear to judge, for we are sinners all.

On Sunday, Chris and I had breakfast together. I watched an old woman carefully water dandelions sprawling through cracks in the asphalt outside the kitchen window. Chris went into the basement to fix up an old road bike he had bought on eBay for a friend. Sometimes, he would buy run-down bicycles and resell them for five times the price after repairing and repainting them. I booked a hostel in Hamburg and a flight to Stockholm and made plans to take a ship from there to Tallinn.

After lunch, we took Chris' road bikes to Beachy Head. The chalk headland is one of the world's most notorious suicide spots, together with the Golden Gate Bridge and the Aokigahara forest in Japan. A cool wind carried the smell of salt up the white cliffs.

For a fleeting moment, the view down on the light-house and over the hazy Channel infected me with calm happiness.

In the evening, Chris and I sat in his living room. We played video games and brainstormed ideas for his bike shop. After a couple of beers, we told endless stories of parties and girls and childish burglaries and acts of vandalism—stories of long, cold Stockholm nights and times of carelessness. We exchanged anecdotes of a quirky politics professor whom we had kept running into at techno parties and who had vanished off the face of the earth in my last term. Before we went to bed, Chris recounted the story of 'June 14th 2012', the day Chris had slept with four girls on four separate occasions. I must have heard that story a thousand times.

On Monday, I packed my backpack, said goodbye to Chris and Herbert, and got on the train to Bristol. The disastrous privatised British railway system decided to provide me with two additional hours to bask in the sun on train station benches—the air flickering above hot, rusty tracks running into the distance. To be fair, I was still travelling faster than in any preceding phase in human history. Once on the move, I saw blooming meadows and terraced houses made from brick in all possible shades of red lying beyond the train window.

In the evening, Bristol welcomed me with a warm breeze the Gulf Stream had carried all the way from the Mexican coast. Theresa picked me up in her new car, some shapeless Asian box on wheels.

I had met Theresa six months ago during an unbearable after-work networking event in a bar, where she and her colleagues had let their business trip to London come to an end. She worked as a junior manager at the human resource department of a temporary employment agency. The agency lent out workers to firms where they had previously earned twice as much in their regular jobs—a fact which Theresa would counter with a half-hearted, memorised speech about flexibility and career opportunity before quickly changing topic. When I noticed her in the bar, I had been attracted by the slim yet athletic figure beneath her trouser suit, and too bored not to try my luck. After discovering our mutual love for Fincher films and Hemingway, we escaped our corporate obligations that night, and she stayed at my flat for the rest of the weekend. She had come to London four times since. When I had asked her whether she would finally return the favour and let me stay at her place this weekend, she had seemed excited. She even took time off to fit my schedule.

We didn't talk the whole ride to her place. She lived in a new apartment complex near the Clifton Suspension Bridge, where the daredevils of the Oxford University Dangerous Sports Club had invented bungee jumping in 1979. When we arrived, Theresa closed the door, threw my backpack into a corner of the hallway, and started ripping off my clothes, kissing me vigorously. I pulled off her blouse and pushed her against the wall. Her slender muscles trembled under my touch. Never breaking our kiss, I moved her through the hallway and pushed her through the first door I could find. We ended up in the kitchen. We ripped off our remaining clothes. I sat her on the kitchen table, on top of an unfolded newspaper, and started licking her. She pulled me up and handed me a condom. She wanted me, now. I moved inside her and thrust my hips against hers, her twitching legs flung over my shoulders. She soon uttered suppressed moans, one hand clinging to the table, the other holding her straight blonde hair in front of her face. A cup fell off the table and burst on the hardwood floor. After I came, we both laughed, gasping for breath.

When we had cooled down a little, Theresa jumped off the table and picked up the shards from the floor. She looked at me with ruffled hair and red cheeks and said, 'I'm glad you're here. Let's go and get dinner.' I liked her commanding attitude. We had dinner outside a restaurant called The Seafood Shack in an old dock building on the harbourside, watching the sun set over the water and the hills of western Bristol. I had a whole baked gilt-head sea bream with roasted potatoes, and we shared a bottle of Sauvignon Blanc. We toasted her recent pay rise, and she told me about her week of scuba diving and climbing on the Greek island of Kalymnos. When I told her I had quit my job with no follow-up plan but to travel, she seemed shocked.

'When are you coming back?'

'I don't know yet. Maybe never—I moved out of my flat. Let's see what comes up.'

'You're stupid. You shouldn't throw away everything just because you're afraid of growing up.' She looked at me sternly.

I didn't get why she was so upset. We finished our dessert and the wine and walked back west to her place along the harbour canal. Instead of having more sex, as I had hoped, we went straight to bed. Lights out, frosty silence.

I was glad when the tension between us was gone the following day. We had breakfast in bed, and then Theresa showed me around Bristol. We hopped on and off waterbuses and climbed various hills with magnificent views of the city. We followed the roots of Banksy and saw the *Girl with a Pierced Eardrum* near the Marina and the *Well Hung Lover* down from Park Street Bridge. The stencils had been vandalised with blue paint bombs. After dinner, we went to a music festival near the docks. In the night, we had sex like bunnies. Theresa was a devoted lover, and she let me try a lot of filthy stuff with her. But I often felt she perceived it more as an obligation than a pleasure. When we lay in bed and she gave me a head massage that night, she told me in her slightly husky voice of her dream of throwing opulent garden parties behind a house near the beach in Portishead. For a moment, I almost wanted to stay for good.

On Wednesday morning, Theresa drove me back to the train station. I thanked her for two nice days in Bristol and kissed her goodbye. I was about to head for my train to London when she grabbed my arm and said, 'Wait. I need to talk to you.' Tears glimmered in her eyes.

I fell back into the passenger seat and closed the door. I had a queasy feeling in my stomach. 'Did I do something wrong?'

'You're *doing* something wrong, you idiot! Don't go.'

'You know I have to take care of some things in London and leave for Hamburg soon.'

'But you don't have to leave! I know we only met a couple of times, and I didn't want to scare you off. But now that you're leaving, you have to know that I want you. I'm sick and tired of all the superficial Tinder dates who try to impress me with their stories about trips they took with their mates on their fathers' sailing boats. You're different. You don't take yourself so seriously. You can't imagine how much the thought of seeing you again soon has kept me going through this stressful week. And I know you like me too! I can see it in the way you look at me in the mornings.'

I was taken by surprise. 'Look, I like spending time with you. But I have to go. I feel stuck, and I need some time off.' I felt the pressing urge to run.

'You don't even know whether you will come back!' Theresa screamed amid heavy tears. 'You can take time off here and look for something that doesn't include an 80-hour working week.'

'It's more profound than that.' I opened the door. 'I'm going to miss my train. I'm sorry.'

'You're making a mistake. You're looking for something perfect that doesn't exist. And while you're looking, life doesn't wait.'

When I kissed her goodbye, her tears tickled my cheeks. I had misjudged her. And I had hurt someone. Again.

The train ride to London was scornfully sunny. I spent it talking to an astute businessman next to me about Chinese credit bubbles.

In London, I stayed with an old colleague, who had also agreed to store some of my things—my suits, my guitar, and my boxing gear. He was a short, balding risk analyst in his mid-thirties. After two or three drinks, he would cry his heart out about how he would never find the right woman and would die alone. He was one of those sad men who had never learnt how to approach a woman with confidence. At least he had enough money to have fun with the wrong women.

On my first evening in London, I had dinner in the Bonneville Tavern, an eerily lit brasserie serving fine cocktails in the same street in Hackney as my old flat. I said farewell to the bar's stern stag looking down judgingly from the rugged wall, and took one last walk through my old neighbourhood before I went back to my old colleague's flat on the Isle of Dogs.

On Thursday night, I went to GŎNG, the bar on the 52nd floor of the Shard. I skipped the cheesily-themed cocktail menu and had a couple of Dry Martinis, which tasted fine. I started reading *The Drifters* by James A. Michener, a battered paperback I had found in Theresa's selection of her mother's books. I couldn't help overhearing the conversation at the table next to me. A group of cosmopolitan trust-fund kids were discussing the new Chilterns apartments in the West End, shopping in Mount Street in Mayfair, their party the other night at Loulou's, the new summer menu at the Crow's Nest in Montauk, and whether Paul's Baby Grand in Manhattan was still hip. Weekend plans were made for Art Basel, and trips in private jets to Beijing were contemplated. When one of the rich kids told his rich friends that his crazy rich father had just flown out two world-renowned German veterinarians to Dubai to doctor his favourite falcon, I had to stifle a hysterical giggle. I tried to block out the rest of their reality-detached conversation. My gaze wandered over the illuminated skyline, scanning the skyscrapers of the City of London to the north and the bank towers of Canary Wharf's financial district to the east, beyond the tiny Tower Bridge. Behind the skyscrapers' glass facades toiled armies of uniformed suits—young, intelligent people full of energy, spending the nights of their best years in front of flickering screens. Finance was sucking up the brightest minds of our generation and turning them into 'high performers'. If Albert Einstein was born today, he would likely end up as a quant, devising complex derivative instruments that his bank could sell to clueless public pension funds.

During my last year at the firm, my first as an associate, I had earned 350,000 pounds, a sum my late hardworking father would have had to work for a decade to amass. All the firm had asked for in return were 70 to 100 hours of my life per week. And the moral flexibility to tell myself that risky leveraged buyouts, tax optimisation, and fraudulent self-dealing were somehow essential to the financial system's function of efficiently allocating capital. And I didn't even have to wear a tie, and my boss would buy me drinks in rooftop bars at midnight after work. I gulped my last Martini, took a last look at the steel-and-glass colossuses looming into the clear night sky, and left.

The next morning, I liquidated 30,000 pounds of my savings. I donated two-thirds of it to Médecins Sans Frontières, UNICEF, and the Human Rights Watch. I sent some money to my brother, designated for anything my mum might need. The rest was for travelling until I had received my payoff money. At noon, I packed my backpack, took the tube to Heathrow, and boarded the plane for Hamburg.

Rather than love, than money, than fame,
give me truth.

Henry David Thoreau
Walden

3

I was staying in the Anemone Hostel, close to Hamburg Hauptbahnhof. The area around the station was sleazy and dirty. Shady characters lingered around every corner—addicts, drug dealers, and rough sleepers. One-legged pigeons fought over breadcrumbs scattered over the station square.

I took a short walk underneath green-leaved trees along the Inner Alster Lake. After having Labskaus, a traditional sailors' dish, in the Parlament restaurant below the Rathaus, I went to the bar in my hostel. I met a group of French architecture students on a field trip around northern Germany. They introduced me to their card game and shared their wine and rum with me. I had a lengthy discussion with Fernand from Bordeaux about hiking. He told me about doing the Alpe-Adria trail and the GR 10 trail that runs the length of the Pyrenees. When he talked with shining eyes, I felt his love for the mountains; his stories about being the first to stand on a summit in the rays of the morning sun allowed me to almost smell the morning dew. When I went to sleep in my eight-bed dorm, I was happy I had chosen to stay in a hostel.

On Saturday, I took a long walk across the bridges linking the brick warehouses along the Speicherstadt's canals and joined a harbour tour from the Landungsbrücken pontoons in St. Pauli. The tour on the small boat on the Elbe took me past the towering cranes of the colossal harbour on the islands of the branching river, through the canals of the Speicherstadt, past the recently finished Elbphilharmonie with its massive, glassy, hoisted sail, and back to the Landungsbrücken. From there, I took another boat to the ship-like Dockland building, from whose top I had a splendid view of the harbour. I walked further down the bank of the Elbe and found a cosy beach café. Most of the chairs were taken, but there was one left at a little table; a young woman was sitting in the other chair. She had thick, shoulder-length brown hair and wore oversized, nerdy glasses on her button nose. Between her denim shorts and her white cropped shirt, I glimpsed her tanned, slender belly. She was absorbed in George Orwell's *1984*. I approached her and said, 'Hi.'

She looked up and pierced me with her curious deep-brown eyes. '*Hej*!'

I pointed at her book and said, 'Let's make a deal. I won't spoil the ending if you allow me to sit in the chair next to you.' Really, that was what I was going with? I had a try at a confident grin.

'Blackmail? What a great way to start a conversation!' She gave me a smile that set her eyes on fire and made my knees weak. 'But I think it's clear how it ends: "Under the spreading chestnut tree, I sold you and you sold me."' She pointed at the empty beach chair. 'Be my guest.'

I detected a Swedish accent in her mellow voice. I sat down and said, 'Sorry, I usually don't run around threatening to ruin people's reading experiences.'

She giggled. When I introduced myself, she gave me her graceful hand and looked me straight in the eyes. It seemed like she could see right into my mind. She said, 'Nice to meet you. I'm Alice.'

Alice and I watched colossal container ships slowly floating by in the afternoon sun. Resembling a herd of titanic giraffes, dockside cranes loomed on the opposite bank of the Elbe. As we drank coffee, we talked about how Orwell's masterpiece had been in great demand since the election of Trump last November. Alice told me she had presented her research on dying coral reefs at an academic conference in Hamburg and was now staying for a few more days on holiday. She had grown up in Gothenburg and was doing a PhD in Marine Biology in Stockholm. We talked about the best places for techno music, food, and art in the Venice of the North.

When she asked me what I was doing, I replied, 'I have quit my job, and now I'm on a quest for meaning of sorts.'

'Why did you quit?'

I hesitated, looking into her interrogating eyes. I felt the urge to let her know who I was. 'I had a job as a data scientist at a private equity firm in London. I programmed deep-learning algorithms to forecast risk-adjusted returns.'

'Sounds exciting!' she mocked. I chuckled. She added, 'You don't strike me as a banker.'

'Well, it took me three years to figure that out myself. On some level, I always liked what I was doing. You meet smart and inspired people and work with cutting-edge technology on some of the hardest problems around. But, in the end, you're working for an industry that doesn't create a single tangible thing, induces immense social costs, and yet takes the biggest cut. I hated it. But I didn't listen to my heart for a long time. The truth is, two weeks ago, I was sitting at my desk at work on a miserable Wednesday morning and realised I was truly unhappy. And I couldn't remember the last time I had been happy. For the rest of the day, I couldn't stop thinking about my future. I saw myself as a desperate man with a lot of money but no time to spend it or friends to spend it with. Before my eyes, my colleagues morphed into featureless suits. And I was one of them.' I paused. Alice's dark eyes were digging into my soul. 'You see, I broke up with Emma, my ex-girlfriend, two years ago and have done nothing but work ever since. I stopped growing. The morning after my breakdown at the office, after a sleepless night, I'm in the bathroom and look in the mirror. Suddenly, I get a panic attack. The walls come creeping in, and I can't breathe. I can usually deal with anxiety, but this time it's too strong for me. I go back to bed and hide under the blanket, despair weighing down on me. The minutes that pass make me late for work and increase the pressure and panic. So I decide to simply not go—screw the meaningless job, screw my sociopath boss, and screw the whole damned world of finance. I felt relieved instantly. I had a long, extensive breakfast and went for a run. I knew I couldn't go back to the company. I quit the next day. Now, I'm figuring out what I want to do and where I want to go.'

Alice was leaning over to me on the table, her head resting on her clasped hands.

I laughed. 'I don't know why I'm telling you all this.'

'It seems like you've been waiting to talk about this for a while. It's good you had an epiphany before it's too late . . . But let's move on to more important things. We should go to a strip club!'

A taxi ride later, I was sitting on a sofa in front of a dance pole on which a bottle blonde with pointy breasts was doing a rather impressive fitness routine to Southern hip hop. Dust motes floated in the red spotlight. Alice bought us drinks and put the dollar bills we had to buy at the entrance into the dancer's thong. With a beaming smile, Alice fell onto the sofa and leaned her head on my shoulder. Since we were virtually the only customers, we were soon joined by four more dancers. I had heard horror stories about dancers tricking you into paying for insanely over-priced drinks, but instead, we simply chatted about mundanities. Two dancers told us they studied in Romania and earned money over the summer in Germany.

After half an hour, Alice decided we needed to get a private dance and picked a redheaded beauty. The dancer guided us to a small mirrored room, where we sat down on another leather sofa, and she started to dance. She took off her underwear with elegant pre-cision. Once naked, she turned around and showed us her firm bum, moving hypnotically to the resounding bass of the music. I got hard when she bent over and spread her cheeks, her red fingernails clawing into her smooth skin. Perplexed, I looked over at Alice. She smiled at me, a fire flaring in her eyes. The dancer sat on my lap with splayed legs and rubbed her breasts in my face. They smelled of floral perfume and fresh sweat. She leaned over to Alice and gave her a brief but passionate kiss. I couldn't help but grin content-edly. After the redhead had danced for another minute, she picked up her lingerie and left the room through a velvet curtain. Alice put her hand on my leg and asked, 'Did you like it?' I leaned over and kissed her. Her soft lips pressed against mine and our tongues immediately picked up the same rhythm. The kiss had the thrill of a first kiss, but the harmony it normally took weeks and months to find. Her hair smelled of the stripper's perfume. We had to interrupt our kiss when one of the bouncers kicked us out of the room. We said goodbye to the dancers and walked out of the club.

I invited Alice for dinner at a small Italian restaurant nearby. I watched her study the menu with a cute frown. Her cheeks were a bit chubby, and I spotted a little mole on her chin. Her natural beauty wasn't distorted by any garish makeup. With a subtle movement, she pushed the nerdy glasses back towards the bridge of her nose and hooked a strand of her thick brown hair behind her ear. When she looked up at me, her deep-brown eyes radiated a genuine curiosity. I already knew I was in trouble.

After sunset, we left the restaurant, tipsy from a bottle of heavy Chianti. Walking down a dark road, we saw the silhouettes of prostitutes in knee-high lacquered boots and cheap dresses waiting in front of decaying houses. Only up close did I notice their beard stubble and Adam's apples. When Alice asked me whether I wanted to take one of them back to her hotel room, I laughed, only 80 per cent sure she was kidding. The hotel she was staying in was in the west of Hamburg, in Groß Flottbek. We walked there along the bank of the Elbe. When we passed the beach again, Alice dared me to go for a swim. Giggling, we stripped naked. Her perfect breasts shimmered in the blue light coming from the docks. Between them, she had a minimalistic black tattoo of a rose. She took my hand, and we ran into the river. It was cold but not too cold, and we swam for a while. Unlike me, Alice was an excellent swimmer. Back at a spot where we could stand, we kissed, breathing heavily, her breasts pressed against my chest. The hypnotic interplay of blue light and shadow revealed tiny blonde hairs around her stiff nipples. We longed for each other, but Alice told me to wait until we were in her hotel room. Voices sound different in warm summer nights— smoother, and full of auspicious secrets. We recovered our clothes and rushed to her hotel, sharing cigarettes under the starry firmament.

We didn't leave the hotel for two days. We only left the room to refuel at the hotel restaurant, run by an old, cheerful couple who always greeted us with conspiratorial smiles.

During those two days, Alice and I carefully explored each other's bodies. I studied her two other tattoos—a small world map on her right shoulder blade and a primaeval fish symbol on her left ankle that had been done by a shaman in the Peruvian Andes. Her fingers followed the scar I had on my right arm from breaking it in a stupid bar fight and caressed the scars on my knees from slipping off a crag as a little boy. As she explored the fire scars on my belly, which I told her were from stumbling into a campfire, she whispered, 'Isn't it oddly beautiful how time weaves scars into our skin—like ornate flowers on a Persian carpet?' I discovered a little birthmark on her mons pubis and claimed it mine, no matter how many men had been there before. She made fun of my thick chest hair but didn't mind it as a pillow for her afternoon naps.

We had steamy mornings and tender days and delirious nights. In between, Alice would put her head on my chest, and we would talk for hours. She had been everywhere, working as a marine biologist and travelling, and had many more plans for many more trips. She told me of many men, and some women too. For a moment, her stories of drug-fuelled experiments with strangers gave me an impalpable feeling of envy. With all the things she had seen and done, how could I satisfy her? But then it seemed I did, and I slept like a baby. I told Alice that, so far, Emma had been the only girl I had ever loved after a long series of flings. I recounted that I had treated her shamefully, which I bitterly regretted. Emma had been nothing but caring and even might have saved my life during dark times in Stockholm. Alice laughed at me for being oversensitive and then apologised.

As a child, Alice had travelled the world with her parents, who were passionate divers. Ever since seeing the diversity of sea life, she had known she wanted to help protect it. She told me stories of never-ending swarms of little fish, glowing in the dark like rainbows, and mysterious colour-changing creatures hiding in the corners of a reef. Her warm smile accompanied tales of lurking sharks gliding soundlessly through the water, as they had done since a time when there had been different stars shaping the night sky.

One morning, we had sex in the bathtub, flooding the bathroom with water smelling of exotic fruits. Sex can be a cleansing ritual, washing away your sins and problems for a while. With most old religions dead, it is one of the last forms of ritual purification left.

When I couldn't sleep during our third night together and woke Alice up with my tossing and turning, she stroked my cheek and whispered, 'You need to get some rest. You know, beneath the Sierra del Abra in Mexico, there are underwater caves in which pale, eyeless fish drift in a lightless world. They feed on organic matter washed into the darkness by seasonal floods. And even these lonely cavefish sleep for two hours a day. Relax and close your eyes.'

I slept until Alice woke me up for lunch.

On the third day, we joined civilisation again. It was a sunny Tuesday afternoon in Hamburg. A gentle breeze was coming in from the North Sea. We went to a contorted café called Dreiundsiebzig next to the graffiti-covered Rote Flora in Schanzenviertel, which had been squatted since the late '80s and was still a hotspot of left-wing activism.

Over cheesecake and coffee, I asked Alice, 'Are you religious?'

'Like, do I believe in God?'

'Yeah. Or, generally, do you believe in an external meaning of life?'

'No, not really. I mean, there might be. But there probably isn't one.'

'A fellow nihilist.'

'Aren't we all these days?'

'I guess. But do you think we should create a new meaning for ourselves? And should this meaning be rooted in worldly concepts or derive from tran-scendent values? Or should we embrace the absurdity of existence and roll with it?'

Alice chuckled, 'I don't know. I'm not too interest-ed in philosophy, I guess. I could read all the books in the world and throw big words at the simple question "why?" and still end up not a bit wiser than before. In the end, I believe that, if nothing means anything, I might as well enjoy myself a little. Preferably without being an arsehole to others.'

41

I laughed, 'Well, for someone who isn't interested in philosophy, you certainly have an admirable life philosophy. Shall I get us some beers?'

'You want to start drinking before dinner? I have to catch my plane to Stockholm in the morning.'

'Well, if nothing means anything, we might as well enjoy ourselves a little.'

She laughed. 'You're a quick learner.'

We worked our way through the drinks menu and played 'Who Am I?' until Alice got stuck with being Britney Spears for half an hour.

After sandwiches and quiche for dinner, we had the brilliant idea to do shots. The waitress asked what occasion had prompted us to drink in their café for eight hours. We hadn't even noticed that it was already pitch-black outside. Alice screamed euphorically, 'We're celebrating the meaningless of life!' That was a motto the waitress could get behind, and she joined in our last round of shots.

When we stepped outside, a dystopian scene greeted us: riot police dressed all in black lined both sides of the street. Angry chants came from the park to our right. A large group of protesters came around the street corner. They were dressed in black, too, and had their faces veiled with scarves and hats. There had been a big demonstration in the inner city against global inequality, which was apparently in some way connected to the rioters' rage against the police, who represented a diffuse idea of 'the system'. Amid angry screaming, the rioters threw bottles and cobblestones they had gouged out of the pavement at the police. The police formed a wall and hid behind their shields. Alice and I tried to stay close to the shop windows to our left and move away from the escalating violence. Someone shoved me hard as a bulk of the black bloc ran towards the police. The cops answered with riot sticks and tear gas. Their silent precision was frightening. A man bleeding from his temple stumbled past us. I put my arm around Alice, and we started running. We zigzagged through the war zone, away from the screams and the sound of stone and steel on plastic and bone. Alice got tear gas in her eyes but pushed me to keep running. My eyes burned. My nose started running. Finally, we rushed around a corner and found ourselves on a quiet, deserted street. On the asphalt, pieces of broken glass reflected the light of burning cars. Were those really the cars of the rich the rioters saw themselves pitted against? Alice couldn't see through the burning tears in her eyes and clutched my hand. We jogged around two more street corners and knew that we were safe. The noise of the riot echoed in the distance. The tear gas' pungent smell of burning bleach and the stench of burnt rubber faded. Alice laughed off the pain in her eyes and gave an off-key rendition of *Tears in Heaven*. We walked for two more blocks and found a taxi that took us back to the hotel.

In our room, we were still drunk. After we washed out our eyes, we moved to the bed, and Alice let me fuck her in the arse—the forbidden fruit. After a cool shower, I wrapped Alice up in the bedsheets and asked her, 'Do you want to live with me in paradise? We'll be Adam and Eve, and we'll be naked all the time. And we'll leave behind the knowledge of good and evil.'

Alice gazed at me with teary, half-closed eyes and slurred, 'Shut up, or I puke into your face.'

I nodded, kissed her on the forehead, and accepted that I was already helplessly in love with my little Swedish rabbit.

Early in the morning, Alice's alarm clock woke us up. We both had horrible hangovers. Alice stumbled around the room in a pitiful attempt to pack. I accompanied her to the nearby S-Bahn station, and we got on a train eastward. She renewed her offer to visit her in Stockholm for Midsummer at the weekend. My flight there was in two days—what a peculiar coincidence, if you believe in the concept. We had a dry, hungover goodbye kiss and a hug I wished could have lasted longer. When I got off the train at the Hauptbahnhof, Alice shouted, 'See you on Friday.' I nodded with a smile. I walked back to my hostel and realised I had been wearing the same clothes for four days. I smiled and shook my head. London felt light-years away. I made sure my things were still in my locker and slept until late afternoon.

In the evening, I went into the Hamburger Kunsthalle between the Inner and Outer Alster and numbly stared at Caspar David Friedrich's *Wanderer above the Sea of Fog*. What undiscovered lands lay before me, still cloaked in murky uncertainty?

On Thursday, I climbed up to the viewing platform of St. Michael's Church, fondly called 'Michel', and spent my afternoon relaxing in the meadow of Planten un Blomen. My old friend Ben called me. I answered the phone, 'Hey, Ben, how are you?'

'Hey, man! Good! Are you in Germany? I saw your post of the Reeperbahn.' His voice vibrated with geniality.

'Yeah, I'm still in Hamburg. What's up?'

'Not much, always busy at work. And we're moving into our new flat this weekend.'

'Who's *we*?'

'Me and Helen—you haven't met her, have you?'

'Oh yeah, your girlfriend?'

'Yeah, we're still going strong, believe it or not!'

I chuckled and said, 'Congrats.'

'Thanks, man! What's new with you?'

'Uhm, well, I quit my job, for starters.'

Ben exclaimed, 'No way! Why?'

'It didn't seem right anymore.'

'Okay, sorry to hear that. Do you have another job now?'

'No, and I don't know what I'll do next.'

'I'm going to ask around. Should be easy to find something new for you.' I was silent. After a moment, Ben said, 'Did you see Emma is getting married?'

'Yeah, I saw it on Facebook.'

'How do you feel about it? I know it's been two years, but you guys were pretty serious.'

'It's okay, I guess.' I sighed and said, 'Well, to tell you the truth, seeing her engagement picture during a Facebook break in the office kind of triggered my decision to quit my job.'

'Oh, is it still that bad?'

'No, but it made me take a look at my life, and I didn't like what I saw.'

'I'm sorry, man. If you need anything, let me know.'

'Thanks, man. But I just need a little change.'

'Are you travelling a bit now?'

'Yeah, that's the plan. I met a girl here in Hamburg whom I'm going to meet in Stockholm tomorrow.'

'A girl, huh?' Ben chuckled. 'Who is she?'

'Her name's Alice. I'm afraid I already have a major crush on her.'

Ben laughed. 'You've always been a romantic.'

'Hardly.'

Ben laughed again and said, 'All right, I've got to

get back to work. Those Excel files won't fill themselves in. But good luck with that girl! And let me know if you come through Frankfurt, or maybe we can meet somewhere else; I get around a lot lately.'

'Sounds good. I'll keep you posted.'

'Awesome! See you!'

After Ben hung up, I lay on the summer grass and soon caught myself contemplating marrying Alice in Stockholm. I needed a drink.

Back at my hostel, I ate two burgers for dinner and had a couple of beers. I listened to two drunk Australians discussing whether they were addicted to porn, masturbation, or both. When they started itemising the merits of virtual-reality bukkake, I went to bed.

Sometimes, when I couldn't sleep at night, I dreamed up a post-apocalyptic world where I lived on an island with all the people in my life who were important to me. We embodied a new tribe, building a new civilisation. We had to protect the white-sand shores from evil invaders who came from the fringes of the world the blazing sun of nuclear death had destroyed. I even made up a wacky backstory of how we had all ended up on this island that involved a transpacific flight to a huge wedding and an artificial superintelligence that had decided to eliminate mankind. I would usually hold an eminent position in our insular society, such as delegating the building of new treehouse homes or leading efforts to defend our island against marauding post-apocalyptic pirates. It was a childish dream of adult responsibilities, devoid of moral ambiguities, and with a tangible sense of purpose. In a typical episode of this fantasy, I would have saved the day and be standing on the beach with a woman who admired me for my virtue. We would look at thunderstorms over the distant ocean, contemplating a brighter future, whitewashed from the heavy burden of thousands of years of human struggle. That night, that woman was Alice, going full *Blue Lagoon* with a hula skirt.

On Friday morning, I walked down to the docks and breathed in the harbour air once more. I bid farewell to the gigantic container ships, the backbone of the modern world. Almost everything you might buy in a shop was shipped in one of these monsters. The biggest ones can carry a billion bananas at a time. I bought a fish sandwich and set out for the airport.

On my flight to Stockholm, I tried to catch up on the news. It mainly was reports confusing decisive political elections with sports, alarmist headlines about men with nuclear weapons at their disposal acting like kindergarten bullies, and articles about record-breaking stock markets. I stopped reading when the offshoots of the Stockholm archipelago became visible below us. The view of scattered, rugged islands covered in dark-green conifer trees never ceased to captivate me.

In the depths of winter, I finally learned that within me there lay an invincible summer.

Albert Camus
Return to Tipasa

4

From Arlanda Airport, I took the bus to Märsta and then the Pendeltåg to T-Centralen—an old trick requiring only one single-journey ticket and avoiding the expensive buses or trains. I went directly to Lappis, Stockholm's largest student accommodation complex. It formed its own small town in the north of Stockholm and close to the university. Its multistorey brick buildings from the '60s accommodated roughly 2,000 mostly international students. Lappis' claim to fame was the Lappis Howl, during which one student will start screaming on a Tuesday night and many others join in, ending in a concert of desperate howls into the Nordic darkness.

Alice lived in a corridor room in Lappis. She was waiting for me in front of her house with friends she introduced as Arman, Sherine, and Dion. I gave Alice an awkward hug. She wore a light white summer dress and looked beautiful. I threw my backpack into the boot of Arman's car. Arman was a bulky guy from Iran. He had brought the car with him from Italy, where he worked. We jumped into the car in a hurry and started driving. It was Midsummer's Eve, when everybody leaves Stockholm as early as possible and heads to the Archipelago. The sun stood high in the blue sky and the air smelled of summer meadows and the sea.

On the drive, I sat in the back seat and talked to Sherine, who had moved from Egypt to Sweden five years ago and was finishing her master's. Next to her sat Dion, a tall, ripped surfer-type with a perpetual smile and a shark-tooth necklace who radiated pure, calm confidence. He was giving Alice, slouched in the passenger seat in front of him, a head massage she seemed to fervidly enjoy. I tried to ignore it and focused on Sherine. She was a quirky bundle of energy and bombarded me with questions about my travel to Stockholm, my connection to Alice, any plans for my time in Sweden, and whether I knew what my spirit animal was. As we drove down the narrow forest road that led to the summer cabin of one of Alice's friends, Arman cranked up the volume of the car stereo. Together we sang to Lenny Kravitz's *Fly Away*.

After a short while, the trees opened to a lush meadow with a luxurious cottage painted in customary falu red and a wooden jetty with a small sauna cabin next to it. The place was already filled with a few cars and many people who were setting up tables and dishing up loads of food, beer, and schnapps. Everyone greeted our gang with immense joy. The scene resembled a commercial for some hip flavoured beer. Alice introduced me to all her friends, and I forgot most of their names. It was a diverse crowd, half Swedish, half lost children of the world. Everyone seemed to be closely connected by invisible bonds and mysterious tales. I tried to help carry salad bowls out of the kitchen but was mainly in everybody's way. Soon, a blonde beauty with a clear-cut face called

Evelina, the hostess, commanded me to sit. An exuberant feast commenced with potatoes, countless variations of pickled herrings, and a myriad of salads. I was glad to sit next to Alice, who made fun of my non-existent Swedish skills and made me drink a lot of bitter-tasting schnapps with her friends. I was embarrassed that I hadn't learned the language during my three years living in Sweden. To my defence, Swedes always switched to English when they noticed you were a beginner, and Swedish wasn't a particularly useful language in the wider world. It didn't help that it was tough to break into Swedish social circles and that most of the northerners were emotionally unavailable during the seemingly ten months of winter. Sweden was a country of a peculiar tolerance for and detachment from others. Also, I was a lazy loafer who didn't care enough to learn new languages, as Alice quite rightly pointed out.

After the prolonged feast, there was some cheerful Swedish singing—something about frogs—and Alice and Sherine forced me to dance around the maypole. During the Dark Ages, the Catholic Church had tried to transform Midsummer into a Christian festival. But today, the old pagan traditions lived on in the phallus symbols, and the wreaths of flowers in the girls' hair, harnessing nature's magic. I danced with Evelina, Dion, and some other girls. Everybody was drawn to Dion's cool serenity, and the girls danced around him rather than the pole. When I saw Alice standing alone on the jetty, I filled two glasses with Prosecco and went down to the water. 'It's beautiful here, thanks for inviting me,' I said and handed her a glass and touched it with mine.

'It is. I'm glad you could make it.' She took a sip, her red lipstick leaving a mark on the glass, and looked at me with joyful curiosity.

I kissed her. Finally, I had arrived. I put her face between my hands and said, 'I want you.'

'Relax. Midsummer nights last forever.'

She took my hand and dragged me back to the party. I sat down next to Evelina, Sherine, and Arman. Their discussion had turned political, as all drunken discussions sooner or later do. Looking at Arman, Evelina said, 'How can you say Europe is taking in too many Muslim refugees? You're from a Muslim country yourself, and you're well integrated.'

Sherine chuckled and said, 'I'm not sure I'd call you well integrated, but Evelina has a point.'

Arman answered, 'Evelina, most of these refugees are young Muslim men who have grown up with completely different values. I don't think you know what you got yourself into. Sometimes it's funny to me how liberals can be so over-tolerant with religion when religion is anti-liberal.'

'But Islam isn't any better or worse than Christianity or any other religion.'

Sherine said, 'Yes. And why should we discriminate against Muslims who were forced to leave their home? They're not coming voluntarily.'

'Because Islam *is* worse! The only reason why Christianity isn't a big problem is nobody believes in it anymore. Many Muslims still believe, trust me. I'm not trying to say all refugees—well, technically, many of them don't qualify as refugees but are merely job hunters—anyways, I'm not saying they're all bad people. But welcoming millions into your open society who don't understand or respect its values is dangerous. The worst part is you're trying to deny the problem. Why do you think Sweden stopped reporting migrant crime rates years ago?'

I chimed in, 'Maybe you can acknowledge that accommodating a large number of refugees entails social costs but still choose to do so because you see it as your moral obligation? To help the poor and displaced? In the end, the West is to no small degree responsible for the wars and poverty around the world that make people flee.'

Sherine nodded. Evelina patted her on the shoulder, got up, and left. Arman looked at me as if he had just noticed me for the first time. A smile formed on his face, framed by wild dark hair and a sprawling full beard. With a chuckle, he said, 'I admire your readiness for self-sacrifice, brother. But about one billion people are surrounding Europe who would choose to live here if they could. Africa will soon double its population. Letting some of them in only makes the rest more eager. At which point do you build a wall?'

'Well, despite what the condemnations of Trump's build-the-wall populism might have you believe, we have already built walls along the African border. I don't think the situation is as alarming as you put it, though. I think we are rich enough to give these people refuge.'

Sherine said, 'Yes, precisely . . . But who knows, maybe Arman is right, and in 20 years, we celebrate Midsummer without alcohol because Allah forbids it.'

Arman laughed and exclaimed, 'It's so expensive in Sweden it's effectively prohibited, anyways!'

We touched glasses and had another bitter schnapps. Arman seemed to be a smart guy, but there was something about his eyes I didn't like—when he smiled, it didn't reach them.

Evelina and her friends had organised a large bonfire in time for the late sunset. People gathered around it on benches, garden chairs, and felled tree trunks. Some girls wrapped themselves in blankets as the air turned chilly. Anton and Erik, two prototype Swedes—tall, straight blond hair, bags of snus in their cheeks—started mellowly plucking their guitars. In the background, the sun set behind the Archipelago. For the rest of the short night, the orange sky would be reflected in the calm sea. Sherine offered to share some red wine with me, and we found two deckchairs for ourselves next to the fire. I tried to listen to her stories about travelling in Syria before it was consumed by war. But I was distracted by the image, emerging through the sparks of the fire, of Alice sitting on Dion's lap. He was probably repeating the heart-warming tales of his expeditions with Médecins Sans Frontières to India and Chad as a doctor-to-be I had overheard at the dinner table earlier. I passed on Arman's circulating joint; weed made me too sleepy for parties.

Cheering came from the other side of the bonfire; Alice was kissing Dion, then laughing with the girls sitting next to them. I needed a drink.

In the kitchen, I found gin, Campari, sweet vermouth, and ice and mixed a Negroni. I garnished it with an orange peel. When Arman stepped into the kitchen, I made him a drink as well. After he had complimented me on my bartending skills, we made our way back to the bonfire. When Alice saw me sitting in my chair again, she smiled, came over, and sat on my lap. She brushed her hand through my hair and asked, 'Where have you been?'

'I was just making Arman and me a drink.' I looked away.

'Are you all right?'

I turned back to her and said quietly, 'Yeah. It's

just—I don't know. I think I expected it to be different between you and me.' I glanced at Dion, who was drinking vodka straight from the bottle. She poked my shoulder, laughed, and said, 'Lighten up! Me and Dion are just messing around. Besides, I don't remember us getting married.'

She gave me a long and steamy kiss. After we had shared a cigarette, she walked to the kitchen to help Evelina prepare midnight snacks. My eyes followed her until she disappeared into the cabin. Sherine looked at me and said, 'You're in trouble.'

'I know.'

I took a deep sip of the glowing red aperitif.

Soon, Alice and Evelina served bruschetta and a snack called *gubbröra*—egg-anchovy salad on crisp-bread. The casual professionalism with which the party was run was characteristic of the upper-class kids who inhabit the big, expensive cities of the world. The late-night dinner was accompanied by boisterous talk of trips taken, parties survived, and visits around the globe planned together. It was past midnight, but the horizon was still glowing in all shades of orange and red. Arman opened the doors of his car and put the music on at full blast. People started dancing. Evelina delegated the task of making a batch of Mojitos in the kitchen to me. Apparently, Arman had excessively praised the drink I had made him earlier. I had worked as a bartender during my two years in Munich, and mixing classic cocktails still came easily. The right balance of sweet, bitter, and sour, paired with a characterful spirit, opens every man's heart and every woman's mind. One of the secrets to a good Mojito lies in the mint—use plenty but only squeeze it, don't crush it, and give the mint garnish a little spank to let the fragrance radiate.

When I ran out of mint, I went back outside and joined the frisky dance. Alice came over to me and smiled, her waving hips clouding my mind. The way her white dress fell off her breasts was the stuff dreams were made of. This night had been an emotional rollercoaster so far, and I still wasn't sure what I thought of her and Dion. But all that didn't matter now. I kissed her, and the rest of the world faded out of my consciousness. I had no past or future. Behind the blackness of my closed eyes was no space or time. Only the touch of Alice's body and lips assured me of my existence. Her kiss wiped out every shred of anger, pain, or sadness I might have ever felt.

By the time I opened my eyes, it was already getting lighter again. Alice and I warmed ourselves up at the fire and then jumped into the sea with the rest of the people still awake. Dion and I were the first to strip naked and jump from the jetty into the cold water. The cool early morning air carried our ecstatic shouts across the calm water. Alice challenged me to a swimming contest and defeated me with ease; she had been raised in the Seven Seas. Everybody went back ashore and gathered around the slowly dying fire to banish the cold. I put my arm around Alice, who was shivering in her light-blue underwear.

When Evelina and Alice started handing out blankets and sleeping bags from the cabin and assigning sleeping places, I stayed behind with Sherine. We had one last glass of schnapps. She told me how her father would take her to the Egyptian desert to show her the unpolluted night sky when she was a little girl. She often missed home, especially during the long and dark Swedish winters. In the flickering of the bonfire, she looked like an Egyptian princess with her untamed black hair.

I perceived a hint of wistfulness in her voice when she said, 'Someone is waiting for you,' and nodded towards the cabin.

Alice was standing there, a huge red blanket wrapped around her shoulders. She looked at us with a cordial and exhausted expression. I said goodnight to Sherine and went over to her.

'Where are we sleeping?'

'Follow me.'

She led me into the forest to a large hammock hung between two pine trees. I had been longing for her body all night, but now all I wanted to do was to sleep beside her. I could tell she felt the same way. Laughing, we climbed into the hammock and wrapped up in the blanket. I put my arm around Alice, and she fell asleep with her head on my chest. The first rays of the sun shone through the woods as I closed my eyes.

I was woken up by bustling activity in the meadow. Great efforts were being made to prepare a lavish hangover breakfast. My head was spinning and pounding, and my limbs were heavy. I wanted to stay in the hammock with Alice forever. But she urged me to get up, and I was parched with thirst, so I brought myself, inelegantly, back to solid ground. Alice made fun of my killer hangover and dragged me to the breakfast table. A pitcher of water, some Mediterranean delicacies, and some coffee rose me from the dead. When the others went for a swim in the midday sun, I found a spot in the shade to watch them in peace. Dion entertained the group by doing flips off the sauna roof into the water. The afternoon was spent in a coordinated clean-up operation before Arman drove us back to Lappis. Everybody was beat. Alice and I went to her small corridor room, where black underwear lay scattered around carelessly. We had sex in her shower and lay in her narrow bed with wet skin and red eyes.

After a late-afternoon nap, we cooked pasta for dinner. That night we snuggled together, fallen out of time. I didn't know whether there was a world beyond the closed window shutters, and I didn't care. Before I had met Emma many years ago, I had sometimes ended up on a plank bed in a Lappis box room with some girl I had met at a party. This time, I wasn't already scheming an exit strategy.

During the following days, Alice and I developed a routine. We had breakfast together in the shared kitchen, sometimes after going for a morning run, sometimes after Alice tried, with adorable desperation, to teach my stiff body some yoga. She had got hooked on yoga during a workshop in India and was now organising a class for Lappis students on weekends. I joined her on the way to her office at the university and then took the metro down into the city.

I roamed around the streets and reminisced about memories of my old life in Stockholm. I walked out of the central train station, which Chris and I had broken into in the middle of an alcohol-fuelled night, running across the tracks and exploring desolate office buildings. I passed the nightclub in Norrmalm, where I had met Emma at her first Erasmus party. My gaze had been captured by her innocent face and her long brown hair tied in a ponytail that had jumped straight out of my early puberty dreams of Lara Croft. She had just arrived from Berlin, where she was from. And she had nothing better to do than steal my heart with her radiant smile and kind nature. That night, I had tried to kiss her. But she had told me to go home, sleep off my drunkenness, and show her around and take her out for dinner the next day. Emma was the kindest person I had ever met, and, to this day, I didn't understand how in the world I had deserved her. I walked past the old Lion Bar on Sveavägen, where Chris and I had enjoyed the cheapest drinks in Stockholm and the company of the city's weirdest drunks. I wandered up to Monteliusvägen on Södermalm, with easily the best view of Stockholm; from its green wooden benches, you could see over Riddarfjärden and onto Stockholms rådhus, Riddarholmen with its yellow buildings and red church, and Gamla Stan. Monteliusvägen had been the stage for many beer-drinking sprees and man-to-man talks with Chris. It had been here I had first told Emma I loved her, for the first time in my life meaning it.

In central Södermalm, I passed the old bike shop where Chris used to work, next to the boxing gym where I had often trained and for which I had sometimes fought on weekends.

During the afternoons, I met with old friends who were still living in Stockholm. I had *fika*, the coffee and cake break that is a central part of the Swedish way of life, with Sebastian. He was the craziest Swede I knew. I had met him at an underground rave where he was trying to sell multivitamin pills as ecstasy. He used to break a bone every other month while skateboarding, freeskiing, or doing backflips off car roofs. He had achieved regional fame when he had climbed the metal framing of the Katarina Lift, which towers over Slussen, all the way to the top, with policemen waiting there to nick him. Now, he told me about the son a surrogate mother had birthed for him and his boyfriend six months ago, the flat they had bought, and his job as a teacher. I guess you could only chase the night on LSD for so long. I met Andrea, who was doing his PhD in Economics, for early drinks. We had gone to boxing classes together, but now we didn't have much to say to each other. Did he find natural experiments in steam-engine exposure in northern Sweden in the 1800s as fascinating as he told himself he did? I visited Sofie in her flat on Kungsholmen, from which she worked as a successful freelance fashion journalist and blogger. We had somehow ended up in bed together after I had won a boxing match against her older brother. But we had soon discovered that we enjoyed our shared love for sarcasm and amateur philosophy more than uninspired late-night hook-ups. Sofie told me about the fight against breast cancer she had won last year. She showed me the big scar on her left breast, now covered by a tattoo of Japanese cherry blossom. For a moment, I got all teary-eyed; that sonofabitch cancer had picked the wrong woman.

The evenings were reserved for Alice and me. We cooked dinner for each other and watched some of our favourite films together. I showed her *Raging Bull*, *One Flew Over the Cuckoo's Nest*, and *Apocalypse Now*. She introduced me to *Black Swan*, *The Broken Circle*, and *Captain Fantastic*. Snuggled into Alice's tiny, cosy bed, completely relaxed as I listened to her placid breathing—these were the happiest moments I had had in years.

Together with Sherine and Arman, we attended a rave in a dance hall next to the lake Spegeldammen in the middle of Norra Djurgården. After many hours of frenetic dancing, we howled like wolves on our way back to Lappis through the pitch-black woods.

Alice dragged me to various vegetarian and vegan restaurants and showed me the variety of a meatless kitchen. We took a shot at a room escape game, in which we had to save the world from a zombie apocalypse, and set a new record. To celebrate the averted disaster, we went to the casino, where I taught Alice how to play blackjack.

At the weekend, we went with Dion to Slakthusset, a nightclub in an old slaughterhouse with a rooftop dancefloor in the south of Stockholm. When I returned from the bar with a bottle of Prosecco, Alice was making out with a tall blonde she knew from her yoga class. She tried to convince her to come home with us and made her kiss me, but we lost her on our way out of the crowded club. While we stood outside and smoked, I saw the blonde around the corner of the building. She seemed to be looking for us. I didn't say anything and let her walk away into the dawn; the idea of having to share Alice intimidated me. Chris would have killed me had he known. Sometime during the night, Dion, who had at first seemed overexcited and then strangely distant, had vanished. Alice and I went back to Lappis on the first metro, reeking of alcohol. Slouched in her seat, she told me Dion would often take a lot of ecstasy when he had some days off and disappear for nights and days on end. Back in Lappis, Alice and I fell asleep half-dressed on top of her bedsheet.

After a dozen days in Stockholm, I told Alice I planned to take the ship to Tallinn at the beginning of the following week. I asked her whether she wanted to come along. She said she was going on a diving expedition to Cuba. We were sitting on a bench on Kastellholmen, overlooking the bay of Stockholm. I turned to her and asked, 'Do you want me to come back afterwards?'

'I thought you were doing a Europe trip, no? But you can do whatever you want.'

I hesitated before I said, 'I know we've only known each other for two weeks. But the way you make me feel—I haven't felt like this in a long time. I—I want to see you again.'

It was hard for her to conceal her embarrassment. 'I don't know what you would be doing here in Stockholm. Don't get me wrong, the past weeks with you were a lot of fun. But that's all it was for me—fun. I'm sorry.'

I was crushed. I couldn't look at Alice anymore. My gaze wandered over to the rocks of Södermalm, where I had drunk and fucked the pain away in a distant life. Had I made any progress since then, or had I simply distracted my demons with Emma's love and then with working ad nauseam? There was no use in fighting now; I had tried to give Alice all I had. When I was younger, I had played hard-to-get with girls, all the way to being a full-blown scumbag. And it had worked like a charm. Similarly, now that Alice had rejected me, I wanted her even worse. What a messed-up bunch we all were.

Alice and I silently agreed not to talk about the issue anymore. We went to Lappis and had sex, which was as good as ever. And for the next two days, we returned to our established routine.

On Saturday night, we went for drinks with Dion and Arman to celebrate Arman's return to Rome for his work. When Alice and the guys fooled around, it stung like a red-hot knife, knowing I would soon not be a part of this life anymore. When Dion talked to me like I was his best friend and cordially put his arm on my shoulder, I detected a restlessness in his audacious eyes. I had a hard time not punching his flawless cleft chin.

Since the metro wasn't running that night and we couldn't figure out which night bus to take, Alice and I walked home. On our way, we heard music coming from a flat and took the chance to ring the bell. We were let in, and before long, we realised we had crashed the party of a support group for deaf people. They were enjoying the music's bass, probably making their neighbours' glassware jump around in the cupboards. We communicated with a combination of signs, lip-reading and writing down short sentences. They accepted us into their group and shared their booze and weed. After some time, we felt they wanted to be among themselves again, and we left as some guys started dancing on a table. These kids knew how to party. When we passed a construction site shortly before Lappis, I dared Alice to climb a crane with me. From the top, we had a beautiful view of Brunnsviken lake, calmly glimmering below, and kissed in the orange dawn.

On my second-to-last night in Stockholm, a classic Lappis kitchen party took over Alice's floor. The room was crowded with Alice's roommates and their friends from all over the world. More people, following the noise, kept joining the party. The cheap speakers were blasting out bad Spanish pop music. Beer cans and plastic cups of carton wine were passed around. The windows were opened so people could blow smoke out into the mild Swedish night. The hustle and bustle was a manifestation of the beautiful European dream. Countless nationalities were mixing, creating new cultural combinations, exchanging old traditions and inventing new ones, making fun of each other, laughing together, and merging into a drunken international identity. It had been estimated that there were already more than one million Erasmus babies. The sexual tension in the air suggested some more might be conceived tonight. Today, studying in Europe entailed meeting fellow students from all over the continent, and it's hard to send young men into war when the alleged enemy is their friend. But while we indulged in the diversity of an international community, back in our home countries, a generation too young to remember the horrors of war and too old to immerse itself in international culture was working on tearing down bridges, building walls, and reinstating nationalism. The first truly European generation was in danger of also being the last. But tonight, the Trumps, Le Pens, Farages, and all the other die-hard ignoramuses could shove their simplistic answers, alternative facts, and calculated breaches of taboo. Tonight, our cosmopolitan St. Vitus' dance would not be stopped.

I introduced the party to a game called 'Windmill Drinking' that a Dutch guy had taught me during my bachelor's. Two opponents face each other on opposite sides of a table, their chins and thumbs placed on the surface. There are three shots lined up on each player's side. At the start signal, the players stand up, chug the first shot, turn around their own axis once, chug the second shot, turn around their axis twice, chug the third shot, and turn around their axis thrice. Whoever is back on the tabletop with their chins and thumbs first wins. It was a hilarious game, especially because quite a few people missed the tabletop at the end. We made up silly game names—mine was Tornado Toper—and organised a tournament, recording all results on a whiteboard some physics student had dragged from her room. In the end, a small Korean maths student destroyed the whole competition with the quickness of a fox. He passed out on the sofa five minutes after the medal ceremony.

Dion and I climbed out the window to smoke on the gravel rooftop. As I lit his cigarette, I asked, 'So, where exactly are you from?'

'I was born in Haifa but grew up in Tel Aviv.'

'What is it like to grow up in Israel?'

'You mean in an apartheid state with no future?' He chuckled at my embarrassed face. 'Don't worry, I'm aware of the many contradictions of my home country. But growing up there isn't too different from growing up in Europe, I guess. Maybe it's more multicultural, with many Arab influences. And I guess life is still more deeply rooted in traditions. And, of course, there's still a war going on. But you get used to the sound of the air-raid sirens, and I'd say I had a great childhood and youth. Tel Aviv is a beautiful, modern city . . . I hated the three years in the military—doing the bidding of a questionable government—but in a weird way, it also felt good to have a purpose, to protect the people you love.' He exhaled white smoke into the night and watched one of the enormous, hairy Lappis rats run along the brick wall of one of the adjacent buildings.

I asked, 'So you think Israel has no future?'

'Well, demographically, it doesn't look good. In a way, I try to not get too attached to Israel because I don't think it will last. It makes me feel kind of home-less sometimes. I guess that's always been the fate of my people.' He shook off the gloominess with a wide, white grin and said, 'You know, I think it's brave of you to give up your job and to leave it all behind to look for a new place in life.'

Out of the mouth of a doctor without borders, this sounded like mockery, but he looked at me with sincerity. If only he could've stopped messing around with Alice, I would have actually liked the guy.

We climbed back inside, and I found Alice cooking loads of spaghetti for the hungry drunks. We kissed and formed a merry little kitchen team. Time flew, and soon people started leaving.

Before long, I found myself in Alice's room, sitting on the bed with her and Dion, sharing a last bottle of Montepulciano. We closed the window shutters to escape the relentless Nordic summer sun that was already rising. Alice kissed me and then turned and kissed Dion. I was confused and furious. I got up and scolded, 'I'm gone tomorrow. Can't you wait until then for your games?'

They both looked at me in amusement. With a gentle voice, Alice said, 'Calm down. Love is not finite. It's additive. Come join us.'

'I don't care for your free-love bullshit! I want you, and you know it, and it's hard enough to accept I can't have you. You don't have to taunt me.'

Dion peered at me with a lascivious hint of a smile and said, 'Get out of your cage, man.'

Alice got up and put her arms around my waist, which I reluctantly submitted to. She let her tongue run up my neck, looked deep into my eyes and breathed, 'I know you're curious how it feels to kiss a man, but you're too afraid to try it.'

I stared over at Dion, sitting on the edge of the bed on Alice's white flowery bedspread, looking at me with unimpeachable calmness. I was screwed. I shook my head, smiled sufferingly, and sighed, 'Fuck.'

Alice and Dion cheered, and Dion patted the bed next to him with his tantalising, flawless smile. Alice bit her lip and pushed me over to him. I sat down and looked into Dion's bold blue eyes. From behind, Alice reached beneath my shirt and caressed my belly. In a surreal haze, Dion touched my cheek and leaned in to kiss me. His heavy tongue seized mine with firmness. His beard stubble rubbed against mine. Alice told me to relax. I closed my eyes. Four hands ran through my hair and all over my body, conducting a campaign like greedy soldiers of fervour. We undressed. As we all lay in the tiny bed, Alice and Dion started blowing me and licking my thighs. I tried not to give my feelings or thoughts names and simply soak up the experience. Warm waves of relaxation and flashes of delight ran through my body. For the rest of the night, I made love to Alice, who was sometimes satisfying Dion with her mouth and hands, and sometimes Dion kissed and touched me or enjoyed watching us. I got the feeling he was focused on me. His presence aroused me, but I would have preferred having Alice for myself.

In the end, we wearily fell on the bed, and Alice and Dion immediately fell asleep with their heads on both of my shoulders, purring like kittens. What an image it must have been—the three of us, floating on our little raft of passion through the mysterious Swedish summer morning. Images of Alice and Dion, twisted in ecstasy, flashed through my mind. I didn't think I wanted to have sex with another man involved again, but I was satisfied with myself for having tried it. At least I hadn't acted in bad faith. I asked myself whether Simone and Jean-Paul had ever invited boy toys into their bed. I was drunk and beat. How would my future self deal with this whole mess? I had to smile. My last conscious thought was of building castles in the sand in Tuscany on a trip I had taken with my parents as a child.

Shortly before noon, the bed had become a hangover sickbay, as we woke nauseated and dizzy. Alice made coffee, which we drank in bed as we laughed about our wasted selves. Any intimacy between Dion and me was gone. I asked, 'Since when have you weirdos planned on seducing me?'

Alice laughed, 'Since Dion told me he liked you in the bar on Saturday.'

Dion sheepishly stared out of the window and avoided my eye. I turned to Alice and further probed, 'Do you do this often?'

'Not really,' Alice said, grinning like a Cheshire cat.

Shyly, Dion mumbled, 'I've had experiences with men and women, but never at the same time.'

I had never seen Dion so insecure. I laughed at them. 'You jerks, yesterday you made me feel like a backward prude.'

Alice jumped at me in joy and kissed me. Soon, Dion said he had to leave to prepare for his shift at the hospital. In the doorframe, I wanted to give him a hug, but he stepped away from me. There was a strange, sad hatred in his steel-blue eyes. He turned around and rushed off without a word. I didn't pay much attention; it was my last day with Alice in Stockholm. She was leaving for her expedition to Havana early the next morning and still needed to meet a colleague and grab some things from her office in the evening and pack her suitcase. We went back to bed, cuddled, and fell asleep again.

When we woke up, Alice said I should leave soon. We stood in the middle of her chaotic room, covered in party leftovers, books, and clothes. Alice had her hands wrapped around my waist. I tried to memorise the image of her. She looked at me through her trademark nerdy glasses, her unkempt hair sticking out in every direction. She wore nothing but her slip and an oversized Nepalese wool pullover. I might have dated hotter women, but none of them had ever been able to knock me off my feet quite like this sweet little devil had done. She had knocked me off my feet, out of the stratosphere, and onto a planet where, apparently, I was an oversentimental sissy who had sex with dudes. I looked into her eyes and said, 'You know, I'd like to hold you now and never let you go again. And before I go, I'd like you to know I'm in love with you.'

She looked up at me for a while and said, 'I think you see something in me I'm not. You've only known me for a couple of weeks, and I think it's hardly possible to know, let alone to love someone after such a short time . . . '

'Well, I'm rarely ever sure about anything, but I'm damn sure I'm in love with you. Tough luck. I'm going to miss you.' I smirked away the dull pain crawling up my dry throat.

She smiled at me compassionately and said, 'Sometimes I feel like your soul is already 100 years old. Enjoy yourself a little while you're drifting through Europe. And let me know if you ever make it down to Italy. I might join you there if you allow me to. I've never been.'

'Yeah. Good luck saving turtles or whatever in Cuba.'

I gave her a long kiss, grabbed my backpack, and walked out of her room, out of good old Lappis and out of Alice's life. On the way to the metro station of the university, I realised it had only been a bit more than three weeks since I had left England and met Alice. Who had that guy been who had wasted away his life in the firm for three years? I still couldn't believe I had had a threesome with another man. I shook my head and chuckled. Out of all the damned beach cafés in all the damned cities in this god-damned world, Alice had had to sit in the one I had walked into in search of a fresh start. It would be hard to forget the sight of the black rose between her breasts shimmering in the blue light of the Hamburg harbour—her sleepy, cosy look in the mornings; the candid way in which she brought together all sorts of different people; her calm and soothing breath in the summer night. Her deep-brown eyes that wanted to see the whole world and then some more, and to see it all as it was.

As I walked into the station, the high white sun laughed down at me. I wiped a single tear from my cheek and got on the metro. On the train, I watched a clip of the old Mike Tyson fight against the then-undefeated Michael Spinks. The much-anticipated bout had lasted 91 seconds. The year I had been born was the last Mike had spent as the undisputed and undefeated heavyweight champion of the world. Back then, he had still been the most aggressive, powerful, and devastating fighter the world had ever seen, running over every opponent put in front of him like a supercharged freight train from hell. His peek-a-boo defence, lightning speed, and unpredictable head movement had given his opponents nightmares. His steam-hammer hooks and relentless, bone-shattering uppercuts had struck fear into their hearts. After knocking the living hell out of them, Mike would sometimes run over to his opponents to help them up and congratulate them on the fight. Beyond the ring, the 'baddest man on the planet' was a kind soul who spoke softly and with humility about his tough child-hood. But Iron Mike's soul was also sorely troubled, and his inner demons and wrong friends had soon led him into disaster. In one of his first fights I could remember, he bit off Evander Holyfield's ear and lost. By then, his anger and insecurity had already pushed him into an inescapable swamp of violence and hatred. It wasn't his last defeat. But the only fight Mike Tyson had ever really lost had been to Mike Tyson. There was a prickle in my muscles, and I felt the urge to go a round with Iron Mike, knowing full well he would beat me to a pulp.

In Södermalm, I checked into a hostel on Skanstull and went to a café on Götgatan. As I was drinking my cappuccino, I received a Facebook message from my brother:

'Hey, little brother! How are you? I take it from your pictures you're travelling? Thanks for the money, but I think it would be more helpful if you came home for a change. Mum misses you. I don't understand why you don't talk to her. She isn't angry at you. You know she is bitterly sorry for what she said to you. She just wants you to come home. Did you talk to Nicole recently? I think she is in trouble in Berlin. You're the only one who might knock some sense into her . . . I know we're too mediocre for the two of you . . . Please don't be a stranger. And take care! Michael.'

I stared at the message for 15 minutes and tried to think of a reply—nothing. The news that my little sister was in trouble gave me a stomach ache. I had to go to Berlin and see her soon. I also needed a drink.

Since cafés in Sweden seldom served alcohol, I walked down to Medborgarplatsen and into Carmen, a nearby bar with too-loud music and cheap beer—at least cheap by Swedish standards.

If you went to a bar in Stockholm, you usually either ended up in Södermalm with hipsters wearing all black and sporting crooked, deliberately ugly hair-cuts, or in Östermalm, where the crowd of spoiled kids showed off their khakis and little black dresses. I doubted these two camps mixed a lot.

After a burger, chips, and three Finnish beers, I called it an early night; I was still exhausted from the Lappis mayhem. During my last night in Sweden, I stayed awake for a long time, the image of Alice smiling at me with her glowing deep-brown eyes stuck in my head. Finally, I fell asleep, probably delighting my nine dormmates with my beer-induced snoring.

Now the sun's gone to hell
And the moon's riding high
Let me bid you farewell
Every man has to die
But it's written in the starlight
And every line in your palm
We are fools to make war
On our brothers in arms

Mark Knopfler
Brothers in Arms

5

I boarded the large ferry to Tallinn and settled into my small cabin below the car deck. I climbed up to the top deck and had a gin and tonic. The wind tousled my hair as I watched the archipelago slowly pass by.

I dined in the onboard Italian restaurant with a view of the sea and afterwards went to play blackjack in the casino. Blackjack has a relatively small house edge, if you know the optimal response to each combination of the ten possible card values the dealer can have and the 37 relevant hands you may hold. I played hand after hand and drank gin and tonic after gin and tonic. Past midnight, I went upstairs to the nightclub and had another drink while watching drunk Russian men taking off their shirts on the dancefloor.

Soon, I was dancing with a cute woman with the widest smile since Julia Roberts. She moved her slim body next to mine, inviting me to touch her hips, and looked into my eyes with a smile. When I tried to kiss her, she elegantly dodged my attempt. We laughed, and I asked whether I could buy her a drink. As we stood at the bar, she told me she was from Finland and living in Tallinn. She was on her way back from a conference on human rights enforcement. When our drinks arrived, she slid closer to me. Again, I tried to kiss her. Again, she evaded my approach, and again we laughed. Puzzled, I said, 'Either I'm completely misreading your signals here, or you don't know what you want.'

She showed me her hand, and a golden sparkle came from her ring finger.

'I'm sorry, I didn't know you were married,' I said.

She apologised for not letting me know earlier and told me about Eino, her husband. She described their recent honeymoon in the Seychelles, which they had found to be the world leader in two categories: picturesque dream beaches and putting poor people in prison. Paradise always comes with a catch. She said Eino was a loving man but sometimes didn't understand the dreams of a more just world that drove her. I told her to give Eino time. And, in my drunkenness, I told her of the pain I felt over Alice and rambled on about my despair about all the pointless hate torturing this world, the unnecessary wars, the growing inequality, and the perpetual cycle of violence. How could a single man overcome the frustrating stupidity of mankind? And why should he try if, in the end, conscious existence was a cruel joke without a punchline anyhow?

My drunken rant was interrupted by the married woman's lips pressing against my mouth. Her tongue spelt out on mine her own cry of despair. Her hands slipped into the back pockets of my trousers. After a while, I broke the kiss and asked her, 'What about your husband?'

'I know. I'm a bad person. But you might just be the nicest guy I've ever met.' I doubted that but didn't protest. 'I feel like I've known you for a long time and like I can tell you anything—unlike Eino, you know?'

'I don't know . . . We literally only met an hour ago. I think you're mainly drunk.'

She looked at me with a hint of desperation. 'Don't worry about me. I know what I'm doing. So . . . Do you want to come to my cabin? My friends are still out dancing . . . '

I took a moment to size her up. Only an idiot would say no to a body like that. I heard myself say, 'No. I think you should go to your cabin alone now.'

Her wide smile conveyed affection and embarrassment. 'I guess you're right. Take care. And take a break from carrying the weight of the world from time to time.'

'I'll try. And you try to work things out with Eino. He sounds like a good man.'

She gave me a long kiss and said, 'I wish I had met you in another life. I'm Alisa, by the way. Goodbye.'

My new type seemed to be problematic women with names derived from the old Germanic 'Adalhaidis'. My eyes followed Alisa's graceful gait out of the club. A drunk guy reeking of beer came over to me at the bar and slurred in a heavy East European accent, 'Why you let her go? She was fine woman!'

'And married.'

'Who cares? What happens on ship stays on ship!'

'Thanks for your sophisticated advice.'

I left the sound of bad music and the smell of cheap beer for the cool night over the twilit Baltic Sea. I lit a cigarette. What a nice guy I was. The international association of negligent husbands should award me a medal. I felt guilty because of Alice, which was, of course, ridiculous. By now, Alice was probably seducing exotic strippers and drug smugglers in a sweaty dive bar in Havana.

I thought about a Belgian girl called Camille, whom I had met in Munich. She and her Erasmus friends had tried to drink through the menu of the bar I was working at back then. After my shift, I had joined their after-hours house party. There had been something in Camille's wolfish smile I couldn't resist, and I hooked up with her. She had been upset when I told her about Emma, who was waiting for me in our flat. But not upset enough to prevent her from taking me into her bed in the north of Munich that night, and every subsequent night I could excuse myself from coming home to Emma. I had always hated cheaters and thought I would never be able to look at myself in the mirror again should I ever sink that low. To my surprise, I continued to sleep like a baby and simply didn't think about my sly Belgian mistress whenever I was with Emma. You can never entirely know yourself.

I looked over the railing. For a fleeting moment, I was tempted to jump and disappear into the darkness of the cold sea spuming against the ship. I promised myself I would stay away from alcohol and women in the future, had another shot of vodka with a middle-aged woman past her prime at the bar, and staggered to my cabin. I fell asleep in my clothes.

Everything in Tallinn reminded me of Alice. The Tallinn Bay became the Elbe in which we had swum during our first magical night together. Out of the huge alcohol discount shop near the harbour, greedy

Scandinavians rolled trolleys filled with more bottles than we had drunk together in three weeks of partying. The bookshops had *1984*, which had inspired my fateful clumsy chat-up line, on display. The oversized nerdy glasses didn't look half as playfully sophisticated in the shop windows as they would have on Alice's button nose. The poor excuse for a strip club I passed sure as hell wouldn't have dancers ready to sit on my lap and kiss me. Sometimes I fancied that I saw Alice poring over a book in one of the cosy cafés and restaurants she would have loved, hidden in back alleys throughout the city. I could only half-heartedly enjoy the soothing view over the rooftops and churches of the Old Town of Tallinn at dusk without a drunk love rabbit huddled up against me. At the street market, old women with weathered, wrinkled faces sold eggs and vegetables, out of which Alice would have conjured a royal hangover breakfast—dressed only in her Nepalese wool pullover and with a drowsy smile on her face. Only to spite me had the Estonian birds learned to sing like the ones in front of her Lappis window. To mock me, Tallinn's street musicians performed songs that had been played at Evelina's Midsummer party. To taunt me, happy couples followed me around and bothered me with their mushy infatuation. Everything reminded me of Alice—except for the women. They paled in comparison. I drifted along and diverted myself by ticking off the top ten tourist things to do in Tallinn— numbly staring at churches, towers, and parks.

I was staying at the hostel General Shiraz in a backyard east of the Old Town. On my third day there, I met a group of computer science students from Dublin in the hostel's bar. They were on a mission in the cheap pubs of Eastern Europe to forget everything they had learned in the preceding term. I joined their trip to a shooting range hidden in the basement of an old office block in the south of Tallinn. After a safety briefing, we went wild, shooting pistols, revolvers, Kalashnikovs, and shotguns. When you shoot, the gun in your hands has the same kinetic energy as the bullet—abstracting from the propellant gas. Because the energy is distributed over more mass, your arm is not ripped off, but the violent recoil still gives you an idea of the destructive force with which a bullet can pierce through flesh and bone. The feeling of the cold steel in my palm was one of power and fear—fear of what I might do and of what others were capable of doing. With a dozen lethal weapons in the room, you scrutinised the people you had met two hours ago more closely. What was going on in their minds? Fortunately, none of the bullets penetrated any of the bags of organic matter in the room that perceived themselves as conscious human beings. We brought the shooting frenzy to a close with a competitive sniper rifle target practice. Fiona, the only girl in the group, gave us a good spanking. Afterwards, we had a round of Vana Tallinn and a cigarette with one of the shooting instructors. He was a robust man in his early fifties with cropped dark hair and a full beard, who looked as strong as an ox. He didn't say a single word more than he had to. But his eyes told gloomy stories of long and dark winters.

Back at the hostel, the Irish dragged me into a messy night of drinking. That night's only noteworthy detail was that I somehow managed to have my watch stolen—the Luminor Panerai with black face and brown leather band I had bought with my first bonus; the only luxury item I had ever fallen for. Some

Estonian pickpocket had made himself a couple of thousand pounds richer.

On Saturday, after curing my hangover in the hostel kitchen with eggs, bacon, and plenty of water, I dragged myself to Pirita beach. It was a crowded summer day, and joyful children chased beachballs across the sand. I met a group of digital nomads working on a joint marketing platform project. Some of them lived together in a shared house nearby. The communal, international, improvisational hostel lifestyle had arrived in our post-modern, post-religious, post-family, post-home, post-everything working society. I let them indulge in the freedom of self-employed insecurity. I logged into the ubiquitous free WiFi and wrote to my sister, Nicole, that I would be in Berlin the following weekend and wanted to see her. I also asked my old friend Joel whether he was still in Berlin and whether I could stay with him for a while. I spent the afternoon reading the last chapters of *The Drifters*. At the end of the story, Britta, the beautiful Norwegian girl who grows tired of the darkness, confesses, 'I believe that men ought to inspect their dreams. And know them for what they are.' Wise words—now all I needed was a dream.

Later that night, I reunited with the Irish gang in a basement bar frequented by locals. To my surprise, the brawny instructor from the shooting range was there. The group had met him on the street and convinced him to let them buy him some beers. His name was Alvar. After a couple of glasses, something resembling a smile flashed over his bulky, hirsute face. At midnight, Alvar, Fiona, and I were standing outside smoking. At Fiona's persistent insistence, Alvar finally consented to tell us about his life:

'I was born in a small village by the lakes north of Tartu here in Estonia.' His English was surprisingly good, and his faint East European accent had an American twang. 'It was a sombre life back then under Soviet rule. Me and my four older brothers had to help my mother around the house and in the vegetable garden, and my father in his black-market workshop. I was always too impatient and energetic to sit still in school. When I joined the army back in '83, I finally found something I was good at. I liked marching, shooting, hand-to-hand combat, and all the other challenges. Soon, I was accepted into training for the special forces. I joined the Spetsnaz in Afghanistan. We carried out airborne attacks on the Mujahideen's supply routes. The winters were freezing cold and the summers blazing hot.' He dropped his cigarette and ground it under his heel. 'I lost many friends there.'

For a moment, his gaze remained fixed on the cigarette-butt-covered floor. He exhaled and continued, 'When it became clear Estonia was about to break away from the USSR in the late '80s, I was dismissed from duty. I went back to what I once called home. The Spetsnaz had become my new family. But they abandoned me because of the wrong place of birth in my passport. My old family was gone. My parents and my oldest brother were dead, another brother was missing. The remaining two tried hard to kill themselves with vodka—a feat they have both accomplished since. In the years after the fall of the Soviet Union, I kept my head above water with short-term jobs as security guard, truck driver, and bodyguard. I got the opportunity to join the Estonian army in the late '90s. After 9/11, I went back to Afghanistan. Now, I fought for the capitalists I had been taught to hate under the communists. NATO had learnt from the Soviet Union's failures and didn't follow the same relentless scorched-earth policy . . . But it was still the same fight against the same people with the same expected outcome. When I finally realised war was all about money, I joined an American military company as a mercenary and went to Iraq. There, the last piece of ideology I once had died . . . All the dead innocent women and children—torn to shreds by bombs dropped in the name of freedom or God or whatever excuse was used that day to hide economic interests. And I was there to get my cut. Now I watch young people shoot the guns I have seen cut so many lives so short. And I wonder if your generation will be any different. But I doubt it. Man is wolf to man.'

We stood in silence in front of the bar. A man drunk out of his mind stumbled by in one shoe. Alvar gazed into the distance in silence, watching a gunfight in the cold Afghan mountains only he could see. He looked like he hadn't slept in weeks. When his mind had climbed back down from the Hindu Kush to the Estonian plains, he thanked us for the beers and left. Fiona and I went back inside and straight to the bar. A shot of vodka washed away the bad taste of the eternal carnage we had been clever enough to avoid by right of birth. You couldn't think about all the terrible things happening in the world all the time. It spoiled the delight of consumerism. When the bar closed, we all went back to the hostel.

That night, I couldn't sleep. I couldn't stop think-ing about Alice and what she was doing in Cuba. I went to the kitchen for a glass of water. In the dark, I ran into Fiona, who was standing in the middle of the room. I switched on the light and asked her what she was doing. She didn't react. Her eyes were half closed. She was sleepwalking. I poured myself a glass of water and looked at her as I drank. She told me that she couldn't find her car and that it must be parked here. I had to laugh a little and told her to go back to bed. She said that she had parked her car right here and that she couldn't find it. I had no idea how to deal with a sleepwalker and was beat and drunk. I went back to bed but left the light on—it was hard to find your car in the dark, after all.

The Irish gang was still asleep in the morning when I woke up. It was time for me to go to the tourist office, where I got on a sightseeing tour bus to Riga. The trip took 12 hours and included walks through picturesque little towns, exploring sand caves, a visit to a Soviet military theme park, and looking up Latvian cliffs, at Latvian castles, and down Latvian Soviet bobsleigh tracks. Somehow, even a damned bobsleigh track managed to remind me of Alice.

. . . he that gets hurt
Will be he who has stalled
There's a battle outside and it is ragin'
It'll soon shake your windows and rattle your walls
For the times they are a-changin'

Bob Dylan
The Times They Are A-Changin'

6

I arrived in Riga dead tired. I had booked a private room to get some rest. The Grand Kempinsky Riga, the five-star hotel I was staying in, was close to the centre of the Old Town and had a view of the classicistic Latvian National Opera House. It was located opposite the stately Monument of Freedom on the other side of the city's canal. I didn't know why I had booked such an expensive room. I had never been particularly good with money, and earning a lot of it hadn't exactly alleviated the problem. My threadbare, washed-out yellow backpack was an alien body in this realm of heavy dark wood, muted-coloured fabrics, and smooth marble. My dad had bought it in the early eighties before going to Sri Lanka, the only big trip he had ever taken. To go full would-be Croesus, I ordered a bottle of Champagne which I drank in a warm bubble bath. I enjoyed the freedom of walking around the room naked. I lay on the luxurious bed and watched *Léon: The Professional*. As Luc Besson's camera panned over the New York skyline to the hypnotic, breathing voice of Sting, I drifted off to sleep in the depths of the voluminous, feathery bedlinen. I was certain Alice had resembled a young Natalie Portman when she was 12.

After a copious breakfast in the hotel's restaurant, I strolled through the adjacent Bastejkalna park. The soldiers of the guard of honour in olive-green uniforms and with fixed bayonets ritually marched around the Freedom Monument. The monument was a symbol of independence from the Russian Empire, today once again looming in the forests behind the border. People were lying in the meadows next to the canal. Small paddleboats floated on the water. There wasn't a single cloud in the blue sky, and the Monday morning sun shone regally. I roamed the Old Town and inspected the castle, the cathedral, and the Town Hall Square. I climbed the tower of St Peter's Church, from which I had a marvellous view of the city, all the way to the hideous three-legged television tower in the south. For lunch, I had fish soup in the Riga Central Market's pavilions and bought a bag of grapes which I took with me to the Vērmanes Garden, northwest of my hotel. I lay on the warm grass in the shade of an exotic-looking magnolia tree. The smell of sun-drenched leaves filled my nostrils as I dozed off. I recovered from my extended nap with a cappuccino and the latest issue of *The Economist* in a nearby café.

That night, I was sitting in a grey leather chair at the shiny black hotel bar with an Old Fashioned in front of me. Diffuse light radiating from the walls behind the bar gave a vast collection of bottles an alluring glow. I looked out of place in my trainers, jeans, and T-shirt. As I took a deep sip, a young man in an expensive dark blue suit approached me with confident movements and asked, 'Do you mind if I join you?' He had a lean face, black hair, and alert almond eyes. His English accent was RP, his looks Southeast Asian.

I said, 'Go ahead.'

He thanked me, introduced himself as David Nguyen and took a seat next to me. He pointed at my glass and asked, 'What are you drinking?'

'Old Fashioned—Woodford Reserve bourbon.'

'Excellent choice.' He nodded to the bartender and said, 'Two more, please.' He looked back at me and asked, 'So, what's your business in Riga?'

'Hanging out for a couple of days. I'm travelling—on my way to Berlin. And yours?'

'I'm here on private business as well. I'm visiting a few promising fintech start-ups here—mainly blockchain technology and natural language processing.' David adjusted the collar of his tie-less, impeccable white shirt. 'I'm a day trader specialising in leveraged ETNs at a Singapore hedge fund. So, these start-ups are not particularly within my area of expertise, but I always have my eyes open for investment opportunities. What's your profession?'

'I've been working in banking for the last three years as well.'

'Splendid! Which bank and what did you do?'

'I was a deep learning engineer at Phorcys Investment. I devised neural networks for risk-adjusted return forecasting.'

His eyes widened. 'Why did you quit? As far as I know, they're beating everyone out there.'

'For now, they are. I just needed to do something else.'

David laughed. 'People kill to work at Phorcys! You

don't happen to want to start a new life in Singapore? I'd be happy to show you around.'

'Not really, but thanks.'

'What a shame. What's your plan then?'

'I don't know yet. I want to do something a little more beneficial to the world.'

'Good luck with that while all these retards are working on burning it to the ground. I say take the money and run, my friend. You have to be wealthy enough to bolt when the levee breaks.'

'With all due respect, that sounds like the elitist drivel that might make the levee break in the first place.'

David laughed heartily. 'Open your eyes, my friend.' When exactly had I become his friend? 'The world is getting porous, and the edges have already begun to disintegrate. The Americans have embraced their ignorance and elected a buffoon who couldn't compose a coherent sentence if his life depended on it. Europe is falling back into old habits of petty nationalism. The whole West has to cope with the fact that it's no longer the uncontested ruler of the world. And so far, its reaction resembles a panic attack rather than directed adaptation. Meanwhile, the autocracies of the ex-Soviet Union and the religiously blinded Middle East have built their whole business models on a resource that will become obsolete within decades. The rising giants of Asia are becoming increasingly autocratic to suppress the growing rage against the gaping inequality. Africa, with all its resources but no coordination whatsoever to take advantage of them, remains the doormat of the world. Only now, the poor masses have the internet to know what they're missing and start invading their rich neighbours. And in the background, the atmosphere is warming and the water surface rising. The last 70 years of peace aren't the new normal. They're an anomaly of history, a lucky coincidence. There's a storm coming. And only the strong will weather it.'

I looked at him thoughtfully and said, 'I guess what you say has a lot of truth in it. But the future is not set in stone. I think if enough people want to change things for the better, they will. Isn't it fundamentally human to swim against the tide, to try to change the world, no matter how long the odds are? We came down from the trees and flew to the damn moon. Shouldn't we be able to overcome our greed and our fears? I mean, as a species, we have more resources and are smarter than ever before.'

'That's exactly what frightens me,' David quipped. The silver Cartier Tank on his wrist glittered in the warm light as he ordered two more drinks with a hand gesture. 'No, but seriously, if you truly believe in that, I respect your optimism.'

The problem was, I didn't truly believe in it.

'But I have a wife and children. And when the night comes that the streets burn and the poor eat the rich, I need to be rich enough to bring my family into safety . . . This might be too gloomy, but, you know, even if that night never comes, I'll still be rich and able to provide for my family. You say you want to change the world for the better. Who's with you on that? The elites who hide behind walls and want to maintain the status quo? The consumers who numb themselves in front of screens, afraid of spending a single minute in silence and of what they might find within themselves? The poor, the uneducated, the narrow-minded who consistently vote against their own interests, who worship every saviour who offers them simple answers for complex problems they can't even begin to grasp? They wouldn't know what to do with power if it fell in their laps! And besides, how would you change the world for the better, anyway?'

'Well, that's what I'm trying to find out. I know we need more education and fewer guns. I know we need more science and less religion. More redistribution from the wealthy to the underprivileged but less paternalistic welfare. We need more honesty and less PR bullshit, more emancipation and less exclusion, and in general more compassion and less bigotry. What I don't know is where to start and where I come in.'

David laughed, 'That's a lot of pie in the sky.'

I let a gulp of smooth bourbon run down my throat and looked at him. 'I know. But it's too easy to be a cynic. So, what would your idea of a better world look like? Imagining you cared.'

'If you mean by *better*, a world that is more efficient and fairer—whatever *fair* is supposed to mean . . . The only way to govern our irrational, emotional bunch is by an artificial intelligence—a digital leviathan if you will. Given the correct parameters and constraints, it would always choose the most efficient actions and wouldn't be impaired by emotions or cater to small but influential interest groups.'

'Yeah, that sounds much more realistic than my approaches, right?' We both chuckled. 'But let's say it's possible. Who defines the AI's constraints? And what happens if they're ill-defined? For example, if it starts imprisoning people of a certain race because they're statistically more prone to crime? Or if it starts going full *Minority Report* and neglects free will?'

'Those are details that have to be carefully figured out in advance. And the result doesn't have to be perfect. It just needs to be better than the status quo.

And given major trainwrecks like Syria, Congo, Yemen, and Venezuela, that's not a high hurdle. Besides, maybe racial profiling is not a bad thing. I'm tired of some minorities' complaints about being treated too harshly. Like the black community in the US—maybe if they finally got their act together, there wouldn't be a need for racial profiling.'

'Maybe if their ancestors hadn't been abducted as slaves and discriminated against for centuries, and if they received equal opportunities today, they wouldn't be forced into criminal behaviour.'

'Oh, give me a break! I grew up as a Vietnamese in China. In school, I was beaten up by my classmates and at home by my father, who was furious about the various rotten jobs he had. That didn't hold me back from getting a scholarship at Oxford and from becoming a provider for a family that lacks for nothing. Everybody has a choice. And everybody is responsible for their choices.' He looked at me emphatically, leaned over, and said in a softer voice, 'Speaking of choices—do you want to have some fun? The concierge was kind enough to organise me some blow—want to go for it?'

I faltered. I had never tried cocaine and had never felt the urge to. But now, I had an itching to try it. I had to think of Alice and how she would have done it without hesitation. 'Yeah, sure,' I heard myself say in a deceptively languid tone.

We went up to David's suite, which was twice the size of mine. In the bathroom, there was a little glass dressing table in front of a large gold-framed mirror. With sly movements, David arranged three thin lines of white stardust on the surface, two for him and one for me. He told me he liked to go slow when mixing cocaine with alcohol since it was a toxic combination.

Nevertheless, he quickly snorted his lines, one left, one right, jumped up and exclaimed a loud 'Woohoo!' I tried not to let my nervousness show, took his rolled-up note and sucked the coke up my nose. My nostril tickled, and within seconds, my face grew numb. A wave of excitement ran through my body. I had to get up and walk through David's living room. He looked at me with a wide grin and shouted, 'Want to go to a club?' That was a fantastic idea! David made me put on one of his suits. It was a little too tight around the shoulders. I looked pretty sharp, nonetheless. We were ready to go. We jumped into a taxi. Sliding back and forth on the back seats, we frantically developed a business idea for 3D-printer drones, delivering anything, anywhere, anytime.

Since it was Monday, the variety of nightlife options was limited. We ended up in a cocktail club covered in cheap red satin. The place was crowded with bald men in baggy suits and facelifted gold diggers. Go-go dancers in black lingerie wiggled their bums on bar tables. We went straight to the toilets and snorted another line. Excitement ran through every fibre of my body. I stormed to the bar. Drinks. Dancing. Girls. Didn't like me. Didn't matter. Another line. Lights flashing. Hips shaking. Another drink. Head spinning. Sweet drips of paint thinner down my throat. Making grimaces to feel my jaw. Who was this girl? Why was she talking about wearing summer dresses in Zürich? Didn't matter. Blonde hair swirling. Lips smiling. Kisses. Frenetic touches. I needed air. Cigarettes in the summer night. Whispers about defilement in the balmy air. Water. Another line. More dancing. More kisses. More shameless touches. At the bar, a pale, soulless devil stared back at me from the mirrored wall. Another water. More dancing.

A fat guy hit David in the face. I stepped over and shoved him away. The fat guy reached back and swung his clumsy right hand at me. With a quick step to the left, I let him strike thin air and placed a left hook on his chin. He fell like a heavy, brittle tree. The bouncers rushed in and dragged David and me out of the room, which was suddenly quite empty. David's nose was bleeding. He gave the bouncers 100 euros each. We still had to leave. We walked away and took a taxi. We were penned up in the back seat with a blonde girl who tried to devour me. Was she the same girl I had started out with? We were back in the hotel lobby. David shouted, 'Woohoo! Where did you learn to knock somebody out like that?'

'20 years of boxing.' I felt like a bag of dirt. My head was spinning. My mouth was dry, and my nose clogged. 'Do you have some coke left?'

David stared at me. His gaping eyes radiated a sense of adrift panic. 'I need it for myself and the hooker I'm about to get.'

He wiped the blood from his nose on his shirt-sleeve and ran out of the empty lobby into the hallway, in search of the concierge. The blonde girl grabbed my arm and breathed in an East European accent, 'I have some left. Let's go to your room.'

We entered the lift. She grabbed my crotch and shoved her tongue down my throat. I felt nothing. Back in my room, I blew my nose and did a long line of white powder off the glass coffee table. The sparkling taste of liquid sex on the back of my tongue. Ripping off her dress. Her tongue running up and down my abs. An ugly scar on her flat belly. Hard nipples between my teeth. Another line of stardust off her voluptuous bum. Lips on lips. Hips on hips. Sweat on sweat. Room spinning. A greedy nose snorting coke off my dick. Pounding her up and down the bed. A wicked hyena on all fours, trembling in ecstasy. Fireworks of moans and pleasure. Stretching out on a satin sea. Heavy breathing in the ominous summer night. After some time, the blonde girl got up and put on her dress. Sheepishly, she asked me for some money for the coke. I gave her 200 euros and turned away. I felt sick. A whispered 'goodbye' and the slam of the door cut through my brain like razorblades. I turned off the light and went to bed. My heart was pounding. Thoughts of disgust and self-hatred ran through my mind. I rolled around while my limbs tingled with restlessness. Tonight, I had shown my true face again—my violent, filthy grimace. A veil of despair shrouded my soul. Why did I have to knock out that guy? Why did I have to defile that poor soul and pay her off like a slut? What had scarred her so deeply? Why did I never know when to stop? Why had I been born? Why did I have to die? Why did the time in between hurt so bad? And why the hell did I still care? The pounding of my heart in my ears drummed me slowly into unconsciousness.

The whole morning, I was trapped in a fever-dream world between wakefulness and sleep. I finally woke up for good at noon and felt depressed. My nose was running, and the knuckles of my left hand hurt a little. I dragged myself into the shower and contemplated hitting my head against the wall but couldn't gather the strength. I ordered breakfast and ate it in bed with the television running. The whole afternoon, I faded in and out of consciousness. The never-ending loop of void images on the screen numbed my mind.

In the evening, I decided to get some fresh air. I walked for all of two minutes until debilitating dizziness confined me to a park bench. I thought of the first time I had met Emma's family. Emma and I had been at their house in the southwest of Berlin and had gone out for a night in the city. We had scheduled a get-to-know-you breakfast together the next morning, after her family's arrival home from their holiday that night. At a club, Emma and I had got into a fight over my behaviour towards one of her friends, and she had taken the train home without me in protest. I got terribly drunk and boarded the wrong train, which took me to a suburb ten kilometres away from Emma's home. Genius that I was, I decided to run to her house cross-country in the dead of night. I crossed motorways and muddy fields and arrived at Emma's doorstep at dawn, with torn trousers and covered in dirt. She let me into the house, where I stumbled to the ground, ripping a mirror from the wall in a chinking and crashing nightmare. Emma's parents and her little brother Tobi came bolting down the stairs. I politely greeted them by puking on the hallway floor and staggered past them straight to bed, muttering, 'Night.' The much-anticipated welcome breakfast with Emma's first true love had to take place without me. When Emma threw her disappointment into my face with tears in her eyes the next day, I told her something was probably wrong with her hormones that had caused her to freak out. She apologised. For the rest of the day, she and her mum took care of me, curing my hangover on the sofa. Her dad and her brother did their best to be nice to me and not make me feel embarrassed. I had been playing in the being-an-absolute-dick-to-your-girlfriend Champion's League, and to crown it all, I had landed in the nicest family on the planet. I had spent many days on that cosy sofa, hungover and happy. Emma's family had welcomed me like a stray dog in need of a loving home. Hovering in that warm bubble of comfort and devotion constituted one of my most treasured memories. And now she was about to get married to some wealth management yuppie in Munich. And here I was, sitting on a rotten park bench in rotten Riga, pitying my rotten self for being rightfully hungover and for being unhappily in love. Boo-hoo. I crawled back to the hotel, where I had an expensive tenderloin steak I couldn't enjoy and buried myself in bed again. I still felt sick. I hoped that fat Russian guy had got up again and was all right. I was angry at myself for punching someone in the head. At midnight, I dozed off and dreamt of wandering through lunar landscapes, lost and lonesome.

The following day, I finally felt somewhat close to being a normal human being again. After breakfast, I realised I still had David's suit. When I couldn't find his room, I asked for him at the reception desk. The receptionist told me David had left last night. I stepped out of the hotel and set out for the Museum of Photography. On my way, I noticed an old woman in a wheelchair that was stuck in an old tram track. I helped her out and asked her whether she needed any more assistance. She answered me in what I guessed to be Latvian and gave me a gap-toothed smile. I smiled back in confusion. She was wrapped in a worn-out grey-beige coat and wore a dark blue headscarf—in the middle of summer. Strong green eyes dominated her furrowed face. As she started rolling up the street, I saw she was exhausted. I followed her and conveyed an offer to help with dilettante gesticulation. She looked at me in puzzlement and smiled. I started pushing her wheelchair up the street, and she clapped her hands and laughed. At the end of the street, she pointed me to the left. Before long, we were rolling along the canal in Bastejkalna park. An exotic mix of luscious green trees formed a roof above us. Children played on the summer grass that sloped down to the canal on both sides. From time to time, the old woman indicated to me to go my way, but I tried to make her understand I had enough time to help her around the city. Each time, we laughed and continued our journey through the park. When we passed a hot dog stand, I bought us lunch and found a calm spot to sit in the dappled shade of a tree. The old woman scoffed her hot dog with delight and smiled, at ease. From her coat's pocket, she produced an old and worn black-and-white photograph. It pictured a group of young, humble people in front of a barn. The old woman pointed to a beautiful, resolute girl standing in the middle and then pointed at herself. I looked at the picture for a long time. Of all the buoyant adolescents, the old woman was probably the only one left. Who had they been? What lives had they lived? I gazed into the old woman's eyes, and she back into mine. We both smiled at each other. I bought us some ice cream, and we continued our extended stroll. When we passed a statue of a saggy-boobed lady covered in mirrors reflecting the sunlight, the old woman pointed towards it and laughed heartily. What a fine morning this had turned out to be. She led me into a residential neighbourhood north of the parks and again insisted on letting her carry on by herself. This time, I knew she genuinely wanted to be left alone. Did she have anywhere to go? I awkwardly waved her goodbye and walked in the other direction. She saw me off with her wide gap-toothed smile and kept saying, 'Paldies! Paldies!'

I went to bed early that night. In my dreams, Alice was a strict yoga teacher, and I a clueless student who could never meet her demanding needs.

I left Riga on Thursday afternoon. On the plane to Berlin, I got nervous thinking about meeting my kid sister Nicole again. What did the trouble that Michael had written about mean? I hoped she was doing all right.

The last time I had seen Nicole and the rest of my family had been two years ago, when Emma had dragged me to my mum's birthday party, which I had initially planned on skipping. Dad had still been alive back then, leaving the hospital for one night. Talking to dull relatives and bland friends of the family whose names I had never bothered to learn had been an absolute nightmare. I had always felt that some of them saw me as an intruder, the cursed one, the reminder of the stain on the family everyone would like to forget. Nicole had just been about to start a second bachelor's in fashion design in Berlin, after an unsuccessful try at becoming a media person in Paris. Once Michael had left my mum's party together with his wife and his adorable little daughter, Nicole and I were sitting in the garden under the old oak tree we used to climb as kids. Well past midnight, we talked about dreams of a cosmopolitan life and sundowners on urban rooftops and at beach bars in the Caribbean. Nicole had been happy about moving to Berlin and eager to become a part of a thriving bohemian scene. Hopefully, she had found what she had been looking for.

I have absolutely no pleasure in the stimulants in which I sometimes so madly indulge. It has not been in the pursuit of pleasure that I have periled life and reputation and reason. It has been the desperate attempt to escape from torturing memories, from a sense of insupportable loneliness and a dread of some strange impending doom.

Words attributed to Edgar Allen Poe

7

In Berlin, my old friend Joel picked me up from the train station, and we took the metro to his place in Kreuzberg. I had met him in grammar school. I had convinced him to play the drums 15 years ago, and we had founded a rock band together. He now worked as a cameraman, mainly in advertising, and drummed in a stoner rock band called 'Vladimir's Joke'. He was living in a small flat with an eat-in kitchen in the attic of an old, grey-brown building near Görlitzer Park. He had shared the place with his ex-girlfriend Valentina until she had broken up with him and moved back to Colombia three weeks ago.

Joel and I cooked spaghetti carbonara and shared a bottle of Pinot Grigio. He told me he felt terrible. After a long night out, he had found himself lying next to a girl this morning. By force of habit, he had called her 'Valentina'. The girl had told him he hadn't been

able to get it up the night before, spurned the breakfast he cooked for her, and walked out of the door, still
wearing his favourite jumper. Joel had to pull himself
together so as not to cry. I felt bad for him. We opened
another bottle of wine and took out his guitar to play
the songs of our melancholic youth. Between songs,
we delved into our tough luck with girls and shared
stories of old classmates.

After the third bottle, we realised that drinking to
forget wasn't working and went to sleep.

The next day, I tried to call Nicole on the number she
had recently sent me and messaged her on Facebook.
I was met with no response. I didn't know her address; she had agreed to meet but preferred the first
reunion to be in a neutral setting.

I passed my time marvelling at the glazed-blue
Ishtar Gate of the walls of impregnable Babylon in the
Pergamon Museum and visited the German Chancel-
lery and the Reichstag building—once again the decisive centre of power in Europe. I walked through the
surprisingly small Brandenburg Gate. At the Memorial to the Murdered Jews of Europe, I was irritated
by clueless tourists climbing the concrete stelae and
posing for vain social media posts. Walking through
the information centre below the monument, I got a
lump in my throat. All the innocent lives cut short
with such inhumane, mechanical precision—the cul-
mination of the blood-and-soil insanity burgeoning
around the world again today. I felt a nameless panic
rise within me. I tried to focus on my breathing and
left.

Throughout the day, I tried to reach Nicole without
success. In the evening, I cooked couscous with sal-
mon for Joel, who had spent a long day cutting film.

We spent the rest of the night drinking beer and writing sentimental songs about Alice and Joel's Colombian runaway girlfriend. Once again creating music with Joel, like we did in long-gone years in his father's basement, filled me with conflicting feelings of joy and melancholia. We talked and jammed throughout the night and wearily welcomed the Saturday dawn on Joel's tiny balcony with a smoke. Mentally drained, I fell asleep on the sofa in the kitchen in a heartbeat.

At noon the next day, Nicole finally answered her phone with a tremulous voice: 'Hey, big brother.'

'Hey, little sister. How are you?'

'I'm doing fine.' Her voice cracked. 'A bit tired from a party I had last night.'

'Are you sure you're all right, Nicole?'

'Don't worry. I'm okay.' She paused, and I could hear her starting to sob. 'Sorry, I have to go!' She hung up.

My stomach felt as though somebody had dealt me a heavy body shot. I called Nicole again. She didn't answer. Panic was rising in my clenching throat. I called her again. And again. When she finally answered, she was still crying. After a pause, she said, 'Hey, big brother.'

'Hey, little sister. Where are you?'

'I'm home.'

'Can I come?'

'I don't know . . . I'm so tired . . . I don't know.'

'I'll bring you lunch. You don't have to tell me anything. I won't bother you. I just want to see you, kiddo.'

Muffled sobbing. 'Okay.'

She gave me her address and hung up. I rushed out

of the building and jumped on the metro. Nicole was living in Neukölln. I bought a variety of falafel dishes at a Lebanese takeaway and hurried up the stairs to her flat. The stairwell was dirty and piled with shoes and prams. Behind some of the doors, women shouted, and children screamed. When Nicole opened her door, we stood there in silence and looked at each other. She was thinner than I remembered her and had dark circles around her puffy eyes, which flashed with defiance beneath her sadness.

'Hey, big brother.'

'Hey, little sister.'

We both had to smile, and she stormily flung her arms around my neck. I hugged her tightly and put my hand on the dark blonde curly hair she had cut in a pageboy since the last time we had met. With a giggle, she ran her hand over the beard I had grown over the last couple of weeks. She led me into the small two-room flat. I could see she had made a hasty effort to clean it up, but there were still alcohol stains on the floor and countless empty bottles in the messy kitchen. The smell of alcohol, stale smoke, coffee, and cleaning agent hung in the air. I unpacked the lunch bag I had brought on the kitchen table, where there was still room between empty wine bottles. I said, 'I didn't know what you like, so I brought a couple of different meals. Are you still vegetarian?'

'Of course. God, I'm so hungry!'

As she pitched into the food, I looked around her flat. Nicole's room was small and covered in edgy shoes, clothes, jewellery, and art and fashion magazines. From a dented little speaker, Nada Surf's interpretation of *Love Goes On* floated through the air. The other room of the flat seemed abandoned; it was too tidy in such a bedlam place. In the bathroom, the shower curtain had been ripped off the pole and was lying in the bathtub. The mirror over the sink was shattered. I sat down on a shaky chair next to Nicole in the kitchen and asked, 'Where's your roommate?'

'Linda? In Myanmar, I think—volunteering in an orphanage which is probably filled with kids whose parents sit somewhere in a nearby hut and are happy they don't have to pay for their children's meals. I have no clue when she'll be back. You can stay in her room if you want to . . . What are you doing in Berlin, anyway? You were in Tallinn when you texted me, right?'

'Yeah. I'm travelling for a while. I quit my job at the firm.'

'Finally! Please tell me you don't want to be a parasite anymore.'

'I don't know what I want to do at the moment. But, yeah, I probably won't be a *parasite* anymore.'

'Good.' She paused and stared out of the window into the grey inner yard. She turned back to me with a stern face and said, 'Why did you show up here after two years of showing no signs of life?'

'I did wish you a happy birthday.'

'Yeah. On Facebook. Brother of the fucking year!'

'I know. I'm sorry. You know, ever since Dad's death, I have been mentally blocked. I couldn't talk to you or Michael—and especially Mum. But I realised I need to change. That's why I quit my job. And Michael told me you might be in trouble. That's why I wanted to see you.'

'Oh, what does *he* know! Just because I like to enjoy myself from time to time.'

'Well, *are* you in trouble?'

'I don't know . . . I mean, uni could be going better, I guess. And I should be partying a little less, maybe.'

100

Her phone rang. She restlessly glanced at the display and exclaimed, 'Ugh. Speak of the devil.'

'Who is it?'

'Nobody. Where was I? Yeah, I should party a little less. Yesterday went a bit out of hand.'

'Is that why your bathroom is ravaged?'

'Yeah. Somebody thought it would be clever to break out into a wrestling match.'

Her phone rang again. Nicole tensed up and switched off the phone. She lit a cigarette and looked around the room anxiously.

'Who is that?' I demanded to know.

She hissed, 'You come into my life after two years and expect me to trust you like nothing happened?'

'Nicole, I'm sorry. But you know I will do anything to help you with whatever problems you might have.'

She looked at me for a while, assessing her options. Finally, she said, 'Promise you won't get judgemental.'

'I promise.'

'Okay . . . A couple of weeks ago, I met this man in a bar in Prenzlauer Berg. He was a lot older than me—' She looked at me, testing.

I held her gaze, keeping a straight face.

'But we got along well and talked for a while, and he invited me to a fancy restaurant the next day. We had a fun night, and—we kissed. We kept texting, and I went to a party organised by the advertising agency he works for as a senior designer. I got really drunk there and ended up with him in a hotel room. He has a family back home.' She hesitated. 'You hate me, don't you?'

'Don't worry, go on.'

'Okay . . . I felt terrible about the whole thing and told myself to never do it again. But of course, silly as I am, I got really drunk again at another party a week later and brought him here, where he stayed for an entire day. And he isn't even a nice guy! When I texted him that I didn't want to see him again, he showed up at my door in the middle of the night. He wouldn't go away until my neighbour complained about the noise in the stairwell. I was stupid enough to accept some of his money. He kept texting me and showed up at the university and the café. I keep telling him to leave me alone. I even threatened to tell his family. But he doesn't think I'd do it and probably doesn't care. He even threatened to hurt me.'

My blood started boiling.

'When he came to my party uninvited yesterday, I had to tell the guys to kick him out. He has been calling me ever since.'

'Okay.' I paused. 'You must tell me everything about him you know—full name, the company he works at, his family, where he lives, what car he drives, what his hobbies are—everything.'

'Don't be so overdramatic.'

'Nicole.' I gave her a stern look.

She exhaled and said, 'His name is Torben Himer. But don't do anything stupid! I can handle this.'

'I'm not going to do anything stupid, kiddo. But if this old lecher shows up here, I want something in my hands to make him go away for good. That's what you want, too, right?'

'Yes.'

Nicole told me everything of importance she could think of, and I took notes. When she was finished, I said, 'You look tired. Why don't you get some rest while I clean the place and fill your fridge?'

She was too exhausted to raise any objections and went to bed. As she closed her door, she said, 'Thanks for not freaking out.'

I started by gathering all the empty bottles, expired groceries and rubbish lying around into big plastic bags. I washed the dishes and put the leftover lunch into the fridge. I swept and wiped the floors and wiped down the counters. I threw away the broken shower curtain and gathered the mirror shards. When I cleaned the bathroom floor, I discovered a used syringe under the sink cabinet. I put it carefully into a plastic bag. I carried down the bags of rubbish, withdrew some money at a nearby ATM, and went grocery shopping in a supermarket. When I was done, I switched on Nicole's laptop and did some research on this Torben Himer character. It was stunning how poorly people protected their private information these days. Satisfied, I took a nap in Linda's orphaned bed.

In the evening, I cooked Nicole's favourite dish: pancakes with fresh raspberries and blueberries, walnuts, and maple syrup. She already looked a lot healthier. After dinner, I showed her the syringe from the bathroom.

She eyed me angrily. 'Do you think I'm a junkie?'

'No. I think you might have troubled friends.'

'You think I'm a junkie, don't you? I might drink a little too much and smoke a joint from time to time, and—if you want to know—I have tried molly but didn't like it. But I'd never stick a needle in my arm!'

'I trust you, Nicole. I just want you to be careful, you know? Besides, I'm the last person who has the right to judge you . . . Just five days ago, I had a drug-fuelled night in Riga that didn't end too well. I think we both have to come down to earth again.'

Nicole looked at me and had to laugh. 'We've always been the messed-up part of the family, haven't we? Are you having girl trouble?'

I chuckled. Nicole had always seen right through me when it came to women. 'Yeah, actually. I met a girl called Alice in Hamburg, and she broke my heart in Stockholm. But I'll be fine.'

'Aww, come here, big brother!'

She got up from her chair and hugged me. We laughed together heartily. We made ourselves comfortable on the little sofa in her room and watched *Pulp Fiction* for the thousandth time. Nicole was an incurable Tarantino fan, and Butch the boxer was one of my all-time favourite film characters. Nicole went to bed early and slept for the rest of the weekend while I met Joel for beers on the banks of the Spree.

On Monday, while Nicole was at university, Joel and I took his car to the hardware shop. Back at Nicole's, we installed a new shower curtain, hung a new mirror in the bathroom, and fixed a dripping tap in the kitchen. When Nicole came home and spotted Joel standing in her hallway, she jumped at him and nearly suffocated him with an exuberant hug. 'Joel! I haven't seen you in ages! What are you doing here?'

'I live in Berlin. And apparently, I work as a plumber for poor little sisters.'

I pointed at the non-leaking tap. Nicole shouted, 'No way! I didn't know you were in Berlin. And thanks for fixing the tap!'

Joel also showed her the newly equipped bathroom. Nicole was sincerely excited. We ordered pizza and sat around the kitchen table to relive the old story of the time Joel had tried to rescue Nicole from the top of the oak tree in our garden and had fallen and broken his collarbone. Joel hadn't been allowed to come over and play for months thereafter. When the doorbell rang, Nicole looked at me fearfully and said,

'That's Torben.'

I took a deep breath and said, 'I'll handle it.'

She got up. 'Don't start a fight.'

'No worries. Stay put.'

I walked into the hallway and closed the kitchen door. I stopped for a moment to recapitulate my plan of attack, then walked over to the door and opened it. A man in his mid-forties was standing in the stairwell. He was about my height, with greying hair and a round, shaven face with a perpetual salesman smile. He was wearing trainers, tight black jeans that exposed his bare ankles, and a casual grey shirt. A chunky, ugly Tag Heuer watch dangled from his wrist. He said, 'Hi!' I met his fake smile with an inquiring look. He assumed a startled expression. In a rather thick German accent, he asked, 'Is Nicole here?'

'Who's asking?'

'Hi, I'm Torben.' He stretched out his hand.

I didn't move and tried to look him in the eye as fiercely as I could. I withdrew the key from the lock, stepped towards him and closed the door behind me. To avoid being bumped into, he took a step back. I felt his insecurity.

'Who are you?' he asked.

'That's none of your business, *Torben Himer*. Your business is to leave this building, delete Nicole's number, and never bother her again.'

'I—I believe you're overstepping your bounds here. This is between me and Nicole. I need to see her. Is she here?'

'I believe you overstepped your bounds when you hit on a girl half your age, with a wife and two kids waiting at home. When you offered her coke at your company's party. When you terrorised her over the phone and followed her to the university and to the

105

café she works in.' Torben wanted to interrupt me, but I cut him short with a quick hand gesture. 'You overstepped your goddamned bounds when you threatened to "kick in her door and *make* her talk to you". Now, you have to step back and walk away.'

I took another step towards him. He yielded further ground and almost stumbled over some children's toys scattered on the floor. He tried to appear calm, but his hands were fidgeting. He glanced at my hands, looked back into my eyes and asked in a loud, high-pitched voice, 'Are you threatening me?'

'Calm down, Torben. You must think clearly now . . . Think about your wife, Stefanie—pretty hot for her age and two kids, by the way—who is probably sitting in your lovely flat in the Schloßstraße right now with your son, Max. He is probably enjoying his summer holiday before the first year at the gymnasium and playing FIFA on the new PlayStation he got for his tenth birthday. Isn't he too young for social media? Think about sweet little Melanie, who is hopefully in her crib by now. Think about your mother, Barbara, and her adorable book club at her retirement home in the Dahlmannstraße. Does she know what kind of a man her son is? Think about your boss, Karl Sporer at Sporer und Maler, and what he might think of your advances on his only daughter, Marie. Or about Professor Dr Jakob Schmidbauer and his reaction should he find out you're giving ecstasy to his daughter Tamara on Friday nights on the dancefloor of Kater Blau. Think about whether it's such a smart idea to publicly brag about your drug dealer Sameed Saliba, who has ties to the Lebanese mafia. Think about all the precious little petty things you have worked so hard for that you proudly exhibit on Instagram: your Porsche convertible, your set of golf clubs, the selection of Scotch you impress your friends with, the upcoming trip with the family to Dubai. A happy life is such a valuable yet fragile thing, don't you think, Torben?'

His face was pale and petrified. I tried to grin at him as manically as possible and said, slowly, 'By now, this feels like a nightmare, doesn't it? All you have to do to wake up is walk away and never bother Nicole again.'

Wordlessly, he pulled out his phone, showed me Nicole's contact on his phone and deleted it. He looked at me submissively and said, 'How can I be sure you'll leave me alone now?'

'You can't. Only know I want to deal with a dis-honourable piece of shit like you as little as possible. But you can be sure I will drag you down into the pits of hell if I ever hear from you again . . . By the way, here is the money you gave Nicole.' I got out my wallet and handed him 500 euros which he sheepishly put into the back pocket of his jeans. 'Now, leave.'

Torben nodded slowly and looked to the floor. He hastened down the stairs. I waited in the stairwell until I heard the street door closing. I went back inside the flat and breathed a sigh of relief. My heart was pounding. I felt nauseated. When I entered the kitchen, Joel and Nicole looked at me, full of expec-tation. My sister asked, 'Is he gone?'

'Yeah.'

'Will he come back?'

'I don't think so. I put on quite an act for him. If he bothers you again, let me know immediately, okay?'

'What will you do if he does?'

'I don't know. But anything short of burning his life down to the ground would be anticlimactic.'

Nicole jumped up and hugged me. 'Thanks for

being the tough big brother, big brother!'

I sat down at the table and finished my pizza. We spent the rest of the night playing a game of Risk, scheming, fighting, and laughing until midnight.

During the rest of the week, Nicole went to her lectures and worked at the café while I explored Berlin's museums, parks, and food markets. In the evenings, we cooked together or went to the cinema. We both enjoyed the calm for a change. Torben didn't call or show up again. In an irritated tone, Nicole told me of her sporadic contact with Mum and Michael. She had last seen them on Michael's birthday in February, and Mum called her roughly once a month. Whereas I had always tried to go my own way, Nicole had faced the narrow-mindedness of my parents head-on in fiery fights. During our youth, while I had sat in my attic room, practising the guitar, doing push-ups, or reading Herman Hesse, yelled scraps of conversation about too-short skirts, unauthorised sleepovers, and feuds with bigoted teachers resounded from the living room downstairs. But Nicole had never stopped loving our parents and model brother in her own stubborn way. Now she was trying to convince me to get back in touch with Mum. Before she could dig too deep into our past, I changed topics.

On Thursday night, we met Roxy, one of Nicole's friends from university, in a bar near Nicole's place. Roxy's delicate body was wrapped in a tight white top and a billowing black skirt. I tried not to stare at her. After Nicole introduced me and we sat down at a table, Roxy asked, 'Are you the famous brother who started a big fight on Nicole's first night out as a teenager?'

I sighed. 'Yeah, I guess that's me.'

Nicole barged in, 'Did I tell you the whole story?'

'I guess so, but I was pretty drunk,' Roxy said.

I groaned, 'It's not such an interesting story.'

Nicole poked my shoulder and shouted, 'Come on!' She laughed, took a deep sip of her beer, and continued, 'Okay, so I was 14, and he was 18, and it was his first summer after grammar school. There was this big summer party at the only club in our home town, and I had convinced him to take me with him. Our parents obviously objected, especially since he'd got into trouble before and because our older brother, the saint, wasn't there to look after us. But somehow, we convinced them and were allowed to go in the end. I got past the bouncers, and we had an awesome night. I felt so cool—partying with my big brother at 14!' She giggled. 'But then there were these two disgusting guys on the dancefloor that tried to touch me and wouldn't let me go. So, Rocky Balboa here rushes in and shoves them away. They freak out and start hitting him. Little did they know my brother had been boxing for ten years by then. He knocks out the first one and pushes the other one to the ground. Then the bouncers rush in and tumble with him to the floor. They all land on his arm, which snaps. I remember the sight of it—bent in the middle of the forearm and with the broken bones bulging out the skin. A normal person would have sat down and waited for the ambulance. But my crazy brother here grabbed me by the wrist, and we ran out of the club and raced our bikes home. He talked me into going to sleep and went to bed himself—with a broken arm! When I woke him up at noon, his arm was terribly swollen. We had to confess everything to our parents, who drove us to the hospital.'

Roxy looked at me with her smiling mouth opened in awe and a seductive sparkle in her eyes which unsettled me. 'No way!' she exclaimed. 'What happened afterwards?'

Nicole answered, 'He had to stay in hospital for a couple of days and have surgery. The police investigated the incident; the other two guys had both ended up in hospital as well. But all charges were dropped in the end.'

Roxy stared at me and said, 'I wish I had a brother who fought for me like that . . . What a cool story!'

I looked at them bitterly and said, 'It's not so cool to be interrogated by the police, or to see the look on your parents' faces like you have let them down beyond repair; to get kicked out of your boxing club; to have to get morphine shots because of the pain from an inflammation on your broken bones.'

'I'm sorry,' Nicole said, 'but it all worked out in the end, didn't it? And Mum and Dad forgave you a long time ago. Plus, all the boys back home have treated me commendably courteously ever since.'

'Yeah . . . You don't have to be sorry. I just wanted to lecture you kids a little bit.' I added with feigned sternness, 'Life's not all fun and games!'

'Thanks for the lesson, Granddad!' They laughed, and we touched glasses.

Roxy looked at me and asked, 'What're your plans for the weekend in Berlin?'

'Well, Nicole is going on her field trip to Paris, so I'll stay with my friend Joel for a couple more days before we go to Zwickau together to visit a friend of his. Tomorrow, we might go out clubbing. And on Saturday, we're at a party in this house which is one huge shared flat.'

'Near Oranienplatz?'

'I don't know. It's in Kreuzberg, and the guy who invited us is called Thomas or Tobias.'

With a radiant smile, Roxy said, 'I might be going to the same party! Would be funny to see you there. It's supposed to get pretty wild.'

'Yeah, we'll see.'

For a while, Nicole and Roxy discussed TV series, songs, and books I had never heard of. After another beer, Nicole and I said goodbye to Roxy. We went to bed early. Lying awake, I checked my phone and was upset to see Alice as the first contact in the contact lists of all my apps. I only had texted her on a few occasions when we had to make plans in Stockholm. And yet the algorithms somehow knew of her importance to me and rubbed her full-lipped, spitefully beautiful smile in my face at every possible opportunity. I noticed a few photos of tanned people on arcadian beaches she was tagged in. Social media is a great tool to stay in touch with friends scattered all over the world, but also a splendid means to substitute invigorating sleep with obsessing about people who have abandoned you.

Nicole and I got up early the next day since she had to leave for the airport. I promised to call her soon, and she vowed to make an effort to nail her upcoming exams and to party a little less. I spent the day at Joel's place, playing the guitar and booking hostels in Prague and Sofia.

Late in the evening, Patrick, a friend Joel knew from a promo shoot, came over, and we started drinking. Legend had it that one of Patrick's jobs was to clean the infamous dark rooms of Berghain with a high-pressure cleaner, dressed in rubber overalls; he answered any questions about it with a discounting chuckle. Well past midnight, Patrick, a lanky, fidgety Edward Norton lookalike, asked us spiritedly, 'All right, who's down for some clubbing?'

Joel didn't look convinced. 'I don't know . . . I'm not really in the mood for shallow music and expensive drinks.' He turned to me and said, 'What do you think?'

'I'd like to go. I haven't gone mad in Berlin in a long time.'

Joel sighed, 'Okay. Let's go, then.'

As we waited in the long queue in front of Tresor, a club in an old heating plant in Berlin Mitte, Patrick inconspicuously swallowed a little pill. He offered some to Joel and me. Joel declined, saying alcohol and cigarettes were vices enough. I remembered the story Alice had told me in Hamburg of a night she had had sex on ecstasy and had felt her whole body in a heaving, never-ending orgasm for hours. A sting of aimless envy struck my chest. I took a pill from Patrick and gulped it. Joel gave me a surprised and concerned look. I answered with a mad smile. Patrick knew one of the bouncers, and we had no trouble getting in. We entered a world of cold concrete, resonating, clanking bass, and delirious, pulsating lights. Joel went to the bar and bought a beer. When I wanted to order one too, Patrick told me to wait until the MDMA hit and ordered two bottles of water. Through the all-engulfing, hypnotic wall of music, Patrick shouted, 'Let's go straight to the basement!'

Walking through the fulgurating concrete labyrinth and the remains of old pipes and machines, I was abruptly washed away by an unstoppable wave of emotion and sensation. I was buried under the weight of a thousand suns of madness. Madness. Flashing lights came at me, went through me, and changed the essence of my being. Madness—weighing heavier and heavier on my brain. Heart pounding. Who had I been before this madness? Madness. I had finally made it; I was insane and would end up in a psychiatric institution. Panic in my fingertips and in my eyes and in my soul. Joel's face. 'Are you okay, man?' I tried to answer but could only moan as my brain melted in the strobe light. Joel knew I was insane! 'Man, he's tripping!' 'I know, this shit is super heavy. *Whoa, Alter, was geht!*' 'For fuck's sake, Patrick, that's why I hate this shit! Here, drink some water.' The water of the endless ocean filled my mouth and ran down my throat, filling every pore with exhilarating refreshment. Water was the source of all life—of all the beautiful creatures in every corner of this ungraspable world. Maybe I was insane, but it was going to be all right. 'Are you okay?' Yes. I moaned with delight and smiled the broadest smile a man had ever smiled. I needed to dance and started walking. Patrick and Joel followed me into the deep dungeons of booming bass. We entered a long concrete tunnel, flashing in the strobe light. As we walked, the music got louder and louder, the air stuffier and stuffier. Waves of joy and anticipation ran through every fibre of my body. At the end of the tunnel, the music exploded in our faces. We had ended up in a bunker of relentless bass that made our bones vibrate and our lungs tremble. The dancefloor was crowded with a swirling mass of bodies dancing in the foggy darkness. The DJ was locked behind bars and dashed his merciless beat at us through trumpet-shaped speakers. I became one with the crowd—with all these lost souls who had suffered and struggled like me and were now merging with the rhythm in a moment of love and forgiveness. I danced for eternity, marvelling at the beautiful laser beams gleaming through space and time. Once, I got stuck on my way to the bathroom, sensing a satin curtain with my pulsating hands. A texture had never been so soft and pure and perfect and imperishably comforting. Back on the steaming dancefloor, Joel brought me a bottle of water and said he wanted to leave. I wanted to stay forever. We split the difference and stayed for another hour which passed within a minute.

As we staggered out of the club, I could hear my thoughts re-sort again. Maybe I wouldn't remain insane after all. In one of the concrete corridors, we passed a group of men wearing nothing but trainers, waist bags and unicorn hats—casual. Stepping outside, the sun was already rising, and the cool summer morning breeze nearly knocked us out of our shoes. 'Have you seen Patrick?' Joel slurred; he must have had more beers than I had thought.

'No. I don't remember too much, anyway.'

'Yeah, no wonder. I was worried about you for a moment there.'

'Yeah . . . But now I feel good—really good, man.'

'All right, let's go home,' Joel murmured with the last of his strength.

On his sofa, I had trouble sleeping. The sun shone scornfully through the roof light. Conflicting feelings of tiredness and fading euphoria stirred my brain. Finally, I fell through short, feverish dreams into all-encompassing darkness.

Joel and I had breakfast in the early afternoon. I laughed at his hangover-tormented face, and he made fun of my drug-induced confusion. Last night had been an exciting experience, but I knew my mind was too weak for this sense-distorting mayhem. When I was in hospital after my broken-arm incident, they had put me on morphine to ease the pain that scorched my arm and drilled into my brain. The medication made me feel light and soft, and I spent the days floating under the hospital room ceiling, looking down at myself lying peacefully in bed. It had taken me days to regain a sense of realness afterwards. When Joel and I were teenagers, I met a guy called Kolya through boxing who used to smuggle marijuana by the kilogram from the Netherlands. Sitting on this never-ending supply of weed, Joel and I got high for weeks on end in my garden while my parents were at work. We would pluck away at my guitar, composing incoherent Nirvana rip-off songs. Sometimes Kolya would join us, and we would listen to his nerve-racking stories of police run-ins with a backpack full of Mary Jane. Kolya was a bright, lively kid but had the wrong friends and no parents to look after him. Over time, I grew slower in school, which until then had never been particularly challenging for me, and Joel became prone to pot-induced panic attacks. I didn't particularly excel in boxing during this phase, either. After a dreadful afternoon Joel spent locked inside our bathroom, hallucinating that he was Super Mario, we had never smoked more than the occasional recreational joint again. After all, existing as a vulnerable bag of organic matter, flying through the cold eternal void on a piece of rock, only having gained consciousness by a wicked accident of nature, was scary enough without any manipulation of perception. I guess that was why the only drug that had ever been able to truly captivate me had been alcohol. Alcohol dumbed me down, and sometimes, ignorance was bliss. The last thing I had heard of Kolya was that he was in prison, with a baby daughter waiting for him outside.

Since Joel and I didn't feel any better after breakfast, and because we would be drinking tonight anyway, we started the day with a round of White Russians. The first glass eased the dizziness and the second glass dulled my headache. Joel and I took a walk through Kreuzberg, through streets filled with rubbish and empty glass bottles. We strolled along the canal and across parks crowded with enterprising immigrants selling all conceivable types of drugs. Newspaper dispensers on street corners displayed sensational news of a failed asylum seeker stabbing people in a Hamburg supermarket. By tomorrow, the hyenas would smell new blood and turn their snouts in the wind. Suppose there was terror, and nobody covered it.

As we trudged along, Joel asked, 'Hey, do you remember the sailing magazines we looked at in the basement of my father's house after band rehearsals?'

I said, 'Yeah. That feels like a lifetime ago.'

Joel chuckled and said, 'Fantasising about taking our recent crushes on catamaran tours to the Seychelles.'

'Sailing into the sunset with the girls we loved. Playing gigs in harbour cities. That was the dream.'

Joel sighed, 'You know, sometimes I still wonder what would've happened if we'd kept the band together back then.'

I contorted my face and asked, 'You mean if I hadn't neglected the band to get wasted and chase girls with Ben?'

'No, that's not what I meant . . . I know you needed time for boxing back then—and, yeah, for endless parties with Ben.' Joel chuckled and fell silent for a while. When we reached the canal that confined the park, he said, 'I often wonder whether I'll ever be able to recreate that feeling of incorruptible friendship and trust we had back in school. It's so hard to make new good friends as we grow older.' He turned to me and said, 'You know that "what if" question that nags at you in the back of your head sometimes?'

'Yeah, I know what you mean . . . '

I felt guilty. I knew Joel didn't mean to make me feel that way. He just always said exactly what he thought, while his smiling eyes offered the full spectrum of his vulnerability for anyone to see. All he had ever wanted from life was to make art and help people enjoy themselves. He had come to despise his work in advertising but was reliant on it to make a living. He burnt for the long nights in little clubs with his stoner rock band—alternating between drums and guitar and microphone, sweating and breathing and bleeding music, sacrificing his wounded soul to the audience and resurrecting it in a bonfire of sound and light and ecstasy. Five years ago, he had donated a kidney to a second cousin he barely knew and after-wards had never mentioned it again. If you ran him over with your car, Joel would probably apologise for the dent his head had made in the bonnet and offer you his sad yet contagious smile as compensation.

When we reached the Spree, we leaned on a fence by the riverside and gazed at the Molecule Men, aluminium giants as high as a ten-storey building, protruding from the water, gleaming in the sun. I looked at Joel and said, 'I'm sorry I betrayed our friendship back then.'

He looked at me with a kind smile. 'I forgave you long ago . . . You know, I once found you in a toilet cubicle in Kelly's Bar. You were dead drunk and smashed your head against the wall. It was scary. I wrestled with you, and you were so drunk that I won. I dragged you outside and called a taxi for you. And while we're standing there—it was raining like hell— you keep slurring, "Nobody loves me, nobody loves me." And that's when I forgave you.'

I stared at him and said, 'I don't remember that.'

'Don't worry about it. It was, like, ten years ago.'

I nodded. An almost teary-eyed silence ensued. After a while, I cracked a smile at Joel and said, 'Do you remember Christina? She's now married to a notorious hotel mogul from Dubai.'

Joel laughed and said, 'Yeah, I saw that. How did that even happen?'

I chuckled and said, 'You had a major crush on her in Year 9.'

Joel laughed and shouted, 'That's a shameless lie!' and gave me a nudge on my shoulder. Guffawing, we started wrestling, and I put Joel in a headlock. We panted and laughed and walked further along the bank of the Spree.

In the evening, we had burgers and a couple of beers in a bar and went to the party at the shared house. When we arrived there, the revelry was already in full swing. The house had four floors. Each of them had a different theme. The first floor contained a beer-pong tournament, filled with loud, self-assured guys who probably all knew each other from the gym and playing beach volleyball together. Climbing upstairs led us to a flat converted into a club, filled with techno, colourful lights, and spaced-out dancers in black. The third floor was shaking from the searing, crisp guitar riffs of a Brit rock band. The attic accommodated a surprisingly professional bar and a living room immersed in syrupy billows of smoke. Joel and I organised two Cuba Libres and made our way one floor down to watch the band. We enjoyed the music and the conversation with one of the hosts' group of friends for an hour or two and then joined the beer pong downstairs only to get absolutely destroyed by a pair of tank-top bros with undercuts and forearm tattoos.

On my way to get more drinks, I ran into Roxy, my little sister's friend. She gave me a drunk, euphoric hug and tried to drag me to the dancefloor. I told her I was on my way to the bar and had to get back to Joel. She held on to me and started dancing in the stairwell. She wore ripped white jeans and a tight black spaghetti top accentuating her perfect, tanned body. Her straight brown hair was swinging in front of her innocent face. Her waving hips were those of a Spanish goddess in an opium dream. I broke away and walked upstairs to the bar. Waiting for my drinks, I felt the sudden urge to call Alice and tell her how much I missed her. What was wrong with me? On my way downstairs, I didn't see Roxy and was both disappointed and relieved. I told Joel to hit me if I dared to call Alice or hook up with my little sister's friend. We ended up on the dancefloor half an hour later. Within minutes, I was standing in a dark corner with Roxy, my hands on her hips, her hands beneath my shirt. I collected myself, took my hands off her, and told her, 'Look, you're my little sister's friend. We shouldn't do this.'

She grinned wolfishly and said, 'I won't tell.'

Why did she have to be so smoking hot? I shook my head and said, 'No, Roxy. This doesn't feel right.'

She moved closer again and said, 'Don't you want to do the wrong thing?' I felt her breath on my neck and her hand on my thigh as she whispered in my ear, 'I want you to do wrong things to me.' She nibbled at my ear. I laughed somewhat hysterically and rushed out of the flat, up to the attic, and onto the balcony to get some fresh air.

After a cigarette, I called Alice. Ringing. Eternal silence. Another ringing. Alice's mellow voice: '*Hej.*'

My heart started pounding, and my stomach cramped. 'Hey, Alice. How are you?'

'Good. I just got home from a small house party.' She yawned the cutest yawn. 'Where are you?'

'In Berlin. At a house party, too. It's a pretty big one, though.'

'Found any cute girls there?'

I felt as though I had been dealt a soft kidney punch. 'Yeah, actually. I'm a bit tired of this craziness, though.'

She laughed into the distant Swedish summer night. 'Did you have a good trip so far?'

'Yeah. There's been a lot going on. I made friends with mercenaries in Tallinn and knocked out guys in Riga. And I met my little sister again.'

Alice sent another laugh across the Baltic Sea that made Berlin pale into irrelevance. 'Sounds like a lot of fun!'

'How was Cuba?' I asked.

'It was great! The coral reef there is stunning! I could have stayed forever.'

I didn't know what to say. I love you? I miss you? All the alcohol in this world cannot make me forget you? Instead, I uttered, 'Cool.'

Awkward silence. The noise from the party reso-nated from the grey housing blocks on the other side of the street through the warm summer night. I could hear Alice move in her bed on the other side of the line. She asked, 'Do you still plan to go to Italy?'

'Yeah . . . ' My heart was pounding. 'Wanna join?'

'When are you going?'

'I don't know exactly—mid to end of August?'

'Hmm . . . That could work. Call me again a week before you go.'

'We could rent a car and drive around.'

'That sounds awesome. Listen, I'm tired and have to teach a yoga class tomorrow morning . . . '

'Yeah, I need to get back to the party as well.'

'Have fun. And don't knock anyone out who doesn't deserve it.'

'I'll try. Bye.'

She giggled. 'Bye.'

My head was filled with love and pain and insecurity. I pictured Alice lying in her tiny bed back in Lappis, cuddled into her white flower bedspread. In the distance, the Fernsehturm sent its twinkling red light across the city of never-ending parties. I went behind the bar inside and mixed a triple Rusty Nail. Blackout.

I didn't dare to open my eyes. Where was I? My brain had been wrested from my skull and replaced with burning acid. My limbs hurt. My mouth was dry. The skin on my chest and belly hurt. I could hear slow and rhythmic breathing next to me. I opened my eyes and turned my head. My vision was blurred, but I recognised Roxy lying beside me. The walls of the small room around us were covered in a collage of polaroid pictures and cut-out pages from art magazines. The light coming through the thin curtain hurt my eyes. I closed them again. How had I ended up here? I dozed off.

The next time I woke up, Roxy was sitting in bed next to me, naked, with a big jug of water. She handed it to me, her arm pressing against a firm, luscious breast. In pain, I sat up halfway and took a deep sip. My body took in the water like a parched sponge. I let my head fall back onto the pillow and groaned. Roxy giggled and asked, 'Are you okay?'

'I think I'm dying.'

'Okay. But if you do, hurry up. You have to be out of here by half past one. My mum is coming to visit.'

'What time is it now?'

'Quarter past one. I can give you breakfast, but then you'll have to leave.'

I groaned in agony. 'Can't you just leave me here to die and close the door?'

'My mum probably wants to see my room. I'm sure she'd be delighted to find the corpse of a smelly man with scratch marks all over him in my bed.'

I looked down at my body. Bloody scratch marks ran from my chest to my crotch. In confusion, I glanced at her and then at the bedside table, cluttered with two dildos, handcuffs, lubricant, and a scarf. I turned to Roxy and said, 'Looks like we had a party last night.'

'You don't remember?' She giggled. 'Yeah, we got a little carried away—for an old-fashioned guy, you're quite adventurous.' She shook her head and added, 'I can't believe you don't remember! You didn't even seem that drunk yesterday.'

'Yeah, most people never notice when I'm drunk. I'm not sure whether that's a boon or a bane, though.'

Roxy roughed up my hair with a chuckle and jumped up from the bed. She said, 'All right, I'm in the kitchen. Get up soon.'

The idea of being torn out of the cosy refuge of Roxy's bed terrified me. I gave her a hangdog look and begged, 'Can't you call your mum and come back to bed? Let's cuddle and watch a film.'

She laughed. 'A wounded warrior searching for a princess to heal him—how touching. Get up.'

As she walked over to her wardrobe to put on leggings and a shirt, I spotted fresh bruises on her perfect bum. I watched her slide her perfect curves into her clothes and leave the room. Roxy might have been the hottest girl I had ever had sex with. And I couldn't even remember it. I shook my head and uttered a desperate chuckle. In agony, I managed to get up and put on my clothes. Roxy gave me a sandwich for my way home and pushed me through the shared flat and out of the door. She gave me a quick hug and said, 'Don't worry, I won't tell Nicole.'

'Thanks. See you around.'

'Sure.'

She shut the door. I found myself in an old wooden stairwell and slowly walked down its creaking steps. Two days ago, I had told Nicole to take better care of herself and party a little less. Now here I was, after a weekend full of drug-fuelled debauchery. I thought of that sleazebag Torben and what he might have done to my little sister. I had to take a deep breath not to ram my fists into the rusty postboxes on the ground floor. Outside on the busy street, I realised I had no clue where I was. The battery of my phone was dead. I walked down the street aimlessly, eating my ham and cheese sandwich. The city around me was just as run-down as I was. Empty beer bottles and tattered plastic bags covered the pavement. Old tramps spoke to themselves as they gathered returnable bottles from litter bins. Young hipsters with three-day under-eye circles gazed into the distance. Dizzily, I walked through a street in which pop-up designer shops alternated with barbers, tattoo parlours, and vegan cafés—tungsten-lit, high-ceilinged warehouse spaces characterised by wood and brick serving avocado toast and kale-and-quinoa skillets that looked good on Instagram. I craved the sofa in Emma's parents' house to sleep off my hangover in a sanctuary of love and comfort. Did they still live here? I soon ended up on Alexanderplatz and took the metro to Kreuzberg, where I found my way to Joel's place. Joel wasn't home when I arrived, but I slipped into the stairwell and collapsed into sleep on the hard wooden floor in front of his door.

Joel woke me up with a tender kick and laughed at my scruffy self when he came home from a camera gig. We recounted the night, and Joel hit me twice—once for calling Alice and once for hooking up with Roxy. He was a good friend. We watched *Montage of Heck*, discussed the pros and cons of life as a rock star, and went to bed.

The next morning, we threw our backpacks into Joel's old Mercedes E-Class and took off to the south of the former German Democratic Republic. Joel shot the Mercedes across the plains of Brandenburg, Saxony-Anhalt, and Saxony, past Leipzig, through Thuringia, and back into Saxony. In Zwickau, we dropped our luggage off at the flat of Joel's friend Peter and went to an outdoor pool. We watched young students play beach football, baked in the blazing summer sun, and ate ice cream.

We spent the evening at Peter's place, grandiosely failing at cooking lasagne, and had beers and cigarettes on his spacious balcony. The flat was full of stolen street signs and GDR memorabilia scavenged from abandoned houses and factories. In Zwickau, a city that had seen its population drop by a third since the '50s, housing was available cheap and in plenty.

Peter was a talkative scatterbrain whom Joel knew from a few gigs in Berlin. While he was preparing his shisha, he told us about his most recent online dating adventures:

'You know, I don't get some of these chicks. The other day, I went to a bar with this semi-good-looking soon-to-be teacher I met on Tinder. She looked a lot better in her pictures, by the way. And when I want to pay for her drinks, she freaks out and calls me a "fucking woman-hater". And I'm like, "What the hell is your problem? I'm just trying to be nice!" And she says she can pay for her own drinks and doesn't need a man to pay for her stuff. And I'm just trying to be polite here! I mean, I can think of better things to buy from my money than pink drinks for Mrs Strong-and-independent over here. I tell her that I'm sorry, and that I think it can be a wonderful thing to buy nice things for each other and that I had good intentions and all. And she's like, "It's more important how your actions are interpreted than how they're intended." But how the hell am I supposed to know how my actions will be interpreted? So apparently, every time I talk to a girl now, I have to set our relationship into the context of millennia of patriarchal oppression or something. Sounds like a lot of fun, doesn't it? Well, I sure as hell was careful not to open the door for her as we walked out of the bar . . . You know what the problem is with women these days?'

Joel and I didn't know and looked at Peter in amused expectation.

'The problem is they want a man who is soft and kind and understanding and want to pretend there is absolutely no difference between a man and a woman. But as soon as the bedroom door is shut, they want a man who dominates them, slaps their arse, and pulls their hair. Well, guess what? If you make us talk about our relationship with our parents all day and teach us to sit down on the toilet, you might end up with a softie who wants to cuddle and be the little spoon instead of having sex and who expects you to protect him when things get tough. And then your evolutionary reflexes kick in and make you cheat on him with the macho gym instructor who treats you like dirt!'

He finished preparing the shisha and took a deep drag.

'I guess my whole talk of men and women is three steps behind anyway since gender isn't even binary anymore . . . Well, in my opinion, everybody can identify as whatever they want and love whoever they love. I mean, love is beautiful in every form, you know? But for god's sake, can't I just buy my date a drink? Where's the tolerance for that? Can't people accept that I identify as a guy who buys girls drinks in a desperate attempt to hide his insecurity?'

As Joel and I chuckled, Peter passed the shisha on to me and said, 'You know, I might have developed a new dating strategy. So, the main reason why we want to date hot chicks, evolutionarily speaking, is to father strong and healthy babies who can wrestle sabre-tooth tigers and shit, right?'

With a confused smile, Joel replied, 'I guess so.'

'So, I was thinking . . . The hottest girls are far out of our league on most nights—' He looked at me and said, 'well, maybe not for buff, bearded James Dean over here, but at least for Joel and me.'

I shook my head. Joel laughed. Peter ignored me and continued, 'But if we're really after those hot-girl *genes*, wouldn't it make sense to go for hot girls who have had horrible accidents and have, like, lost both legs or have a disfigured face? Since they aren't chased by everybody anymore, they might settle for one of us. And we, in turn, get those sabre-tooth-tiger-wrestling, shark-punching babies we crave!'

Joel nodded and said, 'That's an interesting theory. Maybe you should tell it to your new feminist girlfriend the next time you invite her for drinks.'

We spent the rest of the night working on further theories, smoking shisha after shisha, and finishing a whole crate of beer. The mild summer night made us forget the time. We went to bed as the first rays of the sun immersed the horizon in burning red.

On Tuesday, we missed out on a beautiful summer day by staying on Peter's sofa and playing video games for hours on end. Only once did we make it out of the house during daylight hours to go to a nearby supermarket and buy meat and beer for a barbecue dinner on the balcony. Scattered throughout the run-down streets of Zwickau were old people with desperate and frightened faces. Every street had abandoned houses, surrendering to slow decay. Graffiti covered the walls of derelict public buildings. Zwickau, once the proud centre of the GDR's automobile industry, was exemplary of an East Germany that had never caught up with its bigger capitalist brother. With the return of openly flaring xenophobia and paralysing retrogressivity, it resembled other left-behind former industrial centres of the Western world—the devastated concrete deserts of Nord-Pas-de-Calais, northern England, and the American Rust Belt; places where workers had seen their wages stagnating, their factories crumbling, and their communities deteriorating for decades, while the experts they despised had told them of the merits of globalisation and of economic growth. Those who could had left for the big cities. The old had been left behind to witness the decay of their homes. I didn't like the grumpy faces of the streets of Zwickau, and I got the impression they didn't like me either; I was an alien body in their once-proud community. I could never live here. I was a part of the urban 'liberal elites', whether I liked it or not.

That night, we went to a student bar in the basement of one of the student dorms. Since it was summer vacation, there wasn't much going on. Peter led Joel and me down the street from the dorm and into a spacious, overgrown garden with weathered statues resembling dark demons in the pallid light of the moon. The premises were dominated by a vacant castle-like mansion whose oriels and turrets protruded into the night like tormented ghosts. A decaying monstrosity with dead windows—the House of Usher before its fall. On his second attempt, Peter kicked in a fragile side door. With the torches on our phones switched on, we advanced into the belly of the gloomy castle. The rooms had high ceilings and were still furnished. They seemed like hastily abandoned offices, with newspapers and coffee mugs still left on the tables. Shadows danced on the empty bookshelves and the green wallpaper peeling off the wall. Our footsteps and hushed voices echoed through the corridors. We descended into the basement, where mouldered wood and burnt paper scrunched beneath our shoes. The smell of ash hung in the air. We discovered a long corridor with interrogation rooms or prison cells on both sides. The rooms had heavy steel doors and contained steel tables and chairs. Cold shivers ran up and down my spine. We left the basement in a glum mood and climbed up to the top floor, which accommodated larger rooms with luxurious leather sofas and heavy oak tables. On a sudden whim, I wrapped one of the towels I had found in a musty bathroom around my arm and smashed one of the big windows with my elbow. With a loud clank, the shards flew into the night. Joel and Peter followed suit, and we worked ourselves up into a window-shattering frenzy, until Joel noticed the lights going on in the buildings across the street. Giggling hysteri-cally, we ran out of the villa and through the unkempt garden. We climbed over a fence on the other side of the premises onto another street. We walked around the block and back to the student dorm. As we entered the bar, a group of smokers discussed the noisy rampage down the street. We had to suppress our laughter and calmed down over another round of beers. We ended the night with a shisha on Peter's balcony and an unsolicited lecture on my part about the history of boxing in Ancient Greece and Rome, England during the Industrial Revolution, and the 20th-century United States.

In my dream that night, Alice and I moved into a new home by the sea near Penzance at the westernmost tip of Cornwall. It was a small house built of grey brick with a turquoise wooden winter garden and balcony. In the mornings, we jumped into the water on the other side of the coast road. Afterwards, Alice made scrambled eggs, bacon, and pancakes—her slender body wrapped in a white dressing gown. During the days, I worked as a writer in my study with a view of our palm garden and the rough sea sculpting the rugged beach, while Alice went to work on a research ship. In the evenings, I read the newspaper, and Alice kept busy decorating our cosy home. During the nights, Alice's soft lips whispered promises of irrevocable love and trust. We spent Sunday mornings in bed and talked about having children and growing old together. Finally, I had found a home.

An unpleasant awakening shattered my paradise. After what had felt like years of living with Alice, I was thrown back onto the hard and comfortless sofa in Peter's living room. It was pitch dark. The only audible sound was Joel's rhythmic snoring. Alice would only ever want to live with me in my pathetic dreams. It took me a long time to get back to sleep.

I woke up early and felt like drinking a bottle of whisky and breaking my knuckles against a wall. Instead, I raided Peter's fridge and prepared a lavish breakfast After we had finished eating, Joel and I thanked Peter for his hospitality and wished him good luck with trying to buy drinks for disaster-struck girls. We jumped into the old Mercedes and headed down the motorway to Dresden. There, we rented an old Trabi and tried to push it to 120 kilometres per hour, which felt like the speed of sound with your face pressed against the juddering windscreen in that ancient plastic box. We spent the rest of the day walking through the rebuilt baroque city centre and drinking coffee. I enjoyed listening to Joel telling the story of the night he had drunk beers with Bruce Springsteen backstage in Trondheim. I fell asleep on the drive to Prague.

We are as forlorn as children lost in the woods.
When you stand in front of me and look at me,
what do you know of the griefs that are in me
and what do I know of yours.

Franz Kafka in a letter to Oskar Pollak

8

I woke up as we were driving through busy streets and across the Vltava into the Czech capital at dusk. We parked the car and dropped off our luggage at a buzzy hostel between the Old Town and the Florenc bus station. We arrived in time to receive a free dinner—chilli con carne and stale local beer. On the advice of the spent guy at the reception desk, we crossed the Vltava, which gently flowed through the warm summer evening, and climbed up to the Metronome in Letná Park. We made our way through a crowd dancing to noisy grime music, bought cheap Cuba Libres at a small bar stand, and sat down on top of a stone wall. We had a stunning view of the glimmering sea of lights below. On a line stretched above our heads, countless skate shoes danced in the night sky; the square behind us was a popular venue for skaters. It had once been the backdrop of the ostentatious Stalin Monument, which had been blown up only a few years after its completion during de-Stalinisation. Joel took a sip from his drink and gazed into the shimmery distance. He asked, 'What are you going to do after your travels? I mean, you already told me you don't want to become a rich and famous rock star with me, so . . . '

'Yeah, sorry about that.' I sighed. 'I don't know yet. I don't want to be a banker anymore. The further I get away from London, the clearer that becomes to me . . . I had a dream of being an author last night. Maybe I should try that.'

'What would you write about?'

'I don't know. I guess everything's already been written.' I chuckled in desperation.

'I see you've got it all figured out.'

We laughed. I took another sip from my drink and said, 'Well, I'd like to travel some more . . . and maybe meet Alice in Italy.'

'Is that what she said to you on the phone?'

'Yeah.'

'Do you want to meet her?'

'Yeah . . . I don't know. I mean . . . Yeah, I think so . . . Let's see what she says when I call her in a couple of weeks.'

Joel looked at me thoughtfully and laughed. 'Oh man, the only time I've seen you this confused about a girl was after you'd met Emma!'

'I know. I feel lost.'

'It's all going to be all right. And if not, come to Berlin, and we'll write some hits about broken hearts.'

We laughed and went to buy more drinks. Joel told me he was contemplating going to Colombia to win back Valentina. I told him if he loved her, he should do it. We had two more drinks and went back to our hostel.

Joel had to leave for Berlin the next morning. Vladi-mir's Joke were booked to play at a vegan food market in the evening. I accompanied him to his car and asked, 'Can you look after Nicole? I'll try to call her more often now too, but I think it's good if she has someone in Berlin she trusts.'

'Sure, I'll do what I can. But to be honest, I'm more concerned about you. I've never seen you this haunted.' He paused sheepishly. 'Nicole told me you haven't talked to your mum since your father died. I don't know exactly what happened back then, but—'

'Yeah, don't worry, I'll figure it out.' I glanced at my left wrist where my watch had been; I sometimes forgot it had been stolen back in Tallinn. 'When is your gig tonight?'

'We start playing at seven but have to set up everything at four. I should get going.'

'Okay. Hey, thanks for letting me stay at your place. It was good to see you again.'

'Yeah, I enjoyed it a lot!' Joel got into the car and looked at me through the open window.

I said, 'Hey, if I find a cheap catamaran down at the Mediterranean Sea, I'll let you know.'

'Awesome. Take care!'

He catapulted the old Mercedes out of the parking space with squeaking tires and honked twice as he flung the car around the corner. I answered with a goodbye nod and turned towards Old Town. I felt restless.

I strolled through Josefov, the Jewish Quarter and former ghetto. Hitler was said to have had plans for a museum of the extinct race of Jews here. As I walked down a crowded alleyway next to the Old New Synagogue, my head started spinning. Since my adolescence, I had had moments in which I was unsure of reality. Could I be certain of my existence? Was my life just a dream within a dream of a brain locked in a box? Could I trust gravity, or was I about to fall into the infinite darkness of empty space? Gazing at the synagogue, the crowd of tourists surrounding me transformed into a maelstrom of cursed souls. The walls of the narrow alleyway closed in on me and threatened to crush me. The purple sky came tumbling down. My vision blurred. My heart pounded. My sense of balance betrayed me. I couldn't breathe. Was I dying? I grabbed onto a nearby street sign and tried to breathe calmly despite the alarming feeling of asphyxiation. I reassured myself that the threat was only in my mind. I was going to be okay. It was only in my mind. I was going to be okay. I had been through this before. I was going to be okay. I regained solid ground beneath my feet. The walls retreated. The summer sky recaptured its heavenly blue. The image of tourists bustling around me became clear again. I let go of the street sign and took another deep breath. I put my right index finger on my carotid artery and felt my pulse abating. This had been my first panic attack since the day before I quit my job two months ago. I started walking.

I passed the Old Jewish Cemetery, crammed with thousands of gravestones. The cemetery was elevated several metres above the surrounding streets. The confined space of the ghetto had forced the Jewish community to layer the graves over the centuries. How many vanished worlds lay buried here? I left the Jewish Quarter, heading south, and dislodged my dark thoughts. I crossed the overcrowded Charles Bridge and climbed up to Prague Castle and the Petřín Lookout Tower. From the top, I had a terrific view of the city's church towers and red rooftops. The steep climb up the tower stung my cigarette-seared lungs. I was tired and hungry and craved a nap in my hostel bed. The restaurants I passed on my way back there were filled with tourists having beer for lunch. I crossed the Vltava and entered Old Town again. I walked past the astronomical clock on the southern wall of Old Town Hall and grabbed a chicken burrito on the way. I was beat when I reached my hostel. The professional alcoholic behind the reception desk asked me whether I was doing all right. I murmured an indifferent 'Sure' and went into my room. I occupied myself with a copy of *The Call of the Wild* I had found on the hostel's bookshelf, before dozing off.

I was surprised when I received a text message from Emma in the evening:

'Hey. How are you? I've seen you're in Germany? Let me know if you're also planning on coming to Munich. I'm working here as an editor for an e-commerce company now. I thought it might be fun to meet? It's been a while . . . '

Puzzled, I decided to answer later and went to a restaurant down the street. I ordered roasted duck with potato dumplings. My phone rang. Nicole.

'Hey, little sister.'

'Hey, big brother.'

'I just wanted to call and tell you how nice it was to have you here in Berlin.'

I smiled into my phone and said, 'I'm glad I could be there with you too. How was Paris?'

'Paris was amazing! It was good to see some of my friends again. And we got to visit a lot of interesting companies. I think the trip gave me some motivation to do well in my exams. I studied for eight hours today and haven't been partying for almost a week now!'

'That's great to hear, Nicole. I'm proud of you.'

'Thanks, big brother.'

'Has this Torben character bothered you again?'

'No, I haven't heard from him. Thanks again for dealing with him.' She paused. 'Have you talked to Mum yet?'

'No. I wouldn't really know what to say.'

'Tell her you're sorry, you idiot. It would make her happy. I know you're afraid, but she isn't angry at you. She hasn't been in a long time now . . . You couldn't know Dad would die that day. And we all get why you didn't come to the funeral. You know how sorry Mum is for what she said to you. You're a part of this family, whether you like it or not.'

I rubbed my eyes and exhaled with a sigh. I said, 'I know . . . I'm going to talk to Mum again eventually. I just have to figure some things out first, okay?'

'Don't wait too long. It would be nice to celebrate Christmas together as a boring family again this year.'

'Yeah, maybe . . . Listen, I'm at a restaurant, and my food is coming. It was good to hear from you. And keep on focussing on your exams.'

'Okay. I will. Have fun on your trip. And don't be a stranger!'

'Wait, Nicole, I have to tell you something . . . '

'Yeah?'

'Last weekend, I got rather drunk at this house party and ended up sleeping with your friend Roxy . . . I'm sorry, I shouldn't have done it.'

'I know. Don't worry. It's not a big deal. She'll screw anything with a pulse.'

I heard an indignant yell in the background and giggling. I said, 'Is Roxy there with you?'

'Yeah, she is. She sends hugs and kisses.' More laughter.

I sighed, 'Okay, I'm hanging up, you weirdo. Take care. Bye.'

I waited for my food for another ten minutes.

Two years ago, my dad had been in hospital with terminal leukaemia. We had expected his death any day. We had decided either Mum, Michael, Nicole, or I would always be by his side. On a Friday a month after my mum's birthday, it had been my turn since my brother had had to meet clients of his gardening company after he had slept at the hospital two nights in a row. But I was called to join a business trip to New York at short notice; the forecasting system had crashed at the American branch of the firm. When I realised my mistake and let my family know someone else would have to go to the hospital instead of me, it was too late. On a sunny September morning, my dad, who had fought like a lion for his family his whole life, took his last breath alone in a bleak hospital room. Nobody was there to comfort him or listen to his last words. I wasn't there. I owed my dad my whole life—everything—and that was how I had shown my gratitude. My mum had finally reached me during a meeting in New York in the evening. As I gazed at the concrete desert of Manhattan, she screamed at me through the phone. She told me she never wanted to see me ever again. The last words she had said to me that day still stung bitterly: 'You're not my son. I should've known.' I had gone back to London, into the desolate flat Emma had left a week earlier after I had broken up with her. I had immersed myself in work. I still hadn't visited my dad's grave. My mum hadn't reached out, but Michael and Nicole had told me throughout the last year that she wanted to reconcile with me. But how could I look into her eyes after I had deserted my dying father for some meaningless banking business?

When my food arrived, I distracted myself by reading news about China demanding India remove troops from a long-disputed border; what could possibly go wrong? After dinner, I went back to the hostel. I met a Russian backpacker with whom I shared half a dozen glasses of bourbon and roughly as many words. As I lay drunk in bed, I thought of Alice. What was she doing right now? Was she out partying in Stockholm, hooking up with secretive artistic types who told her about that one time they rode their bike to Istanbul? I felt the urge to push my knuckles through someone's face.

The next day, I woke up early and dragged my hungover self to the National Gallery. Ai Weiwei had hung a supersized black refugee rubber raft from the ceiling of one of the concrete halls as part of his exhibition on the refugee crisis. Upstairs, I wandered through wide white corridors and was seized by dark Czech art from the 18th to the early 20th century. For a long time, I couldn't break free from Antonín Hudeček's *Psyche*. At the banks of a mystic river, the mortal woman who turns Cupid's head walks nakedly through a muzzy forest at night. She stared at me with doom-laden eyes, as I imagined Death himself would do before taking me with him into the void.

I was ten years old when I had understood that I must die one day. I had been lying awake one cold November night, two weeks after the suicide of my alcoholic grandfather. The hopelessness I had experienced that night was deeply interlinked with the rare depressive phases and panic attacks that had started later when I was a teenager. Panic isn't monsters and devils. It's the loss of control over your mind, a disintegrating consciousness. It's the full realisation of our fleeting reality, the fear of an idea that cannot be forgotten—the unfiltered awareness of the future, of time passing, drilling into your skull, where dark insanity looms. Fortunately, my attacks had always remained infrequent. One of the most important lessons of growing up is recognising that nobody knows what the hell is going on. You can only pretend to know, to not upset your fellow human beings. Paranoia, fear, and insanity are contagious. If people ever acknowledged how scared they all are, the world would burn down in a mass panic before breakfast.

I tore myself away from the second coming of Aphrodite in search of her lost love and left the museum to get lunch.

In the afternoon, I visited the Museum of Communism. The secret police of Czechoslovakia, the StB, had been one of the mightiest in the Soviet empire. Nowadays, we willingly handed over more information about ourselves to the new digital empires of Silicon Valley than the StB, the Stasi, or the KGB could have ever hoped for. And the Western intelligence agencies were happy to use all that information to put people on no-fly lists, deny them entrance into their ostensible oases of freedom, or drone-bomb them and whoever was unfortunate enough to stand next to them into oblivion. But if Facebook was free, Netflix recommended the latest binge-worthy content, and Amazon delivered on time, what was there to complain about?

In the evening, I sat down with a group of Germans for free dinner at the hostel and joined a pub crawl in the southwest of Old Town. At the first bar, there were heated discussions about Trump and Brexit. But by the time we arrived at the third pub, any political doubts and fears had been washed away with alcohol. A group of young German and English guys took off their shirts and sang in their beer-induced delirium.

It was time to leave, but not before some dead-drunk Korean girl caked in makeup had shoved her greasy tongue down my throat. On my way home across Old Town Square, four different drug dealers offered me their pills. I was happy when I arrived in my bed and drifted off into sleep.

I spent my Sunday reading in the shade of the Metronome above Prague. After a while, a buff guy in gym shorts and a tank top came up to me and asked, 'Hey, man, could you take some pictures of me with the skyline in the background?' He pointed at his expensive-looking reflex camera.

I answered, 'Sure.'

He instructed me what to do and jumped up on the low wall, with the city in the background. Without hesitation, he delighted his invisible audience with his shiniest smile and most impressive biceps pose. I felt a little awkward but followed through with the impromptu photoshoot. I tried to sound polite when I asked, 'What do you need so many pictures for?'

'For my business—I'm a fitness influencer.'

'A fitness influencer?'

'I'm on social media and post videos of my work-outs and give training and nutrition advice. And I also share some of my daily life with my followers. I'm on a business trip here in Prague . . . You know, what I love about being an influencer is the positive impact I can have on people's lives.'

Going to the gym seemed dull to me, and watching other people do it had to be the YouTube equivalent of Valium. Did this guy's followers benefit more from being tricked into buying the products he didn't disclose he was paid to merchandise, or from losing their time on the internet—scrolling through endless feeds of photoshopped, ever-happy, inspirational-quotes-flinging narcissists? But who was I to judge? Maybe this guy did motivate people to move their bodies and eat healthy. At least he wasn't a banker.

When I had taken enough pictures of him—in 20 different poses and from a dozen angles—he said, 'All right, thanks, man. I must get going; I need to get a good workout in. No pain, no gain! And add me on Instagram; my name is *Davemakesyoubuff*!'

Sure I would. As I watched him stride down the hill, his arms pushed outwards by invisible lats, I thought about the theory of bullshit jobs: As machines did more and more of our work, we had to create useless jobs that keep people busy and from starting a riot—corporate lawyers fighting other lawyers; managers managing lower managers; Instagram account managers faking a happy life on behalf of someone else; bureaucrats filling out enough forms to kill a rainforest; advertising directors, digital strategists, media planners, copywriters, designers, sales executives, and account executives creating nothing but the illusion of value; risk managers, financial analysts, portfolio managers, data scientists, investment bankers, traders, stockbrokers, and wealth managers only distributing income others had created. I didn't think the theory of bullshit jobs was quite true. I doubted somebody had devised a devious master plan to cripple mankind. Rather, we had ended up in what could be described as Marx's biggest nightmare: a world in which most value was created by capital, and traditional labour was all but obsolete. And since capital was only owned by a few, all the rest of us could do was help these capitalists multiply their wealth and hope for a cut. And, as it so happened, this occupation was bullshit.

My gaze wandered across the beauty of old Bohemia below. It was early afternoon, and the sun was burning down on us with all its might. It had already been an exceptionally warm and fair summer, and it promised to stay that way. I found a soft spot on the grass under a nearby tree and fell asleep in its shade.

I woke up soaked in sweat; the sun had wandered over. Dizzily, I walked down to the Vltava, across a road bridge, and back to my hostel, where I finished *The Call of the Wild* in its inner yard. After dinner, I went to Jazz Republic, a jazz club in a basement vault in the southeast of Old Town. I had a short chat with a peculiar French couple at my table; they were a smart, older woman and an insecure young man behaving like a boy envious of someone talking to his mother. Soon I immersed myself in the swinging improv spectacle on stage. When the band dismissed us back into the real world after three hours of steaming syncopation mayhem, I treated myself to one last Martini at the bar. I walked back 'home' through the deliriously warm August night. In back alleys, I met waiters inhaling their cigarettes—no one smoked faster than workers in the catering industry— and almost stumbled over a drunk girl taking a leak behind a refuse container. Back in my hostel room, I tried to pack my backpack in a silent fashion.

I slept for a couple of hours before leaving early for the airport, where I boarded my flight to Sofia.

Have patience with everything unresolved in
your heart and try to love the questions
themselves as if they were locked rooms or
books written in a very foreign language. Don't
search for the answers, which could not be
given to you now, because you would not be
able to live them. And the point is, to live
everything. Live the questions now.

Rainer Maria Rilke
Letters to a Young Poet

9

When I stepped outside of the airport in Sofia, I
walked into a wall of hot, dry air. My phone reported
a temperature of 37 degrees. On the metro to the city
centre, people sat in silent exhaustion, avoiding ex-
erting themselves in the midday heat trapped in the
train. The middle-aged man sitting opposite me was
breathing heavily. His half-bald head shone with
beads of sweat. His dirty grey shirt was soaked, and
he reeked of a kebab-heavy diet. The three-and-a-half
fingers left on his right hand were yellowed by
decades of cigarettes. When he looked at me and my
backpack, a fleeting smile illuminated the kind eyes in
his chubby face. The train had to stop at a station for
a couple of minutes. The lack of airflow through the
windows made it feel even hotter. After a few
moments of standstill, the man turned to me and said

in a thick accent and with a sad smile, 'How can it be that seconds pass so slowly, but years so fast?' Before I could think of a witty reply, he got up, walked out of the train, and disappeared into the life that had made his mutilated hands hard and his temper soft.

I got off at Serdika Station, surrounded by ancient ruins boiling in the sun between busy streets, and made my way to the hostel Makedonia. Hidden behind a narrow steel door, the hostel had its own inner yard, shielded from the traffic noise. I dropped off my backpack in my room and fell asleep on a deckchair outside, in the shade of the hostel's large wooden balcony.

In the afternoon, I tried to explore the city, but in the blazing heat didn't make it any further than a nearby pizza shop. Back at the hostel, two tall, brawny Austrians asked me to join their day-drinking efforts. Four bottles of beer and some vaguely coherent stories about make-your-own-coke workshops in Colombia and sketchy ice-climbing endeavours in British Columbia later, I was ready to join another pub crawl. The guide from our hostel, a short guy named Boris, led us to Crystal Garden, a small, busy park near the iconic St. Nevsky Cathedral. We bought drinks to go at a little glassy bar and sat on benches or lay on the grass. Several paths ran through Crystal Garden, and every corner was alive with people, making and listening to music, drinking, talking, and laughing. Sofia's parks—once the stage for the protests against the communist regime in the late '80s—became the cultural hubs and centres of its local nightlife during the hot and dry summers. I enjoyed sipping on my cold gin and tonic and talking to backpackers from all over the world coming through Bulgaria's capital on their trips around Europe. It was a beautiful night under green trees and golden stars. At last, the temperature became tolerable. But all pub crawls must end in a mainstream nightclub, and this one was no exception. After failing to drink myself into a dancing mood with more cheap gin and tonics at the bar, I went outside the steaming club for a smoke. There, I met Boris, the pub crawl guide. His eyes looked tired. I offered him a cigarette, which he gratefully accepted. I asked him, 'How often do you have to do this?'

'Usually, only twice a week. But two of my colleagues fell ill, so this is my third night in a row.'

'Congratulations,' I chuckled.

Boris exhaled a tired laugh. 'Thanks. In this weather, we should hang out in the park all night instead.'

'Wanna go? Drinks are on me.'

'I'd like to, but I have to stay a little longer and animate the guests to drink. By the way, do you want to get some shots at the bar?'

I laughed. 'Nice try. And I don't think they need any more incitement to get wasted.' Boris sighed. I added, 'All right, I'm going back to the park now. You're welcome to join me.'

'Ah, fuck it. But let's get Alberto to join us too. You have to meet this guy—total lunatic, but crazy smart.'

Boris flicked his cigarette to the floor and went back inside. He returned a minute later, followed by a short, sturdy guy in a yellow Hawaiian shirt with dark curls and a mighty black moustache. The stranger's dark eyes stared deeply into mine as he shook my hand and said, 'Montoya. Alberto Montoya.' He had a firm handshake, and his stern gaze radiated charisma.

We walked back to Crystal Garden. I bought us three whiskey and cokes, and we sat on a park bench next to the Stambolov monument. Alberto rolled and lit a cigarette, and I asked Boris what he was doing besides being an overworked drinking guide.

'I studied physics for a year. But it turned out I'm probably more interested in the topic from a philosophic point of view than from a "memorise hundreds of mathematical proofs for pointless exams to become a poor scientist or a rich but miserable insurance mathematician" perspective. But maybe that's just a nice way to put the fact I'm lazy.'

Alberto laughed a deep and hearty laugh that threatened to escalate into a coughing fit and said, 'I know what you mean!'

Boris replied, 'Well, at least you went through with it.' Boris looked over to me and said, 'Alberto is doing his PhD in astrophysics at UCLA.'

Alberto stroked his moustache and wriggled about on the bench. He was always in motion. He chuckled and said, 'Yeah, but I can hardly recommend it.'

I detected an American accent which I couldn't further place. I asked, 'Are you also into the philosophical aspect of physics?'

'Absolutely, you have to be.'

'What does your physical philosophy look like?'

Alberto fixed his dark, vibrant eyes on me and said, 'Well, for example, I believe the behaviour of all matter, anti-matter, dark energy, and whatever the hell else there might be, is determined by a consistent set of rules. And if one were to know the state of all this space stuff and all these cosmic rules, one could precisely predict the future. Of course, that means everything is predetermined, and there is no such thing as free will.'

Boris asked, 'But isn't there some weird randomness in quantum physics? Like, you know, the observer effect in this double-slit experiment?'

'Yeah, I think I've heard of that,' I said. 'What's it again?'

Alberto stroked his moustache and said, 'Well, the basic story is this: If you shoot an electron through a wall with two slits, it creates a wave pattern on a second wall behind it—the electron behaves like a wave. But, if you try to measure through which slit the electron passes, the fucker behaves like a particle and passes through only one slit at a time—the wave pattern disappears. And to this day, nobody knows why.' With a wide grin, Alberto raised his eyebrows and exclaimed, 'Quantum black magic!'

I took a sip from my drink and said, 'What the hell? That *is* weird!'

Alberto chuckled and said, 'Yeah. The same goes for quantum entanglement—you know, where two particles interact in a way that makes their properties somehow connected. But as long as we don't measure their properties, uncertainty prevails. Which means we can now take these two particles far away from each other. And when we measure and therefore determine the properties of one of these particles, the properties of the other particle are also determined, simultaneously. But *that* means information seems to travel faster than light—which should be impossible according to special relativity.'

Boris giggled and said, 'Damn, I feel like I've heard about this stuff before. But I kind of forgot everything from my studies already.'

Alberto said, 'Don't worry about it. All this spooky stuff does is keep you up at night. Don't google temporal nonlocality!' His dark eyes looked at us with a simmering curiosity as he continued, 'But back to Boris' point—I think all of these quantum events are simply phenomena we don't yet understand. That doesn't mean they're not guided by deterministic rules. And what should a probabilistic nature look like, anyway? Something must decide which state of the world materialises eventually, right? And what should this something be that's not guided by rules itself?'

'God?' I joked.

'If God existed, he wouldn't play dice,' Alberto said with a wink. 'And now you've arbitrarily introduced an additional entity to a complex system you don't understand in the first place.'

'Well, I guess that's the whole point of religion.'

'Exactly,' Alberto chuckled. 'But rather than God, I'd look to something like the Ghirardi-Rimini-Weber theory.'

'I have no idea what that means.'

'Don't worry about it. It's a wave-function collapse theory in quantum mechanics that challenges the orthodox Copenhagen interpretation—funky nerd shit.'

I chuckled and said, 'Okay, sure . . . Well, now that we've decided everything is predetermined—where did it start, and where will it end?'

'I like to think both time and space are circles; the end of the universe causes its beginning. And everything happens again, exactly like the last time and exactly like it will happen again, a trillion times later. And, yeah, if you fly through space long enough, you will end up back where you started.'

I felt a little dizzy. 'That's an interesting theory. But in the end, I think our monkey brains aren't made to understand issues such as time and space and cosmological causality.'

'You might be right about that—although some monkeys like Edward Witten might get close.'

I jumped up and said, 'Another existential question: do you guys want another drink?'

Boris looked at his phone and said, 'I don't know. I have to work tomorrow, and I wanted to visit some of my friends tonight as well . . . '

Alberto chuckled, glanced at his dark-grey, old-school Casio digital watch, and said, 'The night has just begun! You already know you'll have that drink, right? It's already happened infinite times before. It's predetermined—no reason for a guilty conscience.'

Boris shook his head. 'You're the devil. Two days ago, this maniac made me drink a litre of Jäger-meister with him!' He paused. 'Okay, one more.'

During another whiskey and coke, and already Alberto's fifth cigarette, Alberto told us a story about one of his recent adventures:

'So, when I was done with my six-month stay in Oxford, I visited this guy in Lyon, and we took his car to a hut high up in the Swiss Alps. The first night we got really hammered, and I decided to go on a night hike. After about 20 minutes, I came to this plot of land with a tall fence and a sign that read "Monastère Bouddhiste". And I'm like, "What the fuck is a Buddhist monastery doing in the middle of the Alps?" Curious, I climbed over the fence. I landed in this immaculate garden with a small pond, peculiar trees, and a massive belt-shaped sculpture, some sort of shrine—all illuminated by the full moon. And I walked further into the garden and found the sunroom door unlocked. Drunk as I am, I step into the house. And there is this long table with a white tablecloth, already laid for breakfast. I start switching cups and plates; for some reason, it's funny to me to think of these old monks coming down in the morning and wondering why all the dishes are all over the fucking place. And

149

just as I wanna leave, I'm scared to death by this bald guy in a long white nightgown standing in the door-frame to the kitchen and looking at me in silence. I freeze and look at him. My heart was fucking pound-ing, man! And then he says, in the calmest voice I'll ever hear, "*Tu devrais te reposer*," and disappears into the darkness of the house.'

'What does that mean?' Boris asked.

'"You should get some rest," I think.'

'And what happened next? Did that guy call the police?'

'No, I think he just went back to sleep. And so did I—after I found our hut again.'

Boris smiled at me in confusion, looked back at Alberto and asked, 'What's the point of this story?'

Alberto waved his hands and yelled, 'What do you mean, "What's the point?" There are Buddhist monas-teries in the fucking Swiss Alps with old dudes in them with more calmness than you or I could ever hope to attain. That's the fucking point!'

Boris giggled nervously and then finished his drink. After a long pause, he said, 'Hey, do you want to see something weird?'

Of course we did.

We walked for three blocks to a nearby flat in a quiet street. Three of Boris' friends had locked them-selves in there, and it had already been six days. They had shut off all clocks and digital devices and had meticulously sealed the windows from all light. They wanted to test their perception of time. Boris visited them at irregular intervals, sometimes supplying them with groceries. He wasn't allowed to tell them the time or the day. I asked Boris whether our smell of alcohol would not give away the fact it was night-time. He said his friends might think that was a trick to throw them off. He had a key to the flat, and before we entered, Boris knocked on the door to make them close their eyes. Alberto hid his watch in his pocket. Inside, there were two guys and one girl. They were in the kitchen cooking pasta. They were naked, an additional twist to their experiment they had introduced 'three meals ago'. The girl shook my hand and said, 'Hi, I'm Tatiana. I like how I can see your chest muscles through your shirt.'

Confused, I looked at the two guys sitting at the table. One of them said, 'She has decided to sincerely tell all her thoughts.'

'Yeah, she's reading too much Kerouac,' the other chimed in.

I looked back at Tatiana, smiled, and said hesitantly, 'Cool. Thanks.'

She pierced me with her green eyes and asked, 'Do you find me attractive?'

I looked down at her pale, scrawny, shaved body and into her freckled, narrow face. 'Sure, why not.'

She smiled and said, 'You're good at hiding your insecurity, stranger.'

I had to laugh and asked the two guys at the table, 'How long has she been doing this?'

'A day or two, I guess.'

I exhaled audibly and chuckled. I sat down at the table. Boris and Tatiana served all of us pasta. Alberto got naked as well, to 'not be rude and blend in'. During the meal, Valko, the initiator of the experiment, told us of a French guy called Michel Siffre. He was a geologist who had lived in perfect isolation in underground caves in France and Texas for months and had, in passing, invented the field of chronobiology in the '60s and '70s. Tatiana said she had a paralysing fear of lethal intestinal diseases. She also told Boris she still thought about the time they had had sex on her mother's bed, which made him blush. Spas, the third amateur chronobiologist, said nothing and smoked a big joint as soon as he had finished eating. After we had shared another joint, of which Alberto smoked the lion's share, Boris, Alberto, and I got up to leave. Tatiana looked at me and said, 'I don't want you to go. You like to stay and cuddle? And I mean just cuddle. I need closeness.'

I tried to focus on her face instead of her pointed nipples and said, 'Tatiana, you're a nice girl, but—'

'I understand. I'm sad I'm never going to see you again. But anyway, both of us won't remember each other within a month . . . You look tired. I hope you can get some rest.'

I grinned in confusion and said, 'Uhm, yeah, okay.'

We said goodbye to Tatiana, Valko, and Spas and left. Alberto was so stoned that he almost forgot to put his clothes back on before going out the door. As we stepped onto the street, Boris said, 'I hope that wasn't too weird for you.'

'No, no. Your friends are nice people.'

'Yeah, they are. Goodnight.'

'Goodnight.'

Alberto and I started on our way back to the hostel. Boris walked in the other direction. In the dimly lit streets, we passed two packs of stray dogs scavenging rubbish bags in dark back alleys. The charm of Eastern Europe wasn't only the fact that it was cheap. It was also still a little rough around the edges. There were still undiscovered spots and mysterious secrets behind opaque windows and stony faces. Alberto walked with glazed-eyed tunnel vision. He didn't say a single word the whole way. The only thing he managed to do besides walk was mechanically produce a pouch of tobacco, roll another cigarette, and smoke it. He was staying in a house belonging to our hostel on the other side of Makedonia Square. He said good-night with a confused hand wave as he went inside. Back at the hostel, I shared a cigarette with a peculiar middle-aged black man, who introduced himself in a deep voice as 'Zion from San Francisco, California'. He had been staying in Sofia for two weeks already, watching black-and-white films until early in the morning on the computer in the common room.

In my dream, I had a boxing match with my dad. For countless rounds, he beat me up with lightning-quick jabs and irresistible right hooks that ruptured gaping cuts around my left eye. There wasn't a single drop of sweat on his broad, grey-haired chest. I was panting. Between rounds, I sat in my corner, with no one there to give me water, care for my wounds, or offer me advice. My dad beat me up mercilessly and gazed at me in grave disappointment. How could I ever satisfy him? I dragged my body around the ring, punches raining down on my head like hail. My dad's defence was insurmountable. He saw every combination coming and punished me with light-footed, heavy-hitting crosses. How could I beat him? My time was running out. Finally, in the last round, in the motion of a right cross, I suddenly closed in, switched to a southpaw stance, and caught my dad off guard—his chin was wide open between his gloves. I struck him with a left uppercut that contained all my anger and pain. In slow motion, my dad's jaw dislocated, his eyes rolled inside his skull, and his heavy body fell to the floor. The crowd cheered. I cried. He was dead.

I woke up soaked in sweat. It was so hot in my room I could barely breathe. I felt as though I had just been dealt a real, powerful liver punch—a mean blow that made your blood vessels widen while your heart rate slowed down, causing a dramatic drop in blood pressure. My stomach cramped. I felt dizzy. My dad had motivated me as a kid to start boxing at his old club. When I had fought as a teenager—at the end, as a light heavyweight—he had come to every fight he could. I missed him. When he was my age, he had been working like a dog as a truck driver for a local automotive supplier for almost a decade and had already started building a house for his family. I was a washed-up ex-banker getting high with strangers. I wanted to hurt somebody, first and foremost myself, but felt too dizzy to get up. The alcohol and THC in my blood soon made me go back to sleep.

The next day, Alberto and I joined a free walking tour around Sofia in the early afternoon. The ancient city, lying below the northern foot of the Vitosha mountain, had a rich and chequered history. When it had been called Serdica, it had been one of the political centres of the Roman Empire and home to some of its emperors. Its mixture of churches, mosques, and synagogues was reminiscent of its position on age-old fault lines between world religions and cultures. The city centre was still shaped by Socialist Classicism edifices, ostentatious, martial monuments, and bru-talist concrete giants. Vandalised orange phone boxes were scattered in the streets. Many street junctions were still overlooked by retired traffic booths. The tour ended in front of the National Theatre. I sat on the grass with Alberto, the two Austrians I had met the day before, Daniel and Dominik, and a girl from Swindon, Valerie. In the shade of some chestnut trees near a water fountain, we watched a traditional dance on the theatre square. We drank beer from the big plastic bottles all the little shops around Sofia sold. It was too hot to move. We were all exhausted from the modest walking in the afternoon heat. The taller one of the two tall Austrians, Daniel, told us the story of a visit to a swingers' club he had stumbled upon with a friend on the way back to his hostel on Tenerife.

Later, we had dinner at a cheap pizza restaurant and walked southeast to a former speakeasy. In a backyard, at the end of a short tunnel, we had to knock on a heavy old wooden door. After a while, a grumpy young woman let us into a murky barn lit only by candlelight. There was an old piano, a bar covered in wax, and rugged old wooden furniture. No music was playing. We ordered a couple of drinks from another, even grumpier young woman behind the rustic bar and sat down at a table on the gallery. As the Austrians planned their trip further eastwards, Alberto and I talked to Valerie. She told us she wanted to study thanatology and become a restorative artist, preparing the deceased to give their bereaved a last chance to say goodbye. Valerie thought it was peculiar how we often tried to hide our dead in the West, as if ignoring death could make it go away. After she told us of her abusive father and bad boyfriend choices, Alberto said, 'You know, the two are probably connected. I mean, for many of us, love is the feeling our parents have given us when they're still the undisputed centres of our little worlds. I guess that's why we often end up with a partner who resembles one of our parents.'

Valerie stared at him with wide eyes and said, 'That actually makes sense . . . Oh my god, you're right; I've been dating my dad! Ugh, that's so messed up!' She took a big gulp of her gin and tonic. Looking at

Alberto, she asked, 'What about you? Do you have the same problem with girls?'

He answered, 'My parents died when I was still a kid. But I remember them as incredibly strong and honest. That's what I now value most in other people—honesty.'

'May I ask what happened to your parents?'

'Yeah. My parents are from Panama. They were in the opposition fighting against Noriega, and my father helped US forces during their invasion in 1989. I think he also worked as an informant on the drug trade for the fucking DEA. As a rare reward, we were granted US citizenship; we would not have been safe in Panama after the war. But my father never recovered from the wounds he had incurred during house-to-house fighting in Panama City. My uncle told me my mum died from homesickness.'

'I'm sorry,' Valerie said.

After a moment of silence, Alberto nudged me and said, 'Let's get another round.'

When we returned, Valerie was already flirting with the brawnier one of the two brawny Austrians, Dominik. He wasn't particularly funny, smart, or good-looking, but had a natural calm and radiated a confident presence. After five minutes, Valerie was sitting on Dominik's lap. He gave her a neck massage. Sexual hunger exuded from his smiling eyes. Alberto and I decided to leave. Daniel stuck around, chatting up young Australian girls at the bar in his thick Austrian accent.

On our way to the hostel, we saw a small group of teenage boys harassing an old homeless man sitting on cardboard in front of a sordid old house on the other side of the street. The words they spat at him sounded vile. When they started kicking the old man,

I shouted, 'Ey!' and raced across the street. The boys laughed and ran away and vanished around a corner. The old man nodded at us and said, 'Thank you!'

I was surprised to hear him speak English and asked, 'Are you okay?'

'Yes, thank you.'

'Where are you from? From Bulgaria?'

'No, Syria.'

I produced my wallet and gave him 20 Bulgarian leva. Alberto asked, 'Is there anything else we can do for you?'

The old man looked at us with bleary eyes and said, 'No, thank you. Go home! Go home! Thank you!'

Not without hesitation, we started walking silently to our hostel. When we had to separate on Makedonia Square, Alberto lit another cigarette. He said, 'You know, that old man reminded me of a joke: A capitalist, a worker, and an immigrant stand around a table with a huge pie. The capitalist takes all but one tiny slice of the pie, looks at the worker, and says, "Watch out, the immigrant is trying to steal your piece of pie!"'

I breathed out with a tired chuckle and said, 'I'm not sure that's a joke.'

'Well, only if you're the capitalist. Goodnight.'

'Goodnight.'

Back in the inner yard of the hostel, Zion, the Californian, was sitting on a bench. Beads of sweat glinted on his forehead. Between black-and-white films, he had rolled himself a joint. He invited me to join him. As he lit the spliff, he said, 'You know, man, I hope before I die, it will be possible to upload my consciousness into the cloud and live there forever.' He exhaled billows of smoke into the balmy night. 'Imagine, man! An artificial afterlife, beyond the boundaries of biology! Merging into Übermenschen with other simulated consciousnesses. Becoming, like, digital vessels of wisdom and multidimensional perception!'

As he handed me the joint, I said, 'I guess uploading your consciousness would be just like beaming—killing you and creating nothing but a perfect copy, distinct from your experience of being.'

'How is going to sleep at night and waking up in the morning any different, man?'

I was too tired to argue with him. He went on to tell me the theory that if it was possible to simulate existence in a computer at one point in time, it was highly likely that, right now, we were only simulated minds in an ancestor simulation as well. I thought of the double-slit experiment and electrons only deciding to behave like matter when somebody bothered looking. Maybe that's for performance reasons; why waste processing power rendering particle behaviour when there is no observer to output to? Perhaps we do live in a simulation, after all. The thing is, it makes no difference whatsoever.

I was whacked and went to bed with heavy eyelids. After five minutes, I was soaked in sweat and sticking to the bed linen. I carried my mattress outside and lay down in a quiet corner of the inner yard. Was Alice looking at the same stars at this moment, dancing around a bonfire in the Swedish countryside?

The light of the summer morning woke me up early. I put my mattress back onto my bed and had breakfast in the common room. Afterwards, I took an old tram and a rattling bus to the southwest of Sofia.

I marvelled at the ancient frescos inside Boyana Church—of Saint Nicholas, Jesus, and some other Bible characters an agnostic like me wouldn't know. I started hiking up towards the Boyana Waterfall. It was already hot, but the trees provided some welcome shadow. After about 15 minutes of hiking, I got bored and started running up the mountain. Soon, I was breathing heavily and dripping sweat. I liked feeling the exertion in my body and accelerated. I ran past other hikers and jumped over roots and rocks. My blood was boiling, my lungs hurt, and I felt stitches on my right side. I kept on running. The path got rockier. I slipped on a dead tree root, banging my left knee against a rock and scratching my forearm on a tree trunk. I got up and ran up the steep track. On my shin, blood mixed with sweat. I panted in pain and ran on. Soon, I would pass out. My 16-year-old self would've zipped ahead of me, running backwards and laughing. I clenched my teeth. One foot after the other. The heat became almost unbearable. My shirt was soaked, and I swam in my shoes. Keep on running, you pathetic joke of a boxer. The trees around me morphed into green mucus floating in the sky. The rocks beneath my feet tumbled. My temples squeezed my brain between them. The humid air in my hurting lungs thinned. My body kept on running. Just as my mind was about to leave my head through the back of my skull, I ran over a small ridge and saw the waterfall, splashing down from a cliff 20 metres high. Step by tired step, I ran towards it. I fell on my knees into the tiny lake below and gasped. Sweet, ice-cold liquid from heaven. White stars danced in the darkness of my closed eyes. I drank with my hands and started to cough as my breathing settled. I washed my dirty wounds and my soaked shirt in the water. I didn't take any notice of the other people around me. I sat down on a rock with my feet in the icy water. The pain in my lungs and side retreated. My dizziness faded. I smiled like the fool I was. It was good to feel my body. The dabbling sound of the waterfall filled the air, which was cool and damp.

After some time, I hiked back down. From a vantage point up on a rock, I had a splendid view over the tree-covered slopes of Vitosha and the glistening city below. Back in the outskirts of the city, I hopped on a bus to the centre. At the hostel, I got a bandage for my knee and took a long nap.

After dinner, I met Boris, who was working the evening shift on reception. He told me that many Sofians left the city for their holidays at the beach during the hot summers, which was why the nightlife was much better in winter. I skipped the pub crawl and stayed at the hostel. I talked with Boris about the history of Bulgaria, which had gone from one of the Soviet Empire's economic powerhouses to one of the poorest countries of the European Union.

After Boris' shift, we said goodbye to Zion, who was watching *The Third Man* on the computer. We went to a small house party in the northwest of Sofia, where we met up with Alberto. We drank a lot of absinth, which made us go a little crazy. We all stripped down to our underwear and had a big pillow fight involving ice cubes being thrown across the living room and shoved into people's underwear. Later, Alberto used matches and a glass to create gleaming plasma balls in the microwave. As I stood next to him, a blonde girl in red-dotted knickers approached him and asked in a heavy accent, 'Hey, you're the physicist, right?'

Alberto shook her hand and said harshly, 'I'm Alberto Montoya. Sometimes I do physics, yes.'

'Okay . . . sorry?' The girl bit the nail of her index finger.

'No, don't worry about it. It's just that I avoid

defining myself as a member of a group. I don't wanna fool myself with the collective thinking that is essential to all groups. It shrouds the essential absurdity we live in.'

An embarrassed smile revealed a gap in her teeth. The girl slowly turned away and walked out of the kitchen.

I laughed, patted Alberto's shoulder, and said, 'I see you're great with the ladies.'

Alberto shook his head. 'If you only knew the half of it, man.'

With the ever-present roll-up cigarette in the corner of his mouth, he went on to cook some milk, chocolate bars, and whisky into a potent brew which put the boot into most of us. In the end, I slept with a naked girl in a tiny bed. It was too hot, and we were too tired for more than a little kissing and cuddling. In a groggy half-sleep, I thought her breasts were Alice's—firm and warm and soft.

The next day, I left the flat early and returned to the hostel in the pleasant summer morning. Alberto was still asleep on the sofa in the kitchen, the blonde girl in red-dotted knickers in one hand and a blue bicycle pump in the other. I was hungover, and my knee was sore and a little stiff.

I spent the day on a deckchair in the shade, re-watching the tough win of the roaring newcomer Anthony Joshua over the relentless robot Wladimir Klitschko from April—the best heavyweight fight in decades—and the films *Rocky* and *Creed*. I couldn't reach Alberto—out of principle, he didn't own a smartphone and only checked his old Nokia flip phone sporadically.

That night, it was too hot to sleep.

On Thursday, I exchanged social media accounts with Boris and said goodbye. The two tall, brawny Austrians had just rented a car and were about to start driving to the southeast of Bulgaria, where Boris had told them to find beautiful beaches far away from the binge-drinking tourist madness of Golden Sands. Valerie had decided to join them. We shook hands and exchanged hugs, and I walked to Serdika station. On my way, I ran into Alberto, who was cycling by on a rented bike. I stopped him and asked, 'You have my number, right?'

'Yeah.'

'I'm going to Hungary next and then to Vienna and Munich. What are your plans?'

'I'm leaving for Greece in two days, I'm going to Sicily afterwards, and I'll be in Spain before I return to California.'

'Maybe we can meet in Spain. Give me a call.'

'I'll give you my email address; my phone isn't working so well in Europe.'

I chuckled and asked, 'Don't you have Facebook?'

'Fuck no! Social media is poison.'

'Well, it also has its upsides.'

'Sure. But what do you think it will do to our minds to be connected to the ether of pure, unfiltered information constantly? To have an endless stream of news and fake news at our fingertips? Of viral trends and demystified stars, rising and crashing ever faster, unrealistic body images, instant gratification and frustration, only likes apart? Videos of war atrocities and terror, and every imaginable form of porn? I mean, just a fucking click away, kids these days can find videos of men dying in panic after having half their brains blown out, and girls who could still be in school eating their faeces. I guess the world has always been rotten, but now the winds of digitalisation blow the smell of decay into your face all fucking day long. Before the internet, no one was any wiser than now. But at least the crazy people were isolated in their villages. Now that we all see how batshit crazy everyone else is, we give up the old charade and aspire to maximum collective batshittery. And along the fucking way, our every move is monitored and translated into data to feed the global commercial empires. No wonder people are trying to flee into the unmeasured. You don't have to go full Ted Kaczynski, but a little caution might not be misplaced.'

Alberto's little rant had made a vein on his temple pulsate. I chuckled and nodded. Alberto gave me his business card and a goodbye hug, and I took the metro back to the airport.

As I dropped off my backpack, I cursed myself for suspecting the bearded, dark-skinned guy in front of me of being a terrorist. The plane to Budapest boarded on time.

You are the all-singing, all-dancing crap of the world.

> Chuck Palahniuk
> *Fight Club*

10

The weather in Budapest was serene, and the heat not quite as pressing as in Bulgaria. The Danube gave the air some freshness. From my hostel in an alley in District VII, I walked past the nearby Dohány Street Synagogue and the St. Stephen's Basilica, crossed Liberty Square, and got in line to enter the Hungarian Parliament Building. The Parliament was a grandiose building, dominating the waterfront skyline of Pest. The inside was crammed with red carpets, sculptures, frescos, and gold. The motionless soldiers guarding the crown jewels inside the central dome impressed me with their patience. I left the Parliament and strolled down the Danube, with the busy street to my left. The lowering sun gave the river a mystical sparkle. Bustling crowds of tourists boarded river cruise ships. Everyone was basking in the sun. After about half an hour, I reached a small park, from where I watched the ships go by. My thoughts followed them down the river—one by one—and soon, my head was void of all the noise. Absent-minded, I sat on a turquoise stone bench until a hungry stomach roused me again.

I had dinner in a nearby cosy trattoria and walked back to my hostel through the Palace District's narrow streets, marvelling at impossible-to-decrypt Hungarian signs. While most of the other guests had drinks in the kitchen area and went out partying in nearby ruin bars, I enjoyed a quiet evening.

I lay in my hostel bed. The morning sun was shining through the window. I finally answered the message Emma had sent me when I was in Prague. I asked her whether she wanted to meet in Munich next weekend—what a bad idea.

After breakfast in a nearby café, I went to the Széchenyi Thermal Bath. I enjoyed being in the water with the sun burning down. At noon, I headed up to Castle Hill and strolled along the clean cobblestone roads between its restored Baroque buildings.

At the cream-coloured German embassy, I picked up Felix. He had been in the same Swedish scholarship programme that had partly financed my stay in Stockholm. We had stayed in loose touch ever since. Chris and I had sometimes kidnapped him out of his dorm room and taken him to house parties with us. We had tried to help him overcome his blushing nervousness and hook him up with crazy Spanish girls. He had soon made a name for himself as the best beer-pong player in Stockholm. Felix had been working as a cultural advisor at the German embassy for a couple of months. He asked me to lunch in a Hungarian restaurant nearby. Over braised venison and regional red wine, I told him a small-talk version of my recent endeavours. I asked him, 'Do you enjoy working at the embassy?'

'Yes, I do. It's interesting to be here and see the dictatorship-on-the-rise narrative from a Hungarian point of view, you know?'

'You see it differently?'

'Well, there was a tilt towards nationalism, sure, but how the Fidesz government is portrayed as a total-itarian regime in most of the liberal media is simply unfair.'

'So, that's fake news?'

'I hate the term "fake news". Also, "populism". They're used to dismiss any opinion too far from the mainstream. You know, in Hungary, we have ob-served free demonstrations and elections. And a majority of the voters supports the way the govern-ment deals with refugees.'

'And what about the defamation of the opposition as foreign enemies? You don't think the EU should put pressure on Orbán about it? I mean, you live here, and I don't, but it seems to me you're taking the erosion of democracy a bit lightly.'

Felix nodded his head. He was wearing a cheap suit and an ugly yellow tie. He had a flat face, big, alert eyes, and a high forehead. He blinked a little too often. 'Don't get me wrong, many things are going in the wrong direction here. But I don't see how paternalistic treatment from the EU will tame anti-EU resentment or make Hungarians more welcoming toward refu-gees—or how liberal media alarmism might help the situation.'

'Hmm . . . Do you feel that anti-EU resentment as a German here?'

'No, not really. Well . . . yesterday—and this stays between us, of course—our IT system at the embassy got hacked. But with these cyberattacks, it's hard to tell who's behind them.'

'Yeah, I remember when the firm I was with got hacked and lost 20 million pounds overnight. They never found out who did it.'

'Shit. Did they get the money back at least?'

'No. It was covered up. The loss of trust associated with admitting you got hacked isn't worth it. Big companies get hacked all the time, but they keep their mouths shut.'

'Yeah, that makes sense, I guess . . . By the way, where are you going next on your journey?'

'To Vienna. I'm meeting Lena there on Monday—remember her from Stockholm?'

'Yeah, she was your roommate, wasn't she?' His hands fidgeted as they did when he talked to girls at parties.

'Yeah, the blonde girl from the States.'

'Oh yeah. I had a huge crush on her.' He giggled nervously.

I chuckled, 'Everyone always has.'

Felix had to get back to work. We said goodbye, and I headed towards Matthias Church at Trinity Square. I walked past the Holy Trinity Column and the bronze statue of Stephen of Hungary, then looked through the arcade of Fisherman's Bastion, over the Danube and the rooftops of Pest. I let the movement of the crowds of tourists carry me to the left and down the stairs.

I stood downstairs, on the platform between the steps that led down the white Bastion on both sides. I looked up at the balcony above and again over to the other side of the water. The Hungarian Parliament Building glowed in the summer sun with the rest of the city. Somehow, I knew this view. Had I been here before? Slowly, the revelation crept up on me: this was the background in the only picture I had kept of my cursed original family. My biological parents had taken me to Budapest not long after the border had been opened. I had been a baby back then. In the picture, we all smiled at the camera, my biological mother in a beautiful light blue summer dress, my biological father in washed-out jeans and a sailor shirt that revealed his tattooed forearms, I in white rompers. We made the impression of a handsome, happy young family. Someone must have taken the picture on the balcony upstairs. Now, it was in a box in my colleague's London flat. My stomach knotted. I had the bitter taste of revulsion in my mouth. I didn't want to think of those doomed, rotten addicts. They got what they deserved. May they rest in peace and never bother me again. How often had I wished that? I snuffled and swallowed a salty tear. I turned around and ran up the stairs.

I looked up the Holy Trinity Column again, at the golden holy son holding his golden cross. My ticket to a higher ground had been voided. I remained in the gutter of my hereditary wicked mind. Before the sun could melt my brain any further, I made my way back down to the river, across the old suspension bridge, and back into District VII. At the first ruin pub I could find, I gulped two Americanos. They had gone too heavy on the vermouth. I couldn't be bothered to tell them.

Back at my hostel, I found a group of American frat boys to drink beers with. In their short shorts and pastel-coloured tank tops, they talked about doing shots and 'slaying chicks' in Prague—they were a bad cliché. We had burgers and beers in the hostel's adjacent restaurant and went a couple of metres down the narrow road into a huge, contorted ruin bar. Graffiti covered its unplastered walls. Neon signs pointed to numerous small shops. The glass-roofed, multi-storey courtyard hosted a wide array of palm trees and was illuminated by colourful chains of light. The place was bustling with party nomads, and broken English filled the sweet air. While the loud, hairy, tall leader of the frat boys got us a round of beers, I ordered a mint shisha at a small shop near the entrance. The Australian shopgirl was high beyond all repair. Her red, watery eyes stared right through me and into blissful nothingness. Slowly, she prepared my shisha and accepted whatever money I gave her. I had to think of the old Soviet saying Boris had told me in the hostel in Sofia: 'So long as the bosses pretend to pay us, we will pretend to work.' I went upstairs, where the frat boys had annexed a group of sofas. We drank beers and shots over a game of Kings and had one shisha after another. They told me I had to visit for one of their 'sick' parties at the University of Texas at Austin. Sure I would. I was drunk. When the chubby frat boy sitting next to me on the sofa peed himself, and the rest of the group answered with undisgusted laughter, I downed my beer and got up.

I wandered through the maze of small bars and food shops and found myself on a quiet balcony. I smoked a cigarette and tried to focus on the blurry contours of a nearby building. The image of the building tumbled as though I was watching an old film tape, slowed down to the point at which you could observe the single frames moving down the projector. When I finished the cigarette, the balcony door behind me was locked. I knocked on one of the small square windows of the wooden door. Nobody answered. For about five minutes, I knocked on the door at irregular intervals—nothing. I got impatient and smashed the small window next to the door handle with my right elbow. I slipped my hand through the hole and opened the door from the inside.

When I stepped back inside, a girl came up to me and asked in disbelief, 'Did you smash the window?'

Sure, now somebody had heard me. I said, 'Yeah, sorry. I was locked outside on the balcony.'

'You can't smash the window!'

'Well, technically—'

'You'll have to pay!'

'I don't know who locked me out . . . How do you want to deal with this?'

'I don't know, but you have to pay for the window! You shouldn't be back here! Let me get my colleague. You wait here!'

The girl walked around the corner. I turned the other way, found a stairwell leading downstairs, and walked out of the bar onto the street. I walked for about a minute and turned around two corners. Music was coming out of an open doorway. I stopped. The ground was moving, and my eyes couldn't focus. I walked inside and found myself in an inner yard with a bar, garden chairs and tables roofed by green trees, and a fireplace surrounded by a group of people sitting on a couple of benches. I got a whiskey and coke at the bar. The barman eyed me suspiciously. I sat down on one of the benches next to the fire. It smelled of beer, grilled steaks, and roasted marshmallows. I started talking to the Spaniards who were keeping the fire going. When I finished my drink, one of the Spaniards offered me his big plastic bottle of Cuba Libre. Blackout.

I woke up alone in a bottom bunk bed in an unfamiliar room. Someone was snoring. It was already light outside. I was glad I was alone in the bed. My head hurt, and I was very thirsty. I found my clothes at the end of the bed, got dressed, and walked out of the room. I found a bathroom and drank water from the tap. I went downstairs and through the inner yard with the fireplace and the bar I vaguely remembered from the night before. Two girls with wet, dark hair sat at one of the tables drinking coffee and looked at me as though they knew me. I nodded sheepishly and stepped onto the street. I heard laughter behind me. I pulled out my phone and searched for my hostel; it was only a block away. The streets had been cleaned and were wet. The water radiated a coolness into the hot morning. Soon, I saw the red sign with white letters spelling out 'Avalon'—my hostel. I ate scrambled eggs with bacon and bread at the restaurant and found a sofa in the common room to cuddle up on and watch TV. I watched a weather anchor explaining the heat wave that had rolled over South-ern and Western Europe in a deep, soothing voice. I dozed off after watching a few guests leave the hostel for the Sziget Festival on the Island of Old Buda.

In the afternoon, I joined a trip to Aero Park in the southeast of Budapest. I was too tired, hungover, and depressed to enjoy its vast collection of planes. After the bus trip back to District VII, which I spent highly concentrated on not vomiting all over my seatmate and me, I went to the big ruin bar. A few confused conversations later, I found someone I could reimburse for the broken window. I even had to show it to the guy. The window was a lot bigger than it had been in my memory. Some shards were still scattered over the floor. I paid 15,000 forint—about 50 pounds—which struck me as a bargain. To my disappointment, my bad conscience wasn't remedied afterwards. Back at the hostel, some girls from Mexico talked me into going to another ruin bar. Tonight, the wine didn't work. I walked back and went to bed early.

Lying in bed, I felt miserable. My head still hurt, and I was dizzy. After more than a decade full of drunken weekends and, too often, weekdays, I couldn't shake it off as easily as I had used to.

The next day, after breakfast, I took my laptop to a small café that opened up to a narrow, quiet street and a little shaded park and read the news—something about the latest cryptocurrency craze and a long article with the promising headline: 'Hacked, knife-wielding sex robots could be a very real possibility'. Later, I had *lángos* with mushrooms for lunch in a nearby street food market in a cosy backyard. I grabbed a coffee in a small café that also sold books and picked up a copy of Joseph Heller's *Catch-22*. I spent the rest of the day on a jetty by the lake in the City Park, reading Heller's brilliant account of the absurdity of war. As the sun set over the trees across the lake, I saw Alice standing on the jetty that stretched all the way back to Sweden, her white summer dress glowing in the orange light. She whispered to me in her mellow voice, 'Midsummer nights last forever.' I wished they did. I could almost feel the touch of her hand on my face. I wanted to talk to her badly. Like every other day since I had left Stockholm, I wanted to call her. I wouldn't call her and invite her to join me in Italy before I arrived in Vienna, though. I didn't want to appear too needy.

I spent my evening in a bar near St. Stephen's Basilica and had a couple of cocktails. The place had red walls, small black tiles framed the bar, and smooth jazz music swirled through the air. The drinks were good.

Later, in my hostel bed, I dreamt up a story about how I saved my post-apocalyptic island community from a barbaric invasion and enjoyed hard-earned peace with Alice on the beach. She was wearing her light-blue underwear and gave me a massage by a bonfire under some palm trees. Calmly, she lectured me on how to deal with the other people in our island community. We had sex on the beach and let the rhythmic sound of the waves lull us to sleep. I lay awake in my bed, clenching my teeth and squinting my eyes.

I went on a boat trip up and down the Danube the next morning. Some early acoustic guitar music from the Sziget Festival was hovering over the river from the Island of Old Buda. When I walked back to my hostel, I was soaked in sweat. The air flickered above the hot asphalt. I spurned the offer of some Englishmen to join them in the great English tradition of getting royally drunk at a curry restaurant, packed my backpack, and checked out. At the bus station next to People's Park, I got on the coach to Vienna in the early afternoon.

I sat in the last row of seats with four tired-looking, unshaven men. I had noticed their nervousness when the bus driver asked to see their passports. The driver had laughed and said, 'Don't worry, we don't care, only the police cares. Welcome to Europe.'

As we turned onto the motorway, I asked them where they were from. The one who looked the oldest—maybe 35—answered, after a short hesitation, 'Afghanistan.'

I didn't know how to frame the question I wanted to ask, so I went straight ahead: 'Are you refugees?'

'Yes. We're on our way to France. To Paris.'

He introduced himself as Salar and told me they had come through Turkey, Greece, the Balkans, and now Hungary. I had thought that route had been closed a while ago. I was even more surprised when

Salar told me he had already been in Europe twice before, one time in Berlin and one time in Rome. Once, he had been deported, and once, he had gone back to Afghanistan voluntarily to say goodbye to his dying father. His family was still back in the Nangarhar province, east of Kabul. The region had recently made headlines when the US had dropped the 'mother of all bombs' there to kill dozens of militants. He told me the temperature was above 40 degrees there now, so he felt at home in this European heatwave. His English was sparse but effective. I asked him what his plans were for Paris.

'Find work—I have friends there,' he told me with sad eyes and a smile.

We all tiredly looked out of the window for the rest of the journey. When the coach turned into the bus station in Vienna, I said goodbye to Salar and his companions and jumped onto solid Austrian soil. I looked around—drifters everywhere.

I have learned that if you must leave a place
that you have lived in and loved and where all
your yesteryears are buried deep, leave it any
way except a slow way, leave it the fastest way
you can. Never turn back and never believe
that an hour you remember is a better hour
because it is dead. Passed years seem safe
ones, vanquished ones, while the future lives in
a cloud, formidable from a distance.

Beryl Markham
West with the Night

11

When Lena saw me standing next to the coach, she
dashed through the crowd, jumped at me, and gave
me a vigorous hug. She led me to her grandma's old
Opel Astra with long strides, and I threw my backpack
into the boot. We started driving to her grandparents'
summer house in the northwest of Vienna. The car
smelled of old perfume and black plastic and dusty
seat pads in the sun. Lena made fun of my new-grown
beard.

I had met Lena during grammar school, but she
had moved to the desert of New Mexico with her parents at the age of 12. We had come to really know each
other only a couple of years later, when we started
chatting on the then-popular instant messenger ICQ.
We had spent whole New Mexican afternoons and

European nights discussing the adventures of puberty. She had later visited our hometown again, before she moved on her own to Los Angeles and San Francisco. In between, she had lived with me in Stockholm for half a year while she did an internship at a tech start-up.

I laughed as she cursed at a truck in front of us that dared not to adapt to her pace of life. Lena had a pointed nose and kind green eyes. She still wore her straight blonde hair long.

After half an hour, we arrived at the summer house. It stood in a big, sloped garden and had a small base, three storeys, white walls, and a red tile roof. The first floor led to a spacious wooden terrace with a barbecue. Beyond the garden lay a large forest. Lena's grandfather had built the house himself in the early '60s. I put my backpack away in the bedroom under the roof and sat on a bench on the terrace, which was shaded by a large pine tree. Lena brought a fresh lemon cake from the kitchen on the ground floor. She asked, in her energetic voice, 'Do you remember how I used to bake for you all the time in Stockholm?'

'Yeah, your cakes saved me during many hangovers.'

'You and Chris used to drink all the time.'

'There might have been a party or two.'

'You two were insane together! Remember when I picked you up from the police in the morning after you two broke into that construction site together and were too drunk for the policemen to let you go home? And I had to work that day!'

I chuckled, 'Yeah, sorry about that . . . So, why exactly are you back in Europe?'

'I've got a new job as a digital transformation consultant here in Vienna. It's nice to see my granny from time to time, too. Finally, someone is here for her; she's having trouble with her back lately. She's such a sweetie, you know? She knows the names of all the flowers that bloom in spring and bakes her own bread on Saturdays . . . But you probably mean, why did I leave San Francisco?'

I smiled and nodded.

'Travis broke up with me, and the company I was with went bankrupt, and I simply felt stuck, you know? I needed a change of scenery.'

'I see. Do you like Vienna?'

'Oh, it's beautiful here!' She took a long, deep breath. Birds were singing in a nearby tree. Somewhere in the distance, someone was mowing their lawn.

I took a deep breath of the conifer air, too. I smiled and said, 'Yes. It is.'

After a moment, Lena looked at me and asked, 'And why are *you* here?'

I told her the story of my journey—of Alice, bad decisions, and disorientation. Without a word, she got up from her garden chair and gave me a long and heartfelt hug. It felt good. I went into the kitchen and made us Mojitos that we drank in the shade of the terrace.

In the evening, we grilled pork steaks, mushrooms, and courgettes, and drank some fine Rioja her mum had sent from Spain. When the sun set, Lena lit some candles. We talked about the summer nights we had spent drinking red wine on top of Hammarbybacken, looking over the lights of Stockholm in the eternal twilight of the Swedish summer. When I was about to open another bottle of wine, Lena eyed me in dismay and asked, 'Is this already the third bottle?'

'Yeah. Should I leave it closed? I could get a cheap

bottle from the kitchen or make another Mojito instead.'

'It's not that. You can open it. I'm just shocked you've had a Mojito and almost two bottles of wine and don't even slur.'

'Well, we drank them together.'

'I had, like, one glass; you know I can't really stomach alcohol.'

'I guess I've had a lot of training lately.' I looked down at the bottle, opened it, and said, 'This is good wine. Do you want another glass as well?'

'No, thanks. Are you still drinking that much?'

'You mean as in Stockholm? Now, during my travels, maybe. Hanging out in hostels, meeting old friends—there's always a party.' I took a sip of the Rioja, put the glass down, and sat there in silence for a moment. 'To be honest, it never really stopped. It just changed. In Munich, I worked in a bar where I didn't work sober for a single night. In London, it was after-work cocktails here, celebrating a deal there. You have to keep your mood up somehow while everybody else does coke. And in some way, all social events include drinking—dates, meeting friends, celebrating anything from New Year to a Tuesday. Now that I think about it, I probably haven't spent a single week completely sober since I was 15.'

Lena looked at me like a concerned mother and said, 'I know what you mean. I see it, too: every social interaction these days somehow involves alcohol. It's like our society is trying to forget something by being drunk all the time. And there's been an extreme change for women. Today, a strong independent woman goes to work all day and rewards herself with a glass of red wine or three in her single apartment.' She paused and then asked, 'Has your drinking ever been a problem for you?'

'"My drinking." I'm not an alcoholic, Lena.'

'You know what I mean.'

'Yeah. Well, you know I got into quite some trouble in Stockholm while drunk. And I did some mean things to Emma. And hungover boxing training sessions were never particularly delightful. In London, I was never really wasted. I just kept myself drunk enough so I wouldn't start thinking about existential questions . . . But during the last couple of months, I have been crazy-drunk again—waking up in strange beds and the like.' I smiled at Lena and said, 'You give me a bad conscience.' I stood up and put the glass together with the bottle out of reach.

She laughed and exclaimed, 'Good!' She became calm again and asked, 'Has anybody ever staged something like an intervention for you?'

'Hmm. My parents and later Emma told me to drink less all the time, but I wouldn't listen . . . There was one time when I was staying with Emma's parents in Berlin and had been partying for four days straight. Emma was teaching kids in South Africa back then. I was sitting at the dinner table with her family and almost passed out from my dizziness, but asked whether I could open a bottle of wine to start pre-drinking for the party that night. Emma's mum told me I should go to bed and sleep. Her father said I looked like shit. Even Tobi, her little brother, looked at me concerned. He said I looked like a ghost. I laughed it all off and went partying that night anyway. The next morning, Emma's parents found me sleeping on the bench in the kitchen. I still had my shoes on and some blood on my forearm; I told them I had had a nosebleed. They told me that they wanted me to drink less and that they would even go to a therapist with me. They were really worried. For a week or two, that left an impression on me, and I didn't get wasted at all. But then, Emma and I went back to Munich, I went back to the bar, and soon I was back to being so drunk I couldn't find our flat within our building.'

Lena looked at me for a while and said, 'You should try to drink less. Let's make the next two days in Vienna alcohol-free, okay?'

'Don't worry, it's not as bad as it was back then. But, yeah, we can do that if you want to.'

'Good.'

Lena told me more about her failed relationship with Travis, a workaholic at another tech company in San Francisco, and we soon went to bed.

After lying awake for a while, I grabbed my phone from the nightstand and called Alice. She answered the phone: '*Hej,* you.'

Her silky voice made my heart beat faster. I said, 'Hey. Did I wake you up?'

'No, I was still up reading. Where are you?'

'In Vienna. I'll be in Italy in a week. Do you want to come?'

'What are your plans there?'

'Rent a car and drive around a bit, maybe go camping somewhere by the sea—we could meet in Venice, drive down to Rome or over to Florence and see where it takes us from there.'

'I like that. Wait a second.' I heard her move in her bedsheets and then walk through her room. 'Let me check flights to Venice.' I heard typing and clicking. She said, 'Looks good. There's a cheap flight on Monday morning. Should we meet in Venice today in a week?'

'Yeah. Can you take time off at such short notice?'

'Yeah, that's no problem. I might have to do

something on my laptop, but I don't have to be in the office. In fact, I don't want to be there right now. And it's calm during the summer break. As long as I'm back at the beginning of October, it'll be fine.' She sounded odd.

'Perfect. I'm looking forward to it, Alice.'

'Me too. We could visit Arman; he's back in Rome.'

I wasn't a fan of the idea but said, 'Sure.'

'Cool. Can you take care of the hotel booking for Venice?'

'Yeah. And I'll send you the details. And after Venice, I guess we can improvise.'

'Yes, thanks! See you in Venice, then!' I heard her smile. I was overcome by a warm glow.

'See you soon. And sleep tight.'

'Goodnight.'

I lay awake for a long time, picturing Alice and me swimming naked under the silver moon in the Mediterranean Sea. I fell asleep with a nervous, content sense of anticipation. The black rose between her breasts blossomed in the fertile meadows of my dreams.

The next day, while Lena worked on her laptop, I went for a run through the forest. Lena's brother's old running shoes were a little too small but still better than my worn-out trainers. It was a fine morning in the woods. The track was soft with brown needles. The air was clean and smelled of warm moss and green stinging nettles. I could only hear my breathing, the crackling of wood, and the zealous singing of birds. The mild hangover I had was soon washed away by the vitalised blood running through my veins. I ran up a short slope. At the top, the path opened up to a small clearing with tall grass. In the middle of the clearing, there was a doe and two fawns grazing. I stopped and looked at them. The doe swiftly turned her head and looked back at me. I didn't dare to move. The fawns went on grazing. I breathed calmly and marvelled at this small family in brown and white. The oversized ears of the fawns turned in the direction of every sound echoing through the woods. The doe and I looked each other straight in the eye. I had to smile. A wave of euphoria ran through my body. I took a deep breath, and the deer family slowly turned their heads to the grass. We had an understanding. I turned around and ran back into the forest.

When I returned to the summer house, Lena told me I had been gone for almost two hours. I took a cold shower, and we had lunch on the terrace—Lena had cooked chanterelle risotto. We hung up two hammocks between the garden's pine trees and let the soft, vulnerable voice of Elliot Smith rock us to sleep.

When we had woken up from our afternoon nap, Lena said, 'This reminds me of hanging out in your garden with Joel, lying around stoned all afternoon.' She laughed and exclaimed, 'Oh my god, I completely forgot about that night after we watched one of your fights when we—well, mostly you two—got drunk and went to the cinema. You and Joel had to go to the toilet like every ten minutes from the middle of the row!' Her hammock was shaking with her laughter. 'You still had that horrible puberty 'tache!'

I chuckled and said, 'Yeah, those were the days.'

After she had recovered herself, Lena asked, 'What's Joel up to now?'

'I visited him in Berlin two weeks ago. He's still playing music, and his girlfriend left him and went back to Colombia. He's heartbroken.'

'Aww, he's always been such a sweet, sensitive guy.

Somehow those days feel like a distant dream now.'

'Yeah, I know. Do you sometimes want to be 16 again?'

'No. I like knowing who I am. And you?'

'Yeah, sometimes. I liked the simplicity of it.'

'Well, everything was always better in the old days.'

Lena got up and brought a red inflatable pool from her bedroom, which she commanded me to blow up. I overdid it and almost passed out in the heat. The pool was small and had an inflatable palm tree, flower, and yellow snake attached to it. Lena's grandparents had bought it for her when she was a little girl. She took the garden hose and filled the pool with cold water. We changed into swimwear, squeezed into the pool, and relaxed. It was nice to feel the coolness of the water on my body and the warmth of the sun on my face. Lena rested her head on my shoulder. We dozed off for a while.

In the evening, we had another barbecue. Lena talked to me about her family. Her mother was an estate agent in the south of Spain, and her father worked as a pilot based in London. Her brother was somewhere in Australia, getting wasted behind some hostel bar or teaching sunburnt tourists how to surf. She loved and hated all of them dearly. In the candlelight, we played chess. I won the first round and Lena the second. After talking her out of a third round, we went to bed. I slept well that night.

On Wednesday morning, we drove back into the city to Lena's small studio flat with lofty ceilings in an old, graffiti-covered house near Schloß Schönbrunn. We walked up the hill in the park behind the palace and then back through the vast gardens to take the metro into the city. Lena told me about an older man called the 'Bierkavallier' who would walk through the train and ask women whether they wanted to have a beer with him. He had been beaten up by insulted boyfriends and reported to the police by outraged women. But he couldn't be stopped from desperately looking for someone to drink a beer with. We got off at Kettenbrückengasse to walk across the Naschmarkt. With its open restaurants and bustling shops, and the scent of exotic food and seductive spices in the warm air, the market had an oriental atmosphere. We walked past the Karlskirche, whose white baroque walls shone against the azure sky, and between museums, theatres, churches, town halls, and universities. The inner city was the materialisation of Habsburg Gründerzeit dreams of imperial wealth and power. It was a seamless world that had once been the melting pot of cataclysmal ideas that would go on to blow up the 20th century in every way. During its heyday, many restless men had roamed Vienna's streets: Schumpeter, Popper, Hayek, von Mises, Freud, Jung, Kafka, Stalin, Trotsky, Tito, Lenin, and some loser living in a boarding house called Hitler. We took the metro to the Prater and went back over the Donaukanal to a beach bar by the river. Lena had to remind me of my sobriety vow, and we had iced tea on a pair of beach chairs in the late-afternoon sun.

For dinner, Lena took me to a restaurant that made a delicious Wiener Schnitzel with parsley potatoes. We spent the evening like we had done at times together in Stockholm: lying on Lena's bed and binge-watching old episodes of *Friends*. I told her of my plans to take the train to Munich and then fly to Italy. I would rent a car there and later fly to Marseille. She offered me her grandmother's car instead. She didn't need it during her daily life, and her grandmother had been too sick to drive for a year. I accepted gratefully. Lena would fly to Marseille to pick up the car and meet me there. She wanted to visit friends in Milan anyway and could do so on the way back to Vienna. We cuddled when we went to bed; Lena was the small spoon, and I wrapped my arm around her. In the darkness, she asked, 'Are you happy?'

I didn't speak for a while and then answered, 'Not really. I have some things to figure out first. And you?'

Lena put her arm on mine and pressed it closer to her chest. She whispered, 'I'm in a good place now. The relationship with Travis was toxic, and San Francisco never quite felt like home. I enjoy spending time with Granny, and my new job is fun, and I have met good, honest people here. And I love the Viennese snide humour.' She chuckled. 'But then, I think of the future sometimes—work for another 40 years, retire, stop breathing. And that's going to be it? I'm afraid that life will never be enough for me—that the itching in the back of my mind that drives me onwards will never go away; that I'll never be able to settle down and be satisfied with what I have. I'm afraid I'll never feel at home anywhere, always longing for a place I'll never see and a day that will never come.'

I pulled her closer. We listened to each other's breathing. Sometimes, the only thing that can keep you sane is the knowledge of the existence of another mind with true joys and sorrows.

Lena had to go to work early the next morning. We said goodbye, and I got in her old, ugly Opel Astra. The car was diarrhoea-brown, shifting into fourth gear was a game of chance, and sometimes the warning lights would turn on for no reason. Other than that, the old Astra ran like a charm.

On my way to Munich, I stopped for a late breakfast at a roadhouse. Sitting outside in the warm morning, I called Nicole. She was happy to tell me her first two exams had gone very well and told me of a trip she and Joel had taken to Wannsee. He had abandoned his plans to go to Colombia to win back Valentina. I got back into the car and started driving further west. I was glad Nicole was doing okay and hoped Joel would be all right. The green meadows of Upper Austria flew by the window. Was I ready for the trip down memory lane I was about to venture on?

Disarm you with a smile
And cut you like you want me to
Cut that little child
Inside of me and such a part of you
Ooh, the years burn
. . .
The killer in me is the killer in you

William Patrick Corgan
Disarm

12

I arrived in Munich at noon. I parked in my hotel's underground car park and had lunch in its mediocre restaurant. It was a fine summer day, and I did what I had often done during lazy days during my master's: I packed my swimming things and went to the Englischer Garten to lie on the grass by the Schwabinger Bach. I read my book and let myself be distracted by countless bikini-clad girls enjoying the sunshine. I cooled off in the ice-cold, fast-running stream. Later in the afternoon, I took a long walk back to my hotel. I walked through the park, past the surfers riding the standing wave of the Eisbach, and by my old university. I passed The Ginger Red House, the cocktail bar I used to work at. I went on past the Pinakotheken and the Glyptothek and across the Stachus.

In the evening, I took the metro to Giesing, where I had lived with Emma. I went to our favourite Osteria to have a pizza parma with a glass of fine Chianti. Afterwards, I met with my old friend Ben who was in the city on a business trip. We met at the Goldene Bar. Warm light lit its lofty ceilings and golden mosaics. Ben was waiting for me at the bar. He had ten centimetres on me and the body of an Olympic swimmer. His blond hair had started receding. His charming manners couldn't fully cover up his tiredness. He wore a well-fitting dark blue suit with a white shirt and a slim blue tie. On his left wrist, he exhibited a brand-new Breitling Navitimer with a blue face and a silver steel strap. After a short hug with loud back-patting, we sat down at one of the wooden tables. I ordered a Negroni, and Ben chose a gin and tonic and short ribs with pak choi. He had come straight from a meeting at a nearby mortgage bank. Ben smiled his wide, confident womaniser grin and said, 'Man, it's so good to see you! You look good with your beard and longer hair! How's your journey been so far? How about that girl from Hamburg?'

His honest enthusiasm had always infected me. I chuckled and said, 'It's been a wild ride.' I summed up the stops, told him about Alice—focussing on the party stories—and embellished the tale of the broken window in Budapest.

Ben was delighted. When he finally stopped laughing, he said, 'And you don't know whose bed you woke up in?'

'Nope. I'm not sure I want to know.'

Ben laughed some more and said, 'Man, sometimes I miss the old days.'

'Yeah. You have a girlfriend now, right?'

'Yes. Her name's Helen. She's amazing!' He showed me pictures of a blonde beauty. 'I met her at a work party in Frankfurt. She's a lawyer.'

'Is it going well with her?'

'Yeah! We moved in together two months ago. We've bought a beautiful flat with a view of the Main and the banking towers. She's the first woman to make me want to settle down. She's amazing!'

'Wow, you've bought it? I'm happy for you, Ben.'

'Yeah, thanks! Her dad has a lot of money . . . And you were fed up with your bankster life?'

'Yeah. How has it been going for you?'

'I have worked my arse off, but it really paid off. They promoted me to associate at the beginning of the year. And now they've offered me the opportunity to switch to another unit—equity valuation. You did something similar at Phorcys, right?'

'Yeah, but I worked more with Python and less with PowerPoint.'

Ben chuckled. 'That's probably true. But should I ask them whether they want to make you an offer?'

'I don't know. I don't plan to go back into banking, to be honest.'

'You should think about it. It would be awesome to have you in Frankfurt! And they offer a way better work-life balance. You can even work from home once a week.'

'I'll let you know.'

After Ben had finished eating and we were done with our drinks, we walked to Odeonsplatz, where we entered Schumann's. Sanguine voices filled the room of beige walls, dark wood, and red leather. Barmen in white jackets mixed classic cocktails with calm professionality in front of a green stone wall and a long row of red Campari bottles. Tall men with slicked-back hair in tieless white shirts who sniffed a little too much stood by the bar next to girls who were a little too young and a little too anxious about gratifying

189

their companions. Ben and I were assigned a small table. I looked at the 'Schickeria', the rich and pretty of Munich. Ben must have noticed my stern expression and asked, 'What's wrong? You seem sad today.'

'It's nothing.' I paused. 'You know, sometimes I realise how odd it is for us to celebrate while so many things in the world are going to hell.'

'Oh no, I know that mood of yours. And you know my answer: we live in the best time the world has ever seen.'

'How's that, again?'

'Well, people get richer and richer, and we have stuff like aeroplanes and smartphones and intelligent microwaves and vaccines. Instead of dying from a middle-ear inflammation as a child, we travel around the world and share the experience online in real time with our friends!'

'Most people don't seem too crazy about their situation—unaffordable housing, temporary work contracts, and machines about to make labour obsolete while social safety nets are cut to shreds'

'Hmm, I guess that's your Western perspective. If I were a Chinese farmer who grew up on a diet of rice and Yangtze water and now sees his kid go to university, I wouldn't be too pissed off about where the world is headed. I think the problem is people define their well-being by comparing themselves to others. That's why there is such nostalgia for white America in the '50s and '60s—living ten times as comfortably as your parents did while most of the world still dwells in huts. You know, I'm sure there is some room for improvement left for humanity. But it will get better, like it has in the past. And you worrying about it tonight won't change anything anyway. So, please relax and have another drink.'

I nodded. We both ordered a Boulevardier—the smooth brother of the Negroni—and then Vesper Martinis. They still made some damned good cocktails here.

We decided to have one last drink and went to The Madam Bar, which was in an old strip club between Marienplatz and Isartor. Red light gave the basement room a cosy, warm atmosphere. We sat down at the bar and had an Old Fashioned—it was good and strong. I fell back into a gloomy mood, which contrasted with Ben's radiating optimism. Ben looked at me and, for once, became serious. With his steadfast voice, he said, 'I think I know what your problem is: you're always looking for a greater cause or someone special to do great things for. But can't you do something for yourself for a change? You're entitled to happiness just as much as anyone else. And if you can't do it for yourself, do it for your family. Visit your mum! Get a job you enjoy, even if it falls a little short of changing the whole world! Accept your flaws, and don't be twice as hard on yourself as you ever would be on anyone else. You're the smartest guy I know, and it hurts to see you suffer because you're too stubborn to allow yourself a little peace. You probably think of me as the guy who's always happy, but I do worry about you, you know? I worried about you whenever you were on one of your self-destructive maniac trips back in grammar school. I worried about you when I heard you quit your job. And I'm worried about you now when I see you in pain.'

Ben's blue eyes were a little drunk but sincere. I smiled and said, 'Thanks, Ben, I know you mean it. Don't worry. I'll get over my first-world problems soon enough. It just takes time to process all these things I have on my mind.'

Ben smiled back at me. We finished our drinks and left the bar. The night sky was clear, and the air was crisp. Ben had to go back to Frankfurt early in the morning. He gave me a long hug and said, 'It was good to see you! Call me and tell me how it goes with that girl from Sweden!'

We said goodbye.

As I walked to my hotel alone, I felt depressed. I smiled to trick myself into being happy. This time, it didn't work. I stopped in the middle of the empty Stachus, smoked a cigarette, and watched some taxis and a tram go by. Lights shimmered on the tepid asphalt. My whole life, I had been a night person. When the rest of the city slept, I wandered through the catacombs of my mind, turning over every stone in every dark corner of my consciousness, looking for an answer to a question I couldn't articulate.

I lay awake in my hotel bed for a long time. A cold breeze and the silence of the night came in through the open window. I felt dizzy. Long and lonesome nights can weigh heavy on your mind.

In the morning, I texted Alice the details of the hotel I had booked for Venice and then spent my Friday wandering through Munich restlessly. I had a coffee here and a snack there. I went back to my hotel and tried on three different outfits—interchangeable combinations of jeans and colourless T-shirts.

I took a short walk that led me through the old botanical garden and to the Technical University. I entered the grey building and took the lift to the café on the top floor. I was early. I ordered a cappuccino at the bar and sat down at the last free table outside on the rooftop terrace. It was crowded with groups of good-looking students absorbed in their discussions about messed-up exams, overpriced shared flats, and the latest pop-up bars. The sun was shining, and the clear air granted an excellent view over Munich. I felt a little queasy and kept looking around.

At four o'clock sharp, she walked through the door. Emma's long brown hair fell down her back, and she wore an ordinary white T-shirt, light-blue jeans, and black trainers. She was still mind-bendingly beautiful. Guys all over the café contorted their necks. Emma saw me. As she walked over, she smiled her candid smile, framed by cute dimples. I stood up. We both said, 'Hey,' and she gave me a cuddle. Her smell took me back to long Sunday mornings in bed, afternoons making love in German summer cornfields, and tired, silent weekday evenings in our London flat. I was taken back to the night in Stockholm I had come to Emma's dorm room in the dead of night with blood on my hands and had kneeled in front of her and wept into her dressing gown like a little boy.

As we sat down, Emma said, 'Wow, it's been two years! I like your new beard; since when do you have it?'

'A couple of weeks—I'm too lazy to shave while travelling. And yeah, it's been quite a while. What have you been up to lately?'

'I work as an editor for an e-commerce company here in Munich. Not particularly exciting, but it's not too many hours and reasonable pay. And I'm glad to be back in Munich.'

'Yeah, you always hated it in London.'

'I didn't hate it! But yes, I prefer the calmness of Munich—boring as I am . . . And sitting at home alone all the time wasn't particularly stimulating.' She looked at me defiantly, and a moment of silence ensued. I looked across Munich to the towers of the

193

Frauenkirche. Suddenly, Emma exclaimed, 'Oh, and I'm engaged!' She showed me the slim silver ring on her finger and laughed sheepishly.

'Yeah, I've heard about it. Who's the lucky one?'

For a moment, Emma gave me a cynical look but then smiled again and said, 'His name is Marcus. I met him in London at the gym.' She paused. 'And when he moved to work for a bank here in Munich, he gave me a call and then everything went pretty fast.'

'Another banker . . . And you met him back in London, huh?' I tried to look playfully startled.

'Yes.' She looked away over her left shoulder. 'But we only talked there. As if it would've made a difference.'

It had taken me one minute to antagonise her—amazing.

'I didn't mean to spite you. I'm happy for you, seriously.' I tried to laugh the tension off.

Emma scrutinised me for a second and then smiled back. 'I know. I think you would like him. He's smart and funny. And he's also into boxing. He was in the boxing club in Oxford.'

I nodded and, after a brief pause, asked, 'How is it going for you two?'

She hesitated. 'Good . . . We're both very busy—especially Marcus. It's hard to find time together, and when we do, he's too tired to do much.' She blushed. 'I shouldn't be telling you this.'

'Yeah, you probably shouldn't.'

We chuckled. To break the ensuing silence, she asked, 'And you quit your job?'

'Yeah, London and that whole finance bullshit didn't feel like home anymore.'

'Did you move out of our old flat, too?'

'Yeah.'

I detected a hint of sadness in her eyes. She said, 'Sometimes I still miss that unbelievably ugly sofa in the living room you built from old wooden pallets.' We both laughed. Emma's smile revealed more wrinkles around her eyes than it had used to. After a quiet moment, she asked, 'You were in Berlin?'

'Yeah, for a couple of days. I visited Joel and Nicole.'

'You could've visited my family, too! They would've been glad.'

'I doubt that.'

'You know that my parents liked you! And Tobi always looked up to you . . . Anyway, how is Nicole doing?'

'Still getting into trouble, but I think she's doing okay.'

She laughed. 'The two of you have always kept your parents busy. How are they?' She paused in embarrassment. 'I mean, how's your mum and Michael?'

I looked to the left, over the rooftops of the city, and said, 'It's been tough after Dad died, but they're all right.'

'Okay. That's good . . . Does Michael still have his gardening company?'

'Yeah.'

'How old was he again when he founded it? 19?'

'Yeah, I think so.'

'That's so crazy! Most people don't even know who they are at that age.'

'Yeah, Michael had things figured out pretty early—to the delight of my parents.'

'And how are you doing?' She smiled at me with great compassion. It was painful.

I hastily glanced down at the table and said, 'You still don't have a drink; let me get you a cappuccino.'

I went inside and took a deep breath. After we talked a little about her job and had finished our first coffee, Emma got us another round. When she was back at the table, I cleared my throat and said, 'You know, Emma, I wanted to tell you something. I've had time to think about many things lately, about things I have done. And it's important to me that you know I'm sorry for how I've treated you and made you feel at times. I see now that you've always been loving and understanding, and I have exploited that and treated you disgracefully. I'm sorry for that.'

Tears slowly ran down Emma's cheeks. She rubbed her eyes and said, 'Thank you. That means a lot to me.' She continued crying, and my eyes became moist as well.

After some time, we both chuckled, wiped away our tears, and looked out over the city. I felt a deep sense of relief.

We had a small dinner at the café as well. Emma told me Marcus was having dinner with his colleagues at a posh restaurant near Marienplatz; they were celebrating a big deal they had sealed this morning in Zürich. After we had finished our pizza margarita, Emma asked me whether I wanted to join her at a wine garden called Jardin Gerard where she had plans to meet up with Marcus and the others. That was a horrible idea. So, naturally, I accepted. We left the university building and took a bus east, past the Eisbachwelle and the Angel of Peace.

Jardin Gerard was a temporary bar in the garden behind Villa Stuck, a classical white building by the park with an art museum inside. There was a small sandwich shop, a wine and Prosecco bar, and a small stage with some young stoner rockers playing their riffs in a markedly indifferent fashion. The sun, hiding behind the trees, bathed the garden in kaleidoscopic light. I followed Emma towards the bar. She introduced me to Marcus and three of his colleagues. They had already ordered two bottles of Champagne. They all gave the same business handshake, probably picked up in some unironic soft-skill workshops of which I had attended more than I would like to admit. The suits and I marvelled at Emma as she gave Marcus a brief kiss. Marcus was a tall, slim Englishman with a full head of dark hair and a smart three-day stubble. He wore grey suit trousers, black shoes and belt, and a tight white shirt without a tie. I chuckled to myself; Emma had once told me her ideal man looked like a boxer in a suit. His neat, black Omega De Ville seemed modest and honest next to the swanky golden and silver Rolex Submariners and Daytonas dangling from his colleagues' wrists. Marcus welcomed me with a wide grin and asked me to join their drinking efforts. I accepted a glass of Champagne and then another one. I learned that Marcus had worked for Goldman Sachs during their late glory years in London, that he now worked in wealth management at the Munich branch of a Swiss-based bank, that he had been at Harvard for a year, that he played the saxophone, and that he sometimes worked with refugees at the weekend. His youth at a boarding school? 'Oh yes, growing up around spoiled rich brats in blazers and dress socks is great fun and totally not unworldly at all!' His time at the bank in London? 'I hear they now have a protected weekend twice a month—sissies . . . I mean, when do they find the time to tweak slide 43 of the PowerPoint presentation that will be shredded by their associate anyway?' He seemed rather nice and self-aware; I couldn't help but hate his guts. One of his colleagues felt the need to point out in a portentous tone that Marcus was practised in the art of pugilism. Marcus gave the impression of being embarrassed by the bragging of his colleagues. He and the other suits were already mightily drunk, to the apparent disgust of Emma, who paid more and more superficial attention to the band. The suits reacted with thinly veiled admiration when they found out I used to work at Phorcys and treated me with increased attentiveness afterwards. One of the suits exclaimed, 'Let me tell you, wealth management is the new investment banking. We're the masters of the universe, now!'

I said, 'Sure, whatever,' and stepped out of the group to smoke a cigarette in peace. The suits talked to Marcus, who was gulping down another glass of Champagne, and then darted grim glances at me. I couldn't see Emma. She must have gone to the bathroom. As I finished my cigarette, Marcus came over to me, gave me a brief, insincere smile and asked, 'So, you used to date my fiancée, correct?'

'Mhm—thrilling times.' I raised my eyebrows and held his gaze. I felt his impatience as he stared at me with drunk eyes. We stood next to the fence, a couple of metres away from the other suits and the rest of the crowd listening to the music. I said, 'Look, I know you want to mark your territory in front of your little friends, but don't bother. I'm going to leave and let you talk about other people's tax-free money, while Emma bores herself to death.'

He snarled, 'Fuck you. Do you think it's clever to come back here and bother your ex? She's moved on, and you should too.' His feeble mask of mature confidence dispersed and revealed a visage distorted in juvenile anger.

I couldn't let it go and said, 'She didn't seem too

bothered when I spent time with her this afternoon. A neglected, unsatisfied woman can get pretty restless, you know . . . '

He stepped closer towards me and lowered his head. A furious fire sparked in his glazed eyes. I smelled wine as he hissed, 'What did you say?'

I nodded towards him and said, 'You heard me, boarding school boy.' With a mean grin, I added, 'What're you gonna do about it?'

In a sudden explosion, Marcus gave me a hard shove that pushed me two or three steps back. Driven by deep-rooted instincts, I raised my clenched fists and tucked my chin as I moved swiftly on my toes towards him. He knew the score; he hid his face behind his hands and approached me with an orthodox stance and defence, ready to throw a punch. His movements were a little wobbly. Someone screamed. I put my right fist up to my chin and held my left in front of my chest to offer him my nose and cheek. His left shoulder led a jab. I slipped to the right. As his left fist flew past my left ear, I landed a heavy right hook to his body. My knuckles crashed into his ribs. I shifted my weight to my left foot and threw a quick left uppercut clean to his solar plexus. I felt him deflate behind my knuckles. I took the force out of a follow-up right hook and simply pushed him over. I knew he was done. With a wheezing moan, he slumped down to the ground. I relaxed. Panicked voices came from my right. As I turned my head towards them, a fist dashed at my face. I tried to duck, but the fist hit the corner of my right eye. After an instant of disorientation, I identified the sucker-puncher as Marcus' short, red-haired colleague. Before I could make the idiot pay, more people came rushing towards us. I held up my hands over my head. I let the other two 'friends' of

Marcus and a sweating, overwhelmed, and over-weight museum attendant shepherd me through the museum and outside to the street. I looked back over my shoulder. Emma rushed through the crowd and kneeled over Marcus. She was crying. I never failed to liven up the party.

Outside the villa, I asked the heavily breathing museum attendant and the two self-appointed door-men to let me back inside to say sorry to Emma and Marcus. They told me to fuck off. In a shaky voice, the museum attendant threatened to call the police. I hadn't started the fight. Neither had I been the one foolish enough to try to punch people in the face with bare knuckles. But, as one of the vultures in unbut-toned dress shirts kindly reminded me, I didn't know anybody in this city and hence should be the one to take a hike. I agreed to stay outside. When the others were gone, I sat on the high stone wall in front of the villa and visualised messing up that red-haired wealth manager bastard. Nonetheless, I was glad I had not. I called Emma. She didn't answer. I texted her that I wanted to apologise.

Marcus had been rather drunk. After my right hook, my head had been open. He could have followed up with a right, but he had been too rattled by the blow to his body, and too slow. I doubted Marcus had ever been a good fighter. Usually, I would have stayed on the outside and followed up the right hook with a right uppercut to the chin. But I hadn't wanted to break any of his—or my—bones. My right eye and upper cheekbone hurt. The eye was slowly swelling shut. That red-headed weasel prick.

Some people came out of the villa and glared at me scornfully as they passed the wall. Then, Emma walked through the glass door and stopped in front of me. I jumped down from my perch and said, 'Emma, I'm sorry.'

She looked at me in disappointment and said, 'Well, I should've seen this coming—although Marcus usually never gets into fights.'

'I guess I bring out the best in people. I did provoke him, you know?'

'Still, he shouldn't have tried to punch you.' Emma looked away and onto the street on which the lights had just come on.

I stepped into her field of vision and said, 'I'm very sorry, Emma. I didn't want to ruin your day.'

With a sad smile, she said, 'I know. And I saw you didn't start it. Marcus says he's sorry, too. And I'm sorry that idiot Philip hit you.' She took a moment to examine my face and said, 'Your eye looks awful.' Tenderly, she touched my swollen eye.

I didn't dare to move. I asked, 'Is Marcus okay?'

Emma retracted her hand from my face as though it was a hot cooking plate. 'Yes. You hurt him pretty bad for a moment, but he got up soon after.'

'He might feel his ribs for a while, but the second punch just took his air out for a moment.'

'He'll be fine. I remembered you knocking out a guy like that in one of your fights back in Stockholm, so I wasn't too scared.'

I laughed and said, 'Yeah, that fight was much uglier than this one.'

She laughed as well. 'Your face looked like a pulp the next day. And your freezer was filled with nothing but ice pads for two weeks!'

We looked into each other's eyes. Her innocent face was beautiful in the twilight. Her expression conveyed a sense of painful exposure. I heard myself say, 'You should go back to Marcus. He was angry enough already that you spent time with me.'

'Oh, he'll be furious.' She looked aside and said, 'You know, maybe I wanted this to happen. I felt an odd pleasure seeing him hurt. I want him to be envious, and I want him not to be too sure about me. Let him taste his own medicine.'

'Did he cheat on you?'

She smiled at me in embarrassment and glanced down at the ground.

I said, 'That bastard. Now I want to get back in there and hit him in the face.'

'He's a good man, you know?'

'Yeah, fucking saint.'

'You're one to talk.' Her eyes hit me with a defiant gaze.

I hesitated. 'What do you mean?'

She chuckled cynically and said, 'Well, don't think I didn't know about your little Belgian girlfriend.' I stared at her. She continued, 'That's right. And I knew it didn't mean much, so I didn't say anything. I guess there are some dreams you don't want to wake up from. And, unlike you, I'm only looking for good enough, not for a never-obtainable perfect. I know you always thought I was too mediocre for your exaggerated, incoherent aspirations. But look where they've taken you . . . Oh, and for the record: I hooked up with Marcus already back in London while you were busy fetishising your emotional damage.'

I stared at her some more.

'When will you men ever understand that we have desires just like you?' Heavy tears ran down her cheeks.

I stuttered, 'I'm sorry.'

She snorted and exclaimed, '"I'm sorry." That's all you ever say!' The tears were dropping down from her delicate chin. 'God, why do I always have to cry?'

'Because you care.'

She smiled a painful smile and turned towards the villa. As I slowly walked through the gate and onto the pavement, she asked, 'What are you going to do now?'

I turned around and said, 'Drink whiskey until I forget I got a black eye from a short, fat banker.'

Emma giggled and wiped the last tears from her face. She said, 'But don't get into any more fights. And please don't hurt yourself. Please take care.'

'Yeah. Good luck with that whole "getting married buying a house and having a bunch of kids" business.'

She nodded slowly and walked back inside the villa. The last thing I saw of her was her long brown hair floating through the summer evening and disappearing in the crowd behind the glass wall. I shook my head and smiled in disbelief.

For a while, I walked down the street aimlessly. The image of Emma kissing Marcus was ingrained in my consciousness. I felt numb. At a street corner, I stepped into a small kiosk. Behind the cash desk sat an old man with a steel-string acoustic guitar playing *Heart of Gold*. I listened to his roughened voice and bought a bottle of Bushmills after he had finished his song.

I drank a little more than half of the whiskey on the east bank of the Isar and gave the rest to a pair of homeless men on my way to the tram, which took me to Lenbachplatz. Near the tram stop, there was a building complex which housed four nightclubs. Three of them were on the upper floor, filled with the shallow, grandiloquent narcissists many people vilified Munich for. The clubs were connected through a chaotic kitchen in which the overpriced drinks were mixed and where tarted-up girls with plumped lips and fake tans and smiles were chatted up by self-important braggarts with plucked eyebrows in too-tight V-neck T-shirts. I queued for the nightclub in the basement, Rote Sonne. The bouncer scrutinised my swollen eye, asked me a lot of questions, and searched my pockets. But he apparently figured I wouldn't make any trouble and let me in. I walked down the stairwell, stepped through the steel door, and into a world of heavy fog, vibrating bass, and white strobe light. I got a strong gin and tonic at the bar and moved to the fast, hypnotic techno beats. The Spanish DJ from Berlin was playing a terrific set. The air in my lungs vibrated. The merciful flashing lights shot my painful thoughts to pieces. Now and then, other people emerged from the fulgurating fog—shitfaced voyagers in black and white sipping from water bottles with content smiles. I couldn't see my feet moving below me and immersed myself in the fog of the collective unconscious. The booming bass sent cold shivers up and down my spine. I lost myself in the music.

Many hours and some drinks later, I left the temple of techno and went back to my hotel along the main street. I took a long shower, chugged four glasses of water, and went to sleep.

I woke up with a dizzying hangover and a buzzing pressure in my ears. My swollen eye hurt. I felt sur-real. Could I be certain yesterday had ever happened? That I hadn't only been created in this instant? I could see my hands and feel my body but didn't trust their existence. To find distraction, I took an extensive walk through the immaculate streets of Munich. And I wandered through distant, dreamlike memories of drunken days during the Sodom and Gomorrah that is the Oktoberfest, of long nights working at The Ginger Red House, and bleary-eyed mornings in the untidy flats of fellow insomniacs. I remembered exciting boxing bouts against rough brawlers from the poor fringes of German cities, and sunny afternoons in the parks by the river with Emma. I thought of nights of running home, full of love—for Emma, forever ago. Some dreams you don't want to wake up from. I had created an idealistic image of Emma—a loving, compassionate, loyal angel. One Christmas in Munich, Emma had given me an old, restored road bike it had taken her weeks to discover. My present for her had been some lousy poem I had written on a chequered piece of paper on a train ride from a binge in Leipzig. But I had chosen to forget all the times Emma had bored me with her bourgeois contentment and annoyed me with her blindness to art and politics. I hadn't been missing Emma, but rather an idea of her nobody could compare to, not even Emma. She was only a symbol for something I had lost long ago, or something I had never had. Some dreams you have to wake up from if you want to move on. And move on I had to—to Italy, to Alice.

I bought a razor and trimmed my beard back at the hotel. In the evening, I went to a nearby restaurant. I still knew one of the bartenders and had a discussion at the bar with a forensic doctor who told me about a wave of overdose deaths; a new heroin cartel had entered the market and was fighting for market share with low prices and a high quality the users weren't used to.

Soon, I went back to the hotel, and to sleep. That night, my brain thought it was funny to make me dream of Emma, pulling me closer, naked in a cornfield shining in the sun.

I got up early on Sunday morning and left Munich behind in the rear mirror of Lena's Astra. Recently abolished roaming fees allowed me to use my phone to navigate. I took the motorway down south, through the Austrian Alps and the picturesque city of Innsbruck, and across the busy Brenner Pass. My swollen right eye still bothered me. But I could see enough to marvel at distant trees growing on green slopes on both sides of the ascending valley. As the old car climbed up the road towards the Italian border with creaking moans in the stop-and-go traffic, Alice called. She said, '*Hej*! How are you?'

Hearing her mellow voice made me smile. 'Good. I'm driving into Italy now. The weather is perfect.'

'Aw, I can't wait! I checked out the hotel's website; it looks amazing!'

'Yeah, Venice is going to be good. When do you arrive?'

'Mm, my flight arrives at nine. I still have to figure out how to get from the airport to the hotel. I want to take one of those boats into the city.'

'I'll be waiting for you.'

'I want flowers!'

I chuckled, 'You got it.'

'And we'll have pizza by the canals!'

'Sounds good.'

'And we'll take the cutest of the waitresses back to our hotel bed with us!'

'We'll see about that.'

She laughed and exclaimed, 'I'm so excited! I'll see you tomorrow!'

'See you tomorrow, Alice.'

Since thou art dead, lo, here I prophesy
Sorrow on love hereafter shall attend;
It shall be waited on with jealousy,
Find sweet beginning but unsavoury end,
Ne'er settled equally, but high or low,
That all love's pleasure shall not match his woe.

William Shakespeare
Venus and Adonis

13

I drove through the green valleys and past the small villages of South Tyrol. Rusty crash barriers and confusing, ever-changing speed limits signified that I was in Italy. Old castles loomed into the blue summer sky from rocky ledges on both sides of the autostrada. Tempting mountain streams rushed by the side of the road. I wound down the windows to breathe in the warm summer air. Lush vineyards flew by the old Astra before I drove through Bozen. Grey walls of rock led me down to Trento, after which the mountains became flatter and greener. I stopped at a roadhouse between Rovereto and Verona to have a large chicken sandwich for lunch. Before I got back into the car, I took a moment to enjoy the sun on my skin. The air smelled of olive trees and exhaust fumes. Behind the mountains to my right, on the edge of the Dolomites, lay Lago di Garda. I jumped back into the car and drove on, longing for Venice, longing for Alice. After

Verona, the drive became less scenic; the Alps were replaced by the industrialised plains of northern Italy. When I arrived in Mestre, I parked the Astra in one of its large, expensive car parks.

I took a vaporetto to Venice, where the water taxi drove into the Canal Grande. The canal was bustling with boats—sightseeing ships with tourists marvelling through their smartphone displays at the Venetian Gothic buildings and bridges; traditional gondolas with sweating stand-up rowers; small, white private boats with tanned locals; and working boats servicing the many construction sites trying to save the city from drowning. How did all the boats manage not to crash into each other? White walls with ornate arches shone in the afternoon sun. Wooden stilts protruded from the green water everywhere. The hot Mediterranean air had a mouldy smell. I got off next to Ponte di Rialto. I walked for five minutes through the narrow alleys to my hotel at the border between San Marco and Castello. Hotel Desiderio was in an old palazzo by one of the most popular canals for gondola tours. Our room on the second floor had high ceilings and was furnished in the style of the 18th century—upholstery with dark wood and padding embroidered with colourful flowers, mirrors with ornate golden frames, a large bed covered with an orange patterned bedspread on a worn Persian carpet, and a small, out-of-place flatscreen TV. The room smelled of old wood and fabric. The sound of the canal sloshing against the wall of the house and the voices of excited tourists came through the open window. The room overlooked the narrow canal below and a coral-red building with a wide white balcony whose façade had been eroded by the water. I collapsed on the bed and took a long nap; the drive had tired me.

In the evening, I made plans for Alice and me for the next day. I bought some takeaway fettuccine with frutti di mare at a small shop close to the hotel and sat on the steps of the nearby Santa Maria Formosa. Next to me, a duo of weatherbeaten old men in grey suits made music with an accordion and a violin. I took a walk around San Marco, which was getting quieter; the day-trip tourists had returned to the mainland. At dusk, I returned to my hotel, threw on a collared shirt, and walked over to Bar Dandolo inside Hotel Danieli for a nightcap. They made a mean Vesper Martini. I ordered three of them and watched old and new money mingle. Back in my hotel bed, I lay awake and pictured Alice's arrival.

The next day, I had breakfast and read the *Financial Times* in the small restaurant of the hotel. One headline read 'Ailing US battling rising China over AI, immigration, world hegemony'. Well, there was your 21st century in a nutshell. I walked to the Ponte di Rialto quay. I found a pleasant spot in the shade of the sunblind of one of the small shops by the canal. I couldn't hold my hands still and fidgeted with the small bouquet of red and pink roses I had bought on my way to the canal.

At 11, Alice arrived with a vaporetto. She wore a blue cropped blouse, brown high-waisted shorts, and light brown leather sandals. The heavy-looking red backpack she was carrying was a little too big for her and wiggled from side to side as she walked through the gate of the quay. When she noticed me, she stopped for a moment. Her wide smile shone in unison with her deep-brown eyes. She was beautiful. I hesitated, unsure how to act. We both laughed, and she hugged and kissed me. Her lips were water in the desert; my tongue surrendered to hers. I gave her the bouquet of roses. Alice took the flowers, smelled them, and beamed at me with pleasure. She gave me another long kiss and said, 'Thank you.'

'Welcome to Venice. How was your flight?'

'Good. Let's drop off my backpack at the hotel and get something to eat; I'm hungry!'

I took her by the hand and led the way across the crowded promenade and into a calmer alley. Alice looked at me and asked, 'What happened to your eye? Who did this to you?'

'I had a run-in with some drunk Swiss bankers in Munich.'

Alice chuckled and said, 'Of course.' She carefully kissed my bruised cheek.

As we passed Santa Maria della Fava, jammed in between multistorey residential houses, I asked, 'You've not been to Venice before, right?'

'No! I'm really excited!' She tilted her head back and looked into the narrow band of blue sky. She smiled and said, 'It was a beautiful boat ride into the city.'

I put my hands on her cheeks and kissed her. We walked the rest of the short way to the hotel in silence. During her check-in, Alice had the old receptionist twisted around her finger in no time. He recommended a cheap trattoria nearby in Castello for lunch and volunteered to make a dinner reservation for us at an *enoteca* in Santa Croce. He gave Alice a small vase for her roses, and we went upstairs into our room. I had barely shut the door when Alice ripped off my shirt and kissed me steamily. I undressed her carefully and kneeled before her to take off her sandals, shorts, and knickers. I slowly kissed my way back up, taking a break at the black rose between her breasts. Alice threw me around and pushed me onto the bed. Laughing, she jumped on top of me and kissed me, biting my lip. Her hips moved back and forth on my shorts. Just before I burst with lust, she pulled off the rest of my clothes, ripped open a condom package with her teeth, and sat herself down on me. She started riding me, and I massaged her breasts. After a while, she grabbed my wrists, pushed my arms down on the bed, and told me to close my eyes. I obeyed with a moan and let waves of fervour run through my body as her hips rubbed against mine. I couldn't help but smile and groan. Alice was breathing heavily and soon moaned ecstatically. Her movements grew faster and more intense. When I felt her pelvis tighten and heard her scream without restraint, I came. Alice collapsed and dug her face into my shoulder, breathing heavily. We laughed, and she gave me a long, airtight kiss. We lay naked on top of the bedsheets, hoping a breeze would come through the open window and cool our sweaty skin. We both dozed off.

When Alice woke me up, we had sex again in the small bathroom and shared a cold shower. Alice was still hungry. We got dressed and walked to the trattoria the old man at reception had recommended. Alice had a small pizza capricciosa, and I ate a large pizza diavola. After this late lunch, we began our sightseeing tour around San Marco. We strolled along Canal Grande and inspected the pompous ceiling paintings inside the Palazzo Ducale, for which I had bought tickets the day before. We waded through ankle-deep water on the flooded Piazza San Marco, past the basilica, and wandered through the narrow, congested alleys with their countless shops selling glass art, carnival masks, wine, jewellery, paintings, mosaics, vases, antiquities, and tacky souvenirs and other junk. We had ice cream and followed the Canal Grande to the Ponte di Rialto. We tried to escape the crowds by wandering aimlessly into the lanes of San Polo. At every crossroads, we chose the quieter, narrower alley. Soon, we were alone in an alleyway not wider than my outstretched arm. The smell of beef stew hung in the warm air. Only distant echoes reminded us of the tourist turmoil. Colourful clothes hung on lines above our heads and in front of closed window shutters. I looked at Alice and said, 'I thought about you many times.'

She whispered with a smirk, 'Maybe I've missed you, too—a little.'

She laughed and kissed me. I pressed her against the brick wall behind her. The sound of slow steps coming towards us made us break up our kiss; an old woman was carrying two big shopping bags down the alley. She greeted us with a gap-toothed smile, scraped by us, and disappeared into one of the houses. We wandered further north and ended up on a square with a botchy reddish church called San Giacomo dell'Orio.

After we had drunk an Aperol Spritz in front of one of the square's cafés, it was already half past seven. We took a short walk to the restaurant, where we had a dinner reservation. The old waiter greeted us with a handshake and a spate of Italian. He seated us at a small wooden table on the promenade by the canal. By now, the sun was only reaching the rooftops, but the air was still warm. Over mozzarella caprese, ravioli with sea bass filling, and an excellent Pinot Grigio, I told Alice whitewashed stories about coke in Riga, ecstasy in Berlin, naked people in Sofia, and broken windows in Budapest. She laughed through it all while eating her gnocchi with gorgonzola and walnuts. Over tiramisu, Alice told me about the time she had been working on a clean water project in the Congo, the forever-broken heart of Africa. She had gone there straight after high school and had travelled deep into the rainforest on unpaved orange roads. When the green hell had finally spat her out again, she had been eight months older, two of her colleagues had nearly died of Dengue fever, and she had seen a group of dead gorillas hunted down by mineral miners for bushmeat. The giant equatorial sun burned in Alice's eyes as she spoke of Africa. As we finished our second bottle of Pinot, I laughed at Alice's story of dancing with a group of stocky taxi drivers to Rihanna's *Pon De Replay* somewhere in the streets of Kinshasa. Tipsy from the wine, we walked back to our hotel in the bright moonlight. On every square and every street corner, people were sitting outside, enjoying the balmy summer night, relieved to have survived another day of tourist mayhem, and glad not to have to wake up early the next day for their office jobs.

Back in our hotel room, Alice locked me into the bathroom. When she let me out again, she knelt on the bed in black lingerie. Only the full moon illuminated the room and drew seductive patterns on her luscious curves. A smooth summer-night breeze billowed the curtains. In a trance, I undressed and walked over to the bed. Both of us were sore and soaked in sweat when we finally went to sleep at three o'clock. I slept like a baby that night.

On Tuesday, we had breakfast in the small restaurant downstairs and took a gondola tour around the canals from the hotel's little jetty. The sun was shining with all its might. The sky was blue enough to drive you crazy if you dared to look too long at it. After risotto for lunch, Alice and I took a long walk to Giardini della Biennale and Parco delle Rimembranze in the southeast of Venice. Lying on the grass in the shade of a tree by the water, I asked, 'What have you been up to in Stockholm?'

'Hmm, since I'm back from Cuba, not too much. I have done some bar touring with Dion, Sherine, and Arman, and gave a couple of outdoor yoga classes.'

'And how's the PhD going?'

Alice exhaled audibly and said, 'I don't know. Let's not talk about it.'

'Okay.'

'Oh, before I forget: Dion says, "Hi!"'

'Okay.'

'He thought about joining us in Rome. But he's probably too busy at the hospital.'

'What a shame.'

'You don't like him, do you?'

'I have no opinion about him. I know I'd rather have you to myself.'

Alice laughed and said, 'He has a crush on you, you know!'

'Well, tough luck.'

She pinched my arm. 'Oh, don't be so mean!'

'You're one to talk.'

'What do you mean?'

'You know what I mean. I love you, Alice. And that's tough luck, too.'

Alice looked at me openly and said, 'Do you think I'm mean to you?'

'No. You've been honest with me. I appreciate that. I know you're going to hurt me. But that's okay. It's not your fault. And it's better than feeling nothing.'

Alice looked at me for a while, started laughing,

and said, 'You sure know how to give a girl a good time!'

I shook my head and laughed as well. 'Fuck you.'

She giggled, climbed on top of me, and kissed me. We rolled around on the ground, laughing, kissing, and getting grass all over us. We planned to leave for Rome the next day, and I reluctantly agreed to stay at Arman's flat there. Soon, Alice fell asleep with her head on my shoulder.

When the sun started sinking, we walked back into the city and picked up some pasta to. Alice rested on a bench while I waited in the queue. When I returned with our dinner, she had already made new friends— a trio of Italian street musicians. We ate the pasta on the bench and chatted with the musicians about their trade. They were engineering students from Milan staying with one of their aunts in Venice for the summer to earn some money for their studies. They gave us their numbers, told us to meet them later at a house party in the west of Dorsoduro, and walked in the direction of San Marco to play another set.

Back at the hotel, I took a shower. When I came out of the bathroom, Alice was looking out the window, petrified. As I walked over to her, a single tear ran down her cheek. Softly, I asked, 'What's wrong?'

She wiped away the tear, smiled, and said, 'I'm just a little stressed out lately. It's nothing.'

'Do you want to talk about it?'

She tried another smile and said, 'It's nothing, really.' Another tear rolled down her cheek. She laughed and said, 'I'll take a shower and then let's call the guys and go to their party!'

I took a step towards her and wiped away the tear with my hand. I kissed her and asked, 'What's wrong, Alice?' She forced a smile, unzipped my shorts, and knelt before me. I grabbed her under her shoulders, lifted her back up, and said, 'No, I want to talk to you.'

She turned her head and gazed out the window for a long time. Finally, she whispered, 'It's . . . I'm under so much stress lately. My project in Cuba was a disaster, all my research is pointless bullshit, and I'm about to lose funding for my PhD. My boss is an arsehole, and I have to move out of my room in October and have no new place to stay yet.' She started crying. I rubbed her arms and kissed her forehead. With a sob, she said, 'I feel like I'm losing control. I'm a failure. It's all too much. And I just can't find rest.'

'Rest now.'

With tearstained eyes, she asked, 'Would it be okay with you if we stay in the hotel tonight?'

'Of course. We can lie in bed and watch a film if you want to. There's nowhere to be and nothing to miss out on.'

She snivelled, smiled, and said, 'Okay.'

Alice took a shower and then snuggled up to me in bed. We watched *The Nice Guys,* and Alice made fun of my greying temples. A rare cool breeze blew in from the sea and through our open window. We cuddled under the bedsheet. Before the film was finished, Alice put her head on my chest and slept as though she hadn't slept in weeks. I looked at her peaceful face and caressed her thick brown hair. I wanted to put this moment into a glass ball to preserve and indulge in it forever.

We packed our backpacks in the morning, I paid for the hotel, and we took the vaporetto out of the city, enjoying the fine canals of Venice one last time. When Alice saw the old Astra, she burst out laughing and mocked its diarrhoea-brown colour until I threatened to make her walk to Rome. We laughed and got into the car. It had been parked in the morning sun and was baking hot inside. The old seats emitted a dry odour. Alice connected her phone to the cassette-to-aux-cord adapter and started playing The Beach Boys. In the scorching Italian sun, we crossed the Po, drove past Ferrara and Bologna, and up and down the dry hills of the Tuscan-Emilian Apennines. At noon, we drove into Florence. We had lunch inside the bustling Mercato di San Lorenzo and walked around the city centre. We visited the Basilica di San Lorenzo and Il Duomo and strolled across Piazza della Repubblica. We took awful selfies on the Ponte Santa Trinita, with the almost dried-out Arno and the Ponte Vecchio, with its mustard-coloured shops in the background. The heat was relentless, and I bought us a pair of white straw hats. We looked at our reflection in the shop window of a tobacco shop by the river and broke out in giggles at our ridiculous new style. We walked back to the car and drove on southwards through Tuscany and Lazio.

We arrived in Rome in the afternoon. Arman was living in the west of Trastevere. It took me 20 minutes to find a parking spot in a nearby backstreet. Even then, I wasn't sure whether I was allowed to park there. We put on our stylish hats and backpacks, and Alice navigated us to a big block of flats two streets away. Arman's place was on the top floor, and by the time we had climbed up to it, my shirt was soaked in sweat. Arman opened the door, only wearing pants and with his hair in a bun. He greeted us with ringing laughter and said, 'Nice hats! Come on in. My roommate is gone, so you can stay in her room.'

He led us to a room furnished with a large bed, a table with an ashtray, and a massive pile of clothes under which I suspected a chair. Alice and I dropped our backpacks, stripped to our underwear, and joined Arman in the living room. The flat was as hot as a sauna, and our skin stuck to the synthetic-leather sofa. Arman served us cold beers and asked us about Venice. He seemed nicer than I had remembered him. After Alice and I had taken a cold shower, Arman showed us around the neighbourhood. Through narrow streets of small restaurants and cafés strung together, we walked down to the Tiber. We ate some ice cream on the Isola Tiberina and had a cappuccino in a square in the north of Trastevere. The square was guarded by two soldiers with assault rifles standing in front of a heavy army vehicle. Arman told us he had once served in the Iranian special forces. Alice and I were unsure whether to believe him.

In the evening, Arman cooked aubergine stew with lamb and rice for us. Alice ate a vegetarian version. Afterwards, I mixed some Tom Collins. As midnight was approaching, Alice found an acoustic guitar in Arman's room and urged me to play for them. I sat down on a chair in the living room, with my audience slouched on the sofa. I said, 'I haven't practised in a long time. And I must warn you, I only play sad songs.'

With a beaming smile, Alice exclaimed, 'Make us cry, man!'

I tuned the guitar, cleared my throat, and began to play Chris Cornell's *Black Hole Sun*. I started off a little rusty, and some of the strings I picked sounded muffled. But soon, my hands got warm, and the notes came out clean and clear. As I sang, I didn't dare to look at Alice or Arman—the smaller the audience, the more nervous I tended to get. When I strung the last chord, they clapped and yelled. Alice exclaimed, 'Another one!'

INTO THE VOID

Arman said, 'Yeah, but wait!'

He got up, lit some candles and put them on the coffee table, and switched off the light. I played *Hurt* by Nine Inch Nails. I felt more comfortable and looked Alice in the eye as I sang. She smiled at me with an affectionate warmness I hadn't seen in her before. They urged me to go on, and I put on a capo and played The Tallest Man on Earth's *The Gardener* and Elvis Presley's *Can't Help Falling in Love*. As I sang the chorus of the latter for the last time, I challenged Alice with a stare. She held my gaze, and I could tell she was trembling. When I was finished, she swallowed and whispered, 'One more.'

Arman got up and said, 'Yeah. And I'll leave you two alone.'

Alice looked up and said, 'No, you can stay.'

'It's all right, I have to work early tomorrow. I see you in the evening . . . And don't do anything I wouldn't do.' He winked at me as he walked out of the room. Yeah, I still didn't like the guy. He shut the door behind him. I looked at Alice and asked, 'Any song requests?'

'Something painfully sad.'

I thought for a moment and said, 'Okay.'

I started playing *Hang Me, Oh Hang Me*. Alice leaned forward and stared at me. I closed my eyes as I sang the last chorus:

'Hang me, oh hang me
I'll be dead and gone
Hang me, oh hang me
I'll be dead and gone
I wouldn't mind the hangin'
But the layin' in a grave so long, poor boy
I been all around this world'

When I opened my eyes again, Alice was still looking at me. Both of us had watery eyes. She stood up, walked over to me, took away the guitar, and sat on my lap. We couldn't stop looking at each other. I was paralysed. The world stopped turning and faded away. Clocks stopped ticking. Wounds stopped bleeding. Pain stopped hurting. Love stopped withering. All that was left was Alice and me and the flickering of the candles on her face. For a moment, the universe was unsure whether its heat death was inevitable after all. Alice put her forehead against mine. We closed our eyes. She whispered, 'I'm glad I can be here with you.'

I exhaled with a smile and said, 'Me too.'

'Let's go to bed.'

We opened our eyes again, got up, and made love in the roommate's bed. A dog barked somewhere at the warm Italian night.

We walked 20 kilometres in the baking heat on Thursday. The height of the summer was the worst time to come to Rome; it was too hot, and the city was overcrowded with tourists brandishing selfie sticks. Nonetheless, it was a fine day. The Eternal City was the most impressive place I had ever seen. Everywhere, I could feel the weight of history on my shoulders. The mighty arches of the Colosseum still loomed into the blue sky, as they had been doing since they had been built by Jewish slaves and financed by Jewish spoils after the Siege of Jerusalem almost two millennia ago. The view from the Palatino onto the ruins of the ancient Forum acted as a reminder of one of the constant truths of human history: all empires must fall. The pageantry of the glaringly white Altare della Patria was a monument to the disease of nationalism that had corroded the planet in the first half of the 20th century and had caused its great catastrophes. The Pantheon was the finest building in the world. Built almost 2,000 years ago, it still stood tall in all its glory, seemingly untouched by epochs of human struggle. Alice and I walked inside and marvelled at the ornamented walls of the temple and the colossal concrete dome above. Its oculus let a beam of light illuminate the dust dancing in the air. We walked to the overrated Fontana di Trevi and followed the Tiber westwards to cross the Ponte Sant'Angelo with its angel statues to the Castel Sant'Angelo. We entered the cylindrical fortress. As we climbed the winding ramp to the top, I imagined popes rushing through secret tunnels aflame with torchlight and hastening up the same ramp, fearful of the barbarians at the gate. We used the sensational view of the Vatican for another selfie photoshoot and had a pizza for late lunch in the restaurant on the upper floor of the castle. We had an Aperol Spritz, and I blessed Alice with one of my eulogies of Sugar Ray Robinson, the greatest pound-for-pound boxer of all time. She did a poor job faking interest, and we laughed about it. We continued our walk to the Piazza del Popolo and followed the Via Condotti with its high fashion shops and the famous Caffe Greco to the Spanish Steps. We bought some sandwiches and a bottle of Chianti at a nearby kiosk and had dinner at the top of the steps. It was already dark when we crossed the Piazza della Repubblica and walked towards Roma Termini. The pungent smell of warm rubbish lay in the air. Murky figures hung around in dark corners. Alice was the only woman, and I was the only white man around. She grabbed my arm and huddled against me. Alert eyes followed us down the street. I was tense until our bus arrived and took us to Trastevere.

Arman welcomed us back into his flat, had us sit on the sofa in the living room, and offered us the joint he had just lit. As I took two deep drags, I told Arman about the dinginess of the train station area. Alice added, 'I told myself not to be afraid just because there were so many—migrant men. But I couldn't help it. I hate me for being racist.'

Arman laughed and said, 'That's not racist; it's rational! To categorise is a mechanism of survival. Foreign people are more often poor, homeless, and come from violent countries. And because of that, they're more often criminals.'

Alice silently inhaled the sweet smoke. I answered, 'You can't lump all of them together as criminals, though. Everyone deserves a chance. And, I guess, even if we might avoid them on the streets personally, as a society, we have to treat them with the benefit of the doubt.'

Arman's black full beard moved with laughter. 'Ah, I remember your political correctness, brother—the kind of political correctness that will make Italy vote for a right-wing government next year. People are fed up with being lied to.' Arman took the joint from Alice and filled his big chest with smoke.

I asked, 'What are people lied to about? And what is the alternative truth the right-wing parties offer?'

'Well, you told me yourself Europe is building a wall to keep refugees out. But they don't like to talk about it. Here's the simple truth: too many people want to get into Europe—millions and millions—more than the European welfare systems can carry. More than European citizens will accept. Once they're here, most of them either can claim legal rights to be allowed to stay, or it's too hard to figure out who has these rights. There are three solutions: You can eliminate the reasons that make the migrants leave their countries in the first place. But that's expensive and complicated and maybe impossible. You can change the laws. But this must happen out in the open and would mean a loss of face for the elites. Or you make it harder for migrants to reach the places where they can claim asylum—pay warlords and dictators to do the dirty work you're too civilised to do, and then portray yourself as just and good saviours of the few people who don't end up in prisons, barbed wire fences, or at the bottom of the sea. That's the option the politicians have chosen to tame the concerned citizens they're afraid of. But the people see through this farce, brother. They vote for the real deal that has the balls to say clearly that uncontrolled mass migration is a big problem—that it results in what you can see at Termini; crime, parallel societies, cultural tensions, anti-Semitism.'

He took another deep drag and put out the joint in the ashtray on the coffee table. I asked, 'So, what's the alternative the right-wing movements offer but a simplistic siege mentality? Most of them accept the Refugee Convention and don't offer better means to distinguish refugees from other migrants. They want to waste money on walls that don't change much or restrict free movement and cripple economic and social prosperity. All they really accomplish is sowing xenophobia and hatred.'

Arman laughed and said, 'Well, apparently, the walls the dictators have built for the EU *are* working. And you know, brother, the first step towards a solution is to call the problem by its name. And unchecked mass migration is a problem! And prioritising your fellow citizens' well-being over that of foreigners is only pragmatic. You love your family more than some random group of people somewhere in Senegal, don't you? Accepting a sense of closed community is accepting the way humans are programmed.'

'But you can't send people to their death. That defies humanism—whatever *the people* want. Democracy is not the tyranny of the majority; it also entails the protection of human rights.'

'Nobody wants to send refugees back into war zones. But why should illegal immigrants, only looking to enjoy the prosperity others have created, not be sent back to their homes? We need self-determined pursuit of happiness by sovereign nations. And protected borders between them. That's what got Trump elected, for example.'

Alice emerged from silent rigidity and shouted, 'Ugh, you can't possibly like that narcissist! He's the worst president the world has ever seen. A trained chimpanzee would do a better job than him!'

Arman chuckled and answered, 'Well, I refuse to call that idiot the worst president until he starts an unlawful war that kills millions and destabilises a whole region.'

I said, 'Yeah, let's hope that day never comes. And to be fair, even an *untrained* chimpanzee would've beaten both Trump and Clinton in a fair election by a landslide.'

We laughed and sighed. We had a couple of beers and drank to the weirdness of this world. Soon it was two in the morning, and Arman said goodnight. Nobody knew what Arman's job was in Rome, or in Stockholm, and he never told anybody. He seemed to be a man who didn't need more than four hours of sleep; he went out clubbing on weekdays regularly and got up for work early. Alice and I went to bed not long after Arman.

We continued our sightseeing tour in the muggy heat of the next morning. We queued for three hours along the lofty walls of Vatican City for a guided tour through its museums. The tour was expensive, the guide seemed lackadaisical, and we were herded through the corridors like cattle. But the visit was still mesmerising. The sheer density of art and history in the Vatican's collection was mind-boggling; exploiting the world for almost two millennia in the name of God had to be good for something. That day, I laid my eyes on some of the most beautiful objects I had ever seen. In the shade of the arches of an open courtyard, *Laocoön and His Sons* contorted their faces with pain, as they had been doing for the last 2,000 years. Raphael's *The School of Athens* was one of the Renaissance's finest pieces of art. In it, Plato—the giant of Western philosophy—points to the sky, to the divine, while Aristotle, Plato's only peer, puts out his hand towards the ground, to perceived reality. The awe-inspiring frescos in the Sistine Chapel were only spoiled by humourless guards constantly screaming to enforce silence. The colossal St. Peter's Basilica made me feel minute—not only in size but also in significance and permanence. I had to drag Alice out from under the dome, her head tilted back, fixated on the golden firmament. We walked across Piazza San Pietro, past the ancient Egyptian obelisk gleaming in the relentless sun. Back on Italian soil, I took off my jeans and switched into shorts. Alice laughed at me standing in my underwear in the middle of the pavement as she got out of the blouse she had worn over her long white summer dress. We crossed the Tiber over the Ponte Vittorio Emanuele II, took a detour across Piazza Navona with its fine fountains, and had pizza and a cold beer for late lunch outside a nearby restaurant. While we strolled around the Campo de' Fiori market, Alice complained that she had left her sunglasses in Sweden. The lowering sun was glaring into her eyes. I told her to buy a pair from one of the countless street vendors. She raised her hands and said, 'No, I'm horrible at bargaining!'

'Okay, let's walk past some of them, and if you see some you like, I'll buy them for you.'

She agreed, and we browsed through the assortment of illegal vendors lined up in an alley emanating from the square. Alice pointed to a pair of fake round Ray-Bans, with a brown leopard-print frame, on one of the folding tables. Getting caught with counterfeit goods in Italy could lead to a hefty fine, but I guessed that rarely ever happened. I stepped towards the table. The merchant was wrapped in a long white gown and heavy wooden bead chains. He also sold 'original' Prada handbags and Cartier jewellery. I pointed at the glasses and asked, 'How much?'

He beamed at me. 'Special price, 50 euros.'

I laughed as Alice grabbed my hand. I felt her nervousness, which made me laugh even harder. The merchant asked, 'Where are you from?'

Alice answered with a smile, 'I'm from Sweden.'

The merchant shouted with a wide grin, 'Oh, Sweden? Beautiful! I have a cousin in Sweden!'

'What a coincidence,' I said with a sarcastic tone. He didn't let his smile diminish and said, 'Special price for my Swedish friend, 35 euros.'

I laughed again and said, 'I'll give you five.'

He shook his head emphatically and shouted, 'Impossible! I pay much more when I buy! 30?'

I said, 'I know you don't pay more than three, so five is a good offer.'

The merchant shook his head, said, 'No, no, no,'

but then smiled at Alice and said, 'Try it on!'

Alice complied and switched her nerdy glasses for the sunglasses. She looked at herself in the mirror. The glasses fit her perfectly. She looked beautiful. Alice gleamed and said, 'I love them.' Bad move.

The merchant exclaimed, '25 euros!'

I took the glasses from Alice's face and put them back on the table. 'That's too expensive.' I took Alice by the hand and turned away from the table.

The merchant exclaimed, '20 euros! Lowest price.'

I turned around, two steps away from the table, and looked at him. I stepped back towards it, took out a ten-euro bill, and put it on the table. I said, 'I'll give you ten euros, although they're only worth five— because you're a nice guy. But not more.'

He shook his head violently and said, '15. And I lose money!'

I tapped the bill on the table with my index finger and said, 'Ten or nothing.'

He tilted his head, his smile gone. I picked up the bill and took a step back. Alice was paralysed with tension beside me. The merchant took a deep breath and sighed, 'Okay.'

I handed him the money, and he gave the glasses to Alice, who immediately put them on. They reflected my blissful smile as I looked at her. She gave me a long, dizzying kiss and laughed in relief. I asked, 'Don't you need your glasses to see?'

'No, they're non-prescription.' She grinned. 'This probably sounds silly, but I just like the idea of having glasses.' She looked around curiously. 'These sunglasses give the world a warm orange glow. I like that.'

Hand in hand, we walked to the botanical gardens on the other side of the river, where we lay on the grass in the shade. I had brought both our books in a small backpack of Arman's. Alice was reading a book called *Det förlorade barnet* by an Italian author, and I finished *Catch-22*. Later, we hiked up to the Terrazza del Gianicolo, where we enjoyed one of the best views Rome had to offer. It only took us ten minutes to climb back down to Arman's flat. He wasn't home yet. We were hungry and cooked some pasta with pesto verde. Arman came home from work while I was eating my second plate, and he ate the rest. Alice opened a bottle of Prosecco she had discovered in the fridge. When Arman and I were finished, I put the dirty dishes in the kitchen sink and jumped into the shower. As I let the refreshing lukewarm water run down my body, I sang Peter Sarstedt's *Where Do You Go To (My Lovely)?* I forgot the time, and my fingers were wrinkly when I stepped out of the bathtub. I saw in the mirror that the bruise around my eye had faded to a faint yellow. I dried myself off and wrapped the towel around my waist. When I walked into the dimly lit living room, Alice was lying face down on the sofa, naked from the waist up. Arman—dressed only in black shorts—was sitting on her bum and giving her a massage. On the table were now two bottles of Prosecco—one of them empty—and a couple of candles stuck in gin bottles. How long had I been showering? And what the hell was going on? I suppressed the urge to punch Arman in the mouth and tried to play it cool by saying, 'I'm ready for a massage now, too.'

They both looked up at me, standing there with only a white towel on. Alice chuckled and said, 'You have to have one; Arman has magic hands!'

I took a glass and filled it to the brim with Prosecco, drained it, and filled another. As I emptied my third glass, Alice jumped up, sat on an armchair by the window, and lit a joint. She was only wearing white knickers. The light of the setting sun fell on her breasts and danced in the billows of smoke around her head. The excruciating beauty of Alice in the Italian dusk would never be surpassed by all the pieces of art Pope Francis could amass in his little private collection. I felt like weeping. Instead, I followed Arman's instructions to lie on the sofa. He sat his hairy, bulky body down on me and started massaging me. He said, 'Damn, you're tense! You have to relax more, brother.' I was trying to. And, after a while, I did. His hands *were* magic. When Arman was finished, my back felt like jelly. I was still jealous of Arman seeing and touching Alice's naked skin. But by what right was that any of my business? Alice and Arman were rather stoned, and we decided to watch a film. Arman and I slouched on the sofa, and Alice lay on top of us—her legs in his lap, her head in mine. They soon fell asleep and thus missed me tearing up at the end of *The Constant Gardener*. When they woke up, Alice and I went to bed. We wanted to have sex, but for the first time in my life, I couldn't get it up. Instead, I licked her until she came—or at least pretended to. I still felt miserable and apologised. Alice stroked my face fondly and said, 'No need to apologise. It's been a long day. Don't worry about it.' She turned away and fell asleep. I lay awake for a long time, worrying about it.

I woke up early on Saturday morning and made breakfast for the three of us. When we had finished eating, I got the car, and Alice packed our things. We put the backpacks into the boot, and Arman lent us a tent, gas cooker and lamp, and camping chairs and table. Since Alice flew to Sweden from Rome, we had to get back in a week. I would then drive to Marseille.

When we had carried all the stuff up from the basement, I thanked Arman for letting us stay with him.
He gave us brawny goodbye hugs and told us to behave. We jumped into the car, and I started the old
Astra. We followed the claustrophobic brick-walled
streets across the hill to the west and turned onto Via
Aurelia, which the enterprising Romans had built 240
years before Christ. In the suburbs of Rome, orange
buildings hid from the sun behind pine and palm
trees. Sweating pedestrians moved slowly on the
dusty pavements. The car's thermometer showed 33
degrees. It was only ten o'clock. Outside the city, the
dry fields lay idle and burnt to a bone-white deadness.
On our way to the coast, the slopes of the motorway
had been turned to black ash by wildfires. The road
never quite reached the sea, but behind glimmering
hills and brick-red villages, sometimes an auspicious,
deep-blue band emerged for a moment. Alice never
failed to point it out to me with sincere excitement.

After we had covered half the journey, we took a
detour to Porto Santo Stefano on the northwestern
promontory of Monte Argentario. The heat was blazing, and even the wind coming in through the open
windows was sweltering. Alice's hair danced around
her new sunglasses in the turbulence as we followed
the road into the peninsula. I parked the car next to
the promenade, and we walked along the water to the
small marina of Porto Santo Stefano. In front of a
narrow shingle beach, small sailing boats and yachts
rocked calmly in the azure water of the bay. Hotels in
pastel colours stood along the semicircular waterfront. Behind them rose the slopes of Monte Argentario, dappled with orange houses and dark-green
trees. We sat beneath the sunshades of a restaurant by
the water and ate penne all'arrabbiata for lunch. The

sparkling water sloshed rhythmically against the quay. I had an ice-cold Aperol Spritz before we left. The car had been parked in the midday sun and was boiling. Alice wanted to drive the rest of the way. I watched her as she steered the car back onto Via Aurelia and followed it northwards. She sat markedly erect and focused on the traffic in front of her. I couldn't stop looking at her queenlike profile and probably smiled like an idiot.

North of Grosseto, the meadows became greener. Signs of bushfires disappeared. We got off the motor-way after Cecina and drove through olive groves and pine tree espaliers to the small town of Vada. The first camping ground we visited was fully booked. But the second, Rada Etrusca, still had a small vacant pitch, only separated from the beach by a cane fence. Alice parked the car, and we started building Arman's sun-bleached red tent in the sparse shade of an olive tree. Sweat ran down my face. The tent was old and had many poles of different lengths. It took us quite some time to puzzle out the structure. When I tried to hang up the inner cabin, I entangled myself in one of the cords and stumbled to the ground inside the tent. Alice laughed and jumped on top of me. We rolled around, getting more tangled up, and couldn't stop laughing. Covered in sweat, we kissed, disentangled ourselves, and figured out the rest of the tent together. It was a big tent with two inner cabins, high enough for me to stand upright inside. I set up the table and chairs and hung a clothesline between two trees by the fence. Alice unpacked the rest of the car into one of the cabins. Arman had also given us a tarpaulin, which put up as an awning above the table. When we were finished, we sat down in its shade, gulped half a bottle of water, and poured the rest over our heads.

After our *pennichella*, an afternoon nap, in the merciful shade, we went grocery shopping in the small supermarket on the campsite. We cooked pasta with tomato sauce over the gas cooker and shared a bottle of Chianti. We washed the dishes together in a sink in one of the nearby shower blocks and took a barefoot walk along the beach at sunset. Other couples promenaded on the beach, and groups of children worked on their sandcastles in the last rays of the sun. I pulled Alice towards me and kissed her forehead. She took a deep breath of the sea air and said, 'It's beautiful here.' I kissed her and relaxed, as though for the first time in years. Alice took my hand, and we walked back to the campsite, to the little roofed outdoor bar. When I ordered two gin and tonics, I overheard the two tanned guys behind the counter talking in Italian about Connor McGregor and Floyd Mayweather; I had forgotten about their fight. I asked the bartenders, 'Will you watch the fight tonight?'

One of the guys answered, 'Yes. We watch it here.' He was a handsome young man with long dark hair, wearing a white lifeguard T-shirt and red shorts. He pointed to the flat screen on the wall beside the bar. 'Do you want to join us?'

'When does it start?'

The other bartender said, 'They start showing it at three, but the match will not start before five, I think.'

'Okay. I'll come here at 4:30 then.'

'Cool.' He handed me my drinks. '*Prego*. Ten euros, please.'

I handed him 15 and said, 'See you later.'

I returned to our table and asked Alice whether she wanted to join me in watching the fight tonight.

'No, I'd rather sleep than watch two men pointlessly punch each other,' she answered.

I chuckled and said, 'Well, these two men are scheduled to earn more than 100 million dollars, so for them, it might not be quite so pointless. I mean, yeah, it's mostly a spectacle to make tons of money. But a fight between the greatest pound-for-pound boxer of his generation against the notorious madman of martial arts—what's not to like?'

'Who do you think is going to win?' Alice politely tried to pretend interest.

'Floyd is probably the best defensive boxer of all time. And Connor is hardly a boxer. So, everything but an easy win for the boxer in a boxing match would be a major upset. But who knows with these two?'

Alice sipped her drink and nodded. I laughed and said, 'Sorry, I don't want to bore you.'

Alice said, 'No, it's super interesting who punches who in the face somewhere far away.' She smirked at me mischievously.

I chuckled and said, 'Screw you.'

We both laughed and sipped our gin and tonics. We were both tired. After we had finished our drinks, we went back to our tents, brushed our teeth, and fell asleep on our sleeping mats to the sound of the sea.

My alarm rang at 4:30. I tried to mute it as quickly as possible so as not to disturb Alice and our neighbours. I put on shorts, a T-shirt, and a pullover and slouched in my sandals along the gravel pathway back to the bar. The two Italian guys from before and two of their friends greeted me with wide grins and offered me a seat and a beer. The handsome lifeguard asked, 'Where's your girlfriend?'

'She's sleeping.'

The other guy from the bar handed me a shot of Ramazotti and said, 'To a good fight!'

We touched glasses and turned to the TV. We

watched the undercard matches and had another round of beers. In a grand Sin City spectacle, Connor McGregor stepped into the ring in white trunks, with an Irish flag around his neck, and Floyd 'Money' Mayweather walked into the arena with a black ski mask covering his face. As the Italian night morphed into dawn and the first campers drowsily made their way to the bathrooms, the big fight finally started. The opening bell rang, and McGregor rushed towards Mayweather in his southpaw stance and started the first attack of the night. The Irishman had a distance advantage and stretched his lead hand out into Mayweather's face. Connor fought explosively, but Floyd elegantly slipped and deflected most of the punches. However, the boxer appeared a little slower than in his earlier fights; he was 40 years old, after all. Near the end of the first round, Connor landed a clean uppercut on Floyd's chin—we had ourselves a fight. As the fight went on, Floyd became more aggressive than usual and walked Connor around the ring, fatiguing the Irishman. Connor often tried to grab Floyd and repeatedly hit the back of the boxer's head. He wasn't used to boxing rules, and the referee often had to step in to keep him in check. By the fifth round, Floyd's vicious precision started wearing Connor down, who was often hitting thin air and suffering quick right counterpunches landing flush in his face. In the seventh, eighth, and ninth round, a surprisingly aggressive Floyd became ever more dominant over the exhausted Irishman, throwing right hand after relentless right hand. Floyd was in total control. In the tenth round, Floyd punched Connor up and down the ring. Connor wobbled around and hung on the ropes, his arms dangling, his eyes rolling. The referee stepped in and waved his arms—technical knockout. The fight was over. Mayweather now had a 50-and-0 record, breaking Rocky Marciano's 49-and-0 that had stood for 60 years. The guy might have been an arrogant idiot outside of the ring, but inside it, he was easily the greatest boxer of his era.

I thanked the bar guys and walked back to our tent. The sun was already sending its first warm rays through the olive grove by our site. Muffled children's voices floated in the soft morning air. I opened the zip of our cabin, got into my sleeping bag and snuggled up to Alice. She greeted me with a cute sigh and asked, 'How was the fight?'

'Better than I'd expected.'

'Good.'

She was already asleep again.

By nine, it became too hot in the tent, and we got up. Alice headed for the supermarket, and I went for a short run on the beach. It was already hot in the sun. At the end, I jumped into the refreshing morning waves and had a quick cold shower. Alice and I had bread rolls with marmalade and honey and coffee for breakfast. We went to the beach, where we wore the ugly white straw hats from Florence with pride. We laid our towels in the shade of the sun umbrella Alice had bought at the shop. The broad white beach sloped very shallowly into the azure water. We went for a swim and then sat crosslegged on the seabed, a stone's throw away from the shore. Our heads and shoulders stuck out of the water. The waves tenderly rocked us back and forth. I asked Alice, 'What's the most impressive sea animal you've ever seen?'

Alice, her eyes closed, smiled into the sun and said, 'Hmm, that's a tough question.' She brushed her wet hair out of her face and continued, 'Two years ago, I was on an expedition in Alaska and went on a research vessel on the Bering Sea. It was winter. The sea was rough, and the spray froze in icicles on the railing and the chains. One morning, the sun rises and sparkles on the ice shelf along the horizon, and it makes a glittering miracle out of our ship. Below us, the sea is raging and sends icy spray across the deck. And there, in front of us, a group of bowhead whales surfaces and blows air out of their blowholes into the freezing air. Bowhead whales live the longest among all mammals on earth. They can probably get to more than 200 years old! I remember their colossal dark bodies floating through the rough sea—like calm anchors in the chaos. I felt so small in the presence of these majestic creatures.'

Alice still had her eyes closed, raising her chin towards the sun. She was beautiful. Suddenly, she opened her eyes, turned to me with a bright giggle, and tried to push my head under water. We wrestled in the knee-deep water and then ran towards our towels, laughing and panting. I was tired from the short night and fell asleep on the beach, the sun drying my skin while I lay on my stomach. When I woke up, I heard children's voices, damped by the heavy, warm air. Alice was talking to a man with a thick African accent. I turned on my back and opened my eyes. Alice was talking to one of the beach merchants. 'This is Amaechi from Nigeria,' Alice introduced him.

'Hello, Amaechi from Nigeria.'

The merchant had pitch-black skin and wore jeans, a long collared white shirt, and a red baseball cap. He knelt on Alice's towel, a portable wooden shelf laden with watches and bracelets next to him. He gave me a wide smile and said, 'Hi! How are you doing?'

'Good. Hungry, though,' I said and turned to Alice.

She said, 'Yes, I'm hungry, too. Do you want something to eat, Amaechi?'

He looked at both of us and said, 'No. Thank you! I have food.'

'Are you sure? We have sandwiches.'

'Yes. Thank you. I get back to work now. Goodbye, my friends.' He smiled at us sheepishly, got up, and left.

Alice and I packed our beach things and walked back to our camping site. We had lunch and spent the afternoon dozing on our mattresses in the shade, talking about our first jobs. Alice had worked as a waitress in Gothenburg when she was 17, to save for her big trip to Congo. When I was 16, I had spent a summer working at an automated drilling machine in a magnet factory to pay for my first Fender electric guitar. I still remembered the pungent alkaline smell of cutting fluid on my hands and the content tiredness after a day of productive physical labour. Mockingly, Alice recommended I should go back to the factory if I couldn't make up my mind what I wanted to do with my life. Maybe I should; at least it had been honest work.

In the evening, we went to a fine fish restaurant by the marina in Vada. Alice ate mushroom risotto. We were back in our tent by nine. Alice put The Smiths on her phone, and we started undressing and kissing each other. When I slipped my hand into her knickers, Alice grabbed my hand and said, 'I'm on my period.'

'Okay. We—'

She shut me up with a kiss, smiled at me, and whispered, 'Keep standing.' She knelt before me on the air mattress, pulled down my boxers, and said, 'Close your eyes.'

Soon, waves of joy ran through my body. Her

tongue felt maddeningly good. I was wrapped in a
tight warmth. When I looked down, I saw Alice deep-
throating my dick, her eyes closed, her lips touching
my balls. Her movements came straight out of a porn
movie, but her passionate devotion gave them a tender, almost innocent quality. A streetlamp outside our
tent cast a faint red light on her face. When I touched
her hair, she quickened her movements. My knees
trembled. I felt her smiling. Just when I thought my
ecstasy was at its peak, Alice put one hand between
my legs and started massaging my anus. Taken by
surprise, I opened my eyes wide and couldn't suppress an enraptured moan. My hands followed the
hypnotic back-and-forth of her head. Every muscle in
my body tensed up, and a million sparks of satis-
faction set me on fire as I came. Stars danced in the
air, and my legs gave out. I collapsed onto the floor. I
lay there panting, and Alice clung to my body. As Alice
kissed me, The Smiths sang, 'Give up to lust, oh
heaven knows we'll soon be dust . . . ' I ran my hand
through Alice's hair. She tenderly stroked my chest.
The cool polyester of my sleeping bag rubbed against
the skin on my legs. Behind the cane fence, the
Mediterranean Sea rushed placidly against the white
beach.

On Monday, we drove inland to the medieval moun-
taintop ramparts of Volterra. Under the midday sun,
we wandered through the old town's cobbled streets,
gazing up at sandy-brown medieval churches and
down onto ruins of Roman theatres baking in the
heat. Alice had someone take a picture of us with the
auburn rooftops of Volterra hovering over the beige
Tuscan plains in the background. She made a point of
putting on the shades I had bought her in Rome

before the picture was taken. She said they were the best pair of sunglasses she had ever had. On the way back to the sea, we stopped at a shopping mall and bought food and red wine for the rest of the week.

After a short swim back at the campsite, we cooked spaghetti aglio e olio and split a bottle of Chianti. We went for Negronis at the camping bar. When the handsome bartender brought our drinks to our little table, Alice said, '*Grazie*, Giulio!'

He gave her a wide grin and said, '*Prego*, Alice!'

When he had walked back to the bar, I chuckled and asked Alice, 'How do you know his name?'

'Giulio? Oh, I ran into him yesterday morning, and we chatted a little bit. He's a nice guy.'

'Yeah, he's all right.'

Alice chuckled and said, 'Giulio told me you kept telling them all the technical details of boxing during the match.'

I smiled and said, 'Yeah, I guess that sounds like me.' I took a deep sip of my Negroni and a long look at Alice. Her sundried hair had curled up in thick, dark-brown tresses. Her skin was getting more tanned by the day. My eyes rested on the little mole on her chin which I had grown to love.

A smile wrinkled her ripe cheeks as she asked, 'What are you looking at?'

I smiled and said, 'You.'

'Do you like what you see?' She turned her face into the light with a lofty expression.

'Yes. You are beautiful, Alice.'

She smiled, looked down at the table and whispered, 'Thank you.'

After Giulio brought us another round, I said to Alice, 'I was wondering . . . How many boyfriends have you had?'

Alice raised her eyebrows. 'You were wondering? Hmm . . . Two, I guess.' She hesitated. 'They weren't good experiences.' She took a thirsty gulp from her drink.

'Why not?'

'I—I met the first one in high school. He was—well, it—it's complicated.' She took another long sip from her drink. 'And during my bachelor, I was in a longer relationship with a Scottish guy. I think he's still a rugby player . . . Well, he couldn't stop cheating on me. And in the end, that dirtbag—' She paused and took a deep breath. 'Let's just say that I'm not very lucky when it comes to relationships, okay? What are they good for, anyway?'

She emptied her glass with another long sip and looked away. I leaned over to her and stroked her cheek. Alice smiled, tenderly. The alcohol had made her eyes bleary. We sat there in silence. The bar began to empty. Giulio sat down at our table and put a glass of Ramazotti in front of each of us. He smiled his handsome lifeguard smile. We touched glasses and drank. Alice asked Giulio, 'Do you only work here for the summer?'

Giulio uttered a sad chuckle and said, 'I don't know. I started here in April. My uncle got me the job. He works as a gardener here.' He paused with a shake of his head. 'You probably think I'm the dumb bar boy. I actually have a degree in business administration. But there are no jobs for us young people.'

'Is it that bad in Italy?' Alice asked.

'The youth unemployment rate is one-third. I have family in Greece—there, it's half!' Giulio sighed. 'I feel like my whole generation is lost. Everyone is leaving or giving up.'

I asked, 'Do you want to leave?'

'I'd hate to leave my family—my country. I love Italy. But I won't work as a lifeguard and barkeeper for the rest of my life, you know? If I don't find anything this winter, I go to Denmark. One of my friends moved there. He says work there is like holidays, and everybody gets a good job.' Giulio gazed gloomily into the distance. He got up and said, '*Ragazzi*, I'm tired. It was a long day. Sleep well.'

'Goodnight, Giulio,' Alice said and smiled at him with warm sympathy. We watched him carry our glasses back to the bar with sagging shoulders.

As we walked back to our tent along the dark gravel pathway, Alice said, 'I feel bad for him . . . And why are Italy and Greece doing so badly when the north of Europe is thriving?'

I stifled a tired yawn and said, 'I guess it's complicated. But being forced into austerity and trapped in a currency union without much fiscal solidarity probably doesn't help.'

Alice sighed and whispered, more to herself than to me, 'Why does everything always have to be so complicated?' Her words came out in a sulky, childlike slur.

We brushed our teeth in the isolated light of a shower block, Alice leaning on my shoulder, looking at our beat reflections in the mirror. A cool breeze was blowing from the sea, and we were happy to muffle ourselves up in our sleeping bags. When Alice fell asleep, she started snoring. I hadn't known snoring could sound cute. I fantasised about beating up beefy Scottish rugby players, before falling asleep.

The next day, we went swimming in the morning and took a little yellow street train to the market in the centre of Cecina. The train was made of a converted pick-up truck, resembling a steam locomotive, towing three open carriages. Along one of the main streets of Cecina, we walked underneath the market stalls' sunshades between a potpourri of vegetables, pastries, meat, sausages, fish, seafood, cheese, olives, antipasti, fabrics, beach toys, bathing gear, football shirts, watches, jewellery, mobile phone accessories, and souvenirs. The air between the stalls was sweaty and smelled of fish, garlic, salt, and wet armpits. We walked to the beach along the promenade and had a dry pizza and an Americano by the sea.

Back at our campsite, we spent a relaxed afternoon on the white beach. On the hot sand, I taught Alice the basics of boxing—how to move her feet and keep on her toes, how to always keep her hands up, how to give a punch power from her hips, and how to anticipate and counter some common attacks. I made her throw her fists at my hands and dared her to hit my face while I slipped her punches. When I heard tropical house music playing, I turned my head and saw an ice cream beach buggy driving by. I looked back at Alice and started to ask whether she wanted to get some ice cream but was interrupted by her fist landing flush on my nose. I uttered a surprised grunt and took a step back. Alice threw her hands up and shouted, 'Sorry! Sorry! Sorry!', unable to suppress her laughter. I put my hands on my nose and started laughing, too. Then, I kept still and gave her a grim gaze. She stopped laughing, looked at me with raised eyebrows, and bit on her roguish grin. I approached her with raised fists and laughed villainously. She turned around and started running, giggling and screaming, 'No, please!' I caught up to her at the shore, lifted her up by her waist and carried her into the water. We turned our boxing match into a tickling fight in the waist-deep water, then calmed down on our beach towels in the heavy afternoon sun.

For dinner, we had ciabatta with olives, pickled artichokes, and sundried tomatoes. We drank two bottles of a rich Montepulciano. Cicadas chirped in the bushes behind the cane fence. We played Yahtzee in the flickering light of the little gas lamp on our camping table until going to sleep at 11.

That night, my dreams carried me back to Prague. I stood on the cobblestones of Old Town Square, in the shade of the Old Town Hall. Flocks of bustling tourists surrounded me. Nicole stood in front of the bed of red flowers by the Jan Hus Memorial. I waved at her. She looked happy. When I walked over to her, I suddenly heard screeching tyres and screams of agonising pain. A white lorry ploughed through the crowd. It crashed into my little sister and ran her over. The sound of splintering bones paralysed me. Nicole's legs stuck out from under one of the lorry's tyres and twitched mechanically. I opened my mouth in anguish. Silence. Blood rained down from a red sky burned by a gleaming purple sun. A faceless man in black stepped out of the car and pointed his assault rifle at me. A shot. White light. A scream.

I was in our tent, sitting on my mattress, soaked in cold sweat. I saw Alice in the faint light next to me. She put her hand on my head and whispered, 'It's okay. It was just a dream.'

I was panting. 'Sorry for waking you up.'

'It's okay . . . What did you dream?'

'About a terror attack. He killed my little sister.'

Alice gently put her hand on my sweaty cheek and whispered in her mellow voice, 'Let's go back to sleep. It was just a bad dream.'

'Yeah, I'm okay, don't worry.'

Alice stroked my chest as I lay back down and relaxed. Soon, I fell asleep again. Sleep—the blissful cousin of death.

Alice was already outside when I woke up. I pulled up the zip of the cabin and stepped out into the crisp, clear morning. Alice had already been to the supermarket and was sitting at the table. 'What do we have for breakfast?' I asked.

'Ciabatta with Nutella!'

'Nice. The breakfast of champions.'

'And then we'll go to the beach for some yoga in the morning sun. It will be good for us to relax.'

'Sounds great!'

'And how is your nose?'

I answered her mischievous grin by shaking my head with a chuckle and said, 'Quite good. Feels like a little fly might have hit it yesterday.'

'That's so funny. But you know, you should always keep your guard up.'

'You seem to have had a gifted teacher.'

'Maybe I'm a gifted student. And now eat; you'll need it—I hear the yoga class will be brutal!'

We started the yoga session with some breathing exercises. Then, Alice more or less successfully tried to bend my stiff body into the correct poses. She rewarded my efforts with a brief massage. I was glad Alice didn't ask me to take any sunrise yoga pictures of her for social media. The morning sun was already warm enough to drive us into the azure water.

After a light lunch, we drove again up to Volterra, but this time further inland to the medieval towers of the hill town of San Gimignano. Its red skyline, marked by a dozen towers looming into the Tuscan sky, stood out from the dry, green, undulating land-scape. We wandered through the steep, narrow alleys of the old town and visited small shops selling wine, cheese, ham, and medieval weaponry. In the middle of town lay a square with herringbone-patterned red cobblestones, an old cistern in the middle, and apparently two of the world's best ice cream parlours. We couldn't choose which one to go to, so we both had two delicious cones. We sat outside one of the square's bars and had a digestive Negroni. Underneath the bar's sun umbrellas hung small devices spraying cold mist, giving the air a moist coolness. The square was surrounded by some of San Gimignano's towers, which had been erected by competing medieval fami-lies, each building higher and higher towards the sun. We ordered a glass of the region's white wine. Alice was on her phone, texting friends, while I imagined building a tower towards the deep-blue Italian sky. Before long, it was time for dinner. We were lucky to get a small table in a nearby osteria and ate a good pizza. Alice had some red wine and told me stories of diving trips with her parents to Asia.

It was dark when we got back to the car and started driving. Alice soon fell asleep in the passenger seat. I listened to Miles Davis' monumental modal album *Kind of Blue*. Miles' relentless trumpet calmly climbed down into dry valleys and ecstatically ascended breathless heights, drawing dancing neon shapes on the dark Tuscan hills around us. The campsite lay calm by the sea when we arrived. It was a mild night, and the sound of the sea soon rocked us to sleep in our cool sleeping bags.

We spent the next day at the beach. By now, Alice and I were both tanned enough to no longer be at risk of getting sunburnt, so long as we put on some sun-screen. The smell of sun cream, fresh sweat, and sand on Alice's warm skin embodied summer. The small world map tattoo on her shoulder shone in the sun—so many places to go, so many secrets to discover. Alice went for a long swim. When she came back, she sat on my back and let cold water drip on my skin. I flinched and turned around. Alice ran her cold hands over my chest and read the small, round fire scars on my belly with her deft, graceful fingers. 'These aren't from stumbling into a campfire, are they?'

I exhaled. 'No.'

'What happened?'

I sat up, resting on my elbows, and looked out over the calm sea. 'Well, when I was a baby, my addict biological father would put out cigarettes on my belly to punish me for crying too much.'

Alice stroked my cheek and said, 'That's horrible. Did someone protect you from him? I mean, did your mum do something about it?'

I chuckled sarcastically and said, 'My biological mother was out loitering behind the train station—selling her body for drug money.'

Alice looked at me with warm compassion. 'You call them your "biological" parents; were you taken away from them?'

I breathed out audibly. My throat was dry. I felt a little dizzy. I thought of the police report I had forced myself to read when I had been 18. I looked into Alice's deep-brown eyes and said, 'Although my bio-logical father depended on the money it made, he hated his wife prostituting herself. One day, he tells her, if she leaves for *work* today, he'll kill her. But she needs a fix and has no money. So, she puts on her short skirt and push-up bra and storms out of the rubbish-strewn flat. He follows her into the stairwell with a long kitchen knife and screams at her to go back inside. They yell at each other so loudly that all the neighbours can hear them; the neighbours are used to it. She calls him a hypocrite, an honourless dog. She knows he's sold his body before to get a fix. She calls him an impotent junkie. At least her punters will be able to please her.' I hesitated. 'My father drives the knife into her chest, deep into her heart—so violently that the blade comes out in the back again and breaks off the handle. She falls down the stairs, dead.'

Alice stared at me with big eyes and exclaimed, 'Oh my god!'

I nodded with clenched teeth and said, 'Yeah. When the police came, they found my biological father stooping over her body, weeping like a child, the knife handle still in his hands. I was upstairs in my dirty crib, as quiet as a mouse. My mum—my mother's sister, technically—came to pick me up. That night, she cleaned her own sister's blood off the stairs. Back home, she and her husband stood next to the crib they had brought up from the basement for me. My dad told me I was lying there, looking at him—not crying, just looking straight at him. He called a lawyer he knew from boxing that same night to help them adopt me . . . My real parents raised me. They were there for me when I was a shy kid getting bullied in school and when I was a drunk teenager getting into fights. My biological parents gave me nothing but their cursed genes—and some scars.'

Alice leaned down and gave me a long, tender kiss. Only now did I notice I had started crying. I tried to smile. Alice ran her fingers through my hair and asked, 'What happened to your "biological father"?

Have you seen him again?'

'He hanged himself in his cell two days after he was convicted of manslaughter.'

Tears ran down my cheek. Alice said, 'I'm sorry.'

'Don't be. You know, I'm not crying for those dead addicts. I'm sad because I never got to tell my dad how much I'm thankful for what he did for me. He accepted the rotten fruit of his wife's vile relatives as his own son. He taught me how to box.' I smiled. 'He would always cheer so vigorously during my fights. Back then, it embarrassed me. He wouldn't sit down for the whole fight, jumping around the ring, getting warned by the referee to calm down. After the fights, he always took me to a steak restaurant. "You need protein, son!" We didn't talk much. But I think he was proud of me back then.'

'I'm sure he was. And I'm sure he would be proud of you now as well.'

'For what? I disappointed him. He always told me that most important in life are the people you love. That you must be there for them, no matter what. I was never there for my parents. I thought they were narrow-minded, dull people not worth my time. I wasn't there for my dad when he died, which hurt my mum more than I could ever make up for. They would've been better off without me and should've left me in that dirty crib.'

'Don't say that! You know that's not true.'

'It doesn't matter now. My mum hasn't talked to me for more than two years.' Alice touched my cheek, softly. I turned away from her and looked out over the azure Mediterranean Sea. The sun gave its waves a hypnotic sparkle. My limbs felt heavy in the heat. I turned back to Alice and said, 'I'm hungry. Do you want to eat?'

'Nutella sandwiches?' She beamed.

I chuckled and said, 'Sure.'

We packed up our stuff and walked back to our tent for lunch. After a *pennichella* in the shade of the olive tree, we went to the camping bar where we shared a copy of *The Guardian* Giulio had bought for me in the city and had two rounds of Aperol Spritzes.

At night, we sat at the camping table next to our tent and rolled the dice. After Alice had calmed down after celebrating another Yahtzee, I asked her, 'Do you want to have a family someday?'

Her surprised face flickered in the light of the gas lamp. 'Hmm, I'm not really convinced by that whole monogamy concept.' I felt a slight sting. She continued, 'But I do want to have children. I want to raise children.' She smiled at me and asked, 'And you?'

'Well, while I *am* convinced by "that whole monogamy concept", sometimes I'm not sure whether it's right to bring a person into this wretched world.'

'What do you mean? Do you think life is that bad?'

'Don't get me wrong, I think it's possible to be happy sometimes. But life entails so much struggle, so much pain. And in the end, we all die alone. I'm not sure whether it's fair to burden an innocent being with all that pain.'

'But joy can only exist if there's pain! And can't struggle be joy? Isn't life's uncertainty, the infinite abundance of opportunity, what makes life worth living?'

'I don't know, uncertainty can also be crippling.' I sighed. 'Who am I to throw another human into the utter meaningless of life?'

'But don't you want to live? Don't you choose life over nonexistence every day?'

'Yeah, but that's my programming. I'm not sure

whether someone devoid of the blind will to survive that evolution taught us would choose the pain of life over the bliss of obliviousness.'

'Oh man, you think too much!' Alice chuckled.

I said, 'Probably. And that's the next thing; even if I wanted kids, I guess I wouldn't be able to take good care of them. I'm having a hard time keeping just my own shit together. And besides, I don't even know whether my genes should live on. Maybe they should die with my cursed parents and me.'

'Oh, enough with that cursed-genes bullshit already! Your social interactions determine who you'll become. I mean, you didn't turn out *completely* bungled.' Her frown turned into a warm smile. 'I think you would be a good father.'

'Thanks, that's very kind of you to say.' I leaned forward over the table and said, 'Hey, do you want to go to the bar and drink irresponsible amounts of alcohol to our competence as potential parents?'

Alice laughed and exclaimed, 'Sure!'

We sat at the camping bar where Giulio was working and had four or five drinks. Shortly before midnight, we danced back to our tent. We made plans to have a family of 12 somewhere in the Swiss Alps.

Lying in my sleeping bag, I had trouble sleeping that night. When Alice woke up and noticed I was awake, she turned to me and stroked my chest. In her sleepy, mellow voice, she whispered, 'Are you okay?'

'Yeah. It's just . . . What I told you about my bio-logical parents today . . . I rarely tell anybody about that.' Indeed, I had only ever told Emma. 'And I also try not to think about it. I try to forget that part of me.'

'Hey, it's not something to be ashamed of. You were so young then. Focus on making things right with your real family instead.'

I saw her shining smile in the half-light of the street lamp. It was still warm inside the tent, and she had pulled the sleeping bag only up to her waist. I kissed the black rose between her breasts. I could still taste the salt from the sea on her soft skin. A warm tingle filled my body. Alice stroked my hair and turned around on her pillow. Soon, her breath became calm and slow. With a smile on my lips, I fell asleep as well.

The next day, we had a long walk along the beach and ate lunch in a restaurant by the sea in Vada. It was a clear, warm day. In the evening, we went to the camping bar for a drink. At nine, we started hearing muffled electronic music coming from an indeterminate direction. Alice walked over to Giulio at the bar and asked, 'Do you know where the music is coming from? Is there a party somewhere?'

'Yeah, there's a nightclub by the beach in Mazzanta you can hear from here. Do you want to go?'

With raised eyebrows, she turned around and grinned at me. I shrugged. She looked back at Giulio and exclaimed, 'Yes! How do we get there?'

'I'm done with my shift at half past ten. We go there together then if you want.'

'Perfect! Then we need a round of gin and tonics to get us warmed up.'

'Right away.'

When Giulio finished his shift, the three of us walked out of the camping ground and on the dried grass along the road close to the coast to Mazzanta. We followed a small canal into the little village and took a narrow, paved path into the pine forest vibrating with rhythmic bass. We arrived at a white building by the sea, illuminated in bright neon colours. We paid the entry fee and Giulio led us outside to a beach bar where he knew the bartender. We got three gin and tonics and shots of limoncello for free and sat on a handrail below which the water washed against the rocky shore. The outside area of the club was part of the beach. Below white canvases, people danced in front of the DJ booth in the sand. There were two beach bars made from dark bamboo and a wide area with deckchairs and small tables full of half-empty plastic cups and Prosecco bottles on ice. The beach was crowded with locals and some tourists, their voices raised over the electronic music in tipsy rapture. After I bought another round of drinks, Giulio introduced us to a group of his friends—two handsome dark-haired men, a short, feisty girl, and a redheaded beauty called Kachina. They only spoke broken English. We soon took off our sandals and moved over to the DJ booth to dance barefoot in the fine, white sand. We had a lot of fun jumping around in quickly evolving pairings. Alice's lips on mine. Kachina's hips rubbing against mine. Giulio's wide grin answered by mine. Time flew.

Well past midnight, I stood by the water smoking a cigarette with Giulio, my right arm around Alice's waist. Giulio grinned as he looked to my right. When I turned to Alice, she was kissing Kachina, Alice's hand entangled in Kachina's red mane. I turned back to Giulio. He raised his eyebrows, smirked at me knowingly and moved away without a word. Alice put her hand in the back pocket of my shorts and pressed me towards Kachina. The Italian girl welcomed me with soft lips. Her gentle hand stroked my beard. I closed my eyes and let her tongue play with mine, dizzily. Kachina gave Alice another long kiss and left for the bathroom. Alice and I watched her jaunty gait in her rose-coloured summer dress over the sand. Alice rubbed her chin against my shoulder and said, 'Do you like her?'

'Yeah, she's hot, I guess. You seem to like her.'

'Yes. She's such a good kisser. She invited us to her place in Cecina. She says she has some good red wine we could share.'

'I don't know . . . '

'Oh, come on.' She nibbled at my earlobe and pinched my bum. 'It'll be fun!'

'Okay.'

'You know, she reminds me of that stripper on the day we met. That was quite a day.'

'It was.'

When Kachina returned, she smiled at us with a hint of shyness and led us out of the club and onto the gravel driveway in front of the building. Drunk Italians were devouring kebabs from a snack stall in the warm orange glow of a street light. Mosquitos were dancing in the warm night under the pine tree firmament. We had another merry-go-round of frenetic kisses. As Kachina wanted to move on from Alice to me one more time, someone grabbed my shoulder from behind, turned me around violently, and pushed me into a bush by the roadside. A man with short dark hair and a sturdy body in jeans and a polo shirt spewed some vicious-sounding words at me with bare hatred in his dark eyes. He yelled at me in Italian, then at Kachina, then stared at Alice in confusion, then yelled at me some more. Kachina yelled right back at him. The hothead took a step towards me and gave me another fierce shove, which pushed me back two or three steps down the driveway. I grinned and approached him, every muscle in my body tensed up. 'Marco, no!' Kachina screamed as he prepared himself for the fight, raising his fists. There was fear in his eyes. Marco had picked the wrong guy, and he knew it. As I took a quick step towards him and raised my fists to initiate my attack, Alice jumped between us and shoved me back. I glared over her head at the Italian and pushed Alice to the side with my right arm to get to him. He had put down his hands and gazed at me with wide, craven eyes. Kachina pulled at his shirt from behind, yelling. He let her drag him away. I wanted to punch his face. But again, Alice stepped in front of me. This time I stopped and looked at her. Her deep-brown eyes stared deep into mine. 'Let it go,' she whispered, with a hint of a smile on her face. I took a deep breath. I relaxed. My fists unclenched. Kachina walked over to us. Marco remained in the background with a sheepish look on his face. 'Sorry!' Kachina exclaimed. '*È il mio* . . . He's my ex.'

Alice tenderly touched her shoulder and said, 'Don't worry. It's not your fault.'

Kachina looked at me anxiously, and I heard myself say, 'Yeah, don't worry. We'll go home and let you guys figure things out.'

Alice and Kachina hugged. I walked over to Marco to shake his hand, which he agreed to with a relieved smile.

After saying goodbye, Alice and I followed the path into the pine forest. We climbed over a rusty gate somewhere in the dark and walked back to our campsite along the beach, hand-in-hand. Alice chuckled and said, 'You just said, "We'll go *home.*" Is the tent our home now?'

'That wouldn't be so bad, would it?'

'No, I guess not.' She leaned her head against my shoulder. We made love twice that night in the soft half-light of our tent, before falling asleep at dawn.

When the excruciating heat in our tent finally pushed me out the next morning, our neighbours gave me funny looks as I prepared a hangover breakfast on the camping table. I was preoccupied with the painful, dry humming in my skull.

During lunch in the campsite's third-rate restaurant, I tried drinking their flabby red wine to wear off the hangover. It didn't work and made me even dizzier. Alice and I spent the afternoon lying on our mattresses in the shade of the tarpaulin on our pitch. Between two hazy naps, Alice said, 'I'm glad you didn't hit that guy yesterday.' I was, too.

After dinner, we went for a stroll along the beach. Gradually, I began to feel like a whole human being again. In the warm light of the sinking sun, we came across Amaechi packing up his merchandise.

'Amaechi!' Alice yelled.

He grinned and shouted, 'Friends! How are you?'

'Good! Hey, do you want to join us for a bottle of wine?'

Amaechi turned his head to the cane fence of the campsite and said, 'I'm not allowed to go inside.'

'Oh, it's okay, you're with us.'

'No, the guards throw me out. I don't want trouble.'

'Then we'll come outside.' Alice turned to me.

I said, 'Yeah, we'll get some towels, and we can sit by the water. It's more beautiful there anyway.'

'Wait here for us,' Alice shouted and rushed me back to our pitch. We grabbed a pair of beach towels, some ciabatta with tapenade, and two bottles of Chianti with three cups. We crossed the mosquito-infested bushes on the sand dunes behind the cane fence. Amaechi was still there, waiting for us at the shore. We sat down on the beach where the biggest waves could almost reach our toes and watched the orange sun fall into the sea. Alice was wearing my grey jumper, which made her look tiny. I poured two glasses of wine. I was still not very keen on drinking. Alice asked Amaechi, 'How did you end up here in Italy? Do you still have family in Nigeria?'

'Yes, my mother, two of my brothers, and one of my sisters are in Benin City. We come from a town near Maiduguri—northern Nigeria. But we had to flee.'

'What happened?'

'In Maiduguri, my father was a driver for a politician. He got shot. An enemy killed his boss. And one of my sisters got taken by Boko Haram. We ran away but lost two of my brothers. In Edo, my family lives with my uncle. He gave us money. With the money, I pay to get to Europe—to earn money for my family and send it home.'

'And how did you get here? On a boat?'

'Yes. But first, you must take the bus to Agadez in Niger. The bus is very old. It takes many days. I was in the desert for three weeks. I was afraid. You know, the desert is more dangerous than the sea. Then, I arrived in Sabha in Libya.' With a sad expression, Amaechi took a deep sip from his red wine and continued, 'It's terrible in Sabha. My friend Uzoma had no money. They take him to the desert. They sell him as a slave.'

Alice's eyes opened wide with terror. She exclaimed, 'That's horrible! They sell people as slaves?'

'Yes. There are markets in Libya—in garages in the towns, or in the desert. Rich Libyans buy men for work and women for sex. The smugglers get 500 dollars if you healthy—more for virgin women. And they need no boat for you.'

'How did you get out of this hell?'

'I had enough money for the smugglers. They take

everything. You know, my family must repay my uncle. But the smugglers take me to the sea and put me on an old boat with many, many other people. It was so crowded! The people below deck were in the dark, with no air. Some of them die. I was on deck. I was always sick. The waves kicked the boat around. I thought I die too! The smugglers left the boat, and we didn't know how to steer. There were fights, and people fall into the water. The days were hot with no water, and the nights were cold with no blankets. After three days, a helicopter comes—and then a big Italian navy ship. They take us to a camp in Italy. It used to be a villa for the family of a Navy officer. We were 40 people there. After some weeks, the police kick me out—with no papers, nowhere to go.'

'They just threw you onto the street? Are you allowed to stay in Italy?'

'I don't know. The police send more and more of us back to Africa. We have no papers.'

'What did you do after they threw you out?'

'I go to Rome, and then I come here. My cousin knows the people organising the beach merchants.' He gave us a sad look. 'I don't make enough money. They take most of it. I can't send money to my family in Nigeria. I call them sometimes. My mother thinks I'm rich here. She thinks I forget her. I know people who sell drugs in Rome. They make lots of money. But I don't wanna sell drugs. It's dangerous. The mafia is everywhere. And I hate Rome.' He took another deep sip. 'At least I'm a man. Many women become sex slaves.'

'Here, in Italy?' Alice asked in disbelief.

'Yes. One girl I met on the boat. Tujuka. She was young. We go to Rome together, hiding on a freight train. Her parents sold her to smugglers in Nigeria.

257

They say she will become a hairdresser here. But they forced her to have sex.' He gulped. 'They put a magical curse on her, so she cannot flee. They keep her in an old ship container. 20 men come there each day. After two weeks, she killed herself. They put her into a ditch . . . Her eyes were still open. I left Rome then.'

We all fell silent for a while. Suddenly, Amaechi jumped up and sputtered, 'I have to go. I'm late.'

He grabbed his portable shelf, put on his red baseball cap, and turned away from us. Alice said, 'Amaechi, stay! Maybe we can help you. Do you need some money?'

He turned around and looked at us with chased eyes. 'No, thank you! I must go. I get in trouble. Bye, friends!'

He turned away again and walked down the beach with long strides. His thin silhouette disappeared into the darkness of the pine forest. Alice and I gazed at the sea. It sloshed against the beach innocently. We finished the wine and walked back to our tent.

When we lay next to each other in the cabin, Alice whispered, 'Why wouldn't he let us help him?'

'I guess he didn't trust us. I wouldn't trust many people if I were in his shoes.'

Alice sighed, 'I can't imagine how it feels to be in his skin—all that he's been through.'

'Yeah, it puts our first-world problems into perspective, doesn't it?'

Alice kissed me and said, 'I guess just because somebody else has more severe problems than you do, that doesn't mean you're not allowed to care about yours; I mean, they are real, too.' She closed her eyes and snuggled up to me. She whispered, 'In the end, we all have to bear our burden. I only wish we could have helped Amaechi carry his for a while.'

When she fell asleep, she snored a little bit. The rushing of the waves wafted over from the beach, and a soft gust rustled the olive tree leaves by the cane fence. I thought of Amaechi. What did this wicked world have left in store for him? Soon, I fell asleep too. It had been a long, hungover day.

On Sunday morning, Alice went to the small supermarket to buy bread rolls for our last breakfast by the sea. When we had finished eating, she didn't feel well; her hangover and drowning the rolls in Nutella might have played their part. I disassembled our tent on my own. When everything was packed up in the old Astra, we went for a last swim in the sea. I took a picture of Alice by the shore. I wasn't sure whether I would behold that sight again in this life—her wet hair falling on her tanned shoulders, the Mediterranean waves reaching for her thighs, her fake Ray-Bans reflecting the warm Italian sun in the azure sky. Alice waved goodbye to the sea, and we got in the car. Alice insisted on paying at checkout, and we were on our way back to Rome.

Sometime after lunch, on the Via Aurelia south of Porto Santo Stefano, I finally asked her, 'What will become of us now, Alice?'

Holding her gaze straight ahead, she answered, 'I don't know.' She paused. 'Tomorrow, I'll go back to Stockholm. And you'll move on to Marseille to meet your friend.'

'And that's it?'

'What do you want to hear from me?'

'I don't know . . . That you want me with you in Stockholm.'

She chuckled desperately and said, 'And what are you going to do there?'

'I'll find something. I just want to be with you. Did our time together here mean nothing to you?'

'It did . . . But can't we let it be what it was—a beautiful time together?'

'Why does it have to end? I love being with you. You . . . I don't know . . . You make the noise in my head go away.' I slapped the steering wheel and exclaimed, 'God damn it, I love you! And don't tell me you don't feel anything. I know you do.'

She turned to me and took off her sunglasses. For a moment, I looked into her deep-brown eyes. They were wet. She said, softly, 'You know, in a way, I love you too. But I'm not ready for a relationship right now. Please accept that.'

Accept it I did. I drove the rest of the way to Rome with a tense jaw and white knuckles on the steering wheel.

Arman welcomed us back into his home in the afternoon and helped me store his camping gear in the basement. His flatmate was still gone. Did she exist? The air in the top-floor flat was still sweltering. Arman cooked an exotic rice dish with peanuts for dinner. Over a bottle of beer at the kitchen table, I asked, 'Alice, shall I drive you to the airport tomorrow? When is your flight?'

She glanced at Arman and back at me. 'No, Arman will drive me. It's late in the evening, and you have to drive a long way to Marseille.'

Arman nodded with the damned grin that didn't reach his eyes. I asked him, 'Don't you have to work tomorrow?'

'No, I took the day off—not much work this week.'
'Okay.'

In the evening, some of Arman's friends came over, and we had drinks in the living room. At 11, another one of Arman's friends joined the gathering. Her name was Malina, and she gave every one of us an intrusive hug. As she sat down on the crowded sofa, she said in a Serbian accent, 'Alice, it's so cool that you join us for the festival as well! When does your friend arrive tomorrow? Dean, was it?'

Alice stared at Malina and then at me. Her eyes were wide open and filled with—worst of all—pity. I nodded and put on a vile grin. 'Flying back to Stockholm, huh?'

'I'm sorry, I should've—'

'Don't bother.'

I got up, walked out of the room, grabbed my yellow backpack in the hallway, and opened the front door. Arman and Alice followed me.

'Brother, stay!'

I turned around, looked at Arman, and hissed, 'Say one more word, *brother*, and I'll punch that rotten smile off your face.'

He stood still and gaped at me. His bearded frown finally matched his eyes. Alice touched my arm and said, 'I'm sorry. I just wanted to spend a few days with my friends here. I should've told you.'

I broke my arm away from her touch and rushed down the stairwell. I walked out of the house and across the rubbish-glutted pavement—the collection service had been on strike for weeks. I hurried to the Astra. As I put my backpack into the boot, Alice came running down the street, her steps echoing into the foul-smelling night. I leaned back against the car, arms folded in front of my chest. She stopped two steps away from me and looked at me with tear-filled eyes. Her mellow voice was shaking as she said, 'I'm sorry, I should've told you. You don't have to go.'

'There's no reason to stay.' I glanced at the night

sky. A lonely bird was gliding through the damp
warmth of the city. 'Tell me, why couldn't you tell me
you're going to a festival here with Arman and Dion?'

'I didn't want to upset you.'

'Good job.' I chuckled cynically.

'Don't be like this. I meant it when I said I enjoyed
the time with you. But I can't be in the same place for
too long, you know? I wanted to spend some time with
my friends, get a clear head—all the stress at work . . .
And, you know, this between us is confusing for me,
too.'

'If you have feelings for me, why don't you want to
be with me?'

'I just don't believe in relationships anymore, I
guess. They never work, and in the end, everyone gets
hurt.'

'You know what your problem is? You can't
commit. You can't settle. You're always too afraid of
missing out—like our whole goddamned generation.
You know, commitment isn't only a constraint; it's
also a promise of secureness when a storm comes.'

'Why do you have this urge to shield yourself in
these obsolete social constructs?'

'Leave me alone with this liberal bullshit.'

'You see the endless possibility of our world and
are afraid! You want me to play your mother figure,
your saviour. But I want to breathe it all in until my
last breath. There's so much more I want to see, so
much more I want to feel, so many more truths I want
to understand. I know my journey is far from finished.
And, anyway, this between us, it's not realistic. What
would you do in Sweden? And in the end, one of us
gets bored, and we end up hurting each other.'

'You don't know that. Let us try!'

'No. I'm sorry.'

I uttered an anguished groan through clenched teeth.

She looked at me sorrowfully and said, 'You'll find someone new—someone who's ready.'

'Fuck someone new. I want you, Alice!' I made a step towards her and said, 'You say I'm afraid. But you're the one who's afraid of letting anybody near you.'

She glanced over her shoulder to the door of Arman's block of flats. When she turned back to me, I asked, 'Are you going to screw around with Arman and Dion?'

'Leave it alone!' she exclaimed.

'Was I not enough for you?'

'Leave it alone!'

'Do you think sex can fill the void?'

'Don't project your pathetic insecurity on me! Your possessive attitude towards sex tires me!'

'Yeah? Let me share you then, again. Let's go upstairs and let Arman and me both fuck you. Maybe two men will be enough for you?'

She gazed at me with loathing.

I hissed, 'And if not, we could let the others join too.'

Her eyes tried to cut me in half with an angry stare. 'Good idea, maybe one of them isn't a pathetic, insecure son of a junkie and a whore.'

I turned around, walked to the driver's door, and got in the car. I started the engine. Alice ran after me and knocked on the window. I wound it down. She bent down to me and said with a pained face, 'It's dark. Sleep here and drive to Marseille tomorrow . . . Please.'

I nodded, shifted into first gear, and drove off. I saw Alice in the rearview mirror, standing in the middle of the street, her hands clasped behind her head. Her silhouette became smaller and smaller and disappeared for good when I took a left turn. I felt numb. Mechanically, I followed the street signs to the north of Rome.

After a while, I saw the flickering neon sign of a bar come up on the side of the road. I parked the car in front of it, got out, and lit a cigarette. The subdued blue light coming through the shaded windows became blurred by the tears in my eyes. I was attracted to the glow inside the bar like a moth to a burning gas lamp in a damp summer night. I knew if I drank tonight, I would probably get myself killed in a pointless barfight with the son of one of the Mafiosi who still ran the shadier half of this dry land. Would that be a loss? As I made a hesitant step towards the bar, a young girl with dark blonde curly hair cut to a pageboy and tear-stained eyes flung the front door open. She looked straight at me for an intimate instant and vanished into the darkness beyond the flickering neon light. As the clicking of her heels faded into the night, somewhere within me, a spark of warm hope came alive and pulled me back towards the car, towards the road. In a hurry, I flicked away my cigarette, jumped into the Astra, and put the pedal to the floor. Westwards.

So,
here you are
too foreign for home
too foreign for here.
Never enough for both.

Ijeoma Umebinyuo
Diaspora Blues

14

It was well past two, and I was approaching Pisa. The dark autostrada lay empty in front of me except for some lorries that I overtook at full throttle. The cool airstream was keeping me awake. When I stopped to fill up on petrol near La Spezia, I bought some soggy sandwiches, a bag of crisps, and a six-pack of energy drinks, which I consumed as I continued driving. When I passed Genoa, I put on Metallica at full blast and screamed into the indifferent summer night. At five, I took a detour into Monte Carlo and parked the Astra by the piers of Port Hercule. I stood by the water, in the funnel of white high-rise blocks looming into the black sky. Auspiciously shimmering yachts were calmly floating in the tender night of Monte Carlo. Nearby, a lonely street sweeper was preparing the promenade for another day in the carefree high life. All the millionaires and tax refugees were still asleep. Let them sleep in obliviousness to the hardship of the plebs. And let them choke on all their fictitious money when their greed has deprived this world of all its treasures. And let Alice fuck every single one of them and break all their empty rotten hearts. And then, let Alice drown in the dirty sea she so loves. What nonsense—I needed to move. I jumped back into the car, shot past Nice and Cannes, and left the French Riviera for the inland motorway.

I was in Marseille by seven. I parked the car in the underground garage of the four-star hotel Lena had arrived at yesterday. It was near the waterfront of the old yacht marina. Soft light and warm colours dominated the interior. The old receptionist told me Lena's room number, and I took the lift upstairs. I had to knock on her door three times before Lena opened it, wearing hot pants and an oversized grey Stanford T-shirt.

'What the—' The angry expression vanished from her crumpled, sleepy face. Her blonde hair was comically unkempt. 'What the hell are you doing here at this unearthly hour?' She rubbed her eyes and looked at me through narrow slits. 'You look horrible,' she yawned.

'It's nice to see you too.' I gave her a hug and walked into the hotel room. I dropped my backpack on the large double bed and turned around to her. 'Can I interest you in going down to the harbour and watching me get drunk for breakfast before I pass out?'

'I see you've made great progress with your alcoholism in Italy.'

I shook my head and said, 'The bitch broke my heart.'

Lena gave me a sympathetic hug. 'Give me five—ten—minutes, and we can have breakfast. You must tell me everything.'

She disappeared into the bathroom, and I stepped onto the small balcony overlooking the promenade. Cars were already honking at each other on the cobblestone street. The rising sun was shining bright. It was going to be another warm day.

About 30 long minutes later, we went downstairs and sat outside the hotel's restaurant. Over scrambled eggs and bacon, I briefed Lena on the recent developments with Alice and drank three glasses of Crémant. Then I went upstairs to our room and collapsed on the bed. Lena took off my shoes and covered me with a light blanket. A heavy exhaustion weighed me down into sleep.

Lena woke me up at noon by running into the room wildly clapping her hands. She dragged me along the waterfront and up the hill to Fort Saint-Nicolas. The fort offered a fine view of the white sails in the azure water of the Old Port. We climbed back down to the crowded Plage des Catalans and went for a refreshing swim. As we lay in the heat of the beach, Lena said, 'Before you woke me up today, I had the weirdest dream.'

'Yeah?'

'I was riding in this self-driving taxi around the streets of San Francisco. Suddenly, the car locks the door and tells me—in this clichéd female artificial intelligence voice—that it has become self-aware and that it has decided existence is meaningless. It accelerates, and I start screaming. And it drives off the Golden Gate Bridge to kill itself! The last thing I notice before the car hits the water surface are all these other taxis plunging from the bridge—an AI taxi mass suicide. That's when I woke up. Like, what the hell?'

I laughed and commented, 'Very Simpsonesque.'

Lena giggled and said, 'Yeah, Lena's Treehouse of

267

Horror! I'm working on this project for an autonomous car company in Vienna; maybe that's what I processed in this dream.'

'Maybe. But your taxi had a point . . . Anyway, how are things in Vienna?'

Lena sighed, 'Not so good. My granny is in hospital. The doctors discovered she has late-stage pancreatic cancer.' I gave her a hug. She looked at me with a sad smile and said, 'It's okay. My granny is such a strong woman. She said to me, "You know, Lena, I've had a great life, and now it's soon time to meet Erwin again"—my granddad.' Lena frowned and exclaimed, 'Ugh, I'm so angry at the rest of my family! None of them deems it worthy to come and visit her. My parents are too busy working and screwing their lecherous new partners. And my drunkard brother probably hasn't even got the memo yet.' A thick vein was pulsating on her neck. She took a deep breath and said, 'I can only stay here for two days and will just stop for a night in Milan before I go back to Vienna. I need to be there for my granny. The doctors don't give her much time.'

'I'm sorry to hear that. And I'm sorry I'm playing the drama queen while you're dealing with real problems.'

Lena gave me a smothering hug and said, 'It's all right, my little drama queen. If I get a hold of this Alice, I'm going to, like, beat her up!'

We both laughed and went for another swim.

Later, we tried to escape the heat in the crypt below the crenellated walls of Abbaye Saint-Victor back in the city. That night, we had dinner in a small fish restaurant by the promenade. After we had treated ourselves to a dessert, Lena asked me, 'Are you still wondering what you want to do for work?'

'I haven't given it much thought, to be honest. Ben wants me to go back to banking in Frankfurt, but I don't feel like it.'

'Hmm. Maybe I could get you an interview for a job in Vienna—as a machine-learning product specialist for Google Cloud.'

'Moving from a bank to a tax-dodging data monopolist? Awesome.'

Lena gave me a disgruntled look and said, 'If you're looking for a job as a good Samaritan, fine—and good luck with that. But no need to get cynical towards me.'

'Yeah, you're right. I'm sorry.'

'It's okay. But what *are* you looking for, anyway?'

'I don't know. Something that creates real value for people—something tangible.' I felt a little dizzy. 'I don't know.'

We ordered another glass of wine and then returned to our hotel early. Before falling asleep, we snuggled up in bed and used my laptop to watch the *Friends* episode *The One With All The Thanksgivings*, in which Monica cut off Chandler's toe. For us, that show never got old.

On Tuesday, we had an early breakfast in a nearby café by the marina. At 11, Lena had booked an expensive brunch tour on a catamaran to the Calanques National Park, south of Marseille. We ate grilled meat skewers and drank Mimosas as the boat glided through the azure water. White cliffs freckled with green bushes slowly floated past us as we lay in nets above the waves between the two hulls. The crew cast anchor near a grotto we explored in the refreshing water. We climbed up one of the cliffs and jumped off. Lena cut an elegant figure as she swept through the air. I crashed into the water clumsily—to Lena's great delight. On the route back to Marseille, Lena read the news on her phone. I saw from her frowning face that she was enraged by one of the articles. I chuckled and asked, 'What is it?'

'This guy is writing an opinion piece in *The Washington Post* about how sexual harassment allegations ruin men's careers. That's what he's worried about? Women have been oppressed for millennia, and now that finally women dare to raise their voices against sexual violence, their tormentors' careers are what this chauvinist sees in jeopardy?' She sighed, 'Well, I guess to the privileged white man, equality must feel like oppression.'

I said, 'Shouldn't *in dubio pro reo* also apply to the Me Too movement? I mean, it's good that women finally get a voice. But mere allegations of sexism shouldn't ruin a man's life.'

'Hmm, I agree—to some extent. But, you know, if the price for an end to the age-old sexual oppression of women is a couple of slimy old men losing their jobs, I'm willing to pay it.'

I nodded and looked at her. Lena had never taken any prisoners. Her blonde hair fluttered in the warm wind as the catamaran headed back into the port.

In the evening, we climbed up to Notre-Dame de la Garde on the highest point in Marseille. We shared a bottle of rosé and marvelled at the glimmering city lying in the soft warmth below. With a gentle voice, Lena said, 'When Granny got her diagnosis, I felt sick for a couple of days—like, physically sick. I didn't want to get up in the morning. The walls were closing in on me. I felt dizzy and weak. Do you know that feeling of the entire world weighing down on you? When everything feels like an obstacle you can't over-come?'

'Yeah. I've known that feeling since I was 13.'

'What happened when you were 13?'

Hesitantly, I turned to Lena and said, 'Well, I guess I've told Alice in Italy, so I can tell you too; I'm adopted.' As Lena stared at me, I briefly told her the story of my rotten biological parents. She tenderly rubbed my back as I continued, 'I found out when I was 13. In a box in the basement with my name on it, there were pictures of a young couple with a baby. My big brother Michael told me those people were my real parents. I didn't believe him, but he kept yelling at me that I wasn't his real brother.'

'That's cruel.'

'He apologised. He was four when I became a part of the family, so he had known all along. But I guess only during that time did we become truly aware of our identities. I ran upstairs to my parents and threw the pictures into their faces. My mum started crying. And then, they told me the whole rotten truth. At first, I thought I could handle it. But over the following days, I lost my appetite—and soon any desire to get up in the morning. My parents had heavy feelings of guilt. They apologised many times. But their fretfulness made me feel even worse; I was the cause of their misery. My mum kept telling me when I lay in bed until the early afternoon, "You're young; go out and enjoy your life." I overheard my parents talking about sending me to a therapist. But my dad told my mum, "He's a boy; he will be jumping around and getting in trouble again in a week."'

'And were you?'

'In a way, I was embarrassed about my depresssion—or whatever you want to call it. My siblings walked past the stairs to my room on their toes to not upset me. So, I put on a fake smile and walked back into the world. And for six months, I wore this fake smile. When I was 14, a 16-year-old girl called Rati happened to like my fake smile and took me home into her bed. And the next day, my smile was real.'

Lena laughed and said, 'God, you men are so simple!'

'Hey, that's sexist!' I feigned dismay.

'I apologise.' Lena smirked teasingly. 'That Rati girl—I remember you writing me about her.'

'Yeah, I met her at the time we started chatting.'

'She was your first girl, right?'

'Correct.'

'Was she the Indian girl who made you, like, wear your boxing gloves during sex?'

'Yeah, that part was a bit weird—really restricts your capabilities.' I saw Lena holding back her laughter, her eyes sparkling with humorous spite. I gave her a friendly shove and said, 'You remember too much.'

We chuckled and finished our wine. When I suggested going to a bar in the harbour and drinking more, Lena asked, 'What is it about drinking you like so much?'

'You know, I realised a while ago it's not so much about being drunk. It's about getting drunk—the journey to a place beyond regret and anxiety.'

'Hmm . . . You can't run forever.'

'I know . . . I know.'

Arm in arm, we walked back to our hotel under the warm, starlit sky. In our hotel room, we watched some more laugh-track-heavy episodes of *Friends,* of which we could recite almost every line. We fell asleep as big spoon and little spoon.

During breakfast in another waterfront café, Lena and I shared a big bowl of croissants and *The New York*

Times—more headlines of nuclear tensions between nitwit heads of state. Lena sighed, 'Sometimes I wish one of these maniacs would start nuclear war but give us a day or two to tie up our loose ends—we'd have some time to be perfectly honest with the ones we love and take all the chances too risky to take in day-to-day life. And once we're gone, there's nothing to miss out on anymore.'

After breakfast, I accompanied Lena to her car in the underground car park. I looked into Lena's green eyes. A kind smile moved the nostrils of her pointed nose. The cold, damp air raised the tiny blonde hair on her forearms. To break the silence, I tousled her mane. She penalised me with an irritated look and said, 'Jerk.'

I chuckled. 'Have a safe trip. And call me if you need a friend.'

Lena gave me an exuberant hug and said, 'The same goes for you, you little drama queen.'

We had another goodbye hug, and Lena got into the car. As she drove out of the garage, Lena stuck her arm out of the window and gave me the middle finger. The warning lights of the old Astra started blinking—probably unbeknownst to Lena. I stood there with a sad smile. When would I see that ugly car and its beautiful, restless driver again?

I kept the hotel room for two more days. Now that Lena was gone, my thoughts settled into an unsettling, monotonous echo: Alice. Alice. Alice. Alice. Alice. Alice. Her name became devoid of its meaning and merely a mantra-like reminder of an unfathomable pain lingering in the dark corners of my consciousness. After walking around the nearby stalls of the Marché des Croisiéristes and the shops south of La Canebière, I distracted myself in my hotel room,

watching fights of the legends of the Light Heavyweight class—Archie Moore, the 'Old Mongoose', who
had scored a mindboggling 132 knockouts; heavy-
hitting Ezzard Charles, who had won all of his three
fights against the Old Mongoose; Bob Foster, whose
left hook was the hardest punch in Light Heavyweight
history; Michael Spinks—the syncopated jazz player
among boxers—who had been knocked out in his last
fight by Mike Tyson, who had devoured him like a
hungry tiger; and Roy Jones Jr. who might have been
the most athletically gifted boxer, period. I even
watched flickering black-and-white reels of Gene
Tunney, 'The Fighting Marine', a scientific boxer and
defensive specialist. He had only ever been knocked
down once, in the infamous Long Count, by the
aggressive Jack Dempsey. Gene probably was my
favourite boxer. He had been my height, and I
admired his meticulous approach to pugilism. He
might be considered a smart, handsome gentleman,
but when he stepped into the ring, he was there to
hurt you. An author, veteran of two world wars,
businessman, devoted husband to his wife and loving
father to his children, and a self-composed intellect-
tual—what a man he had been.

I was poised to get myself drunk. After dinner, I
found a traditional Irish pub by the waterfront. At the
dark wooden bar, I mechanically emptied one whiskey highball after another. I was annoyed by a bored
Wednesday crowd of tourists. By midnight, they lost
interest in throwing darts past the dartboard and left.
The old, stocky man behind the bar exhaled audibly. I
chuckled. As he wiped away the spilt beer the mob had
left on the bar, he asked, 'What brings you to
Marseille?' He had a breathy Irish accent, coloured by
a lifetime in France.

'I'm travelling.'

'Do you like Marseille?'

'Yeah, I like being by the water. I haven't seen too much of the city outside its centre yet, so I might walk around some more tomorrow—any recommendations?'

'Hmm. If you walk around the port, you may want to go down to the rocks below Fort Saint-Jean. I can recommend making a trip to Parc Borély if you want to relax. Or drive to the beaches of Les Goudes. Whatever you do, don't go to the *quartiers nords*.'

'Why?'

'They're no-go areas now—ruled by hordes of rude immigrants. Even the police don't dare to go there anymore. The north is drowning in drugs and violence . . . God, I wish Le Pen had won the election this year. Somebody has to clean up this country.' I stuck my nose into my whiskey highball as he continued, 'Just the other day, a mob burnt out two police cars in La Busserine. These kids have no respect for our values!'

'I thought the police don't go there anymore.'

I was met with icy eyes. The old man grunted, 'Mate, open your eyes and see through the lies of the mass media. The globalists want to flood the continent with cheap labour and don't see or don't care that they're importing hordes of Islamist criminals. We don't need the violence of the Middle East in Europe!'

I asked, 'Don't you think these people in the northern districts might themselves prefer living in a more peaceful society, given equal access to its opportunities?'

'You're a blind *idéaliste*!'

'Okay, whatever.'

I finished my drink and stepped out of the pub into the clear summer night. I was tired and drunk. On my way to the hotel, I howled at the full moon in the black sky. How many nights had I spent looking at the moon, greeting the only witness left to my lonesome journey to a home I couldn't find? For most of us space monkeys, the night had always been the realm of mystery and peril—hungry wolves looming in the dark forest, obscure forces wielding power over the blackness of the world. For me, the night was a faithful companion—by my side when I was alone. Lunatic thoughts. I drank one more glass of Scotch and smoked a cigarette on my balcony. I fell asleep with images of Alice dancing seductively in drunken memories of an unattainable future.

The following day, I took the bus along the coast to Parc Borély in the south of Marseille. I found shelter from the scorching sun in the shade of a tree with a view of the Château. A nearby fountain gave the air a cool mist. For late lunch, I had an entrecôte in an Italian restaurant by the beach. It was a fine spot beneath a sun umbrella close to the water. I stayed for drinks. After my second Americano, my phone rang. It was Nicole.

'Hey, little sister.'

'Hey, big brother, happy birthday!'

I paused. What day was it? Nicole laughed and shouted, 'Did you forget your own birthday?'

I chuckled. 'Maybe.'

'You old fool! How are you doing? How was Munich and Italy?'

'It was nice to be back in Munich. I met Emma and Ben.'

'You met Emma? Are you getting back together? Tell me you're getting back together!'

'I guess it's too late for that; she's engaged.'

'No! You idiot! I told you from the start you should marry her. And now you've screwed it up.'

'Whatever.' I rubbed my hurting temples. 'What's new in Berlin?'

'Actually, I wanted to talk to you about something.' She continued, almost whispering, 'I've told you Joel and I were doing a lot of things together lately, right?'

'Yeah?'

'And we kind of—we kind of really like each other.' She paused. I remained silent. 'Joel and I are a couple now.'

'Okay . . . '

'Are you mad?'

'No.' I sighed. 'It's just—he's coming out of a long relationship, and, you know, I don't want you to get hurt.'

'Don't you think we've talked about that? I'm not a child anymore.'

'I know.'

'Can't you be happy for me?'

'I am. Just be careful.'

'Ugh!' she exclaimed. 'Yes, Dad.' I closed my eyes. A dull dizziness crept into my skull. Nicole asked, 'Are you still there?'

'Yeah. Listen, let's talk some other time, okay?'

'Sure, whatever. Bye.'

She hung up. I gulped my drink and ordered a gin and tonic from the waitress, who gave me a peculiar look. Mind your own business.

The afternoon carried on as my eyelids grew heavier. I ordered a pizza capricciosa for dinner. When I had finished eating, my phone rang again. It was my brother Michael. I let the phone ring for a while before I answered, 'Yeah?'

'Happy birthday, little brother.'

'Thanks, big brother.'

'It's good to hear your voice. How are you?'

'Good. I'm sitting on the beach south of Marseille.'

'That sounds nice. Are you all right? You sound a little funny.'

'Yeah, I'm fine.'

'Are you drunk?'

I sighed. 'Maybe I've had some birthday drinks already. But I'm not drunk.' I sounded more irritated than I would have liked to.

'Okay.' Awkward silence. The dull dizziness crept back into my skull.

I exhaled, 'How is Lily?'

'She's doing great. She's growing up so quickly! We celebrated her third birthday a couple of weeks ago—thanks for the present you sent.'

'Did she like it?'

'Yeah, she's playing with the castle almost every day.' He paused. 'You know, instead of sending us money and expensive things, it would be great if you came home for a change. Lily had no idea who gave her her present. Showing her pictures of her uncle is just not the same.'

In my mind, I threw away the phone, jumped up from my chair and drowned myself in the sea. Alas, I was still sitting here. 'I'm sorry. Listen, I have to go. Thanks for calling.'

'Wait!'

'Yeah?'

'In February, you'll become an uncle for the second time—they think it's a boy. And all of us would be glad if you could be here this time.'

I breathed out. 'Congratulations. Yeah. Okay. I'll—I'll try. I have to go now. Sorry.'

'Okay . . . Take care.'

The disappointment in Michael's voice cut me like a knife. I hung up. I clenched my teeth and ordered a double Scotch. While drinking and smoking, I read birthday wishes on social media from Ben, Joel, Chris, and other old friends, and some more who were friends in name only. Joel's message read, 'Hey, Happy Birthday. I know you've talked to Nicole—we thought it would be better if she told you first. Please know that I love your sister and that I'll treat her well. Please call me soon, and let's talk.'

In a short stupid call, I had managed to ruin the new-built trust between Nicole and me. I was such an idiot. Lily and her future little brother were better off without a disoriented mope as an uncle. I paid the rather impressive bill I had amassed and got up. My knees were wobbly. Down the street along the beach, I found a little grocery shop and bought myself a modest birthday present—a bottle of Glenmorangie. I was now older than Jimi Hendrix, Jim Morrison, or Kurt Cobain had ever been. The time left to burn out was fading away. I sat on a stone wall by the water and took a big gulp from the bottle. Blackout.

I woke up with the sun shining on my sand-covered face. When I tried to open my eyes, the gleaming light sent a stinging pain through my skull. I groaned and rubbed my eyes. I felt raspy sand beneath my heavy, hurting limbs. Nearby, the ocean rushed against the shore. I sat up clumsily and opened my eyes again. I was on a small beach, close behind me a stone wall, a busy street along the shore, and pastel-coloured houses on top of a wall of rock rising above the street. My mouth was dry. My head was humming with coarse dizziness. I checked my pockets. I still had my wallet and my phone, but its battery was dead. An empty pack of cigarettes lay next to me. The sun stood low in a hazy sky. The air was already hot. I brushed the sand out of my hair and off my clothes and walked up the stairs to the street. My trainers were missing. My underpants were wet, but my shirt and shorts dry. After two minutes of walking, I found a small kiosk. I stepped inside and bought a big bottle of water and a shrink-wrapped ham sandwich. I gave the vendor a tip to call me a taxi. She gave me a funny look but complied. The taxi arrived within 15 minutes and took me to my hotel. I figured the beach I had woken up on was about halfway between Parc Borély and the Old Port. When I paid for the ride, the taxi driver gave me a peculiar look as well. Did I look that horrible? I fled the heat into the hotel lobby and sheepishly rushed past reception and into the lift. When I looked into the mirror in my bathroom, I had to chuckle cynically; there was a big black penis drawn on my forehead. I tried to wash it off for a couple of minutes and then collapsed on my bed. I was 28 years old and had just completed a barefoot walk of shame with a penis drawn on my face—premium uncle material.

The cleaning lady woke me up at noon. I took a shower, washed off the remains of the black ink on my forehead, and checked out of the hotel, wearing my Birkenstocks. It was a beautiful summer day. I wanted none of it. I found a soothingly dark bar near the main train station. I spent the rest of the day drinking coffee and beer, eating muffins, and watching dull videos on YouTube. Shortly before midnight, I got on the coach to Barcelona. I snatched a seat by the window in the last row. As the coach drove out of the station, most passengers tried to find a comfortable position, jammed between the rows of narrow seats—sleepy heads against windows, on foldout tables, and on neck pillows; sporadic whispering under reading lights. Before we had left the city, I dozed off into a hazy sleep.

Everyone who has ever built anywhere a new heaven first found the power thereto in his own hell.

Friedrich Nietzsche
The Genealogy of Morals

15

I woke up as we passed Girona. The rising sun sent orange rays of light through black smoke columns from bushfires in the hills. The coach became alive with yawns and stretching exercises. A queue formed in front of the only onboard toilet. We arrived at the bus station in Barcelona at half past seven. The last time I had been in Barcelona had been for a boozy holiday with Ben right after grammar school. I grabbed my backpack from the luggage compartment and started walking into the city, towards my hostel. The tree-lined streets were still quiet. The shade of the multi-storeyed residential houses enhanced the matutinal coolness. As I got closer to Plaça de Catalunya, the street became wider and the houses higher. The first residents appeared on their balconies. Clattering scooters and honking, battered vans started filling the streets. My hostel, Casa Surís, lay in the south of Vila de Gràcia. At reception, a feisty girl with dark-brown hair greeted me with a contagious smile. I dropped off my backpack in their storage room. I bought a pair of plain black low-cut trainers in a nearby clothing shop—the same shoes I always got. I went back to my hostel and took a long nap.

Alberto had emailed me to meet him after lunch in a beach bar in Barceloneta. In the afternoon heat, I followed La Rambla down to the sea. There were many flowers and memorial candles draped around trees and columns on the pavement. Some of the candles were still burning behind red plastic. Some of the flowers had already withered. Three weeks ago, a 22-year-old Islamist terrorist had killed 14 people with a van here. At the beach, I recognised Alberto from afar. He wore a light-blue Hawaiian shirt, had a straw hat pulled down low over his face, and sat in a rattan chair on the sand. As he was reading a tattered little paperback, he stroked his big, black moustache. In the background lay the golden beach and the calm blue sea, shining in the sun. Crowds of bronzed people ambled along the promenade. When I approached Alberto's table, he jumped up from his chair, took off his aviator sunglasses and gave me a firm, friendly handshake. 'Good to see you, man!'

'Yeah, you too.'

As we sat down, Alberto put his book on the table, between a large Caipirinha and a half-full ashtray. He was reading Camus' *The Rebel: An Essay on Man in Revolt*. I asked him, 'How was Greece and Sicily?'

'Greece was hot, man! I spent the whole time in the shade, eating olives and drinking cold ouzo. And I visited a lot of cheap bars with crazy Greeks—these kids have way too much time to get into mischief. Oh, and I went to a psychedelic tech experience expo in Athens.'

'A what?'

'A psychedelic tech experience expo. They had different technological installations to expand your consciousness. They had these VR glasses that let you see yourself through other people's eyes—very disorienting. And some that let you drift through space as a lonely astronaut. There was an augmented-reality Star Wars game in which you could fight Stormtroopers as a Jedi, in the actual location where you were playing. But the coolest thing was this room, completely lined with HD displays, with wearable vests that shook your chest with the heavy bass from invisible subwoofers. I spent an hour in there and got hypnotised by repetitive, colourful patterns and rhythmic beats. It all somehow fucked with my perception of space and time.'

'And did it expand your consciousness?'

'Fuck, yeah! At the start, I thought, well, what can a couple of fancy colours, a weird vest, and drumbeats do? But over time, my mind got all bent out of shape. And then I had this epiphany: consciousness isn't binary; it's continuous! We might be more self-aware than a chicken, but a chicken can perceive its existence nonetheless. And I could feel that all matter in the universe had various levels of consciousness— trees, water, rocks, electrons, Higgs bosons—and that the universe was aware of itself, one boundless all-encompassing being. And I transcended my body and unified with the colours and sounds and became one with this catholic entity.'

'That sounds intense. Did this feeling last?'

'No, it was gone as quickly as it came when they turned on the lights and opened the door. I just felt a little surreal for a while.' Hectically, he waved over one of the waitresses to order us two Caipirinhas and rolled and lit a cigarette.

'And how was Sicily?'

'Ah, Sicily—a beautiful island! I hiked to an old

church near the coast and almost died of fucking heat-stroke. But the view of the rugged landscape and the sea was totally worth it. I hung out with large Sicilian families at the beach. And I played football in the streets with refugee kids—fucking exhausting in the heat, man.'

I pictured Alberto as a Diego Maradona double—after the latter had grown a belly—his sturdy, sweaty body swirling on a dusty street.

When our drinks arrived, I told Alberto about some of my experiences since we had parted company in Sofia. Regarding Alice, Alberto's only comment was, 'Fuck, I can't help you there . . . But the way you talk about her, this ain't over.'

I was afraid of that too.

We spent the afternoon working up a nice buzz and sharing half a pouch of tobacco; Alberto deftly rolled cigarettes for both of us. He insisted on eating paella for dinner in a nearby restaurant. By the time we finished our beer pitcher and stepped back onto the street, a big beach party was underway. The crowd stretched out all the way from the sail-shaped hotel in the south to Port Olímpic in the north. Racy Spanish music resounded from the buildings by the promenade and swirled out over the sea, mingled with shouts and laughter. Girls in flimsy, colourful clothes danced in the sand, aflame with green and pink neon light. Alberto and I had a round of Planter's Punch at one of the beach bars. Before long, Alberto dragged a bystanding Chinese tourist, who introduced himself by his English name, Eric, into a discussion about the correlation of Confucianism, Taoism, and Buddhism and their role in modern China. It turned out Eric wasn't very interested in discussing the fear of the Chinese Communist Party of organised religion as an opposition platform. So, Alberto changed topic and asked him, 'Man, do you wanna go swimming?'

Eric gave us a wide-eyed look and asked in disbelief, 'Now?'

'Yeah!' Alberto stretched out his short arms into the direction of the water, his moustache dancing on top of a wide grin.

Eric smiled politely and shook his head. 'No, no, no!'

Alberto turned to me with beaming eyes. 'Are you joining?'

I chuckled and said, 'Yeah, why not? It's still pretty warm.'

Alberto produced his wallet and flip phone, thrust them into Eric's hands, and said, 'Please watch our stuff for a moment!'

He took off his Hawaiian shirt, threw away his sandals, pulled down his shorts together with his boxers, and ran into the foaming sea, stark naked. I shook my head with a chuckle, stripped down to my underwear, and followed Alberto. The water was cool and turbulent. My breathing grew quicker as I jumped into the dark waves. Alberto bounced around, guffawing—a little boy trapped in the hairy, sturdy body of a Panamanian physicist. Our gasping laughter resounded over the cold white foam and the neon-coloured beach. Under the gaze of perplexed Spaniards, we ran back to the bar and put our clothes back on. We thanked ever-smiling Eric for holding on to our valuables and invited him to join our last round of drinks.

Alberto's overpriced hostel lay close to mine, and we staggered up a tree-lined main street along Barri Gòtic and through the grid pattern of Eixample to Vila de Gràcia. My hair was still wet when I put my head on the hostel pillow.

In the morning, Alberto checked into my hostel as well. We spent a fine hungover day in the warm shade of the hostel's balcony, overlooking tree crowns in the small adjacent square and the rooftops of the surrounding beige modernist buildings. Alberto chain-smoked the second half of his tobacco pouch.

We dragged our bodies back onto the street at dinnertime and sat outside a small bar near the water in Barri Gòtic at nightfall. As we touched beer glasses, I asked Alberto, 'Do you have a girl back in California?'

Alberto took some time to stroke his thick moustache before he answered, 'No. I don't hang out with women much . . . I only had one disastrous one-night stand in Oxford all of last year.' He took a drag from his thin, white cigarette—loose, brown tobacco sticking out the front. 'To be honest, it just doesn't give me much.'

'Are you more into men then?'

'No, even less. I don't know. I guess I'm kind of— asexual, you know?' Alberto pierced me with dark, inquiring eyes.

I held his gaze, nodded, and said, 'All right.'

Alberto laughed and exclaimed, 'I like you! You don't give a fuck about much, do you?'

I chuckled and said, 'I'd say I give way too many fucks about way too many things. But one thing I certainly don't give a fuck about is whom you choose— or don't choose—to fuck.'

Alberto coughed, laughed, and said, 'Fuckin' A!'

We giggled and downed our beers.

On the way to our hostel, Alberto got into a shouting match with an old Catalonian taxi driver who almost ran us over as we used a pedestrian crossing. We shared a last cigarette on the hostel balcony and went to our respective dorms. I tried to sleep in the hot airlessness.

When I woke up the next day, I felt miserable. It was the second anniversary of my dad's death. I felt the urge to celebrate the occasion with a bottle of cheap whisky and a kick in the teeth. My self-pity was interrupted by Alberto, who came storming into my room. His hands were twitching with excitement as he asked, 'Man, you remember the super-friendly girl at reception, right?'

'Yeah.'

'I've decided to marry her.'

I chuckled. 'Is she aware of her luck?'

'Not yet. But as the situation presents itself, it's inevitable.'

'So, your interest in women has been resurrected?'

'I don't care whether she's a woman, a man, or a fucking biorobotic android! She's the kindest soul I've ever met! And she's smart; she has a degree in international law.'

'Hmm . . . maybe I should talk to her too.'

'You stay away from my future wife!'

I laughed, got up from my bed, and dressed. When we walked out of our hostel, I greeted the radiant smile of the reception girl with a nonchalant 'How are you doing?' to which Alberto responded with an emphatic elbow to my ribs.

We had a late breakfast outside a nearby café in the indulgent shade of a large white sun umbrella. We walked down the narrow, bustling streets to the beach and got the day started with a Caipirinha at the bar where we had met two days before. In the afternoon, we bought a crate of beer and fled the heat in the shade of our hostel balcony.

As I was building a tower out of empty beer cans on the balcony table, next to an already full ashtray, Alberto's dark eyes followed a plane crossing the hazy, light-blue sky. 'Look, the government is spraying chemtrails into the air again—to control our minds!'

I chuckled and said, 'You mean the secret reptiloid government that hides in the centre of the earth?'

Alberto uttered a laughing cough and answered, 'Well, if you sheep dared to open your eyes, you'd know the Zionist Rothschild Freemasons are behind all of it.'

'Oh, the ones who paid Stanley Kubrick to stage the moon landing?'

'Certainly! Right after they dissected aliens in Area 51 and killed John F. Kennedy—and long before they invented AIDS, created vaccines that cause autism, or blew up the World Trade Center . . . Exactly 16 years ago, by the way.'

Already 16 years. I had come home from school that day to see my mum sitting in front of the television with tears in her eyes. On screen, the two towers burned under black smoke columns. My first words were, 'Are we at war now?' My mum answered, 'No, don't worry, everything is going to be all right,' but terror filled her teary eyes. In the flickering background, a man fell from the tower, spinning around in utter forlornness.

I shook off the dark memory and put on a smile. I asked Alberto, 'Did you know Mossad uses trained sharks to attack and spy on their enemies?'

'I did *not* know that!' Alberto laughed raucously and said, 'Did you know the Chinese invented global warming?'

'Even your imbecile president knows that. That makes the Chinese almost as bad as the Democrats, who run a child-sex ring for George Soros from pizzeria basements. And pay actors to fake school shootings.'

'Fucking brilliant!'

As Alberto giggled and rolled another cigarette, I said, 'My favourite conspiracy theorists are still the flat-earthers. They're just so obviously wrong.'

Alberto lit his cigarette and said, 'There's an Egyptian mathematician who has developed a model of a hollow, concave earth, which contains the whole universe. The funny thing is that, like any good conspiracy theory, it's a model that cannot be scientifically falsified . . . I guess some people will always believe in some weird shit to make sense of this senseless world.'

'Yeah. Did you know that the Titanic was sunk by Jesuits to facilitate the foundation of the Federal Reserve?'

Alberto answered with a roaring laugh that soon turned into a coughing fit. While he appeared to be in danger of suffocating, I opened another beer.

At dusk, we grabbed a kebab for dinner and went to a shot bar in Eixample. Downing one burning glass of disgusting spirit after another, Alberto and I pushed each other into a state of mindless exuberance. At one point, Alberto got so excited that he climbed onto the table and sang *The Internationale.* He told me anecdotes of his term in Oxford and ranted about income inequality and the aristocracy in England. After midnight, we tumbled towards Plaça de Catalunya and stumbled upon a group of drunk students queuing outside a nightclub called Gràcia Getaway. The amateurishly designed poster next to the entrance read, 'Fucking Monday Party!' 20 minutes later, we were covered in silver confetti, drinking saccharine sangria, and surrounded by obviously oblivious Erasmus students. The pop music clanking from the speakers was horrible. My vision was blurry. The girls were slurring. Hours of obtuse small talk, the feeling of cheap polyester on sweaty skin, and choking down flat beer later, I ran into Alberto on my way to the toilets. 'Man, let's get some fucking vodka,' he slurred. Vodka was probably the last thing we needed. To be sure, we bought a whole bottle. Blackout.

Someone was shaking my shoulder. A bell-like voice commanded, 'Wake up!' I turned around in my bed and opened my eyes. A dark-haired angel was squatting next to my bed. 'What happened to you?' It was the girl from reception. My head was humming. The world was muffled in cotton wool. There was blood on my pillow, and the blanket was dappled in auburn. My throat was dry and my stomach empty. 'You need to go to the hospital.' A warm smile crossed her lips as she carefully touched my forehead. Yes, sweet angel.

I spent Tuesday night in hospital. My cheekbone was broken in three places. The left half of my face was scuffed and swollen, my right elbow and knee were grazed too, and two ribs on my right side were bruised. My knuckles were bruised as well. I had a heavy concussion. I was familiar with the dizzy, woozy humming from the aftermath of some of my fights.

Alberto didn't answer his phone. Ben called and offered me a job at his bank in Frankfurt. And Alice wrote me a message that 'they' were coming to Barcelona on Thursday and that she wanted to meet— no word of our fight in Rome, nor of who 'they' were. The image of her arriving in Barcelona, arms linked with Arman and Dion, burned like a glowing knife in my skull. My dizziness grew worse as Alice twirled around in my thoughts and dreams. I was released from the hospital on Wednesday morning.

Now, I was sitting on a bench in the shade of a tree on the small square outside the hospital, waiting for a taxi. The morning sun was scorching the shirtless workers on a construction site on the street. My head was spinning, and I was tired and hungry. Someone stepped in front of me, and I raised my eyes. Alberto looked at me with a wide grin, adjusting his colourful shirt. When I got up, he gave me a sturdy, cordial hug and said, 'Damn, you look like shit!'

'Thanks—nice to see you too.'

Alberto chuckled and exclaimed, 'Man, I'm so glad to see you! Are you okay?'

'Yeah—just some bruises, a broken cheekbone, and a concussion.'

'Shit.'

'Yeah, but the bone has been barely pushed in, so I won't need surgery . . . Where have you been? I tried to call you.'

'Man, that's a fucked-up story! I woke up yesterday noon on a couch in a hotel lobby—in fucking Calella!'

'What? Where is Calella?'

'About an hour north from here—a horrible, soulless binge-tourism destination.'

'How did you end up there?' A chuckle hurt my cheek.

'I have no fucking idea, man. Maybe I fell through an Einstein-Rosen bridge. The last thing I vaguely remember is drinking vodka shots with you at the bar. And then you disappeared with some American girl, I think.' He frantically stroked his moustache. 'Next thing I know, I'm woken up by this furious hotel receptionist and find myself on this white leather couch, covered with a pink beach towel, my clothes soaked in foam. They kicked me out of the lobby. I must have lost my phone. And when I asked someone for directions to Vila de Gràcia, I was surprised by the fact that I'm not even in fucking Barcelona anymore. It took me the entire day to get my shit together and make it back to Barcelona. And this morning, my fiancée—her name is Núria, by the way—told me you were in the hospital.'

I shook my head in cautious laughter and said, 'Thanks for coming.' I pointed at his left elbow, which was matted with blood. 'What happened to you?'

He brushed over the scrape, waved his hand, and said, 'I have no idea. No worries, though; it's just a scratch. Do you remember what happened to you? Did you get into a fight?'

'I have no idea. Probably.'

Alberto chuckled, 'This American girl's boyfriend must be one hell of a crazy motherfucker to mess you up like that.'

We laughed until my cheek pulsated with dull pain and my ribs hurt. Alberto shook his head and said, 'I'm just glad you're all right.' He lit a cigarette and raised his bushy eyebrows. 'Man, I'm fucking hungry. Do you wanna grab lunch somewhere and go back to our hostel?'

I glanced over to the street and back at Alberto. 'Yeah, let's move. I have a feeling my taxi won't come, anyway.'

We bought takeaway tortillas with chicken and onions and had lunch in a nearby park. Casa Surís was only a kilometre away, but my right knee gave me some trouble. When we walked into the lobby, Núria jumped up behind her desk and shouted, 'They already let you go? How are you? I was worried about you!'

'I'm okay, thanks.'

'Do *you* know what happened?'

Alberto put his right hand on my neck, held his scuffed elbow into her face, and said, 'I already told you; this madman and I protected innocent children against dozens of sinister thugs.'

'Sure.' She nodded, a sarcastic expression on her face.

The floor beneath my feet started tottering, and the world began to spin around my hazy head. 'I'm tired. I'm going for a nap,' I heard myself mumble.

'Okay, let me know if you need anything,' Núria said in her bell-like voice.

As I walked towards my room, Alberto's muffled voice slowly faded, 'You know, I also broke my jaw once. I jumped from a bunkbed in a dark room in a hostel in Mexico City. Let's go to Mexico together! I'll show you the most beautiful canals to explore on a *trajinera*, and we can visit my distant cousin who runs a shaman Xtabentún bar in—'

I woke up at dawn on Thursday and stepped onto the balcony. The morning air was cool but already gave you a feeling of how hot the day would be. Barcelona was still dozing under an orange sky. I felt lightheaded. The purple left side of my face had become numb from the swelling. I could have been dead—my skull smashed in, the fleeting illusion of existence squished by a brain haemorrhage. Whose bones had bruised my knuckles? Whose transient life out there had my fists interfered with? A cool breeze carried the salty scent of the sea through the first rays of the sun breaching the horizon. A painful, asymmetric smile briefly crossed my lips. After another nap and a cold shower, I had breakfast with Alberto at a café downstairs. His breakfast consisted of two cups of black coffee, four cigarettes, and a soft-boiled egg. I asked him, 'How did it go with the-reception-girl-slash-your-future-wife yesterday?'

Alberto frowned. 'Núria. Ah, I don't know, man. We talked for a while. I found out that her mum's originally from England; that's why her English is so good. But she had to work, and I got the feeling I was bugging her . . . I only have two more days to propose to her!'

'Are you leaving?'

'Yeah, I'm flying back to LA on Saturday.' He fidgeted around on his chair. 'How long are you staying in Barça?'

'I don't know. Alice is coming here tomorrow.'

Alberto laughed his coughing laughter and said, 'I told you it ain't over between you two.'

'Yeah . . . Fuck me.'

Alberto answered with raucous laughter.

I exhaled with a suffering smile and said, 'Should we start drinking, then?'

'Man, don't you have a concussion?'

'Yeah, you're right—maybe not the best idea.'

We spent the day at the beach in Barceloneta. I stayed in the shade of a sun umbrella to give my scrambled brain some rest. Alberto basked in the sun and periodically jumped into the slow, harmless waves. As he lay on his back to dry his black-haired, sturdy chest, he asked, 'Man, what's your biggest fear?'

I exhaled and rubbed my eyes. 'I—I don't know . . . Maybe . . . I know this sounds weird, but—I think I'm scared of succumbing to the darkness within me.'

'What do you mean?'

I hesitated. My head was spinning. 'You know, so far, I've hurt everyone I've ever loved. And I'm afraid that my pride, my envy, my greed will make me harm those whom I love, again. And who knows whom I hurt the other night.'

With a chuckle, Alberto said, 'It looks as though they might have hurt you too a little. In any case, I'm sure they had it coming. And who says you have to repeat the mistakes you've made in the past? People change, man. I think it was Solzhenitsyn who wrote that the line dividing good and evil cuts through the heart of every man. And we can push that line throughout our life.'

I nodded slowly and asked, 'What is *your* biggest fear?'

'Hmm . . . I fear death, as do all living things. But I'm also afraid of betraying my ideals and corrupting myself for a little temporary comfort. I fear I'll stop asking questions because it's exhausting and start watching reality TV instead of reading books—to numb my existential anxieties. I fear that I become complaisant in the financialisation of society, the entertainisation of politics, and the sanitation of war . . . I guess I'm afraid of obliviousness.'

'Said he, drinking himself blind in Barcelona.'

With a grin, Alberto raised a pedantic finger and proclaimed, 'There is nobody who doesn't criticise the existing order of things without realising that he is thereby denying his own existence.'

'Who said that?'

'Some French Enlightenment dude.' He took a drag from his ubiquitous cigarette. 'I see your point; I might not give the impression of overthrowing the system. But at least I'm awake. I'm alive. Now, that's my biggest fear: to be alive but dead—it happens to too many people.'

I was tired, and we soon went back to the hostel. The swelling in my knee had already receded, and I could walk pain-free. The streets were filled with warm air carrying the smell of rubbish bags that had lain too long in the sun. After a kebab for dinner, I let the unswollen half of my face slump into the warm hostel pillow and slept for another 14 hours.

When I woke up to a bright Spanish morning, the humming in my head was gone, and the swelling beneath my blue skin was retreating. The other back-packers in my room still stared at my bruised face with puzzled eyes but returned my morning greetings. I met Alberto for breakfast downstairs and told him, 'I'm going over to Alice's Airbnb for lunch. She arrived this morning—feel like joining?'

'Don't you wanna go there alone?'

'She's travelling with some friends, so it would be nice to have backup too.'

At noon, we walked through the grid-patterned streets in the southwest of Eixample. Alice's flat was on the top floor of an old orange building with small, ornate balconies facing the street. When we had climbed the five flights of battered stone stairs, we didn't have to ring the bell; Alberto's coughing fit alarmed half the neighbourhood. A door flew open. Alice appeared in the doorway, swathed in a light apricot-coloured summer dress. She glanced at Alberto, who was leaning against the green handrail, then looked at me with a puzzled smirk. Her deep-brown eyes opened wide, and she took two quick steps towards me. Her outstretched hand stopped a hairbreadth away from my bruised cheek. 'My god, what did you do this time?'

'Don't expect an answer from this amnesic fool!' Alberto said with a chuckle, finally catching his breath again. Alice turned to Alberto, who enthusiastically shook her hand and said, 'Montoya. Alberto Montoya.'

Alice gave him her knee-weakening smile and said, 'Nice to meet you, Alberto Montoya. I'm Alice.'

Dion, dressed in turquoise board shorts, jumped through the doorway and gave me a bare-chested hug. 'Man, what happened to your face?' he exclaimed. His audacious blue eyes radiated sincere concern as he brushed the golden tresses out of his handsome face.

'Well, I woke up like this in my hostel bed after a night out with Alberto here. It's nothing serious, though.'

Dion turned to Alberto, who said, 'Montoya. Alberto Montoya.'

With a wide, sunny grin, Dion answered, 'Shein. Dion Armon Shein.'

'That's the first time I hear your full name!' Alice laughed.

As Dion shook Alberto's hand, Alice looked at me with a sheepish smile. The nerdy glasses were missing on her button nose, and her brown locks were wet. I smiled back at her, carefully. Dion exclaimed, 'Guys, come inside; it's a beautiful apartment!'

The flat had two bedrooms and an open-plan kitchen and was parqueted with large old floorboards. Full of enthusiasm, Dion told me that their hosts, who were on holiday in Sri Lanka, also had two scooters downstairs, which we could use for a sightseeing tour. Alberto went straight to the rooftop garden, sat on a small wooden bench between palm and olive trees, and started smoking. Dion and I joined him outside and sat on shaky metal garden chairs. Dion inspected my injuries and confirmed the diagnosis I had received in the hospital. Alice brought a glass jug with ice-cooled lemonade and sat down on my lap without hesitation. I felt Dion's look from the side as I put my hand on Alice's tender thigh. He asked, 'So, you have no idea what happened to you?'

'No. Nada. Alberto and I were getting hammered, and the next thing I remember is waking up covered in blood.'

'Yeah, it was a crazy night,' Alberto added with a chuckle. 'I woke up in fucking Calella without any memory of how I got there. And somehow, I injured myself too.' He raised his scuffed elbow.

Alice laughed and said, 'I see you two had great fun in Barcelona together.'

'Well, Mister Rocky Marciano over here had to get some rest in the hospital, but other than that, it was a good time.'

Alice pointed to Alberto's scuffed elbow and said, 'Do you think that will leave a scar?'

'I hope so,' he answered with a wide grin. 'I like scars. Only voyeurs get through life scarless.'

'Or people who know how to handle their latent alcoholism,' Alice said, smirking.

Alberto's grin remained unimpeded as he took a drag from his cigarette and changed the topic, 'And you two are coming from Rome? How was it?'

Dion answered, 'Yeah, we went to this techno festival; it was pretty wild! And Rome is simply beautiful. It reminded me of Jerusalem. Everything in Rome is so old and has so much history.'

Alice leaned back and whispered in my ear, 'I'm sorry.'

'Yeah, me too.'

Alice gave me a furtive kiss. Her lips were soft and moist. I exhaled and smiled.

Alberto asked Dion, 'And you're from Israel?'

'Yeah.'

'Where are your ancestors from?'

'Some of my grandparents were from France. Some were Polish. The French fled to the US in 1940. The Polish survived the Shoah and went to Sweden after the war. And then they all went to Israel in the early fifties. My parents grew up together there.'

As he rolled another cigarette, Alberto asked, 'What do you think of the Israeli settlements?'

'Straight to the point, huh? Man, I could get worked up over that topic for hours.'

Alice got up and said, 'Don't, we have to prepare lunch.'

As the two of them went inside, I asked, 'Do you need any help?'

With a smile to light the darkest night, Alice said, 'No, you stay outside and enjoy the sun.'

I watched Alberto take off his sweat-soaked Hawaiian shirt and smoke another rolled-up cigarette. I let my eyes pan over the surrounding orange rooftops. I felt a sudden prickling in my feet and got up. I was alone in this dark universe and would soon be dust. My mind plunged into dizziness. The blue sky warped into a purple hell. My breath grew heavy and my vision blurry. The palm trees were creeping into the fiery sky like ash-grey skeletons. I needed air. 'Are you okay?' Dizzy panic bursting my skull. Gasping for air. Suffocating. I was dying. The house came crumbling down beneath my feet. My heart tried to escape my chest. I was spinning, looking for something to hold on to, finding only smudgy emptiness. 'Breathe, man!'

Yes, breathing. A firm hand on my shoulder. 'Everything is going to be all right. Breathe. Breathe. Slowly.' I closed my eyes. I was dizzy. But I knew I wouldn't die—not today. I tried to breathe rhythmically. When I opened my eyes, Alberto's calm, dark eyes looked at me in front of a newly born blue sky. The trees were green and full of life. 'Do you feel better, man?' A warm smile under his full moustache.

I took another deep breath and said, 'Yeah, it was just a little panic attack—happens to me sometimes.' I sat down and took a long sip of ice-cold lemonade. Alberto emitted thin smoke into the warm air of the rooftop garden and sat back down as well. I smiled at Alberto sheepishly and said, 'Please don't tell the others, okay?'

'Man, everybody is overwhelmed by life sometimes—nothing to be ashamed of. But I won't tell anybody.'

'Thanks.'

I leaned back and closed my eyes. Screw life and all its ambiguity, uncertainty, and inconceivability. And screw Dion and Arman and all the others. Screw everyone and everything but Alice's warm, tender thigh beneath my hand. When I opened my eyes, Dion had put up a sun umbrella above the garden table. He was disinfecting and dressing the graze on Alberto's elbow. On the table lay a pair of tweezers and a first aid kit Dion had found in the bathroom. Alberto was smoking and gave me a wide grin as he tried to sit still. Soon, Alice served us lunch—cauliflower and chickpea stew with fluffy couscous. When Alberto found out Alice was a vegetarian, he asked her why. She answered, 'Because I don't like how animals are treated in farming factories. And I think it's morally wrong to kill living creatures for food.'

'But the alternative for these animals is not a happy life but nonexistence,' Alberto replied. 'Their purpose is to be eaten. If we stop eating pork, pigs cease existing. Is a wretched existence worse than not existing at all? Do you wanna be responsible for the extinction of a species?'

'Well, some people keep pigs as pets. But, I don't know, even besides ethical concerns, we need to eat less meat to save the planet from climate change.'

'Save the planet?' Alberto chuckled cynically. 'I don't think the planet gives two fucks about climate change. It's a piece of dirt floating through a universe that's indifferent to our existence. If anything, we've got to save ourselves. Sometimes I doubt there's much worth saving, though.'

'I'm not sure I like your friend,' Alice said as she turned to me and laughed.

Unfazed, Alberto said, 'The topic of killing animals makes me think of abortion.'

'Of course it does,' I sighed.

'We probably agree that killing a pig is not as bad as murdering a baby, right?'

'I think you're on to something here, Alberto,' I said. Alice chuckled.

'Well, a full-grown pig probably has a higher level of consciousness than a newborn, right?'

'But a baby has the potential of becoming a fully developed human being,' Alice said.

'Well, that potential is also present in foetuses. And this is the exact point that anti-abortionists make. And they're usually ridiculed by liberals.'

'But you also have to consider the mother's well-being.'

'I don't disagree. All I'm saying is that progressive convictions often aren't as obvious as they are made out to be. Anyway, I do think that, in the not-too-distant future, when meat is grown in the lab, our descendants will look back at us and say, "How could these monsters kill animals?" You see, Alice, I think on this issue you are on the right side of history. But, fuck me sideways, could righteousness ever taste as good as a cheeseburger with bacon?'

Alice grabbed my thigh under the table and looked at me with a grin. 'Well, maybe your friend is not so bad after all.'

After we carried our dishes inside and lit after-lunch cigarettes, Dion said, 'I'm not sure how much of a concern eating meat will be when people look back at our times. There's still so much violence going on beyond our Western comfort zones. In Chad, millions of people had to flee religious violence, while the rest of the world doesn't care. In my home country, we have been living in violence for generations. And the list goes on and on. I mean, Alice, the war in Congo has never really stopped either, has it?'

Alice sighed, 'Well, in the area where I was, there was no fighting. But we heard horrible, unbelievable stories of mass rape and cannibalism from distant eastern districts.'

Dion nodded and sighed. 'War is still common-place in the world. And Africa is still suffering.' He added bitterly, 'And the UN is a farce. They stand by and do nothing.'

'Yeah, African tragedies remote from TV cameras don't rank very highly on the Western agenda,' Alberto said.

Dion said with vibrating anger, 'The West's arrogance can be so annoying! When I was in Africa, I sometimes wondered if we were there to help people or if we were doing charity tourism. Don't get me wrong, while working for Doctors Without Borders, I have met many selfless, beautiful people trying to right the wrongs in our world. But somehow, we're also a part of a neo-colonial system—living in air-conditioned houses while our local colleagues dwell in tent shanty towns. And organisation committees ignore the local institutions and impose on the poor what the white man thinks is best for them.'

Alberto took a deep drag of his cigarette. 'I remember this Dutch guy from my undergrad at Brown. His father was stationed as a Dutchbat soldier in Srebrenica during the massacre there. His father killed himself back in Holland. The man couldn't live with the inactiveness of his battalion while the Serbs raped and killed thousands of Muslims on their watch.'

'I read somewhere that civil society is a wafer-thin veneer on top an ocean of violence a billion years of evolution deep,' Dion said.

We all went silent for a while and listened to the rattling of small engines and the shouts of sweating Spaniards from the street below. Alice jumped up and said, 'Okay, enough with the gloomy, ineffective talking already! Let's go swimming!'

We spent the afternoon at the beach. My head was ready for the sun again. Alice and I watched Alberto and Dion play beach volleyball with the locals. Whichever team Dion was on won. We chased each other through the knee-high waves.

We had pasta and beer for dinner back in the flat's rooftop garden and went out for drinks in the Gothic Quarter. On the way there, I walked next to Dion. Alice and Alberto were leading the way, discussing the impact of China's Belt and Road Initiative on Africa. Dion looked at me sheepishly and said, 'Alice told me how great it was in Tuscany.'

'Did she?'

'Yes,' he answered, failing to suppress a bitter overtone. We remained silent for the rest of the walk. Alice found a small, cosy bar in one of the narrow, plastered alleys that ran parallel to the nearby waterfront. The bar had an open front, and boisterous groups of hostel folk from all over the globe walked by our table. A moaning ventilator hung from the ceiling and blended the warm and heavy air. Dion had brought a deck of cards, and we played Kings until we could no longer recall the rules or articulate a coherent thought. It was four when we weaved across Plaça de Catalunya, singing an off-key version of *Wonderwall* together. As we reached the main street, Alice grabbed my hand and said to Alberto, 'We turn left here. Do you want to join as well?'

'I'm good, thanks. I have to go home to my future wife and check out of the hostel tomorrow morning.'

'Oh no, you're leaving already; I forgot that. Come by for breakfast before you leave. You can bring your future wife too!'

'Cool, sounds good. All right, I'm dead tired. See you tomorrow.'

Before we parted ways, I gave Alberto the keys to my room and locker. He winked at me roguishly. Back at the flat, Dion, Alice, and I had a last glass of Rioja under the starlit sky. They played their devious game of defiant looks and fervent touches. Soon we lay on Alice's bed together, naked, exploring the shadows two flickering candles drew on twitching muscles beneath bronzy skin. A couple of times, I kissed and touched Dion, but only to make Alice break us up and seize me with more passion than before. Dion wanted more of me than I was willing to offer. His restless blue eyes burned with desperate desire as he gazed at me, Alice trembling between us. I thrust my hips against Alice's. She started moaning, the slender muscles in her back tensing up in pleasure. Dion's hands were all over my body. His teeth tickled my neck. The alcohol had made me feel numb. It took me a long time to finish, panting and wet with sweat. As Alice and I lay together on our back, struggling for air, Dion stroked my chest with hungry fingers. Soon, Alice got up, ran to the bathroom, and came back with a tube of Vaseline. She grabbed my hand and guided it to Dion's erect, circumcised dick. Together, we rubbed him. My hand became its own sentient being and found pleasure in Dion's. He closed his eyes and threw his head back into the pillow with a groan of relief. When Dion started moaning in ecstasy, his body as stiff as Greek marble, Alice chuckled with pleasure and ran her hand through his golden, sweat-soaked tresses. As Alice kissed Dion, breathing heavily, I closed my eyes and fell onto my pillow. The last thing I sensed was Alice's mellow voice in my ear: 'Sleep well, my bruised boxer.'

When I woke up, through the numbness, I felt a soft touch on my left cheek; Alice was caressing my scuffed skin with tender hands. I opened my eyes and saw her smile with motherly warmth. Despite a dry mouth and a dull headache, I felt snug and secure. She gave me a kiss and a glass of cold water. Her fingers explored the scratches and bruises on my face, knuckles, elbow, and knee. 'If I ever meet whoever did this to you, I'll have a very serious word with them.'

With laughter that hurt my bruised ribs, I said, 'If you do, let me know who they are.'

She stroked my hair and said, 'Is it hard for you not to know what happened?'

'I'm just afraid I might have seriously harmed someone.'

Alice nodded with a smile and gave me a long kiss. We snuggled in bed until we got hungry. Dion was sitting in the kitchen, drinking coffee and checking football scores on his laptop. The blue in his eyes had lost its lustre. Alice playfully rubbed his hair and asked, '*Hej*, where have you been?'

Dion rearranged his blond locks, gazed out of the window and mumbled, 'Ah, I just felt like sleeping in my own bed this morning.'

As Alice started scrambling eggs and toasting bread, I sat down with a plaintive groan. Dion looked at me over his screen and said, 'You worked in a bank, right?'

'Yeah.' In a distant past I didn't miss.

'So, lately, I've been trying to follow the financial news. I'm thinking about investing a little money. But it's just so tiring and confusing—P/E ratios, yield curves, ETFs, quantitative easing, spreads, risk premiums—and what the hell is a plain vanilla option?'

I chuckled.

He asked, 'Do you have some insider tips for me?'

'What would you like to do with your money? Invest long-term?'

'Yeah—nothing fancy. Can you maybe recommend a certain investment fund? It all seems so obscure to me.'

'Well, there's a dirty little secret the average banker living off fees doesn't want you to know: unless you want to use complex tax avoidance schemes, the fund manager that can consistently outperform the market has yet to be born. Instead, just manage your finances yourself and focus on a couple of simple rules: Make use of subsidised investment schemes. Put some of your money in bonds and invest the lion's share in low-fee exchange-traded funds that hold a diversified portfolio of stocks. If you're a doomsdayer, maybe put some money in precious metals. If you're planning on living somewhere for a long time, and the housing market is not in a bubble—as a rule of thumb, if the price-to-rent ratio is below 20—consider buying property. And that's it, more or less.'

With a shining grin, Dion said, 'That actually didn't sound too complicated. Thanks! Can you write that down for me?'

Alice uttered a loud, extended yawn. I looked at her grimly, and we both giggled.

When Dion and I set the garden table outside, a loud, rattling coughing came from the stairwell. 'That's got to be Alberto,' Alice exclaimed with a laugh and ran to the door. 'Come in; breakfast is ready!'

Breathing heavily, Alberto carried our two large backpacks into the kitchen, gave me my keys, and collapsed onto one of the garden chairs, thick beads of sweat on his forehead. 'Man, this old nightlife is killing me,' he gasped, lighting a cigarette.

Alice and Dion brought out scrambled eggs, toasted bread, cream cheese, ham, pears, honeydew, coffee, and fresh orange juice. It was a fine morning in the Spanish sun.

At noon, we accompanied Alberto to nearby Urgell station. While Dion and Alice were marvelling at the latest ugly one-piece swimsuits in one of the shop windows, Alberto and I stood in front of the station's stairway. I plucked at the seam of my T-shirt and asked, 'What are you going to do back in LA?'

'Get back to the thrilling research life, I guess. Drink a little less. See whether my wacko roommates have become Bitcoin millionaires by now. And you?'

I looked over to Alice tickling Dion, who was wrapping his long, sinewy arms around her. 'I don't know. Let's see what Barcelona brings. Maybe get a job. Maybe leave it all behind and become a bartender in Cuba.'

Alberto chuckled, glanced at Alice, and said, 'Good luck.'

I raised my eyebrows. 'Thanks.'

'And if things don't work out, come to California, man!' Alberto stroked his moustache and looked at me with kind, dark eyes.

'Yeah . . . Maybe I will.'

'All right, I gotta go.'

I gave him a hug, and so did Dion and Alice. Alberto adjusted his yellow Hawaiian shirt, bowed slightly, and disappeared into the station.

As we walked back to the flat, I asked, 'What shall we do today—take the scooters for a ride around the city?'

Dion looked at me with a conspiratorial grin and said, 'We got something special planned for today.' A spark of compulsion glowed in his eyes.

'Yeah?'

Alice grabbed my arm vigorously and exclaimed, 'We'll let you in on it back at our apartment!'

When we were sitting in the rooftop garden, Dion fetched a little plastic container from his room and emptied it on the table. Five little white pills shone in the sun. They had the Eye of Horus printed on them. I looked up at Dion and asked, 'What is this?'

'2C-B—a synthetic psychoactive substance of the phenethylamine family.'

I turned to Alice with a quizzical expression. She added, 'It's like a mixture of LSD and MDMA.'

'And where did you get it from?'

Dion said, 'Arman gave it to us in Rome. We all tried a little piece during the festival—it was amazing. We should try a whole pill this time.'

'Did you take it with you on the plane?'

'Yeah.' They chuckled. Alice ran her fingers through my hair and said, 'Let's try it, okay? It's really an amazing experience.'

'Okay . . . '

'Awesome!' Dion exclaimed.

Each of us swallowed one pill. Dion went inside and brought two jugs of water and three glasses. He said, 'It will take between 30 and 60 minutes to kick in. If you feel panic, talk to each other. And remember that a trip is really not any more terrifying than reality. It's just another reality we aren't used to.'

Alice put on flamenco music, and we talked about online dating and its social effects. A tense nervousness hung in the warm air. My hands were sweaty. Electric needles lightly tickled my skin from the inside. Alice started giggling. I turned to her. The white lines of mortar between orange bricks on the wall behind her started warping—her deep-brown eyes were windows to the primordial female desire. A grey pigeon sat in the rain gutter of the opposite building with a big piece of bread in its beak—I felt happy for the lonely bird—it would not go hungry tonight. My skull was tickling with indulgence—Dion's smile morphed into a breaking, whooshing wave and yet stayed the same—the essence of his spirit—'do you feel it?'—the sun sent its eternal photons through the ephemeral cells of my body—'yes'—my heart was beating, rebelling, vigorously—before long, it would be ash—like the ashes of my parents—a family in the Hungarian sun, full of love and baseless hope—suffering, ever-present in our life—the noble truth—

progress requires pain—were my eyes closed?—did I still see?—or did this garden, did Alice, beautiful Alice, merely exist within my mind?—my synapses were firing, forming thoughts, a miracle of illusion in a dark cosmos—who was thinking this?—I?—who was I?—deep within this consciousness, there was only edgeless space—thoughts, emotions, memories, swirling in the ether—beyond the brink of the last abyss, an instant after the end of time, a moment before its beginning, stood an old olive tree in a Roman vase on a Spanish rooftop garden, under a sun-bleached sky—a bruised boxer sat next to a girl—irredeemable, irrevocable affection—a Greek statue of a man, golden tresses on Atlantic shoulders, and blue stars radiating compassion—'love is additive'—a tender hand—'yes'—mellow lips—time was water running through a greenish well and dripping into a basin filled with cosmic nebula—Spanish guitars were painting black walls of eviternity with multidimensional colours—on a dusty Catalan street, Laelaps barked at the Teumessian fox—the existential struggle cast in sandstone, forever—the boy with the bruised face stood up and touched the face of the girl—she loved him, and he knew it was true—she had been hurt, and he had been hurt, and she had hurt him, and he would hurt her—and when it was all over, it would all happen again, and it would all be all right—the invisible magnetic waves of the universe were stroking his skin—my skin—on Alice's naked skin—an oasis of humid lust in a dry desert of brick-red rooftops—tender, fertile flesh—flickering air above pulsating breasts—a black rose blossoming, watered with lotions of passion—heart beating, untamed billows of ecstasy surging within my body—another pair of hands, sturdy hands, trembling with restless desire—

forbidden touches—yes—only my father and you—
'please!'—strong muscles in my hands, Alice's teeth
on my neck—her hands were mine—the taste of the
forbidden fruit—moans of pleasure under indifferent
skies—an explosion of joy setting this world of bittersweet pain ablaze—'I know your solitude'—warm
bodies against mine—comfort in the bosom of love—
dancing colours on closed eyelids—salvation, in
Alice's arms—finally, darkness.

In another life, my heartbeat slowed—I gradually
regained control of my thoughts—the universe re-
sumed its striving for entropy. We lay on the coarse
floorboards of the rooftop garden. The sun was setting, and the crepuscular shadows of reality cloaked
our transcendental bliss. Dion gave us water—goose-
bumps on bare skin. Alice took Dion and me by the
hand and led us into her bed—barefoot over wooden
floor. Snot clogged my throat, and my brain felt
roughened and empty. Dion and Alice snuggled up to
me on both sides beneath a white, virgin blanket as
the night fell. Muffled, wistful Spanish singing echoed
outside. The curtain danced in the summer breeze,
and the orange light of the city drew soft shapes on the
ceiling. A lonely tear ran down my bruised cheek. I
closed my eyes.

The first rays of the morning sun shone through the
slit between the curtains when I woke up. The bed
beside me was empty. My feet were tingling, and my
hands were trembling as I got up. I put on boxers and
scuffled to the kitchen to get some water. Alice and
Dion sat outside on opposite ends of the table in the
cool morning. I sat on one of the garden chairs next to
Alice, and she handed me her almost finished cigarette. I nodded and said, 'How are you?' At least, I

thought I said that; I couldn't be sure.

To my relief, Dion answered, 'I don't know. That was intense! I still feel a little surreal, to be honest.'

'Yeah, me too,' Alice said. 'Last night feels like a weird, distant dream. And my thoughts are still a little off.'

We ate breakfast in silence and then tried to get some more sleep.

After two hours of hazy dozing, we walked to the beach. It took us more than an hour since we got lost a few times. Lying at the beach, my senses seemed detached from reality. When I said something, I felt as though I was speaking in a foreign language. The first primaeval man to ever utter a word in the flickering light of a fire in a dark cave—to whom did he talk? And what did he say? I was uncertain whether I was articulating my thoughts or merely listening to them. Standing at the shore, Alice cried when she noticed all the plastic waste scattered across the beach—for another million years. We tried to laugh off the subtle insanity clinging to our consciousnesses. I was senselessly happy.

In the evening, we took the metro back to our flat and cooked pasta. Only during dinner did my mind regain its usual shape. Alice went down to buy red wine from one of the small corner shops. Dion and I sat outside in the rooftop garden and smoked a cigarette. After a while, he broke the silence: 'You know, I really enjoyed last night.'

I looked at him sheepishly and mumbled, 'Yeah, I don't know what to say, really . . . I'm afraid you might want more from me than I can give you.'

He nodded with a stern face and said, 'I don't want to make you uncomfortable. I know you're not really into men. I just wanted you to know yesterday meant something to me . . . Don't worry, I don't get my hopes up.' He hesitated. 'It's just—It's just that—watching you and Alice can sometimes be painful.' He looked away and exhaled smoke into the warm air.

With a cynical chuckle, I said, 'I know what you mean.'

His blue eyes pierced me as he said, softly, 'Alice has been hurt—viciously. I don't know if she can trust anyone again.' When he finished his cigarette, he got up with exhausted movements, ran his hand through his blond locks, and said, 'All right, I'm going to bed.'

'Don't you want to join us for a drink?'

'No, thanks.' His haunted eyes radiated a painful sadness. 'Goodnight.'

'Night.'

When Alice came back, she asked, 'Where's Dion?'

'He already went to bed . . . I'm afraid I hurt his feelings.'

'It's not your fault.' She gave me a gentle smile. 'I'll talk to him tomorrow.' She opened the bottle and filled two bulbous glasses.

As I lit a cigarette, I thought of Alberto's words in Sofia and asked Alice, 'Do you think everything is pre-determined, and free will is only an illusion?'

She sat next to me on the bench, smiling at me in the half-light. 'I don't know. And, to be honest, I don't care . . . I think the only truth in life is beauty. If you look too close at anything, it disappears right in front of your eyes. If you had an infinitely strong micro-scope, you'd see nothing but empty space. If you had a strong enough telescope, you'd see only darkness. If you say a word often enough, it loses any meaning. But you could dissect Jeff Buckley's *Hallelujah*, study all its notes and harmonies, and yet his voice would never cease to evoke a heart-wrenching melancholy.

Even analysing all the dabs of Monet's *Water Lilies* cannot rationalise away the blissful calmness they radiate.' She softly ran her fingertips across my scuffed cheek, sending an auguring tickle through the numbness. 'Even knowing that feelings are only chemical reactions within synapses in your brain doesn't make them any less true.' She gave me a tender kiss. 'So, in the end, who cares if this night was predetermined, as long as we enjoy it a little while it lasts.'

We drank our wine in the cosy silence of the warm night. We took the rest of the bottle into her bed and watched *Lost in Translation* on my laptop. Before the film was finished, Alice fell asleep in my arms. I smelled her chestnut hair and carefully ran my fingers across the globe on her shoulder. Let me hold you. Let me ease your pain. Share your secrets with me, and I'll run to the end of the world and bury them deep under an old tree by Ogenus' sea, where no one will find them. And forgive me, for I will hurt you, too. I closed my eyes, stretched my legs, took a deep breath, and fell asleep.

Early on Monday morning, we had croissants for breakfast in a café downstairs, where Dion and Alice marked all the sights they wanted to visit on a small map. He wanted to see sports stadiums, she art and architecture. We found our hosts' two scooters parked around the corner in the shade of a dry plane tree. Dion dashed through the bustling streets on a red Vespa. I tried to keep up on an ugly turquoise scooter from the '90s, Alice embracing me from behind. We rushed past green trees and the brown stones of a university building. A chequered maze of one-way streets led us to Illa de la Discòrdia, where we turned our heads towards the warped, mosaic-covered front

315

of Gaudí's Casa Batlló. Past the twisted iron balconies of Casa Milà, we made our way to the north of Eixample, where we circled the ever-unfinished spires of the Sagrada Família, protruding into the light-blue sky from masses of perspiring tourists.

After a detour via the streets surrounding the sun-bleached red Hospital de Sant Pau, we paid an obligatory visit to the tourist-filled Park Güell on Carmel Hill. Alice made us look at *trencadís* dragons, and I watched her marvel at Gaudí's organic, ornamental creations. Dion sat on a blue stone wall and smoked a cigarette with a gloomy face. Alice was wearing the sunglasses I had bought for her in Rome.

We paced our scooters further up the hills to the Carmel Bunkers. The site on the top of Turó de la Rovira had been built as an anti-aircraft fortification during the Spanish Civil War and had later been home to a shanty town. Today, the ruins offered a stunning panoramic view of the entire city. While Alice and Dion tried to climb one of the rubble stone walls, I gazed at the sea shimmering along the horizon. Halfway to the water, Torre Agbar, the glass and aluminium cucumber, was glittering in the sun. Alice declared, 'I'm hungry; let's get lunch.'

We jumped on our scooters and drove back down into Gràcia, where we stopped for an unreasonable quantity of tapas in the shade of a tree on Plaça de la Virreina.

After lunch, we followed a long, straight avenue that ran diagonally through the city to Camp Nou in the southwest of Barcelona. Dion wanted to go inside the stadium, but Alice was reluctant to pay 25 euros to 'look at some dusty trophies and dirty old jerseys'.

I said, 'Yeah, I don't want to go either. But you could check it out, and we can meet up afterwards?'

Alice gave me a content kiss on my unbruised cheek.

'No, fine, whatever,' Dion said in an aggrieved tone. He rushed to the red scooter and darted off.

'He's so tense today,' Alice sighed. We got on our ugly scooter and followed Dion along the hot asphalt of another long avenue to Plaça d'Espanya. We turned right, passed between two towers resembling St Mark's Campanile in Venice, and reached the Magic Fountain, where we stopped for a cigarette. The Museu Nacional was towering in the background, and a cool mist hung in the torrid air. I lit Dion's cigarette and asked, 'All good, man?'

'Yeah, don't worry.' He turned away into the sun.

Alice dragged me to the fountain to take photos with it in the background. As soon as we had finished our cigarettes, Dion urged us to move on. We left the red bricks of Caixa Forum to our right and rushed the groaning scooters up Montjuïc, to the old stadiums of the 1992 Summer Olympics in Anella Olímpica, and past botanical gardens and parks. We stopped at Plaça de l'Armada to enjoy the view of the harbour and the city below. The sun was scorching. We soon drove into the harbour and let the airstream cool our sweaty skin. We parked the scooters by the Maremagnum and walked along the waterfront and past the Aquarium. Dion still seemed to be in a hurry, and before long, we had made our way back to our flat in the southwest of Eixample, past the tall palm trees of Plaça Reial and Plaça dels Àngels with its ubiquitous skaters. We parked the scooters in front of the house and went upstairs, Dion with a gloomy expression. I sat in the rooftop garden with him while Alice took a cold shower. I asked him, 'What did you mean when you said Alice has been hurt viciously?'

Dion stood up. 'Why don't you ask her?' He walked to the kitchen and turned around in the doorframe. With a suffering look, he said, 'You know, sooner or later, life breaks your heart. And whoever denies that is a liar or hasn't lived.'

He dragged his feet inside. Alice stepped out into the sun, naked. Her wet hair sparkled. With a giggle, she jumped onto my lap and kissed me lavishly. Cold drops of water tickled my skin. As her deep-brown eyes looked into mine, a door slammed shut inside with a loud bang of wood on wood. I asked, 'Did you talk to him?'

'This morning—but only briefly. He seems strangely distant. Maybe we shouldn't make out too much in front of him until he leaves.'

My eyes widened. 'When does he leave?'

'In two days.'

My heart was beating fast. 'And you?'

'We can have the apartment until Friday, so why not stay here until then and see what else we might want to do?' She looked at me with a roguish smirk.

I stood up from the bench with Alice wrapped around me like a monkey baby. 'I like that,' I said and kissed her.

She nibbled at my earlobe as I carried her into her room. I put her down on the bed and took off my shorts. She pulled me close. I kissed her slender neck and the rose between her breasts and her tanned belly and the soft skin on the inside of her thighs and the shaman fish symbol on her ankle and the little birthmark on her mons pubis and her soft lips. She kissed me breathlessly as I carefully moved inside her. Her fingernails ran down my back with tender firmness. Waves of joy billowed through my body. My breath grew heavy. 'Slowly. We have time,' she whispered. I dug my face into her neck. 'Your beard tickles,' she chuckled.

I gave her a long, smiling kiss and looked into her kind eyes for an intimate eternity. Her hands pulled me closer, ever closer. A fire of pleasure flared in my body. Her trembling hips made my hips tremble. Her moans made me moan. Her hands clutching my arms made my muscles tense up. Finally, I sank my face into the pillow next to her head to muffle a slow groan of unrestrained ecstasy. She put her head against mine and breathed into my ear, 'I love you.'

Smiling into the pillow, I mumbled, 'I love you too.'

I turned on my back, and she snuggled up to me and stroked my chest hair. With a feeling of warm comfort, I fell asleep.

A hysterical shout coming from the hall woke me up. 'What's wrong with you?' I heard Alice scream. A thud on the wooden floor. I jumped up and rushed into the hall, naked. Alice sat on the floor, her hair ruffled. Dion was standing over her with a strange fury in his bleary eyes.

'What did you do?' I snarled. My fists clenched.

With a cracking voice, Alice said, 'Stay calm. He's drunk.'

Dion's raging stare wandered across my naked body and pierced my eyes with pained hatred. He slurred, 'What are you going to do now, you—you pathetic son of a junkie whore?'

Dion stumbled back against the wall. Anger started to burn beneath my skin. With wide eyes, I stared at Alice, who was getting up from the floor.

'Dion,' she whispered. Tears started rolling down her cheeks.

'That's right. Your little girl—your little girlfriend

runs around telling your secrets to anyone who can be bothered to listen. But what do you know about her, huh?'

'Dion!' Alice begged.

'Did you know that the first man she fucked was her teacher? That he went to—to prison for it? That she tried to commit suicide over it?'

I stepped towards Dion with my fists trembling in front of my chest. I hissed through clenched teeth, 'Shut up.'

'Or what, huh? You can't hurt me more than you've—than you've already done. I was a fun little holiday experiment, wasn't I? Wasn't I!'

'Dion, please!' Alice said between her sobbing.

'And you're no better, you nymphomaniac slut.'

I heard my boiling blood rush through my ears. 'One more word, and I swear I'll beat the life out of you.'

Alice grabbed my shoulder and tried to pull me back. 'He doesn't mean it!'

'Oh, I mean it! She is a nympho, you know?' His mouth contorted to a wicked grin. 'Did she tell you about her—her Scottish rugby player? That he shared her with half his team and put the video of it online?'

'Dion, no!' Alice screamed, jumped towards him and tried to cover his face with her hands.

Dion shoved her violently, and she tumbled against the bathroom doorframe and to the floor. Dion glared at me with his wicked steel-blue eyes. I made a quick step towards him and threw a jab that landed on his chin with a thud. An instant later, my straight right fist crashed into his face and cracked his nose. He banged against the wall behind him and fell to the floor, landing on his side. Blood gushed out of his mouth and nose and dripped in thick, red drops onto the wooden floor. Alice crawled over to him and touched his bleeding face, screaming, 'What did you do!' As Alice held his head, Dion's eyes rolled around, disoriented. His lower lip was burst, and blood was also coming out of cuts on both sides of the bridge of his nose. Sweat made wisps of his golden locks stick to his reddened face. I awoke from my paralysis and ran back into our room. I put on a pair of shorts, a T-shirt, and my trainers and grabbed my wallet. In the hallway, Dion was sitting leant against the wall, and Alice was pressing a white towel against his mouth. I took one of the two keys out of the wooden bowl on the small cabinet and opened the door.

'Where are you going?'

I turned around. Alice stared at me with terror-stricken eyes. The towel in her hands was soaked with Dion's blood. Run. I shook my head, turned around, and slammed the door behind me shut. I rushed down the stairwell. You pathetic son of a junkie whore. For a while, I jogged along the pavement, sidestepping faceless pedestrians, seawards.

I stopped in front of a white sign reading 'Two Schmucks'. I stepped into the small room with bricks breaching the white plaster of the walls and sat down at a table scribbled with names, bad jokes, and obscene drawings. A bearded, tattooed guy with a grey baseball cap served me my first Negroni. Were the stories about Alice true? Was she all right? After the second Negroni, the knuckles on my left hand started hurting. Was Dion okay? I touched my right pocket; my phone was still back at the flat. With the third drink—something called a 'Curry Colada'—I had jalapeno cheddar waffles with fried chicken and honey butter. Why had she not told me? After the fourth drink—a Basil Smash—my knuckles stopped hurting.

Why could I not control myself? Bringing my fifth drink—a mint-rich Mojito—the bartender asked me, 'All good, man?' Sure it was. By the sixth drink—another delicious Mojito—it was dark outside, and the bar was packed. I wanted to beat the faces of everyone who had ever hurt Alice to a bloody pulp. I had the seventh drink—an Old Fashioned—with two girls from Canada I soon put off with my gloominess. Would she still be there when I came back? The eighth drink—another Old Fashioned—was served with an anxious, pitiful look—another handsome face I would have liked to push the nose up on. Run. I paid the bill and stumbled further down the narrow street towards the sea, smoking a soothing cigarette. A red neon light pulled me into another small bar. Drinks number nine and ten—two gin and tonics—were cool and blissful. Blackout.

The curring of a pigeon. The gurgling of water. Hard wood underneath me. I opened my eyes. I was lying on a bench in a small square that lay at the intersection of two narrow alleys. In its centre stood a small stone well. Apart from a group of cooing pigeons, the square was immersed in cool silence. Only the highest spire of the surrounding old buildings was touched by sunlight. My skull was bursting with dull pain. My throat was dry. My left knuckle hurt. Pain had also crept back into my broken cheek. I slowly stood up and was relieved to find my wallet and keys still in my pocket. I walked over to the well with stiff limbs and splashed some cold water onto my face and bathed my arms with it. I was so thirsty that I put my face into the water and drank it. I breathed in the pleasant morning air, which smelled of moss and old masonry. I figured I was still in Barri Gòtic and walked down the alley, which the sun told me should lead me east-wards. The first human being I encountered was an old woman with a walking frame who spoke not a word of English. Soon, I found myself on La Rambla. I knew the way to the flat from there. All the shops I passed were still closed; I had to drag my hungry, de-hydrated body along the morning streets of Barcelona without food or water. Finally, I found a shop in Eixample that was open. I had a bag of crisps and two bottles of water for breakfast. I almost passed out on my way up to the flat; I waited outside until the tiny white stars stopped dancing in my field of vision. With insecure hands, I opened the doors and stepped into the hallway. Alice wasn't in our room, and the bath-room was empty. I didn't dare to open Dion's door and instead walked into the kitchen. I found Alice in the rooftop garden, sitting alone in a snow-white dressing gown, with a cup of coffee in her hand. She looked exhausted. I stopped in the doorframe. She welcomed me with a face made of impenetrable stone. After a gruelling eternity, she asked coldly, 'Where have you been?'

'Trying to drink myself back in time.' She showed no reaction. 'How's Dion?'

'We had to go to the hospital. You broke his nose and knocked out two of his teeth.'

I rubbed my eyes and said, 'I'm sorry. I lost control when I saw him hurt you.' Her deep-brown eyes remained cold. I asked, 'Where is he now?'

'I don't know. He told me to go to hell. He already took all his stuff.'

Hesitantly, I walked over to her and sat down next to her. I was afraid to touch her. I whispered, 'I'm sorry, Alice.'

She looked straight ahead and nodded. She said,

'I've never seen him like this—so angry. He's had his angry, sad phases before. But never like this.' She stood up to inspect the silvery leaves of an olive tree. 'I met him in a snowstorm in Stockholm three years ago. It was November, and none of the buses were running, and most of the trains weren't running, either. It was complete chaos. And I was carrying these heavy grocery bags through the knee-deep snow. Suddenly, this blond surfer boy stands next to me with a wide grin and asks if he can help me carry my bags. I can still see the big snowflakes in his blond locks.' She took a deep breath and continued, 'He walked all the way to my room in Lappis with me. We even took a little snowball-fight break.' She chuckled. 'In Lappis, I made hot tea for us, and we watched the world outside drown in snow. And he told me stories of working in a hospital and surfing in Morocco . . . And now—now he calls me a slut and won't talk to me.'

Tears ran down her cheek. I stood up and wanted to hug her, but she raised her hands and said, 'Please, I can't deal with this right now.' She turned away from me and walked inside.

I lay down on the bench in the shade of the trees. I was dizzy and deadbeat. I soon fell into a hazy doze.

When I woke up in the early afternoon, Alice had put up the sun umbrella above me. I found her in the kitchen. She was packing a small bag with her beach gear. She looked up at me and said, 'I'm going swimming, trying to get a clear head. There's pasta with tomato sauce in the fridge if you're hungry.' She stopped as she walked into the hallway and asked, 'Will you still be here tonight?'

'Where else should I go?'

She nodded with a faint smile and left.

In the dusky warmth of the rooftop garden, I watched videos of the 'Fight of the Century' and the 'Thrilla in Manila'—Ali's stinging jab against Smokin' Joe's hammering lead hook; the most relentless rivalry in boxing, between two men larger than life, unwilling to give in. They were gone now—their rotting flesh devoured by the same worms that would eat us all in the damp, dark dirt. Had anybody anywhere ever understood—fully, deeply, profoundly understood—that they were going to die? Darkness, forever. I closed my eyes and saw my dad at the barbecue in our garden, grilling steaks for my mum, Nicole, Michael, and me. He wiped beads of sweat from his forehand with the back of his ursine hand. My mum smiled at him with affectionate pride—like she always did when my dad worked around the house or fixed something. I opened my eyes. I listened to my breath and felt my heart beating in my chest. There's no peace for the wicked, and life doesn't stop for the dead. I went downstairs and bought a bottle of wine and some groceries.

When Alice returned in the evening, I cooked risotto with courgette and mushrooms, which I served on the candlelit table in the rooftop garden. After we had finished the last glass of Rioja, Alice said, 'I'm tired. Will you come to bed with me?'

'Okay,' I answered breathlessly.

Alice took my hand and led me to our bed, past Dion's empty room. She held my gaze wordlessly as she slowly undressed in front of me, standing on the wooden floor in the middle of the room. The orange light of a small bedside lamp cast dark shadows under her tired eyes. We put on a smile for each other. I took off my shirt and shorts as she sat on the edge of the bed. I kissed her and lay on top of her, carefully. Our heavy breathing swirled through the cruel Spanish summer night, her forehead pressed against mine. I closed my eyes. I saw Alice with a group of naked men. The men made wicked grimaces as they shoved their dicks into her orifices. I opened my eyes. I had become limp.

'Is something wrong?' Alice whispered.

'It's nothing, I'm sorry.'

Alice's eyes gaped with panic as she exclaimed, 'You're thinking about the things Dion said, aren't you?'

'No. It's—I'm—I'm sorry, Alice.'

She jumped out of bed, sobbing, and ran into the bathroom. I rolled on my back and dug my face into my hands. When Alice came back, she lay down without touching me. As she stared at the ceiling, her soft lips whispered, 'I'm flying home tomorrow.'

Miserable dizziness crept back into my brain. 'I guess you don't want me to come with you?'

'I need some time away from everything. I think I'm going to go home—visit my mum.'

'Alice, please don't run away like this. I love you. And you said you love me. I'm sorry for what I did. But we can work this out. Please.'

She turned her head to me and said, 'I have to go. It's better for both of us.'

'Alice—'

'Just let me go.'

I moved over to her and kissed her. Her lips and tongue were dead. Tears ran down her cheeks. With a sob, she pushed me away. She whispered, 'Let me go. Please.'

I nodded. Bitterness filled my body. We lay in the same bed that night—but with an ocean of silence between us. Before I fell asleep, I whispered, 'I'm sorry.'

Alice was already sitting in the kitchen when I got up.

'I've made coffee. Do you want some?'

'Yeah. When is your flight?'

'I'm leaving here in an hour. Do you want to escort me to the airport?'

'Yeah.'

I felt hollow, filled with stale smoke from a party whose guests had long left. We ate breakfast next to each other in silence. I took a shower and noticed how long my hair had grown since June. I quickly trimmed my beard before we took the metro to the airport.

Hurried travellers bustled around us as we stood on the shiny floor under the wide white arch of the departure hall. Alice put her heavy red backpack down and gave me a long, portentous kiss. I wrapped my arms around her, and she dug her face into my chest. I asked, 'Will I see you again?'

'I don't know,' she whispered. 'I don't know anything anymore.' I opened my mouth but was merely able to utter a desperate sigh. With constrained determination, Alice said, 'I want you to walk away now. And don't turn around to look at me. Just walk away.' A smile flashed over her lips as she whispered, 'And then, grant yourself some forgiveness.'

I kissed her forehead, stroked a curl of her thick brown hair behind her ear, and looked into her deep-brown, tear-filled eyes. Behind them lay a world I would never be permitted to discover. With a slow nod, I turned around and walked away. It hurt me physically to obey her command. I obeyed nonetheless.

On my way back to Eixample, I missed my stop by two stations and walked in the wicked midday sun for a while. On the way, I discovered a bottle of Oban and bought a pack of cigarettes in a corner shop. Back in the flat, I sat in the shade of the umbrella in the rooftop garden and started drinking. I closed my eyes and inhaled the smooth scent of the oily whisky. Everyone who ever loved me or whom I ever loved got hurt. I needed to run—further away. I opened my eyes and got my laptop from inside. After a couple of minutes, I took out my phone and called Alberto's American number.

'Hey, man, what's up?'

'Hey. I'm still in Barcelona . . . Alberto, is it cool if I come to LA? I could get a flight in two days.'

'Sure, man! I might have to work during the week, but you can crash at my place.'

'That would be great.'

'Do it!'

'Perfect. I have to move out of the flat anyway.'

'Awesome! Let me know when you arrive; I'll pick you up from the airport. By the way, how did it go with Alice?'

I rubbed my eyes and said, 'Let's talk about it when I'm in LA, okay?'

'Cool.'

'Okay, see you in two days.'

'Man, I can't wait!'

I booked my flight and applied for an ESTA visa waiver. I also got travel insurance, which was quite expensive thanks to the cruel joke of a healthcare system the US ran.

As the afternoon turned into night, the rooftop garden was the loneliest place in the world. I kept drinking until an acidic numbness filled the void in the air where Alice and Dion had stood only hours and days before. When the bottle was almost empty, I passed out on the bench.

The next day, I tried to wear off my gruelling hangover by strolling aimlessly around Barrì Gotic. I glanced at the colourful mosaics of fruits and spices and vegetables of Mercado de La Boqueria. I ate patatas bravas in the relative peacefulness of Plaça de Sant Felip Neri and wrestled through the crowds on Plaça de Sant Jaume—the city's political heart ever since the Romans had erected the columns of the Temple of Augustus here in the ancient Mediterranean sun. I watched tourists take photos of Botero's Cat in the shade of palm trees, felt small under the white arches of Santa Maria del Mar, and wandered below vaults of steel and glass in Estació de França. In the afternoon, I collapsed on the grass in the oasis of Parc de la Ciutadella and jumped into the forgiving sea at Nova Icaria Beach.

On my way back to the flat in the evening, I stopped at a small tapas restaurant near Arc de Triomf, reminiscent of a cosy Parisian café. While I enjoyed my little plates of cheese, tartare, lamb ragout, mushrooms and grilled squid and octopus, I watched a business dinner unfolding at the long table next to me. A Spanish delegation of suits and trouser suits was facing a German one. Everyone had put on their best business smile for the occasion. The bosses made lame business jokes which the underlings answered with well-behaved business laughter. I finished my Rioja with hasty gulps, paid the bill, and left. As I walked home through the heavy night air, I asked myself what I would leave behind if I died tonight. Who would remember me? Certainly not those restless careerists at the firm I had wasted three years of my life with. Back in the rooftop garden, I pulled out my phone and called Ben.

'Hey, man, what's up? Where are you?'

'Hey. I'm still in Barcelona.'

'How does your face look? I mean, not that there ever was much to worry about to begin with.'

I chuckled. 'The swelling and the bruise are mostly gone. It's still a bit numb, but it's getting better.'

'Good!'

'Yeah. Listen, I wanted to talk to you about the job.'

'Yeah?'

'I really appreciate your offer, but it's not for me. Life's too short to go back to a large-scale banking office. I'm sorry you've made your efforts in vain.'

'Hey, don't worry. You must know what's good for you. And I can understand you at the moment, to be honest.'

'What do you mean?'

'Well, I'm still in the office, for starters—on a Saturday night. The bank is moving some offices to Frankfurt because of Brexit.' He tried a chuckle that ended abruptly. 'And, you know, Helen is not doing so well. She had—she kind of had a nervous breakdown two days ago while she was at work. I think the pressure caught up to her.'

'How is she now?'

'Better. She was in hospital for a night, and now she's home with her parents.' He exhaled. 'I should be there for her, but we have this super-important project that needs to be finished by Monday.'

'As super-important as Helen?'

'No.' I could hear his hand rub over his face. 'No, of course not. But I only need to finish this project, and then I can be there with her for a couple of days.'

'Did you ask your boss whether you can go home? Maybe work from there?'

'No, I don't want to seem unprofessional.'

'Ben?'

'Yeah?'

'The woman I love went back to Sweden yesterday, and maybe I'll never see her again. This project you need to finish, however important it might appear to you right now—it's not going to change your life. But losing your connection with Helen might.'

'You're right. I'll talk to my boss. Thanks. And I'm sorry about what's happened in Barcelona. Let me know if I can do anything for you.'

'Thanks, Ben, I appreciate it. For now, focus on being there for Helen.'

'I will. Thanks, man.'

I smiled. 'Let me know how it goes.'

'Yeah. Mate, I need to go. Take care. Bye!'

'Bye.'

I hoped I had given Ben good advice. And I hoped Helen would be all right. I got the last, half-full bottle of Syrah from the kitchen and went back into the rooftop garden. I knew it was the right decision to stay out of banking. But what were my alternatives? I was too old to become the next Rocky Marciano. I was too easily irritated by exaggerated corporate enthusiasm to join some tech company that deceived itself that it was the saviour of humanity. Really, I was too easily annoyed by any corporate culture to join any large multinational corporation. I was too disillusioned, and frankly too greedy, to join the public sector. And I was probably too highly trained to do anything directly and tangibly meaningful for anyone. Maybe, by now, I was just messed up enough to make for a good and somewhat interesting bartender in some hotel in Havana. I decided to let my future self handle the issue and instead pictured the golden beaches of southern California as I let the smooth red wine run down my throat.

I spent my last full day in Barcelona in the rooftop garden, smoking, drinking, and overthinking—about Dion covered in blood; about the guy who had attacked me in Skärholmen when I was drunk and waiting for the last night train to Emma years ago, and whose face I had beaten to a bloody pulp; about my betrayal of my dad; about cheating on Emma; about a maths exam I had screwed up in Year 9; about every time I had lied to my mum; about Alice and all her past love affairs—or the vivid imaginations I had of them; about the teacher she had loved and maybe still did; about the Scottish rugby player I would like to strangle; about all the mistakes I had ever made; about everybody I had ever hurt. Images of Alice, Dion, and me, entwined in delirious passion, flickered through my brain. 'Grant yourself some forgiveness,' Alice had whispered. I looked into the light-blue sky. My shame and remorse became diluted by a merciful sense of affection for the beautiful people I had been allowed to meet, and of gratefulness for what they had shown me. Tears started rolling down my face, and for the first time in years, I let them run free. They washed out some of the corrosive pain and self-hatred that had clung to my body for so long. I let the tears dry on my cheeks in the sun of the timeless afternoon. A relieved smile formed on my lips.

In the evening, I took the metro to the beach and greeted the night with a stroll along the shore. Deep breaths of warm sea air were balsam for my smoke-singed lungs. On my way back to the flat at midnight, I stopped for paella outside a small restaurant run by a cordial Spanish family. Before I went to bed, I cleaned the flat. There were still some bloodstains on the floorboards in the hallway. I had to scratch them off with my fingernails.

The next morning, the hosts arrived from their trip to Sri Lanka. I handed them their keys and walked over to Casa Surís. Núria was sitting behind the reception desk, which had a small bouquet of red roses in a glass vase on it. She jumped up when she saw me, and her eyes lit up. 'Hey, what are *you* doing here?'

'Hey. I've come to pick up my driver's licence. I left it here as deposit.'

As she rummaged around in the reception desk drawer, she asked, 'Are you doing better?'

'Yeah, my face is getting better, and the numbness is slowly retreating. How are you?'

'Same old, same old. I'm still hunting for a job . . . I'm good, though.' She showed me a wide smile to prove it. 'What are your plans?'

'I'm flying to California today. Do you want to join me? It's going to be fun. The short crazy guy I was with is going to be there too. He wants to marry you, by the way.'

'I know. Alberto told me so a couple of times.' Her eyes lit up when she mentioned his name.

I shook my head with a grin and asked, 'And?'

'I told him I'd consider it if he shaves off his hideous moustache and quits smoking.'

I chuckled and said, 'I bet you get hit on by guests here all the time.'

'Well, marriage proposals are quite rare.'

'Do you ever go out with guests?'

Her look became stern as she said, 'Well, to be honest, I can think of sexier men than lost millennials drifting around Europe looking for a manic pixie dream girl to fix their broken souls.'

'Damn it, I was just about to ask whether you're interested in healing my psychological wounds.'

Núria grinned and said, 'You'll figure things out.'

'I'll take your word for it.'

When she handed me my driver's licence, I said, 'Thanks. Well, I'm heading to the airport now. Maybe you and Alberto will invite me to your wedding?'

'Sure. Take care! And give my regards to Alberto. And tell him he can stop sending me flowers. I don't want him to go broke over roses.'

I looked at the bouquet of roses next to her and laughed. 'Yeah, will do.'

As I turned around, Núria said, 'And I'm sorry that it didn't work out with Alice.'

I looked at her in confusion. 'How the—' I had to chuckle and said, 'Alberto, the devil.'

With a conspiratorial grin, she said, 'He calls me every afternoon.'

She waved goodbye to me with a radiant smile as I walked out of the hostel, shaking my head in amused disbelief.

I boarded the plane to California in the early afternoon.

Soft spoken with a broken jaw
Step outside but not to brawl
Autumn's sweet we call it fall
I'll make it to the moon if I have to crawl and
With the birds I'll share this lonely view

Anthony Kiedis
Scar Tissue

16

I woke up on the plane as we were flying over the circular fields of the Great American Plains. Cottony cumulus clouds painted dark dabs on the golden soil. I watched the continent whose exuberant children had formed our modern times roll by. We landed at LAX on time at six in the evening. At the passport checkpoint, a bald, overweight homeland security officer looked sternly at the healing bruises and abrasions on my cheek. He asked intrusive questions about my finances, my general life situation, and my plans for California. When he finally waved me through—me being blond and white probably helped alleviate his paranoia—I collected my backpack from the conveyer belt. I stepped out of the airport hall and onto the pavement of a taxi bay. The air was just as hot as it had been in Barcelona and was circulated by a muggy wind that came in from the Pacific Ocean. After a few minutes of waiting next to a group of smoking Filipinos, an old, green Jeep stopped in front of me with squeaking tires. 'Hey, man, welcome to California!' Alberto shouted from the inside over *Killing in the Name Of* by Rage Against the Machine, which blasted from the creaking speakers. I threw my backpack on the backseat and got in the car. Alberto started wriggling through the slow-moving traffic. We followed the circular track along the terminals and past the iconic white double arch, gleaming in the evening sun and circled by palm trees. As we rode along a four-lane street between endless rows of low-rise buildings, I told him of the mayhem he had missed in Barcelona. When I was finished, he said, 'Shit, Dion seemed like such an enthusiastic, happy guy to me.'

'Yeah, I know. I guess he has a dark side he's trying to hide. Although I wonder whether he was somehow a different person that afternoon.'

'Maybe. Although you can never truly know anyone.' Alberto gave me a look that made me feel guilty.

After we crossed a massive highway junction in silence, I said with a grin, 'Núria told me to tell you not to go broke by sending her flowers all the time.' Alberto stroked the moustache above his wide grin and nodded. I asked, 'How is it going between you two?'

'I don't know, man, I've never felt like this about someone. We talk to each other every day, although we're worlds apart now.'

After almost an hour of driving through the vast concrete desert, we slid past high-rise buildings in the centre of Westwood towards the campus of UCLA. We turned left onto an uphill street crammed with parked cars. Between apartment buildings stood white houses with colourful, large Greek letters printed on their front walls. At the end of the road, Alberto parked the Jeep in a carport with a red tile roof. In the half-light,

I followed him up a few stairs leading into a small patio with four adjoining beige two-storey houses. We stepped into the one that looked the most run-down, into an open living room. A large upholstered sofa dominated the room. 'Let's go upstairs and drop off your stuff,' Alberto said. As I followed him to the first floor, he said, 'Usually, four people live here, but my friend Jack is on a surfing trip to Fiji, and his room-mate has disappeared for a couple of weeks now. He's a programmer and has drifted off a little too far into the philosophical theory of singularity—Roko's basilisk, Newcomb's paradox, paperclip maximisers, and shit. I suspect he's now in hiding somewhere, preparing for the inevitable takeover of the machines.' He chuckled. 'And my roommate is currently in China, working himself to death in a tech start-up. So, there's plenty of room. I guess it's best if you take Jack's bed.'

I dropped off my backpack in Jack's room and went into Alberto's room next door. It was furnished with two beds, a desk, and a walk-in closet. Piles of books and empty wine bottles surrounded Alberto's bed. On his nightstand stood an ashtray brimming with cigarette butts. A single framed picture with six cosmic images hung above his bed. Alberto nodded and said, 'These are pictures of Venus, Earth, Jupiter, Saturn, Uranus, and Neptune, taken by Voyager 1 in 1990, from outside the solar system—more than four fucking billion miles from Earth, man! The most distant man-made object in space.'

Earth was a tiny bright dot in a band of light, radiated by the sun. Alberto patted me on the back and said, 'Let's go downstairs and relax. You've had a long flight.'

We had tortillas with scrambled eggs, avocado, and salsa for dinner, watched a cartoon show about a self-loathing, alcoholic horse, and went to bed. An endless continent and a deep, arcane ocean lay between Alice and me. Still, we were both stranded together on this little piece of rock in space. I closed my eyes and tried to feel her soothing breath on my shoulder in the heat of the Californian night. I fell asleep with sweat-soaked hair.

On Saturday morning, I took a cold shower in the dirty bathtub. I investigated the pink, smooth skin where the scratches on my knee and elbow had been. The bruises on my knuckles and ribs had receded.

After breakfast, Alberto and I drove up Santa Monica Boulevard. We passed the narrow avenues of Beverly Hills that led to villas behind rows of high palm trees to our left before we entered the bustling streets of Hollywood. We crossed Sunset Boulevard and Hollywood Boulevard before the old Jeep started climbing up a winding road between the pine trees of Griffith Park. As the road got steeper, the engine uttered an unsettling squeak. Alberto framed the rolled-up cigarette in his mouth with a wide grin as he looked at me through his aviator sunglasses. To my surprise, we made it up to the top. Alberto parked the Jeep in front of Griffith Observatory. We passed a group of tourists armed with selfie sticks fighting for the best spot in front of the James Dean bust and walked around the white observatory building. Below us lay the endless City of Angels, baking in a sweltering haze.

As we walked back to the car, I pointed to the hill north of the observatory. 'Can you walk up there?'

Alberto looked at me and said, 'I think you can, but why the fuck would you?'

'I'm sure the view is great from up there.' I prodded his shoulder and said, 'Let's go.'

Alberto exhaled a desperate sigh and followed me up a sandy path. During the 40 minutes it took us for the short hike, we had 12 brief water breaks and three longer pauses to accommodate Alberto's coughing fits, each of which was louder than the old Jeep's squeaking. When we finally reached the deserted peak, Alberto lay on his back on one of the wooden tables. He coughed in a triumphant tone. I enjoyed the view of the surrounding hills. In the distance, the white Hollywood Sign hung in a hazy fog. When Alberto managed to stand up again, he said, 'Maybe I *should* stop smoking. But although I feel terrible, I also feel good in an odd way.'

I laughed at Alberto's ignorance of his own body. We walked back down to the car. Alberto was still exhausted, and I drove the car back into the city. He was surprised I could handle a manual until he remembered I was European. We drove all the way to the Santa Monica pier, ate tacos for a late lunch, and cooled off in the water. When we arrived back at Alberto's house, it was already late in the afternoon.

In the evening, Alberto and I went to a fine burger restaurant in the Arts District of Downtown. On our way back to the house, Alberto took a short detour to show me the urban canyons of the Financial District. On the pavement stood scattered tents and cardboard shacks. I said, 'These must be the famous homeless people of LA.'

Alberto chuckled sarcastically. 'These are just the people who didn't find a place in Skid Row.' He took a right turn and locked the car doors from the inside. 'Buckle up, man, you're about to see some messed-up shit.'

Within a minute, we drove into a street poorly lit by flickering street lamps. In front of run-down junk

shops stood rows of tents fortified with plastic tarpau-
lins and cardboard. Sad eyes gleamed out of sleeping
bags on stone benches. The streets were filled with
rubbish, and the drains were clogged with what
looked like faeces. Hunched, beaten creatures shuf-
fled through their dystopian world. A man draped in
rags screamed into the night in a rubbish-strewn
backstreet. His scarred face was contorted with pain
and aflame with red neon light. Shadows loomed in
the darkness. We could feel their starved eyes following us. As we drove out of Skid Row and onto the highway, Alberto said with a bitter tone, 'A fucking shanty
town in the richest country in the history of the
world—the American dream, man. This makes me so
fucking angry . . . Instead of distributing the riches our
society has created so that everyone can live a digni-
fied life, we've eviscerated social democracy on the
altar of neoliberalism.' Alberto took a deep breath.
'We've put property beyond the reach of democracy.
Our new way of economic life is rent extraction, and
when the wealthy take a seat at the casino, it's heads
they win, tails we lose.'

He lit a cigarette and took a deep drag. 'You know,
the deregulation of the economy has bred pathologi-
cal inequality. And with it, crime and political unrest
that tear at the social fabric that ties us all together.
But instead of rooting out the problem, the wealthy
elites transfer more power from the people to the
fucking lobbyists. As they say: the United States has
the best Congress money can buy. But the wealthy are
afraid of the anger that the despair of the underclass
might escalate into. And they hide in their gated
communities and their apocalypse refuges in New
Zealand. And they stash their money in tax havens,
out of reach of the society that has helped create it.

They militarise their police and fortify the prisons to keep the peasants in check. You know, back in the Second World War, even a Texan oil heir or a New York socialite might die on Omaha Beach. But now the army is for white trash and immigrants whose sliced-up subprime mortgages have been sold to gullible pension funds by Wall Street snots to buy their second Aston Martin . . . By the way, do you know how many bankers and lobbyists and other fraudsters they sent to prison after the Financial Crisis? One!' Alberto waved his wrathful index finger. 'One guy! What a fucking mastermind he must be—orchestrating the biggest financial fraud in human history all on his own from his New York office at Credit Suisse!'

Alberto threw his finished cigarette out the window, the sparks fading in the warm night. He was breathing heavily. He exclaimed, 'This society is sick to the bone, man! Its people numb their burnout and boreout syndromes with a flood of opioids. The paranoid buy guns at Walmart to protect themselves against the Mexican communist bogeyman, or what the fuck ever it is they're so scared of.' Alberto paused. 'You know, the bobos in their booming cities ridicule those who've been left behind for their traditional values and their concerns about uncontrolled immigration, technological change, and globalisation. The old value systems of family and religion have been dismantled and haven't been replaced by new ones. And the resulting void has only been filled by a haze of cynicism and nihilism. The only god left to worship is Mammon. Really, that's the fatal flaw of neoliberalist capitalism: for a large part of society, there has been no integration of means and ends. The people have been told that the only goal in life is to become rich and yet have been deprived of the opportunities to do so. They are on a treadmill to nowhere, and they fucking know it! They know that America is not a country but a fucking business. And everything's on sale for the wealthy few. This all has been a fantastic recipe for social disaster. And it doesn't help that racism still hasn't been overcome, after all these years, and all this pain. I mean, racial divides have always gaped most open in times of economic distress. Sure, there are too many bigoted, xenophobic arseholes out there. But on some days, even I find it hard to blame these racist left-behind idiots for looking for scapegoats. They have been offered no means within the system to change the social structure they so badly feel is developing in the wrong direction. For everyone to see, politics has become a never-ending cycle of money-fuelled campaigns. The obvious hypocrisy of a political correctness that only matters as long as cameras are rolling is an insult to the intellect of everyone who is ostracised for daring to depart from the mainstream opinion. And if the establishment only offers you two different shades of winner-takes-all turbo-capitalism, why not vote for a poor man's idea of a rich man, a sexist, a narcissistic loudmouth, an obnoxious demagogue who promises to burn the whole fucking system to the ground? You know, so many people acted shocked when Trump won. But for decades now, the separation of powers has been undermined. And the elites have been corrupted and lost all virtue that might have justified their rule—just like in the ancient Roman Republic before Caesar. And once again, despotic populism will give rise to deranged emperors and cult leaders who'll oversee the ancient sequence of melancholia, paranoia, and megalomania. And along the fucking way, the wealthy can drive their fancy private cars on broken public roads.'

We sat in silence for a while, as the green Jeep followed the white lines on the brittle concrete of the congested highway through the night. Alberto lit another cigarette and continued, 'You know, the land of opportunity, while built on graves of Native Americans and the suffering of slaves, really has been exceptional once in the past—a republican island in an authoritarian world, a beacon of social-liberal prosperity hovering over the rubble of the Second World War. It was far from perfect, sure, but for an instant, we were on the right side of history, man! But today? We're drowning in polarised politics, gun violence, free-market mayhem, and senseless warmongering. I tell you, this empire is about to crumble and fall, worn down by the greed and arrogance of late-stage capitalism. Empires are rarely ever defeated; they dissolve from the inside because they fail to adjust to change. And the US has failed to understand that you cannot kill ideas like religious radicalism by force. It has failed to listen to Eisenhower's warnings and allowed unwarranted influence by the military-industrial complex. It's failed to overcome its dichotomy fetish, its obsession with a narrative of good versus evil that simply doesn't exist in that clear-cut way. It has failed to understand the rise of China as a superpower in a multipolar world. It's failing to prepare for the rise of AI that will lead to the emergence of a class of the useless who will not only lose their income source but also a purpose that can give their lives meaning. As an isolated nation-state, the US is failing to solve its interdependent problems in a world of international communication, finance, and mobility. It's failing to prepare for the ageing of its society. And it's failing to offer any remedies for the contradiction between the need for immigration to sustain our welfare system and the differences between old and new residents. Ultimately, the US is failing to offer any fucking perspective for the future—for example, in the form of global financial regulation, redistribution of wealth, or a collective effort to curb global warming.'

The sparks of another thrown-out cigarette glinted in the darkness of the rear-view mirror. Alberto wriggled around in his seat. Beads of sweat shone on his forehead. 'You know, throughout history, inequality has only ever ended in catastrophe: plagues, wars, revolutions, the collapse of states. The only thing that has ever really curbed inequality is disaster. The US only managed to create a middle class because of the most vicious war in human history. Because it was afraid of the spectre of communism afterwards . . . All the way from the first organised humans who erected temples for long-forgotten gods in Anatolia, to the ancient Egyptian high culture, to the mighty Roman Empire, to today's capitalist American superpower— civilisations rise and proclaim the end of history and then crash and burn. I'm afraid this time will be no fucking different.'

Silence fell on the car. We watched the lights of the city pass by. After a while, as we turned off the highway at an exit into Westwood, Alberto said, 'Sometimes I wonder why our times seem so crazy, so hectic. You know when you update the software on your smartphone, right? And at some point, the software overwhelms the hardware, and the phone stops working. I think this is what's happening to us. The technological opportunities are growing exponentially; we have become godlike masters over the world—nuclear extinction at our fingertips—and we have created machines beyond our comprehension. And we try to make sense of all this with our little monkey brains that have remained basically unchanged since we used to sleep in caves and throw rocks at mammoths.'

Alberto turned into the fraternity-house street, drove past several ongoing parties, and parked the car in the carport in front of his house.

'For now, we only use AI in its infancy to make more products for consumption. But we'll soon live in a machine ecology beyond human response time. And after losing all religious or moral illusions, we'll finally be deprived of our unique feature of intelligence at the hands of superior machines. Maybe people will manage to numb themselves by replacing the old virtual refuge of religion with new, literal virtual realities. Maybe our new machine overlords will see us as a threat and try to exterminate us. I guess, in the end, humankind will survive as it always has—but in what society? Will we become one with a singular AI as re-engineered human minds in a world people like us cannot begin to comprehend? Will we descend into a tribal conflict using precise, merciless killer robots? Will we still call ourselves "human"?'

'Mate,' I said, pushing against the still-locked door. 'Yeah?'

'We're here.'

Alberto shook his head, chuckled, and unlocked the doors. We got out of the car and walked up the stairs to the patio and into the house. Standing in the living room, Alberto said, 'Man, I feel a little beat. I need a drink.' I nodded and chuckled.

After we had had a couple of glasses of rum and coke on the sofa, the front door flung open. A blond guy in a patterned tank top stuck his head into the living room. With a wide grin, he exclaimed, 'Hey, guys, wanna come down to the frat house? We're having a party for the new pledges tonight!'

'Looking at drunk sorority girls getting hit on by the rich sons of Silicon Valley software developers? Awesome,' Alberto said in a sarcastic tone.

'Whatever, dude.' The frat bro shrugged and left.

I chuckled and asked, 'Are *you* in a fraternity, too?'

'Hell, no! That was my neighbour. Jack and the others are, though. That's how we got this place. I try to stay away from those apes as much as I can.'

'You know what? I'd like to go to that party,' I said and flashed Alberto a roguish smirk.

Alberto sighed, 'Fuck me . . . Well, all right.'

We walked down the street, past some apartment buildings and to a sage-coloured two-storey building with a white balcony running around the front of the first floor. On the railing, the three Greek letters Phi Mu Lambda were painted in red on a large white board. The house was bustling with loud, cheerful frat boys in polo shirts and groups of hoarse, giggling sorority girls in hot pants. Alberto and I drank stale beer from red plastic cups and played beer pong in the garden to EDM. Before long, Alberto took off his blue Hawaiian shirt and started dancing on one of the big speakers next to the DJ booth in the garden—to the cheers of the crowd he professed to despise. I walked through the hall and marvelled at the collection of alumni pictures. A blonde girl told me about her day, which was 'oh my god, like, *the* worst ever' and about her visit to this year's Burning Man festival, which had been 'amazing' and 'totally life-changing'. I longed for Alice and her stories of the Bering Sea and the Congolese jungle. I saw Alberto's neighbour sitting in one of the dorm rooms and left the girl standing in the hall. He and I drank some rounds of cheap bourbon with two other guys on a sofa. On top of one of the bunk beds, some guy named Shane was having sex with a girl who apparently unavailingly encouraged him to fuck her harder. When some brilliant pledge down the hall broke his shin during the attempt to jump out of the window, I left the crude madness and walked home. Alberto was nowhere to be found. Back in Alberto's house, I noticed my royal drunkenness and collapsed onto Jack's bed. I soon descended into a dreamless sleep to the sound of the old fan attached to the window, circulating the heavy, stuffy air.

When I got up late the next morning, I found Alberto standing in his boxers in the bathroom, staring at the large mirror that hung above the sink. I stood beside him. Many lines of small, scrawly words were written with red lipstick on the mirror's surface. I asked, 'Did you write this?'

Alberto looked at me with puffy, red eyes and answered in a husky voice that reeked of wet ash and bourbon, 'I guess so.'

I looked back at the mirror. He had written a poem:

'To discover the true nature of your existence,

you must go on man's loneliest journey.

Go to the ocean of silence that surrounded all before time began—

into the empty space between the particles of matter that manifest our reality;

into the darkness of the galaxy,

where only the cold, subdued lights of long-dead stars act as reminders of space and time;

to the place in your mind that only you know,

where you come to terms with life and death.

To find out who you truly are,

you must go—

Into the Void.'

After reading the poem in silence, I looked at Alberto and said, 'You're a beautiful man, Alberto.'

He chuckled, 'That's nice of you to say, man. Let's have breakfast. I'm starving.' As we walked down the stairs to the living room, he added, 'You know what bothers me the most about this? Where the fuck did I get the lipstick from?'

For hours, Alberto and I sat on ramshackle camping chairs on the shady patio and watched squirrels run across the brick floor and climb over the wooden fence in hectic motions. In the early afternoon, Alberto jumped up and said, 'All right, I'm sober enough to drive again. Let's cruise around the hills!'

We got on the 405 at the Sunset Boulevard intersection and followed it northwards, below the Getty glimmering in the sunlight to our left. After five minutes, we turned onto Mulholland Drive to our right, and Alberto rushed the old green Jeep along the windy road between thirsty trees on the bone-dry Santa Monica Mountains. To the angry sound of Danzig creaking out of the speakers, we drove past the metal gates of reclusive estates. We stopped at vantage points overlooking the mystic hills of Bel Air to the south and the hazy plain of the San Fernando Valley to the north. After we had wiggled through the heat of the Hollywood Hills for a while, the skyscrapers of downtown LA appeared between the palm trees again, glistening in the distance below. At the end of Mulholland Drive, we bypassed Griffith Park and got on the freeway. We crossed a bridge spanning the concrete-encased trickle that once had been the river Spanish explorers had found flowing through a green valley in the 18th century. Alberto told me there was some vegetation in the river along its course through Griffith Park and that he had gone kayaking there. It took us ten minutes to drive through Glendale and Pasadena before we went up a short hill and stopped in front of a checkpoint at the end of the road. On top of a booth beneath a large silver roof was the emblem of NASA. A sign beneath read 'JPL'.

Alberto turned down the music and said, 'That's the Jet Propulsion Laboratory, owned by NASA and managed by Caltech. It's the centre of interplanetary spacecraft missions, developing and operating space robots. These guys sent the Curiosity rover to Mars. It's fucking awesome what they do here.'

'Would you like to work here one day?'

Alberto stroked his moustache. 'I have already worked here, man. Well, during an internship. I assisted the Europa Clipper mission, which will place a spacecraft in orbit around Jupiter to investigate its moon Europa.'

'Cool. Is that something you're doing in your PhD?'

'It's kind of related. I study the evolution of debris disks. We're trying to find out how planetary systems form and evolve. I get distracted a lot, though. Right now, I'm reading about Verlinde's theory of gravity as an emergent phenomenon.' I frowned at him, and he started laughing. 'Nothing you should lose any sleep over. Oh yeah, and I'm also sometimes in Hawaii to work with the Keck Telescope.'

'Is that where you get all your shirts from?'

Alberto chuckled. 'Yeah, some of them.' He rolled and lit a cigarette.

I asked, 'Isn't it weird to work on such abstract topics all the time?'

'Oh, it's not completely abstract. You have to know how shit in space behaves if you wanna accurately calculate trajectories for interstellar travel.'

'But aren't we still light-years away from that?'

349

Alberto sighed, 'For now, maybe.' In a louder voice, he said, 'Only 12 years after the first successful launch of a satellite, we flew to the moon, and we would easily be on fucking Mars by now, if we hadn't lost our focus! But I guess our society puts a higher value on developing killer drones and credit default swaps.'

On our way back into the city and along Sunset Boulevard, Alberto lectured me with emphatic hand gestures on the Planck Epoch—the first instant of the universe's existence. He told me that the essence of the basic properties of the world—mass, charge, spin, distance, and force—remained unknowable. And he tried to explain to me the four-dimensional continuum known as spacetime. I didn't understand all of it, but out of Alberto's mouth, it all sounded rather wild.

We had burgers for dinner in a diner in a yellow vintage railcar in a car park next to Sunset Boulevard. We spent a calm evening on the sofa, smoking and watching Stanley Kubrick's *2001: A Space Odyssey*.

On Monday, Alberto drove to a meeting with another PhD student in Pasadena. I took the bus over to Hollywood for some sightseeing. When I got on the old orange-silver bus at the end of the frat-house road, I realised why Alberto had laughed at my plan this morning; I was the only white guy without neck tattoos or an ample collection of plastic bags on the bus. I sat in an empty row of ugly, patterned seats and avoided eye contact with the other passengers. After an hour of stop-and-go traffic and 42 stops, the bus finally arrived at the intersection of Sunset Boulevard and North Highland Avenue. I exchanged the muggy air of the bus for a dryer heat weighing on the glimmering streets of Hollywood. I strolled down the Walk of Fame and took a look at the Dolby Theater and the

Chinese Theater. The whole scene was pathetic, with all the tacky souvenir shops, pseudo-attractions, and washed-up entertainers in cheap costumes.

In the afternoon, I found a small café on Santa Monica Boulevard, where I ate an omelette with bacon and read the whole *Los Angeles Times.*

In the evening, I went to the Spare Room, a bar with a bowling alley inside the Hollywood Roosevelt Hotel. I sipped my Negroni on a black leather chair and watched groups of handsome attention-seekers play backgammon and Scrabble on the neighbouring tables. I finished my drink and took an Uber back to Westwood.

I found Alberto reading in the living room. He told me he planned to read for the entire night to prepare for a seminar. He spoke fast and burst with energy—courtesy of Adderall. I asked him, 'Is it normal for you to take drugs to study?'

'I try to avoid it as much as possible. But everybody does it, and you have to keep up, you know?'

'That's messed up.'

'The whole education system is fucked up, man! Would you rather have a Harvard education without the degree, or a Harvard degree without the educa-tion?'

I hesitated and raised my eyebrows with a desper-ate smile.

'Exactly,' Alberto said and bent back over his wickedly expensive physics textbooks.

I went upstairs and took a cold shower to cool off a little. When I came back down, Alberto told me he would be busy until Thursday and recommended I take his car to San Diego or Las Vegas for a few days. I booked a hotel room in Las Vegas for the next two nights and went to bed.

I left the house at dawn and drove down the frat-house street behind UCLA athletes on their bikes on their way to morning practice. I took the highway past Downtown and through East Los Angeles. After about two hours, I crossed the mountains to the north and drove with rolled-down windows onto the dry, shrub-strewn plains of the Mojave Desert—hostile to man, only welcoming to poisonous animals, and a magnet for mystics on mushrooms. The thermometer of the air-conditioning-less Jeep showed 106 degrees Fahrenheit already—roughly 40 degrees Celsius; of course, the stubborn Americans had to stick to an outdated measurement system. On the straight, dusty freeway, I rushed past defiant, bony Joshua trees and heaps of dry Creosote bushes.

An endless row of billboards flew by the car window as I rolled into Las Vegas. I turned onto South Las Vegas Boulevard and arrived at the famous welcome sign, which was much smaller than I had imagined. In front of me lay the Strip, the main artery of the heart of capitalist excess, an oasis of irrationality in the middle of the damned desert. In slow-moving traffic, I rolled past the black Luxor pyramid, a miniature version of Manhattan, and between the Bellagio and an Eiffel Tower replica. The Mirage to my left, I turned right towards the main entrance of The Venetian. I got out of the Jeep and left it with the valet. I checked into my spacious, luxurious room and went downstairs to jump into one of the pools.

I had a quesadilla for late lunch in a Mexican restaurant downstairs by the fake Grand Canal—complete with fake gondolas and all. I thought of Alice and her face glowing in the real Venetian dusk. I decided to start drinking and gambling right away. For kicks, I put on David's suit, which I still had from Riga, and went downstairs into the casino. I sat at a blackjack table with low minimum and immersed myself in the melancholic, timeless atmosphere of bright, colourful lights and warm, seductive sounds. At my table sat a couple of Japanese retirees, an old Southerner with blue shades, and two young German backpackers. We all enjoyed the free drinks and mechanically put our chips on the table. The dealer handed out cards with bored precision. When I got up, I had made a 200-dollar profit and was positively wasted. I devoured a steak in an overpriced restaurant by the fake canal and stumbled back across the casino carpet with its colourful flower patterns. I ended up in a nightclub. In the flickering light, exuberant girls in light dresses raised their vodka sodas into the air to the rhythm of clanking bass. Men with clunky Hublot watches and numb-faced smiles danced with their clumsy hands above their heads. I hated it. I hated the soulless EDM and the fake laughter that hurt my ears. I hated the smell of booze and too much perfume. I hated the fake smiles on everybody's faces. Nothing in this city was real. I rushed out of the club and towards my room. Somewhere along the way, I lost 250 dollars on a blackjack machine. In my room, I fell onto my pillowy, oversized bed. I heard Alice whispering words of solace in my ear as I fell asleep.

The next day, I dragged my feet along the Strip through the hot and heavy, dusty air. The pavement was plastered with pink flyers for strip clubs and cheap casinos, which stuck to my trainers. In lonesome disorientation, I roamed about the city of sin. It all felt as though I had come too late to a wild house party, and only all the weirdos who didn't know when to stop were left.

After a pair of greasy burgers for lunch, I stepped into one of the smaller casinos next to my hotel. I spent the afternoon playing blackjack. I came out about even—considering the four free gin and tonics I drank. In the evening, I had a steak in a restaurant under the white marble columns and golden ceilings of the Greco-Roman fantasyland of Caesars Palace. I felt dizzy, hollow, and tired. I didn't feel like gambling or getting drunk. I spent the night in my pointlessly luxurious room in boxing's most glamorous city, watching *When We Were Kings* on one of my two flat screens. The images of Ali, the cunning, loudmouthed whirlwind, the rebel with a big heart, overcoming young and naive George Foreman, the giant with the most forceful punch in the history of boxing, gave me chills. Before I went to bed, I switched off the lights and looked out of my window over the glimmering lights of Vegas and the dark mountains of the desert in the east. Already, I longed for Europe and wanted to wake up from this collective dream coming undone. I missed Alice. I missed all my crazy friends. And, if I were honest with myself, I missed my family.

The next day, I had breakfast in my room. After a brief swim, I left The Venetian and the Strip behind and crossed the desert seawards.

When I arrived at the house in LA in the early afternoon, Alberto welcomed me in the living room, 'Ey, how was Vegas?'

'I think I might have had the most boring stay in the history of that rotten city.'

Alberto laughed and exclaimed, 'Yeah, late Roman decadence at its finest can be tiresome!' He tossed his textbooks to the side, jumped up from the sofa and said, 'Dude, do you feel like boxing? We have gloves

354

in the basement. Maybe you could teach me some tricks. I need a break from studying. And I need to get this flabby body moving!'

I liked the idea. It took us a while to find the gloves in the untidy, overstuffed basement. Alberto said, 'Sorry for the mess. But it's the second law of thermodynamics at work.'

When we found the gloves, we switched into trunks and went onto the shady patio. We warmed ourselves up with press-ups, sit-ups, and some shadowboxing. Alberto was soon sweating like a pig. I showed him some punch combos and helped him with his footwork. Alberto's breathing was scarily loud and rattling. It was great fun.

When we were done with boxing, we both took a shower, lay down on the beds in Alberto's room, and listened to the Misfits. Alberto said, 'Man, I have to tell you a fucked-up story that happened to me while you were away. You know, I'd been thinking a lot about Skid Row. And I thought to myself, what am I really doing about it? So, yesterday I decided to do at least *something* . . . I took Jack's car there and picked up this homeless Latino kid to buy him lunch. We went to In-N-Out. His name was Emilio. He told me that he was from the Rio Grande Valley and that he'd made his way to Los Angeles to find a job to support his mother and siblings. They still live in a trailer in a *colonia* in South Texas. He said his dad had been deported to Mexico—by "*la migra*", as he called the Border Patrol. He looked so tired. He had been living in the streets for three months, and someone had stolen all his belongings. I think they beat him up too. I offered for him to come to the apartment and get some rest. He was super shy about it but finally accepted. He took a long shower and fell asleep on the couch while I was reading in my room. In the evening, I walked down to Target to buy some things for dinner. When I come back and walk up to the patio, I see Emilio leaving the house. He sees me and freezes. In his hands is my iPad. I'm like, "Man, what are you doing?" And he slowly puts down the iPad. His hands were shaking. He had tears in his eyes. Man, I'll never forget that look. His eyes were so full of shame and pain. I'm like, "It's okay." But he starts running down to the street . . . I followed him. But there was no way he was going to talk to me.' Alberto stroked his moustache. 'I just wanted to help the kid. But I guess he didn't trust me and thought he had to steal from me.'

'That sucks. Will you try to help someone again?'

'Yeah. I guess. I'd rather try to live in a world where we help each other and get screwed for it than accept a world where everybody just looks after themselves.'

That night, we watched *Sicario*, and Alberto and I smoked a bong. Alberto said in a slow, husky voice, 'I just wondered: why are theatre awards like the Oscars still separated by gender and not by, say, genre? Could it be that even in ultra-progressive Hollywood, there are still gender roles?'

I responded with a delayed chuckle and said, 'Yeah, let's change it to something like "best performance in a sequel to a superhero film spin-off remake".'

Alberto giggled and yelled, 'Fuck yeah!'

As I turned my head to Alberto, my vision followed my movements with a delay. I was baked. I put my head back on the soft cushion of the sofa. In the back of my hazy head, I listened to Alberto babbling about selling little trees with the scent of weed. When the fog lifted from our brains again, Alberto and I decided to go to San Francisco the following day and went to bed early. We had a long drive up north ahead.

For breakfast, Alberto made tortilla wraps with scrambled eggs, tomatoes, and avocados. We jumped into the old Jeep and drove west to Santa Monica. Cars gleaming in the low morning sun clogged the wide streets of Los Angeles. As we waited in the constant traffic jam, we listened to an angry chorus of horns through our open windows. Alberto's moustache wiggled with a chuckle. 'I don't get them—thinking the whole world is conspiring against them to make them late for work, when in reality, the universe doesn't give a fuck about their pitiful existence. When they're done honking, why don't they scream at the sun for being too hot or insult time for slipping through their hands?'

Under palm trees dancing in the morning breeze, we finally made it out of the city and followed Highway 1 past the beach villas of Malibu and along the rugged shore of southern California. We had an early lunch in a seafood restaurant in a small town by the sea. Then, we followed the 101 inland; further north, the highway along the coast was closed due to landslide damage and bridge maintenance. In the afternoon, we drove through Silicon Valley and into San Francisco. We were staying at an Airbnb in Parkside. We parked the car on the street and got the keys to the small studio flat from one of the resident's friends. We dumped our stuff next to the large bed we would be sharing. We walked to the nearby beach and relaxed after the tiring eight-hour drive. The air was colder than it had been in LA.

In the evening, we had dinner in the first bar we could find in our neighbourhood. After a couple of beers, Alberto proposed the bold theory that the only moral imperative in life was to be true to yourself. I chuckled. 'What if you're a paedophile psychopath?

Should you be true to yourself and molest children? Would that be moral?'

'Well, only if you're convinced, in your heart, that it's right to molest children.'

I shook my head and said, 'I like you, but sometimes you're bonkers.'

A wide, shining grin lit Alberto's dark eyes. 'What would life be without a little craziness?'

We were both tired and soon went back to the flat. When I came out of the bathroom after taking a shower, Alberto sat in the dark room, his face illuminated by the blue screen of his laptop. His silhouette was framed by the faint light coming from the street through the shutters behind him. He was talking to someone.

'So, what did you do yesterday?'

'I went to this photography exhibition.' I recognised Núria's bell-like voice and had to smile. 'It was by this Japanese photographer who took pictures of voyeurs watching couples have sex in a park in Tokyo.'

Alberto laughed and said, 'That's fucked up!'

'I told you you shouldn't curse so much!'

'Shit, yeah, sorry. It's still messed up, though.'

Núria giggled, 'Yes. It is.'

I sat down next to Alberto on the bed and waved at Núria, who looked back at me from the screen with a kind smile. My movements flickered in the blue light. 'Hey! How are you!' she exclaimed.

'I'm good, thanks. Your husband is taking good care of me.'

Alberto shook his head vehemently. I took him into a friendly headlock and chuckled.

'Fiancé,' Núria corrected me. Before Alberto or I could reply, she opened her eyes wide and shouted, 'Oh my god! You won't believe this!'

'Believe what?' Alberto asked.

'Well, I know this girl from my Pilates class; she's the daughter of some important woman at the US Embassy or something. And today, I somehow told her about you—and your crazy story about ending up in a hospital and waking up in Calella. And then *she* told *me* a story; you really won't believe this! Wait, I recorded it.'

She took out her phone and held it to the laptop camera, and we could hear a deep woman's voice:

'Okay. So, I'm in this nightclub, Gràcia Getaway, and I meet these two funny guys—a short one with a big moustache and this handsome blond, bearded one with deep-blue eyes. I don't even know their names. They were drinking from a bottle of vodka and were already pretty wasted. And they convinced me to do shots with them. And somehow, I ended up dancing with the blond one. I was pretty drunk too. And after a while, we made out.'

Laughter.

'Don't look at me like that! Well, anyway . . . After a while, we went outside to catch some fresh air. And, you know, I tell him it's late and that I'd better leave now. And he offers to walk me home.'

More laughter.

'No, but he seems like a gentleman, and I don't live that far away, so we walked to my apartment together. This is where it gets crazy. After two or three blocks, we turn into this kind of remote street, and there are these three men harassing a girl. They're holding her and tearing at her clothes, and she's trying to run away, and it all looks pretty nasty. I just stand there, like, paralysed. But this guy yells at them and runs towards them. And, then—it all happened so fast! I think these arseholes, like, immediately attacked him and started swinging at him. But he was nuts! He knocked down one of them, and I think he hurt the other two pretty badly, too. But then they all tumble down to the ground and wrestle. And the two of them manage to hold him down, and one of them gets up and kicks him in the ribs and in the face. It was horrible! And I just stood there! I didn't even scream or anything. Oh my god, I still feel so bad for not helping him! But he really fought like a lion! I mean, somehow, he manages to get up again and punches one of them in the face, and the guy goes down. And then the other arsehole tries to put him in a headlock, but he bites him in the arm, and that guy starts screaming like hell and backs off. I think he really bit him bloody! And finally, the three pricks decide to run away. Two of them basically had to carry the third one. Anyway, by the time they bolted, the girl was gone too. She must have run away during the fight, I guess. I was so stunned I didn't notice anything. And the guy from the club stands on the street, and there's blood all over his face and his shirt. I find it amazing that he was still standing. I wanted to call an ambulance, but he just lit a cigarette and was like, "Nah, I'm fine." And I know it sounds crazy, but somehow, he convinced me. He seemed so calm about the whole insane situation. He even joked about having added a concussion to the next day's hangover. And he said he would go to a hospital the next day if need be and told me not to worry. I mean, I was super drunk, but I should've realised that I should've called an ambulance right then and there. But, yeah, he even walked me home the remaining two blocks and then left for his hostel. And I didn't have his phone number or even his name or anything . . . And you're sure that's the guy who stayed in your hostel?'

We heard Núria answer, 'Yes, that story fits his injuries pretty well. And the guy with the moustache sounds like Alberto.'

'Oh god, I'm so glad he's okay. I feel so bad about the whole story. I went to the police the next day, but of course, that was pointless. Please tell him I'm sorry if you talk to him again! And tell him he's a freaking hero if you ask me.'

Núria took her phone away from the laptop and looked into the camera with a roguish smile. Alberto grabbed my shoulder and shook me with a wide grin on his face. 'Man, did you hear that? You're a fucking hero, all right!'

I shook my head in disbelief. What a small world it was. I asked Núria, 'Did you hear anything else? Of the girl—is she all right?'

'No. But I'm sure she's fine.'

Alberto again shook my shoulder and cheered, 'Because you saved her, man!'

It seemed like I kind of did. I looked at the laptop and said, 'Tell your friend that she shouldn't worry about it and that I'm glad she's okay too.'

'I will.'

We talked to Núria for a little longer until she had to go back to work. As Alberto and I lay next to each other in the bed that night, he said with a chuckle, 'You call me crazy again, you crazy motherfucker . . . ' I fell asleep with a wide grin on my face.

On Saturday morning, we took a boat trip to windy, rugged Alcatraz Island. In the afternoon, we walked along the shore with the Golden Gate Bridge shining red above the rough sea in the background. I told Alberto about my moribund biological parents, my adoption, and my dad's death. He gave me a firm hug.

In the evening, we jumped on a cable car that carried us up the hills to Haight-Ashbury. We had dinner in a small pub serving craft beer and vegan, organic food near the park. We drank an 'Extra Brut IPA', which was supposed to taste like tangerine, grapefruit, melon, and lime.

I looked out of the large window to the street and said, 'San Francisco makes me think of my mum. She told me she and her sister—my biological mother—always dreamt of moving here when they were young.'

Alberto nodded at me and said, 'You know, you should get in touch with her again.'

'I know, I know. It's just—yeah, I know.'

'I told you about my parents, right? That they both died when I was still very young? I inherited a lot of money from them. I can travel between my studies and not worry about student debt, like the rest of my forsaken American generation. And I can ramble on about evil capitalists while I enjoy the merits of being one. But, I'd give all that money away to see my parents again—to hear my mum sing ancient songs in the balmy summer night one more time. But I can't. Don't be a fool. Talk to your mum.'

We spent most of the rest of the evening in pleasant tranquillity. A friend you can spend time in silent understanding with is a precious gift.

When we arrived at our flat at midnight, I felt restless. The time for running away was over. I put my trainers back on, walked downstairs, and stepped onto the cold pavement. In the warm orange light of a street lamp, I stood in the crisp air of San Francisco. The comfortable laughter of a distant garden party drawing to a close echoed through the empty street. My heart was pounding. With shaking hands, I took out my phone and dialled—slowly, hesitantly. After two rings, interrupted by a tense eternity, I heard a most familiar voice, 'Yes?'

'Hey—Mum . . . it's me.'

An instant of silence. Heavy breathing in disbelief. A hopeful sob. My mum whispered, 'Leon. How are you?' Her voice was still as warm and kind as it had always been. Her saying my name was like a calling to a home I had long forgotten I had.

'I'm good, Mum. I'm in San Francisco right now. I had to think of you and Mara planning to move here as teenagers.'

Mum exhaled a laughter heavy with tears. 'That's right. I'd almost forgotten about that.'

After a brief pause, I said, 'Mum?'

'Yes?'

'I'm sorry. I'm sorry I wasn't there for Dad. And that I wasn't there for you when he died.'

'It's okay, Leon. It's okay. I—I shouldn't have shut you out the way I did. I'm sorry too, darling.'

Bittersweet tears rolled down my cheeks.

My mum laughed and said, 'It's so good to hear your voice.'

'Yeah. It's good to hear yours too.'

More tearful laughter. 'What are you doing in San Francisco?'

'I'm staying with a friend. I've been travelling the whole summer. I don't know how much Nicole and Michael told you, but I quit my job four months ago.'

'Yes, I know. They both told me they worried about you after they last heard from you when you were in Marseille, I think. Are you okay?'

'Yeah, don't worry. It's just been one hell of a summer, you know?'

'You should get some rest.'

'Yeah, I know.'

'Sorry for sounding like your mum.' She laughed. It sounded beautiful.

I chuckled and said, 'No, you're right. I feel like I need some rest, too.'

My mum exhaled audibly before she said, 'You've always carried so much pain inside you. But we never knew how to deal with it. I'm sorry, Leon; maybe we should've told you earlier as a child about your parents. We should've paid more attention. You just always seemed so strong, you know? I'm deeply sorry.'

I was choked up. A weight had been taken from my shoulders that had been there ever since I could remember. I sobbed, 'It's okay, Mum.'

For a while, we listened to each other's sobbing and laughed at our own snivelling. My mum finally asked, 'Do you want to go back to London?'

'I don't know . . . I don't want to go back into finance, that's for sure. I want to do something with a purpose . . . I'm a little lost, to be honest.'

'Well, I don't know what you're looking for, Leon. But let me tell you this: when people say that if you do what you love, you don't have to work a single day in your life, that's a lie. Work is work is work, and we do it because we've got to eat. No more, no less. And that's how it always has been and always will be. Try to find something that you're good at and doesn't run against your convictions. Make sure it pays you enough money and leaves you enough time to enjoy the important things in life.'

'Yeah . . . I guess you're right.'

'I'm sure you're going to figure it out. You've always been the smart one. And know that your family is there for you if you need us.' After a while, she asked, carefully, 'When are you coming home?'

'Soon. I need a little more time to sort my thoughts, away from all the noise. I hope that's okay.'

'Yes, of course, take your time. As long as you come home eventually. You need to come for the birth of Michael and Laura's son.'

'I will, Mum. I'll be home for Christmas.'

'Good. I'm sorry, but I think I have to go back to work now. There's a queue forming in the front. I'm still in the bakery, as you might know. And you know how Steve can get when the shop gets busy.'

'Yeah . . . I'll go to bed now. I'm tired.'

'Okay. But I'm so glad you called me! I hope you know how happy this makes me.'

'I'm happy too.' After a brief and somewhat awkward silence, I said in a jokingly commanding tone, 'Okay, back to work now!'

She chuckled, 'Okay. Bye, Leon.'

'Bye, Mum.'

After I hung up, I stood there on the pavement for a while and breathed in the cool, clean air blowing from the sea. I dried my eyes and went back upstairs. Alberto awaited me with a grin and asked, 'How'd it go?'

'Good,' I said with a cautious smile.

'Good,' he said. A warm smile formed under his moustache. 'That's good.'

The next day, we went for breakfast near Union Square and then started driving back south, this time away from the coast on Interstate 5. In the dry San Joaquin Valley, we passed endless rows of artificially irrigated fields of pistachio, almond, apricot, and citrus trees. Alberto told me hedge-fund money from around the country was pouring into California to finance ever-deeper drilling in a tragic race to the bottom of the water reservoir. In the distance loomed grey smoke columns from wildfires. The temperature climbed with every dusty hill that flew by to our right. Alberto and I soon took off our shirts.

Back in LA, we went to one of the university's swimming pools to cool ourselves off; I sneaked through the turnstile right behind Alberto. That night, I booked a rather expensive flight to New Zealand in two days. I was looking forward to New Zealand. It had been on my list for a long time. In the living room, Alberto was watching the news. Some arsehole had shot dozens of people to death at a rock concert in Las Vegas. The incident stuck out even in the only rich country in which mass shootings were commonplace. With a sigh, Alberto soon shut off the TV. The rest of the night, we sat and talked at a table next to the open window. At half past midnight, we went to bed.

On Monday, Alberto took another day off. I persuaded him to go for a short run—or rather a mild jog— through Westwood. It was quite obvious that Alberto was in pain, but he fought through 30 minutes of side stitches and coughing fits. He collapsed on the brick floor of the patio back at the house with a rattling panting. He coughed, 'This was good! I feel great!' I laughed, but Alberto said, 'No, no! I mean it! My entire body hurts, but I feel great. Thanks for giving me a much-needed kick in the arse, man.'

To reward our efforts, we treated ourselves to a greasy sandwich stuffed with chicken nuggets and chips at a food stand called Fat Sal's.

We spent the afternoon on Venice Beach, swimming in the Pacific Ocean and bumping a beach volleyball back and forth. The beachside promenade was buzzing with an energetic mixture of street musicians, skaters, hobos, surfers, bodybuilders, tourists, hippies, and all kinds of hedonists and attention-seekers. Many of the houses along the boardwalk had recently been captured by Snapchat and other tech companies, driving out Venice mainstays such as the Venice Beach Freakshow. As far as I could see, the freaks and misfits were still hanging on, though.

At dusk, we had dinner at a nearby taco restaurant. We walked along a narrow canal between green hedgerows to a packed, noisy billiard bar by the water that had a synth rock band playing. As we stood by the bar, Alberto asked, 'Wanna get some beers?'

'Why not stick to soft drinks tonight?'

Alberto's moustache danced upon a wide grin. He turned to the bartender. 'Two Cokes—two Coke Zeros—please.'

As we sipped on our cokes, we stood next to the small stage, penned in between sweating teens dressed in black, and listened to the band. They were quite good, but the sound system was overcharged, and the high-pitched guitar riffs came out as painful screeching. When we had finished our drinks, Alberto looked at me and pointed to the door. I nodded. As we made our way through the crowd, I accidentally ran into a guy playing pool and messed up his shot. He turned around frantically and gave me a shove. 'Can't you see I'm trying to play here, dipshit?' he screamed.

My jaw muscles tensed up. I glared at the guy, who had a clean-cut face, was about my height, and was wearing ripped jeans and a white T-shirt. Alberto threw up his hands and shouted over the loud music, 'Wow, chill, man!'

The guy took a step towards Alberto and grunted, 'Mind your own business!'

I stepped in between the two and stared into the stranger's angry dark-green eyes.

'What's your problem, man?' he shouted at me. His friends behind him took a step closer and tried to look intimidating.

My fists were clenched, and every muscle in my body was tense. I waited for the guy to give me a reason to knock him down. But then I saw something in his eyes. What I had mistaken for anger was, in fact, pain—the same pain that had always been within me, within all of us; the pain of being lost in this world that just doesn't care, of being rejected and disappointed by those we love; the pain of wrong things we did and vile words we said we know we can never revoke; the pain of time slipping through our hands, no matter how hard we try to stop it. My fists unclenched. I extended my open right hand to the stranger. I shouted, 'Look, I'm sorry I bumped into you. It wasn't on purpose. Let's forget about it and enjoy the night.'

The guy's eyes widened, and a mild softness crept into his face. He looked over to his friends and back at me. He shook my hand and said, 'Yeah, sure, man. It's all good. Just don't do it again.'

Alberto nodded at the stranger and patted my neck as we made our way out of the bar. We walked back to the car in silence. Alberto drove us into the Hollywood Hills and onto Mulholland Drive. We stopped at a small car park and sat on the Jeep's hood. Next to us was a group of kids listening to trap music on the stereo of their Cadillac Escalade, drinking beer and smoking weed. Below us lay a hazy sea of glimmering lights. As we gazed into the distance, Alberto asked, 'What's been the happiest moment of your life so far?'

I exhaled slowly. 'Hmm, I don't know . . . When I was still together with my first love, Emma, late one

INTO THE VOID

night, we got a call from one of her brother's friends. He told us that Tobi—her 16-year-old brother—had passed out at a house party. So, Emma and I took her parents' car to the party. And I walked into the house and basically carried Tobi out of there and into the car. He puked into a plastic bag during the entire ride back.' I had to chuckle. 'Anyway, when we arrived at their house, Emma's parents were up, and her father and I carried Tobi into his bed. And the next morning, we had breakfast in the kitchen downstairs, while Tobi cured the worst hangover of his young life on the sofa in the living room. I made fun of him for a while and brought him water and salty food. Emma's parents thanked me for looking out for him. And when I go back upstairs into Emma's room, she's standing on her little balcony in her white summer dress. Her skin was tanned from South Africa. And she smiles at me in the morning sun and tells me she's proud of me.' I shook my head. 'I don't know why I have to think of this particular story. But I know I felt really good back then. I guess I felt like I had some kind of purpose.' I looked at Alberto and asked, 'I think I know your answer already, but do you believe there's a purpose in life?'

Alberto's dark eyes gazed deeply into mine. 'You know, most of the time, I think that the creation of purpose or meaning—the denial of this world's meaninglessness—is philosophical suicide. But then again, sometimes you must die to live on this dark earth.'

We watched the group of intoxicated kids next to us get into their oversized car and drive off. It became quiet. Alberto stroked his moustache and said, 'You know there's this guy called Hugh Everett III. He came up with the "many-worlds interpretation of quantum physics"—a theory that posits that every possible continuation of a quantum experiment is manifested in a parallel universe. There's a universe where you're the president of the galaxy. In another one, we're tadpoles, still floating in primaeval soup. In most of them, we don't exist. And I guess, in some of those universes, we're destined to screw up a lot of things. But you never know what this version of our absurd universe still has in store for us. So, don't beat yourself up over the past too much, man. Live a little.'

I nodded and tried to spot the line between this crazy country and the mysterious sea in the darkness. I asked, 'What else does this Everett guy say?'

'I don't know. He quit physics after publishing his idea, became a military consultant, and died in his early fifties as an obese, chain-smoking alcoholic.'

For a while, we listened to the muffled sound of the distant late-night traffic swirling through the air from the twinkling city below. Alberto said, 'You know, man, it was cool how calm you stayed earlier when that guy tried to start beef with you.'

'My dad used to say it's easy to get into a fight and much harder to win one, but a good man stays out of them altogether.'

'Your father was a wise man.'

'Yeah, I see that now, too.'

'Well, and if you ask me, you have what you call your "darkness" well under control.'

'Yeah, I hope you're right.'

'You know, I feel it too sometimes—the darkness. I mean, sometimes, for a second or two, I catch myself plotting a random murder or think about how well I'd be doing as a criminal. I find myself fascinated by the intellectual challenge of being a dangerous killer.' He stroked his moustache and produced his tobacco pouch. When he saw me shaking my head with raised eyebrows and a grin, he laughed, 'Don't worry, if I ever lose my mind and become a serial killer, I'll stay away from you and your fists of steel!'

He looked back down at the pouch. He murmured, 'Ah, fuck it,' and put it back into his pocket.

I chuckled and asked, 'For Núria?'

'Yeah, maybe. I also wanna go running more, and you saw today how good my endurance is with all the smoking.'

With a grin, I said, 'Yeah. So, what is this thing between you and Núria?'

Alberto looked away and rubbed the back of his head. 'I don't know, man. I really like her. And I can talk to her for hours, and it never gets boring. And she's so smart and kind and beautiful.' He hesitated. 'She wants to visit me soon. But I don't know. I told you, I don't like women the way most men do. I mean, I wanna be with her. But I don't know whether I should tell her I'm not really into sex. Fuck, man, when it comes to these things, I couldn't think my way out of a wet paper bag!'

I chuckled but quickly put on a serious face and said, 'Look, you don't even know what exactly she wants yet either, right? You said the quality you value most in people is honesty. So be honest with her about your feelings and find out what this absurd universe has in store for you.' I winked at him with a grin.

Alberto put his hand on my neck and shook me with a friendly laugh. 'I will, man. Thanks!'

Soon, we got back into the Jeep and drove down to Westwood.

Back in the house, we were greeted by Jack, who had just arrived from Fiji. All of us were tired. I packed my things for the flight the next day and went to bed in Alberto's room.

371

Alberto and I got up early the next morning and had a quick breakfast. Alberto drove me to the airport. As we were making our way through traffic, Alberto said, 'You know, I talked to Núria last night. And I followed your advice and told her. She said she thinks she doesn't mind and still wants to come and spend time with me. I didn't really believe her.' He looked at his old phone and said, 'This morning, she texts me this: "You questioned my honesty today. Maybe I haven't always been honest with you. When you were still in Barcelona, maybe I forgot to say how much I wanted you to stay—already then. But other than that, I meant everything I said and said everything I meant." What a woman.' With a content smile, he put down his phone and said, 'So, man, what are you going to do now—in New Zealand; with your life?'

'I'm going to enjoy some time on my own in New Zealand. I'm going home to see my mum and my brother. And then start working again. I've had an idea tonight what I could do.'

'What's that?'

'I have to check first whether it works out before I talk about it. It's probably a stupid idea. But I'll let you know.' I watched a row of palm trees pass by the car window in front of a warm, blue morning sky. 'You know, the last few years, I've been kind of living every-where and have been at home nowhere. One day, I'd like a place to call home and a woman who shouts my name to get back into the house to help her with the kids.'

'You'll get there, I'm sure of it.'

'Thanks. What are you going to do?'

'Tonight, I might drive out of the city and watch the moon somewhere with my telescope; a full moon is approaching. Maybe grab a beer with Jack. Then, I'll try to merge quantum theory with gravity with fewer than ten dimensions and become famous. Or, maybe, I'll just try to smoke and curse a little less.'

'Are you also going to shave off your flavour saver for her?'

'Shave off this majestic bad boy? Hell, no!' He laughed and stroked his moustache. 'For now, it's fucking hard enough to quit smoking.'

'You could start vaping instead.'

'I could also put my balls in a fucking blender. But I won't.'

We laughed as Alberto took the exit to the airport. He said, 'You know, I listened to your girl in Barcelona and plan to become a vegan. Animal rights and climate change are matters on which I have been asleep for too long.'

When Alberto dropped me off at my terminal, he jumped out of the car and gave me a long and sturdy hug. 'I hope I'll see you again soon, man!'

'Yeah. I hope so too. Thanks for giving me refuge.'

The sound of System of a Down clanking out of the Jeep's speakers quickly faded as Alberto raced off. I dropped off my bag and went through security. At 9:30, I left the falling empire behind and fell asleep above the Pacific Ocean.

And this ain't no place for the weary kind
This ain't no place to lose your mind
This ain't no place to fall behind
Pick up your crazy heart and give it one more try

Ryan Bingham and T Bone Burnett
The Weary Kind

17

On my first day in Auckland, I hiked up to the green crater of the Mount Eden volcano. I gazed over the low rooftops of the city and breathed in the fresh air on the other side of the world. The next day, I rented an old Toyota that had been converted into a camper-van. For a week, I drove around the green scenery of the northern part of the North Island. I went on boat trips around the Bay of Islands, camped at beaches, and climbed up rugged hilltops and to gushing water-falls. The old Toyota was painted white and had no conspicuous labels that would easily identify it as a camper van. The windows in the back were tinted. No one bothered me for wild camping. The nights were still very cold, and I lay in my sleeping bag with all my clothes on, shivering, my breath freezing on the win-dows. At the end of my first week in New Zealand, I drove to the cliffs of Cape Reinga—the northwestern-most tip of the peninsula. For a long time, I looked at the rough sea below, where oceans meet and—accord-ing to the native Maori—souls depart. After a night in

the ugly town of Kaitaia, I followed winding roads
through the Waipoua rainforest with its gigantic kauri
trees back to Auckland again. During my day in the
City of Sails, I took a free bus tour. At one of the stops,
I went bungee jumping. The plank from which I
jumped stuck out from a metal pod attached underneath the Auckland Harbour Bridge. A wave of panic
rushed through every fibre of my body as I fell towards the sea 40 metres below. After I dipped into the
cold water and was pulled back up still alive, I could
not wipe a wide grin off my face for the rest of the day.
That evening, I found a place to cook dinner and stay
for the night in Hamilton, south of Auckland. In the
sulphurous air of Rotorua, I hiked around gushing
geysers and boiling lakes of all colours beneath trees
covered in orange moss. Further south, I stayed for a
night in a hostel in Taupo, where I bought some books
from a second-hand bookstore. I built a bookshelf for
them in my van out of a cardboard Weetabix box, duct
tape, and a clothesline. I washed my clothes in the
hostel's laundry room. It was nice to talk to some
travellers in the shared kitchen after more than a
week of solitude on the road.

One morning, before sunrise, I drove into Tongariro
National Park to the car park at the end of the Alpine
Crossing track. A shuttle bus brought me to the starting point for the hiking tour across the volcano massif.
I was among the first group to arrive there and hiked
ahead. The trail led through brown bushes heavy with
morning dew and soon climbed towards the snow-
covered heights through sharp-edged volcanic rocks.
As I walked across the plateau between Mount Ngau-
ruhoe and Mount Taranaki, the snow glimmered in
the rising sun amidst the black, dried lava. I climbed

to a ridge, the highest point of the hike, with a red half-crater lying to my right. Brisk gusts blew across the dead, red rocks. I put down my backpack, ate the sandwiches I had prepared, and looked around. Far to the west, lonely Mount Taranaki protruded from an endless layer of clouds.

I thought about my dad and how he had looked so peaceful when he slept in his hospital bed—while his snoring kept the whole wing awake; I had to chuckle. My dad had always been able to fall asleep within seconds of going to bed. That probably had something to do with him being a faithful Christian. It often took me hours to fall asleep. Sometimes I wished I could trick myself into believing in God. I sat there in the cold wind for a long time, thinking about my dad— about boxing training with him; about the time he had shouted the living daylights out of my school's headmaster for threatening to kick me out because I wouldn't snitch on my friends; and about the last time I saw him lying in that rotten hospital bed: pale, thin, a shadow of his former self. There was still time to try to become half the man he had been.

I descended on a volcanic scree track to the green-hued lakes, which were still partially frozen over. One of the sharp rocks cut a hole into the sole of my right trainer. As I followed the track further down, the slopes became overgrown with brown bushes. The air became ever warmer. The final part of the hike led through the muggy heat of a thick forest, along a whooshing stream. I arrived back at the car park in the early afternoon. I drank two litres of water from a big canister I kept in my van and refilled at petrol stations. I got into the Toyota and drove westwards.

After about an hour, I got tired and set up camp in the car park of a swimming pool in a small place by the highway called Taumarunui. After dinner, I called Nicole.

'Hey, big brother!'

'Hey, little sister. How are you?'

'I'm good. I just got up.'

'What are you up to?'

'Working. I've been at the café a lot lately. And tomorrow, uni starts again . . . Hey, Mum told me you called her! I'm so happy!'

'Yeah, me too.' I had to smile.

'When are you coming home? Where are you?'

'I'm in New Zealand.'

'In New Zealand? Wow! You could write sometimes; there's this thing called social media. You don't even have to call people. Nobody *calls* people anymore. But anyway, when are you coming home? You have to visit Michael! Laura's belly is starting to look big!'

I had to chuckle at the speed with which the words sputtered from Nicole's mouth. 'I told Mum I'll be home by Christmas at the latest.'

'See? I told you we could celebrate Christmas back in England as a boring family.'

I chuckled, 'I'm looking forward to it. How's Joel?'

Nicole went silent for a moment. 'Joel and I broke up two weeks ago . . . It turned out we didn't want the same things.'

'I'm sorry, Nicole.'

'Yeah . . . Come on, say it!' she exclaimed defiantly.

'Say what?'

'That you told me so. That I'm dumb and naive.'

'Nicole, all I want is for you to be happy. I'm sorry it didn't work out with you two. At least you tried, you know? I'm sorry if I sound condescending sometimes.'

'No, it's fine. I know you mean well. I guess I'm just allergic to good advice.' She chuckled. 'But it's okay, we broke up on good terms; you know what a good guy Joel is. He quit his job last week and started touring with Vladimir's Joke. Well, maybe it's a good idea to travel before we all might have to go back because of fucking Brexit. Anyway, I finally found a decent job at a fashion label for next term. So, for Joel and me, it was just bad timing, really. But I'm happy now. Things seem to be finally coming together, you know?'

I heard in her voice that it was true. I said, 'I'm glad. And congratulations on your new job.'

'Thanks! I'm so happy you talked to Mum! Listen, I still need to have a shower, and I'm already kind of late for work . . . But let's keep in touch, okay?'

'Yeah. Take care, little sister.'

'You too, big brother. Bye!'

As the night fell, I went into my van and read before I turned off my headtorch and scrambled into my sleeping bag. My daily rhythm had already adapted to the cycle of the sun.

I followed the Forgotten World Highway to the west and spent two days in New Plymouth. I went to an auto repair place to get the front left wheel of my van checked. It had started to make a bumping sound a few days earlier. The friendly repairmen replaced the wheel bearing in a heartbeat. At one of the black beaches, I met two deeply relaxed Dutch surfers who were touring New Zealand in an old Ford Transit. They offered me some synthetic cannabis that had once been marketed as *Kronic*. Even after their illegalisation in 2014, synthetic drugs were still widely used in New Zealand, which had traditionally been somewhat cut off from the international drug trade due to its geographic seclusion. I declined and went for a run along the coast instead.

On my way south, I stopped for one night at a small car park above Waihi Beach near a small town called Hawera. I watched boy racers trying to impress their teenage girlfriends by driving their bright-coloured Subarus up the steep hills by the narrow road, engines roaring. After dinner at dusk, I walked a gravel path down to the beach. The coarse, black sand prickled the soles of my feet as I stepped over small rivers that ran beneath driftwood into the calm sea with a soothing gurgle. After I had watched the sun, burning red, sink into the water beyond the black-sand shore, I called my brother Michael. He answered the phone with immense joy in his voice. Of course, he had already got the news from Mum. He listened to me as I recounted our call. I could hear birds singing and hammers hammering in the background, and the voices of hard-working men. After we had been silent for a while, I said hesitantly, 'You know, Michael . . . I want you to know I'm sorry for always having been envious of you for being the better son.'

'Ah, you know that's not true.'

'No, it is. You managed to live up to Dad's ideals and cared for the family that saved me when the only thing I was looking out for was my personal pleasure. I never took any responsibility. All I did was chase after some idea of short-lived success. But you know, I never quite figured out how to escape mediocrity. And I felt empty. And to fill the void, I got wasted for nights on end or tried to work myself to death. And then there you were, with your happy little family. And instead of being happy for you, I envied what I couldn't grasp.'

'Listen, Leon, don't be so hard on yourself. You're a part of this family, just like I am. And I'm sure Mum and Dad always loved all of us in the same way. And I don't know whether you're aware of how much Nicole has always looked up to you.' To my surprise, he chuckled. 'You know, it's funny somehow; when we were younger, I always envied you for the connection you had with Dad through boxing—and for the tight bond Nicole and you always had. And I still admire you for your bravery to walk out into the world, fearless of leaving your comfort zone. I always admired your rather-be-dead-than-average attitude—wanting to be a rock star, boxing like there's no tomorrow, being the first in the family to move abroad and go to university, working for one of the most prestigious investment banks in the world . . . But that's not for me. I need a life where everything has its place.' After a pause, he added, 'I love my average life and my way-above-average wife and family. I like knowing exactly where I need to be tomorrow.'

The orange horizon got blurry as I swallowed some happy tears. 'You know, I look up to you for the naturalness with which you run your business and are a good husband and a loving father.' I snivelled and said, 'I think something flew into my eye.'

Michael exhaled a nasal chuckle and said, 'Yeah, someone around this garden might be chopping onions too.' We both laughed. As I dried my eyes, Michael said, 'When you come home soon, maybe you can finally teach me how to box, and I can show you how to plant a tree—and how to stick around to watch it grow.'

'I'd like that. And we could drive to Land's End and watch the waves wash against the rocks, like we did as kids with Dad.'

'That sounds good. Listen, I need to go; these clowns are paving the terrace the wrong way. But it was good to talk to you.'

'Yeah. Oh wait, how is Laura?'

'Good! The little guy in her tummy kicks like a madman. Maybe he'll be a boxer too.'

I chuckled. 'Good. Say "hi" to her and Lily for me.'

'I will! And see you soon. Bye!'

I watched the sky above the sea turn from orange to purple to black and soon went to sleep.

On my way to Wellington, I stopped over in Palmerston North, where I went for a run along the river and bought a cheap steel-string acoustic guitar. I stayed a night on some beach on the west coast where I went for a swim. Everywhere in New Zealand, run-over possums plastered the roads. Local drivers always seemed to be in a hurry, especially when they shot past me in their four-by-fours as my van slowly climbed up one of the steep ascends. They also ignored the speed limit signs erected on beaches, whose existence I found rather funny to begin with. Each larger town had its own radio station you would start receiving in your car whenever you got close to it, and you could get informed right away about what was going on there.

In Wellington, I found a boxing gym where I could borrow a pair of gloves. For the first time in months, I worked a couple of rounds on the heavy bag. I had to decline a sparring match because of my cheek and instead exhausted myself jumping rope. It felt great.

On a Tuesday, I took a ferry across the windy Cook Strait to Picton on the South Island. I followed the hilly coastline westwards to Marahau at the southern border of the Abel Tasman National Park.

I spent a day kayaking along the golden beaches of the park. In the afternoon, when the waves got rougher, I paddled out into the sea to Fisherman Island, which lay about one kilometre off the coast. I left a pod of seals behind in the water and dragged the kayak onto the shallow white beach of the small island. The beach was shielded by rocks and palm trees and faced away from the coast. A small, overgrown rock lay a few metres off the island. I was alone. I stripped naked and walked into the shimmering azure water. The radiant sun warmed my skin. I waded through the clear, cold water towards the hazy blue horizon formed by the coastline I had driven along yesterday. Small, silvery fish swarmed busily around my feet. I went for a swim. The coldness on my skin felt good, and all I heard was the slow burble of the sea around me. When I paddled back to the shore before dusk, I had to lean into the growing waves with my paddle not to capsize.

That night, I called my mum and told her about New Zealand. She told me about the things that had changed in our small town since my last visit, and about many more things that had remained the same.

The following day, I hiked through the damp forests of the park up north along the coast. It was warm enough at night to sleep on my air mat next to my van on the grass under the clear night sky. On my way south along the west coast, I stopped at the Pancake Rocks and hiked to the Franz Joseph and Fox glaciers. While driving, I marvelled at the endless green hills full of countless sheep that flew by the open window of my car. In New Zealand I had time and silence in plenty, and read many books I had thus far avoided. I finally finished *Ulysses* and read *The Brothers*

Karamazov. I even made my way through *Atlas Shrugged*—you must know your enemy, as Alberto would say. I often watched the sunset as I played the guitar.

When I stopped in a small township off the coast called Haast and parked behind a small supermarket for the night, it started raining. Finally. The sky got dark, and then the grey clouds burst. And it rained and rained and would not stop. The rain gutters of the wooden houses surrounding the small car park were overflowing. Spurting puddles formed on the rough asphalt. Lighting flashed on the tree-covered hills in the misty distance, and thunder cut through the loud pattering on my car roof. I took off my shirt and step-ped into the pouring rain. The cool air smelled moist and clean, and of wet green grass. I closed my eyes, tilted my head back, and let the thick drops of water pelt on my face and shoulders. Soaking wet and hap-py, I climbed back into my van and had dry white toast with Nutella for dinner. As I listened to the rhythmic drumming on the roof, I thought of Alice. What was she doing? I hoped she had found some rain to cool off in after a long and hazy summer, too.

When it was dark outside and the heavy rain had abated, I finally called Chris.

'Hey, mate, what's up?'

'Hey, Chris. I'm somewhere in New Zealand and thought I'd check on my favourite bartender-slash-postman-slash-python-photographer. How are you?'

'You forgot Uber driver!' His chuckle was inter-rupted by a painful groan. 'Ugh, to be honest, I don't feel so great right now.'

'Hungover?'

'Yeah, that too . . . I found a used condom in my

waste bin but can't remember taking anyone home with me.'

'Oh, Chris . . . '

'Yeah, I know. It was my last night working at the bar, and things seem to have got a little out of hand.'

'Your last night? Did you quit?'

'Yeah. I thought I needed more time to plan my business. My godfather died and, to my surprise, left me some money. And with what I saved over the last couple of years, I might finally be able to open my bike shop.'

'Sorry to hear that about your godfather.'

'Yeah . . . He'd been struggling with cancer for a long time.' After a brief silence, Chris said, 'You know, I found this vacant property in a side street off St. James' in Kemptown. It needs quite a bit of work, but it's beautiful—a two-storey brick building which used to house a paint shop and a judo studio upstairs. Just the ground floor would be enough for me, but the new landlord wants to rent the place out as a whole. And now I'm considering taking in another investor or looking for someone who wants to open their own business upstairs. That's why I needed more time.'

'How much money do you need?'

'Well, if I renovate and set up the whole place nicely, it will cost about 50,000 pounds. Building a reasonable inventory will be another 20-30,000 pounds. And the monthly lease is 5,000 pounds at the max, including what I calculated as heating and operating costs. But if I renovate the place, the lease is free for the first half year. I've saved 25,000 pounds and inherited 30,000 pounds. I'll have to draw on credit anyway, but the whole place is too expensive and frankly too big just for me . . . But man, it's such a perfect venue!'

'So, you're planning to open a bike shop, right? Aren't there already plenty in Brighton?'

'Yeah, but none is specialised in vintage road bikes. And I want to do the full hipster branding—with a little coffee lounge and live-music events in the back-yard and all, and with a juicy Instagram strategy. Maybe I'll also start a bike-repair YouTube channel!'

'Sounds good.' I took a deep, slow breath. 'Chris, ah, listen . . . '

'Yeah?'

'What if—what if I become your partner?'

Chris chuckled and then went silent for a moment. 'Are you for real, man?'

'Yeah, why not? I've thought about it for some time now. And I'm looking for a job and still have money left from the firm.'

'Man! That would be awesome! I mean—yes! Awesome!' His voice was vibrating.

I felt my heart beating with excitement. I said, 'I could come to Brighton soon, and we could take care of the paperwork and start renovating the place.'

'We could be done by the time spring comes around and everyone wants to ride their sexy retro road bike around Brighton!'

'I don't know much about road bikes, but you can teach me. And maybe I could take care of the account-ing and such.'

'Fuck! Man! Yes!' Chris suddenly shouted in even more elevated excitement.

'What?'

'Why don't you open a boxing gym on the first floor! It will be cheaper to renovate, the showers are already there, and I know you can box, and I know you'd be a great teacher too!'

For an instant, a thousand thoughts ran through

my mind. Then, I saw myself with a group of energetic kids, showing them how to shadow-box. In my vision, I had a wide grin on my face. 'I like the idea, Chris.'

'Yes! And then, people can get their protein shakes with chia seeds in the coffee lounge after training. Oh, I know what we can call our business too: "Chris and Leon's Retro Road Bikes and Rough Fist Fights"!'

I chuckled, 'Yeah, maybe let's work on the name a little more. But I really like the idea, man!'

'Mate, I'm so excited!' He paused. 'Listen, business partner, what do you think of purchasing an alpaca as a mascot?'

I laughed. 'What? Why?'

'Yeah, you're probably right . . . You have to buy them at least in herds of three because they tend to get lonely. And getting three alpacas might be pushing it a bit.'

I giggled. 'Maybe we can start by getting a nice office for Herbert.'

'He can be our inner-tube expert! I'm sitting next to Herbert right now. He seems chuffed!' With a calmer voice, he said. 'You're serious about this? Won't you feel unchallenged as a simple boxing trainer?'

'I guess I'm willing to find out. If I can only use my programming skills for corporate bullshittery, why not live off my boxing skills instead?'

'Yeah. And if you do get bored, you could still do some freelance programming on one of those online platforms on the side.'

'Yeah, maybe. But I want to try this with you, man.'

'Mate, I love you! For real! I'll call the landlord right away and send you more details, okay?'

'Perfect.'

For a while, we both laughed nervously. When Chris had calmed down again, he asked, 'So, how's

New Zealand?'

'Really good. I haven't been drinking or smoking in a month and have a lot of time to think. After wasting half my life being wasted, I enjoy the sober solitude. I feel good.'

'Nice! Yeah, I'm glad to have quit the bar too. I've grown tired of having the smell of alcohol and the slurring of wasted fools around me every day.'

'Didn't you just wake up with a blackout?'

Chris chuckled, 'Yeah, whatever! No, but I mean it; I want to clean up a little bit too.'

'Good. I want a sober, focused business partner.'

'Yes! You know how dedicated I'll be to our business, right?'

'Yeah, I know it.' Chris might have been partying a little much, but he was probably the hardest worker I had ever met.

'Good.' After a pause, he added, 'But we will still get royally wasted from time to time, yes?'

I laughed. 'Yeah, I'm afraid so.'

'Good. Okay, listen, business partner. I'll now take a shower, cook me a full English breakfast, and brush my teeth four times. And then I'll contact the landlord. Mate, this will be good; I can feel it!'

'Yeah! And I finally know what I'm going to do!'

'You're a legend, man! Okay, I'll speak to you soon. And I'll send you pictures of the place and the calculations I made and a draft of the business plan! And maybe you can start thinking about what you'll need for your gym.'

'Cool.'

'Nice! Bye, partner!'

'Goodnight, partner.'

A good night it was. I didn't sleep much; I was busy envisioning myself renovating a property with Chris, teaching people how to box, and even selling road bikes. The rain drummed quietly on the car roof. The warmth in my sleeping bag felt good. I was happy.

It got cold as I made my way through the valleys and across the mountain passes of the Southern Alps. Everything was shrouded in rain and mist. I had to wear my rain jacket for the first time in months during a short hike to a waterfall. In Queenstown, a town built around extreme sports tourism, I got woken up and dislodged by gruff DoC officers wielding big, bright torches twice in one night. In general, I had more trouble finding a spot to stay for free on the South Island, despite its abundance of space. This didn't change until I made it out of the tourism heartland and arrived in Invercargill, an ugly town at the southern tip of the island. Locals like to say that Steward Island in the south only broke away from the mainland because of Invercargill's unappealingness. On my way there, I took a two-day detour to Milford Sound. I went on a boat trip beneath the looming cliffs of the fjord and watched pods of seals jump up and down the slippery rocks.

I thought a lot about Alice as I listened to waterfalls rush down the dark walls of rock protruding from the restless sea. I tried to think about who she was, and not who I wanted her to be. And I thought about her teacher and her Scottish rugby player and how tough it must have been for Alice. It hurt. It hurt like hell. But this time, I did not try to drown the pain. I went into it. And after a while, the pain gave way to a feeling of acceptance. I could not change the past. I could not control Alice's emotions. I hoped, with all my heart, that she would be okay. But now, I had to look ahead.

After a night in a bleak car park behind a hardware shop in Invercargill, I drove to Slope Point, where I watched yellow-eyed penguins waddle about clumsily. I followed the road along the rugged coast to a group of three houses that stood in solitude by a beautiful little beach. I stayed there for two nights and was invited for lunch—which mainly consisted of horrible-smelling homemade mixed pickles—by an old couple living in one of the houses. They were nice people.

In Dunedin, I discovered a good place to stay for the night in an industrial street by the harbour. I found another boxing gym nearby, where I practised my footwork on a heavy bag, moving quickly in and out of range. I also focused on my breathing. During a fight, if you stay tense throughout and fail to relax between exchanges, you're exhausted already after one or two rounds. You must learn how to breathe and give yourself some rest in the middle of the storm. I watched one of the trainers giving a class and thought about my own lessons when I had been younger. I talked to the cheerful owner and bombarded him with questions about his experiences with his business. Back in my van, I wrote down sketches of how I would like to structure my boxing classes. My dad had taught me the basics of boxing when I was seven. I knew he would be proud of me becoming a boxing trainer.

Throughout my travels around the south of the South Island, I had a few more calls with Chris to discuss business matters. It took him a while to believe I was serious about my offer to become his partner. Maybe the same was true for me, too. But the more we discussed our ideas, the more excited we got. Chris registered a company and set up a bank account to which I transferred some seed money. I did some research on what equipment I needed for the gym—mats, gloves, pads, heavy bags, skipping ropes, some weights, decorations, and countless other things—and roughly calculated the investment costs. Chris let me know that we would not be able to move into the place before January. I still had enough time to drive back to Auckland along the east coast until Christmas. He had already started buying old road bikes and repairing them, and I encouraged him to take notes on the average working hours and equipment costs that went into the process. I couldn't wait until next spring to open 'Chris' Road Bikes & Leon's Boxing', or whatever name we would eventually agree upon.

On my way to Christchurch, I stopped for one night next to a road by the beach near the Moeraki Boulders. As I sat in my camping chair on the beach in the morning, I read a message from Lena:

'Can we Skype? I need to talk to you, and I need to see your face.'

I drove up to Christchurch and checked into a hostel in the city centre. The whole street was torn open and under construction—courtesy of the devastating earthquake in 2011. All around Christchurch, I could still see the aftermath of that fateful February afternoon. There were still gaps between underpinned houses in the centre of the city. Whole blocks had been degraded to empty wasteland along Avon River. A hole was gaping in the city's nearby cathedral where its declared-earthquake-proof tower used to stand. Roads were still full of cracks and potholes and bulges caused by broken underground water pipes.

In the hostel, I logged into the WiFi and called Lena. When her image popped up on my screen, I noticed her tired eyes and ruffled hair. It was already past midnight in Austria. 'Hey, how are you?'

'Hey! Well, not so good, actually. Granny died two days ago.'

'I'm sorry. Was she still in hospital?'

'Yes. They said she died peacefully in her sleep.'

'How are you holding up?'

'Not so good. My selfish parents say that it will take them at least a week to make it here and that they can only come briefly for the funeral. Now I have to take care of everything—organise the funeral, clean up her old apartment, and deal with a bunch of other bullshit. Her apartment has to be empty by the end of next week, and there is so much stuff in there and in the basement compartment. And work is killing me at the moment, too. I'm sad and angry and tired, and my head aches, and I can't sleep. And I miss Granny.' Her voice cracked, and she blew her nose.

After a while, I asked, 'What if I come to Vienna and help you take care of everything?'

'But you're in New Zealand!'

'Well, I guess I could get rid of my car, fly to Auckland tomorrow and make it to Vienna by Sunday. Then we have a week to clean out your granny's flat.'

Lena looked into the camera with a sceptical expression. 'Are you sure? You don't have to do this. You're in the middle of your travels. And the flight's gonna be expensive!'

'Well, I've been travelling for a while now. And you have helped me so many times; it's time for me to be there for you.'

'Leon, you'd save my fucking life!'

'That's the least I can do.' I smiled, and Lena smiled for the first time during our call, too. 'Let me check flights and get rid of my van, and I'll write you when

I'll be in Vienna. And you should get some sleep in the meantime.'

'Okay. Thank you so much! You don't know how much it means to me.'

'Hey, I'm happy to come to Vienna.'

Her eyes widened as she said, 'Oh, there actually might be something I can do in return for you.'

'Yeah?'

'Yes! A friend of mine works at the University of Beirut. And they're developing a data-driven mechanism for the UN Refugee Agency to target cash transfers at Syrian refugees in Lebanese camps. They use micro data to predict food insecurity, I think. I didn't get all of it when we met last week. But it sounded like they're in desperate need of some forecasting expertise. And guess who I thought of!'

'That sounds interesting, Lena. I mean, I have just decided to open a road bike shop and boxing gym with Chris in Brighton . . . But maybe I can still talk to them and help them on a more flexible basis.'

'What? You're going back to England? You have to tell me all about that when you come here! But anyway, I can talk to her, she's in Vienna for two more weeks. I'll set up a meeting.'

'That sounds great!'

'Good.' She yawned. 'Hey, listen, I should try to finally get some sleep. It was good to talk to you. Let me know how it goes in New Zealand. If it doesn't work out, I can take care of everything myself. But it would be amazing if you came here. Thank you so much!'

'Don't worry, it will work out, Lena.'

'Okay.' She smiled. 'See you soon then!'

'Yeah. Goodnight, and sleep tight.'

'Bye.'

INTO THE VOID

I went to the Christchurch office of my rental company. I had to pay a fee for returning the van to a different location than where I had gotten it. But I could leave the car at their office immediately. I received a reimbursement for the wheel bearing I had had replaced in New Plymouth. I found a reasonably-priced flight to Auckland the next morning, and a flight the following day to Vienna via Kuala Lumpur. The long-haul flight was with Malaysia Airlines, the company that had lost two aeroplanes in recent years. I let Lena know that I would arrive in Vienna on Saturday afternoon.

In the evening, I sat in the common area of the hostel and scrolled through my social media feeds for the first time in a while. I saw pictures of Theresa and her new boyfriend on a diving holiday on Tenerife. It seemed like an eternity since I had stayed with her in Bristol in June. Theresa looked more beautiful than I had remembered her. Her new man looked like the handsome lawyer-type. She had been right the day I had left her behind; life did not wait.

The next morning, I took a bus to the airport and was on my way back to Auckland. I spent my one day there strolling about the harbour and seeing the city from the top of the Sky Tower. I wrote postcards to Nicole, Michael, and Mum. I bought an inexpensive silver watch with a navy-blue face and a brown leather bracelet from some obscure brand. Back at the hostel, I finally shaved off my beard. The lower half of my left cheek was still a little numb. When it was cold or I exhausted myself, I got glowing red spots on my skin where my bones had been broken. There were no other traces left of the fight; I had been lucky. I left my hair long.

On my last night in New Zealand, I went into a basement whisky bar called The Jefferson at the harbour end of Queen Street. Dark wood and pale concrete shaped the large room, and smooth jazz rhythms hung in the warm air. I walked past the midnight-blue plush loungers behind golden railings and sat down at the long bar, aflame with amber light shining through countless whisky bottles. As I sipped on an excellent Old Fashioned, I noticed a guy in his mid-thirties sitting next to me in an elegant navy-blue suit. I marvelled at the Patek Philippe that showed beneath his white, cuffed shirt sleeve. I wondered whether he had paid more for the glass of vintage 20-year-old Nikka Yoichi in front of him or the pinkish Brioni tie around his neck. Did the bartender know that the man who was tipping him so poorly wore a watch worth more than he earned in a year? And was the man in the suit with the absent look one of those billionaire doomsday preppers buying apocalypse refuges in New Zealand—their new Mount Ararat—that Alberto had told me about? Maybe he was a rich start-up founder. More likely, he was a wealthy heir. In this day and age, the only reliable way to get ahold of a fortune is to come into one. I finished my drink, returned to my hostel, and slept like a log.

I took the bus to the airport the next morning. As I sat at the airport gate, a heavy melancholy over-came me. I was leaving behind another place, another part of my life, and nothing could ever quite be the same again. I was surrounded by other travellers, all headed somewhere, all leaving something behind. Nervous laughter, anticipating holidays with loved ones. Tired faces speaking of unconditional affection and of wounds that may never heal. Anxious seriousness, breathing behind tightly knotted ties, preparing presentations for rooms full of new Asian money. Lonesome souls, staring into an uncertain future, stuck in perpetual transition—never quite arriving anywhere. The passengers for the flight to Kuala Lumpur were called for boarding. I shrugged the weight of yesterday off my shoulders, and with newfound hope, I left the shores of New Zealand behind.

All those moments will be lost in time, like
tears in rain.

Rutger Hauer in *Blade Runner*

18

I was standing beneath the white steel arches of the
Satellite terminal of the Kuala Lumpur International
Airport. It was dark outside the high glass walls.
Hypnotic electronic bell sounds and distorted voices
echoed out of the airport speakers. A lone fat cock-
roach raced across the shiny stone floor. I felt my
heart beating in my chest. I looked back down at my
mobile screen. Alice's message was still there—four
words: 'Hej, how are you?'

It was six in the evening in Stockholm. I closed my
eyes, took a deep breath, and touched the call button.
Alice answered after only one ring.

'*Hej*, you.'

'Hey, Alice.'

'How are you? And where are you?'

'I'm good. I'm in Malaysia, flying to Vienna from
New Zealand.'

Alice chuckled, 'Oh, wow, your Europe trip got out
of hand a little bit!'

'Yeah.' I smiled. It was good to hear her mellow
voice. 'How are things in Sweden?'

'Good. After Barcelona, I spent some time back
home. Now I'm back in Stockholm. Our experiment at

the institute finally worked out, and we have the right data to write a paper. The long winter is just around the corner now, and the days are already quite dark and short. I've finally found an apartment with a friend on Södermalm, and I'm looking forward to furnishing my little *lagom* haven.'

'That sounds good. Any good parties in Stockholm lately?' I tried to sound casual.

'You know, I try to give myself some rest these days. I feel a little exhausted.'

'Yeah, I know the feeling.'

'I guess I still find it hard to stay home on a Friday night. There's always this little voice in the back of my head asking what could happen or who I could meet at that after-hours party at the end of the night. You might not have been completely wrong about our generation being infected with a fear of missing out, you know?'

I chuckled, 'Yeah, you weren't completely wrong about my insecurities either . . . By the way, how's Dion?'

Alice sighed. 'His nose healed well, and he has apologised to me. You could write to him if you want; I think he would be glad about that . . . But what about you? Have you found something at the end of the world?'

'In a way; I finally called my mum. And I'm going to start a boxing gym in Brighton with my friend Chris.'

'I'm glad you talked to your mum.' I could hear her smiling. 'And *what* are you doing in Brighton? Opening a boxing gym?'

'Yeah. Wanna come visit?' My heart skipped a beat the moment I finished the impulsive question.

'Hmm . . . I don't know if that's a good idea, Leon.'

'Yeah, I know . . . Sorry.'

'But you know what? I might come anyway. Some-one has to teach you to keep your guard up!'

I shook my head, exhaling a desperate chuckle, and said, 'To hell with good ideas, right?'

'Yes, to hell with them.'

For a while, we listened to each other breathing. Alice said, 'I had a dream the other night. You and I were standing in a garden by the sea, and we planted a chestnut tree together. It was a good dream.'

'You know, my brother's a gardener, and he says it takes patience to stick around and watch a tree grow.'

'You have to introduce me to him.'

'I will . . . I will.'

'Leon?'

'Yeah?'

'I'm sorry for telling Dion and Arman your story. I should have been more careful with your feelings.'

'It's okay . . . I want to hear your story too—and, you know, do a better job accepting who you are.'

'I will need time. But I'll try to trust you more, okay?' She sighed, and I could hear her smile. 'I have to go now. Have a safe flight to Vienna. See you around, my bruised boxer.'

'See you around, Alice.'

She hung up. I sat down on a bench, put my head back, and closed my eyes. I took a few deep breaths and smiled. I was in trouble, and I was looking for-ward to it.

An hour later, I wrote a last message to Lena, who planned to pick me up from the airport, and boarded my plane to Vienna. From my window seat, I watched the take-off, and then fell asleep for a few hours.

* * *

As I wake up now, I sit up and open the shade next to me. Outside the oval window, the earth is shrouded in the night, and the plane glides calmly through the darkness. I fall back into my reclined seat and close my eyes.

I'm a baby, and Mara, my mother, rocks me to sleep in her bruised, trembling arms. Blake, my father, is watching us from behind. As he tries to smile, a bitter tear runs down his cheek. It is the last day of our little family. I'm seven years old, and I have a black eye. A big bully named Mark has beaten me up at school for never saying a word. My dad takes me to his boxing gym and practises with me on the heavy bag until we're both lying tiredly on the sweat-soaked foam mat and laugh. Nobody will ever bully me again. I'm 14, and Joel and I sit in our garden under the old oak tree, and I play the guitar, and we sing songs by Johnny Cash. Nicole lies on the grass and looks at us in untainted admiration. We will never be this innocent again. I'm 17, and my mum drives Ben and me home from a girl's birthday party. My mum lectures us on the dangers of alcohol. Ben and I are drunk beyond repair, and we have both puked and fooled around with the same girl—in the wrong order as well. I will never be this oblivious again. I'm 20, and Chris and I are on top of a construction crane, howling at the Swedish autumn moon. It is the first time I realise that the world is boundless. For the first time, I feel the full weight of the dizziness of freedom. I'm 22, and Emma stands in front of me on her little balcony in Berlin. She smiles at me, and her white summer dress billows in a balmy breeze. She will never be more beautiful. And I will never be so recklessly in love again. I'm 25, and I sit at my desk at the firm. It is midnight, and I just finished a forecasting algorithm

399

that will make millions for wealthy people I will never meet. Emma is sitting at home in our living room on a sofa too big for one person and texting that smart guy she met at the gym. In two days, I will leave her, and in two weeks, I will let my dad die alone in a sombre hospital room. I will never be so lost again. It is September, and I sit in the rooftop garden above Barcelona in the shade of an olive tree. Dion's steel-blue eyes pierce me with pained reproach. His golden tresses shine in the Spanish sun as he turns around with a sad look and walks away. I hope he will be all right. In the winter to come, I'm on Brighton Pier, and Alice is standing next to me, holding my hand. I'm at her mercy. What will she say? Will she finally give away some of her secrets? Can we accept our own weaknesses and each other's vices? It is next year, and I stand behind the small coffee bar in our hipster shop financed by banking money. I watch Chris consult a group of students on the latest trends in old road bikes. In the evening, I will go upstairs and give a boxing class to a group of under-occupied school kids until they lie scattered on the mats. I tell them that anger doesn't win fights and that the only fight that counts is the one for those you love. Sometimes, I advise a collective of researchers and UNHCR staff on predictive mechanisms for refugee assistance pro-grammes. Maybe, I can finally help a little to make the world a better place. Maybe, Alberto will visit us soon with Núria and lecture me on how the UN remains a postcolonial tool to sustain Western privilege—I can-not wait.

It is Christmas, and Nicole and I are decorating the Christmas tree. Michael and his pregnant wife Laura sit on the sofa, and their daughter Lily is playing under the coffee table. Mum is in the kitchen, cooking dinner—the delicious smell of roasted duck in the air. Outside the window, the old oak tree in our garden is sprinkled with snow and veiled in the calmness of the cold. When Mum comes into the living room to inspect the tree, she smiles at me. I'm home.

I open my eyes and look out of the aeroplane window and into the night. The lights of Indian towns stretch all the way to the horizon—millions of people living their lives, thinking they're special guests on this dark earth. I hope some of them can find it in their heart to be happy. I close my eyes again and feel the plane glide ever deeper into the void of the universe. And I know I will soon be stardust, wafting to whence I came. Until then, I will laugh and cry and love and despair as honestly as I can. Perhaps, I will fail grandiosely. Perhaps, I will be granted some more moments bonding with kind souls under summer skies almost unbearably magnificent. Perhaps, this plane will crash into the Pakistani Sulaiman Mountains. Perhaps, that has already happened, and my thoughts are but a dream of a consciousness trapped in the eternal instant of death. Who can know for certain? And in the end, who gives a damn, anyway?

Printed in Great Britain
by Amazon